D0229771
123
WITHDRAWN * FROM * STOCK

SEA STORIES

'Typhoon', 'Falk'
and
The Shadow-Line

WITHDRAWN * FROM * STOCK
ABERDARE LIBRARY COLLEGE

SEA STORIES

'Typhoon', 'Falk' and *The Shadow-Line*

Joseph Conrad

WORDSWORTH CLASSICS

This edition published 1998 by
Wordsworth Editions Limited
Cumberland House, Crib Street
Ware, Hertfordshire SG12 9ET

ISBN 1 85326 743 0

© Wordsworth Editions Limited 1998

All rights reserved. This publication may not be reproduced, stored in a retrieval system, or transmitted, in any form or by any means, electronic, mechanical, photocopying, recording or otherwise, without the prior permission of the publishers.

Typeset by Antony Gray
Printed and bound in Great Britain by
Mackays of Chatham plc, Chatham, Kent

INTRODUCTION

This edition brings together 'Typhoon', 'Falk' and *The Shadow-Line* for several reasons. They all sympathetically portray seamen whose solidarity and endurance are tested by 'the sea and all its works' ('Falk', 81). Though the first two were composed in quick succession between October 1900 and May 1901, and the third in 1915, Conrad first conceived of the last story in February 1899, under the title ' "First Command" as a companion to "Equitable Division" (a story of a typhoon)' (**2** 168–9); and the experiences of the young captain who tells the story of Falk are extensively reworked in *The Shadow-Line*. Finally, all three manifest Conrad's mastery of 'the form that needs for its development 30,000 words or so' (**2** 441).[1] 'Typhoon', 'Falk' and *The Shadow-Line* are roughly 32,000, 30,000 and 44,000 words long, respectively. This medium-length narrative – variously called the 'nouvelle' by Henry James, the 'long-short story' by Ford Madox Ford (294), 'the short novel' (Guerard, 295) and, more generally, 'the novella' – was at the turn of the century the 'form' that Conrad liked 'best' (**2** 461).[2] Such terminological variety greatly vexes modern genre theorists but was of no concern to Conrad, who throughout the composition of these works invariably called them 'stories'.[3] None the less Conrad's letters (especially between 1898–1902) anticipate and share James's

1 **1/2/3/4/5** refer to the volume number of *The Collected Letters of Joseph Conrad*.
2 As Shaw notes 'the English language has no equivalent to "nouvelle" or "novella" other than "novelette", which has acquired a disparaging connotation' (20). Whenever possible, as here, I use only the author's name to identify a title. For full details see the Bibliography at the end of this Introduction.
3 See Good, Pasco and Pratt. Conrad, incidentally, rarely used the term novel, preferring 'tale' and 'story', and he did not distinguish in nomenclature between short fiction and novels (Fraser).

delight in 'the possible scope . . . and the possible neatness' (1 237) of 'the shapely nouvelle' (1 227).[4] Thus in a great letter, 31 May 1902, to William Blackwood, who had read the first 14,000 words of 'The End of the Tether' and felt that 'one can hardly say one has got into the story yet', Conrad wrote that his complaint: 'is in a measure correct but on a large view, beside the point. For . . . in the light of the final incident, the whole story in all its descriptive detail shall fall into place – acquire its value and its significance. This is my method based on deliberate conviction' (2 417).

This form appeals to Conrad because it shares the intense end-directedness and patterning of the short story and depends 'upon the reader *looking back* upon my story as a whole' (2 441).[5] It can, therefore, as he said of 'Falk', be 'highly finished' (5 275): yet like the full-length novel, it also accommodates the construction of a series of 'episodes' which enable him to 'indicate the progress' (2 441) of his characters in time and space. Blackwood's criticism also solicited one of Conrad's most important explanations of his artistic aims:

> I am *modern*, and would rather recall Wagner . . . and Rodin . . . and Whistler . . . who . . . had to suffer for being 'new' . . . My work shall not be an utter failure because it has the solid basis of a definite intention – first; and next because it is not an endless analysis of affected sentiments but in its essence it is action . . . observed, felt and interpreted with an absolute truth to my sensations . . . Action of human beings that will bleed to a prick, and are moving in a visible world. [2 418]

I stress Conrad's awareness of method, form and treatment because he was also aware that the subject of the sea itself would smack of 'the light holiday literature' that Jim devours in *Lord Jim*

4 James, Preface to vol. xv of the New York edition of his works (1908–9). *Nouvelle* was first used in the last third of the century in France, and for James it referred to any story between 16,000 and 45,000 words. This length was greatly favoured by the writers James and Conrad most admired, Turgenev, Flaubert and Maupassant. Both James and Conrad knew that this 'bantling' (bastard) form was difficult to place in the periodicals who operated 'the hard-and-fast rule of the "from six to eight thousand words" ' (James, 1227, 1228). Conrad's fondness for the form was encouraged by *Blackwood's Magazine*, which published 'Karain' (17,000 words) in one issue (November 1897), 'Heart of Darkness' (38,000) in three (February–April 1899) and 'The End of the Tether' (47,000) in five (July–December 1902).

5 For this reason, I urge readers who are unfamiliar with the stories to read them first and then return to my Introduction.

(5) and suggest that he was not to be taken seriously as a writer.[6] Thus, in his early essay on Captain Marryat and James Fenimore Cooper, 'Tales of the Sea' (1898), Conrad dissociates himself from the 'exuberant' and 'enthralling' naval novels of the former because for him the sea 'was not an element', but 'a stage, where was displayed an exhibition of valour, and of such achievement the world had never seen before' (*Notes on Life and Letters*, 54, 53). Conrad's sea-fiction, unlike that of his predecessors was not 'a book of adventures or travel with a plot rammed into it' (Reynolds, 163).[7] Rather, as in Cooper, 'the sea inter-penetrates with life: it is in a subtle way a factor in the problem of existence and . . . always in touch with the men, who, bound on errands of war or gain, traverse its immense solitudes' (55). This is so for Conrad, because 'Everything can be found at sea, according to the spirit of your quest – strife, peace, romance, naturalism of the most pronounced kind, ideals, boredom, disgust, inspiration' (*A Personal Record*, 109), and because 'events at sea' test his characters and 'show in the light of day the inner worth of a man, the edge of his temper, and the fibre of his stuff; . . . reveal the quality of his resistance and the secret truth of his pretences, not only to others but to himself' (*Lord Jim*, 10). And 'that,' as Reynolds observes, 'is what Conrad does to the men in his books, be they seamen or landsmen' (167).

LIBRARY

I

At the beginning of January 1900, Conrad, anticipating the completion of *Lord Jim*, planned 'to write 20,000 words' for *Blackwood's* and once again suggested 'First Command' and 'A Skittish Cargo' (conceived as 'Equitable Division' and to become 'Typhoon') as a pair (2 237). Conrad began 'Typhoon' in October, but, as the punning term skittish implies, he anticipated that it would be light and satirical. Then in November, in the same vein, he told his newly hired agent J. B. Pinker, 'This is my first attempt at treating a

6 Messenger is good on how Conrad, late in his career, did not want to be remembered as 'primarily a writer of "sea stuff" '. Behrman illustrates the ways the English were weaned on Victorian myths of the sea as the 'natural home of the Englishman' and 'the scene of our greatest triumphs and dangers' (28). 'Given the importance of the sea and navigation to island Britain, it is rather surprising,' as Tanner remarks, 'how few novelists of the sea have emerged here' (Introduction, xvii).

7 Reynolds was a close friend of Conrad's and a writer of sea-stories. His neglected essay is still one of the finest appreciations of Conrad and the sea.

subject jocularly' (2 304), and, echoing the spirit of the storm story, he wrote that 'the typhoon is still blowing', but lamented, 'I find it extremely difficult to express the simplest idea clearly' (2 307). Conrad finished the story in January 1901 hoping that *Blackwood's* would accept it. Pinker, however, looked to popular magazines of high circulation and poor quality and placed it in the *Pall Mall Gazette* who paid £100 for the serialisation.

The moment it appeared in hardback in *Typhoon and Other Stories* (1903), 'Typhoon' was praised by a reviewer as 'the most elaborate storm piece that one can recall in English literature' (Sherry, 1973, 146). Others hailed 'the most amazing description of the utter madness of the sea when tormented by a force almost as great as itself that we have ever read' (143), and 'the typhoon itself' was regarded 'as the most vital personality of the story' (153). The reviewer who praised its 'most simple manner' (143) anticipated two generations of critics who liked 'Typhoon' but who thought it to be 'relatively simple' (Guerard, 299) and 'one of Conrad's simplest tales' (Baines, 254).[8] Such appreciation damned with faint praise and sponsored a reluctance to engage either the qualities of Conrad's 'most amazing description' or the subtlety of its design. I begin, therefore, with an appreciation of two of my favourite passages in order to show the ways in which Conrad's 'descriptive detail' contributes to the 'value and significance' of the whole story:

> The *Nan-Shan* was being looted by the storm with a senseless, destructive fury: trysails torn out of the extra gaskets . . . weather-cloths burst, rails twisted, light-screens smashed – and two of the boats had gone already. They had gone unheard and unseen, melting . . . in the shock and smother of the wave. It was only later, when upon the white flash of another high sea hurling itself amidships, Jukes had a vision of two pairs of davits leaping black and empty out of the solid blackness, with one overhauled fall flying and an iron-bound block capering in the air, that he became aware of what had happened within about three yards of his back. [38]

As ever in 'Typhoon', this sequence attests to the exactitude, energy and virtuosity of Conrad's style. The particular parts of the sturdy 'full-powered steamship' (30) simultaneously 'speak for

8 The single dissenter, Frederick R. Karl, obtusely laments 'the lack of surprise either of word or structure' (1960, 141). The best essays on the story are by Birrel and Brown.

themselves with overwhelming precision' (15) as they are 'looted', 'burst', 'smashed' and 'twisted' by a gale which combines the senseless fury of a mob and the silent and awesome force of a mysterious power in the surprising, soft pressure of 'melted'. Similarly, the marvellous oxymoron of an 'iron-bound block capering' expresses both Jukes' wild sense of the antic power of the storm and the sheer brio of its composer.

Towards the end of Chapter 2, Captain MacWhirr prepares to combat the storm:

> He threw himself into the attitude of a lunging fencer, to reach after his oilskin coat; . . . Very grave, straddling his legs far apart, and stretching his neck, he started to tie deliberately the strings of his sou'-wester under his chin, with . . . all the movements of a woman putting on her bonnet before a glass, with a strained, listening attention, as though he expected every moment to hear the shout of his name in the confused clamour that had suddenly beset his ship . . . It was tumultuous and very loud – made up of the rush of the wind, the crashes of the sea, with that prolonged deep vibration of the air, like the roll of an immense and remote drum beating the charge of the gale.
>
> He stood for a moment in the light of the lamp, thick, clumsy, shapeless in his panoply of combat, vigilant and red-faced.
>
> 'There's a lot of weight in this,' he muttered.
>
> As soon as he attempted to open the door . . . he . . . found himself engaged with the wind in a sort of personal scuffle whose object was the shutting of that door. At the last moment a tongue of air scurried in and licked out the flame of the lamp.
>
> Ahead of the ship he perceived a great darkness lying upon a multitude of white flashes; on the starboard beam a few amazing stars drooped, dim and fitful, above an immense waste of broken seas, as if seen through a mad drift of smoke. [33–4]

'Typhoon' is jocular, and much of the rich comedy in the story is engendered by 'the hilarity of the active opposition between MacWhirr and Conrad' (Brown, 4), that is, between the literal man who 'expostulated against the use of images in speech' (26) and his creator who delights in the imaginative flights his hero's stolidity unleashes – flights that would irk him as surely as Jukes' use of simile to express his sense of the awful weather ('I feel exactly as if I had my head tied up in a woollen blanket' [25]). The title refers, therefore, both to the ferocious natural elements he confronts and to the circling, whirring storm of words and images that simultaneously tease, engulf and render homage to his 'thick' figure. 'The shout of his name', 'the prolonged deep vibration of the air', 'the remote drum' and 'his panoply of combat' announce both 'the charge of the gale' and MacWhirr's knightly response to its call to arms. Moreover, as we shall see, MacWhirr's 'tongue' and 'voice' will bring order to 'the confused clamour' of the gale. The comedy of the passage, as in the story as a whole, depends upon swift changes of perception. Thus the image 'of a woman putting on her bonnet' is inappropriate to his gender, lack of vanity and to the grim situation he is about to face; but it reinforces his fastidious attention to detail that is stressed throughout the story. Again, his 'sort of personal scuffle' with the door precedes his defiance of an apocalyptic 'great darkness' that threatens to return the world to 'an immense waste of broken seas' from which humankind once emerged. In this respect, MacWhirr's father who has 'a gift for sly chaffing' figures the author who creates a narrator who happily banters with his creation but who, in marked contrast to his father and Jukes, refuses to dismiss him as either a 'half-witted person' (12) or, in the final words of the story, as 'a stupid man' (77).

Indeed, as Conrad carefully explains in his Author's Note (1919), MacWhirr 'with his literal mind and dauntless temperament' was the figure who enabled him after much meditation to illuminate 'the deeper significance' of the anecdote of the cargo of coolies trapped in the hold during a typhoon. MacWhirr provides 'a leading motive that would harmonise all these violent noises, and a point of view that would put all that elemental fury into its proper place' (6). Merely to state his motive – to face rather than to try and out-manoeuvre the typhoon – is, of course, to pose the question that sponsors such different responses among the characters in, and readers of, the story: is MacWhirr 'stupid'? Or, to put it in another way, how are we, finally, to appraise MacWhirr?

The narrator informs us that, 'With a temperament neither loquacious nor taciturn, he found very little occasion to talk . . . the past being to his mind done with, and the future not there yet, the more general actualities of the day required no comment – because facts can speak for themselves with overwhelming precision' (15). And the only sea facts that he can relate to are those he can either see or has experienced, namely 'every-day, eloquent facts, such as islands, sandbanks, reefs . . . tangled facts that nevertheless speak to a seaman in clear and definite language' (19). Such facts absorb him entirely; but they also ensure that, despite 'a conscious effort', he cannot understand 'the terminology' of 'the chapter on storms', because they anticipate with their graphs ('advancing semi-circles . . . probable bearing of the centre') future conditions and 'things' he cannot imagine and has never encountered; and, therefore, he cannot bring them 'into a definite relation to himself' (31). Hence this man who 'had sailed over the surface of the oceans as some men go skimming over the years of existence to sink gently into a placid grave' makes the preposterous decision to face the typhoon and, unwittingly, ensures that both he and his reader are 'made to see all it [the ocean] may contain of perfidy, of violence, and of terror' (22).

MacWhirr's error has led good critics who are knowledgeable about the sea, such as Bonney and Foulke, to dismiss him 'as an unperceptive clod' (Bonney, 35) and, relatedly, to deride both his maxims about 'facing' the storm and his subsequent treatment of the coolies. Such critics appreciate that MacWhirr's mistake is a consequence of his literal mind, but they fail to realise that his lack of imagination is essential to his comic functions as a harmoniser of all the 'violent noises' that the story entertains and as a point of view that puts 'all the elemental fury' he heaps on himself 'into its proper place'. The central opposition in the story is between the 'overpowering concussion and rush of great waters' (36) and the 'few words' the typhoon wrings out of him (69). And every aspect of the story, such as the contrast between Jukes and MacWhirr, the narrator's commentary, the events, and the intensity and variety of the patterning, are designed to ensure that MacWhirr's 'few words' acquire extraordinary 'value and significance'.

Thus Jukes fears that 'his sight might be destroyed in the immense flurry of the elements' (36) and he is reduced to 'a revolt of misery and despair' until 'his wretched struggles . . . become somehow mixed up with a face, an oilskin coat, somebody's boots . . . and finally was himself caught in the firm clasp of a pair of stout arms. He returned the embrace closely round a thick solid body. He had found his captain' (37). The redemptive, spiritual echoes of Jukes' recognition are smartly tempered by the fleshly 'facts' of MacWhirr, which speak with power and 'overwhelming precision' to his terrified suppliant. The same comic mix of the sacred and the profane recurs in the narrator's famous testimony to the power of MacWhirr's 'voice':

> And again he [Jukes] heard that voice, forced and ringing feebly, but with a penetrating effect of quietness in the enormous discord of noises, as if sent out from some remote spot of peace beyond the black wastes of the gale; again he heard a man's

> voice – the frail and indomitable sound that can be made to carry an infinity of thought, resolution and purpose, that shall be pronouncing confident words on the last day, when heavens fall, and justice is done – again he heard it, and it was crying to him, as if from very, very far – 'All right.' [38]

'It is after all,' remarks Conrad wryly in *The Mirror of the Sea* (1905), 'the human voice that stamps the mark of human consciousness upon the character of a gale' (79); and, as 'Typhoon' superbly illustrates, that mark is registered in both humankind's love of images (as in the narrator's play with the 'black wastes of the gale' as a prefigurement of the end of time) and in the vernacular simplicity of MacWhirr's 'All right'. In Conrad's defiantly secular world, however, 'the still small voice' of God that Elijah hears after the wind and the earthquake (1 Kings 19) is echoed and supplanted and 'made to carry an infinity of thought' when MacWhirr finds his 'voice' and, against all the odds, reaffirms a human sense of order and 'puts all that elemental fury into its proper place'. Humankind grants 'the still small voice' of God the power to control the furious elements: MacWhirr's power is much humbler, but it bears witness to what Conrad in his essay 'Henry James' (1904) calls 'the artistic faculty, of which each one of us has a minute grain' (*Notes on Life and Letters*, 13–14), and it magnificently affirms 'the stubborn human presence' (Wegelin, 46).

MacWhirr's 'All right'[9] is the antithesis of Kurtz's withering final judgment, 'The horror! The horror!'[10] ('Heart of Darkness', 149). Moreover, in marked contrast to the latter who 'presented himself as a voice' and for whom only his 'gift of expression' 'carried with it the sense of real presence' (113), MacWhirr is a squat, burly presence who is presented by the narrator and encountered by Jukes as a 'voice' carrying 'resolution and purpose'. In fact, MacWhirr's voice, in a direct echo of Marlow's in 'Heart of Darkness', is a 'voice that would not be silenced' (44); and it resists 'the spell of the storm' that falls upon Jukes, because it is born out of this experience which, in ways the talk of his fellows cannot do, 'unsealed his lips'. And speaking out 'in solitude and in the pitch darkness of the cabin, as if addressing another being awakened within his breast', he says, 'I shouldn't like to lose her' (66). 'He was spared that annoyance' (69)

9 Reynolds notes that this was one of Conrad's favourite phrases 'in letters and conversation, where he can state his intuition without having to justify it' (168).
10 All quotations from 'Heart of Darkness' are from *Youth, a Narrative, and Two Other Stories*.

because, unlike the dismayed Jukes, who tries to 'outscream' the typhoon when he asks, 'Will she [the ship] live through this?' and then feels his cry merely 'added to the tempest waves of the air' (40), his captain's resisting voice is 'the dwarf sound, unconquered in the giant tumult' (41):

> 'She may!'
>
> It was a dull yell . . . like a ship battling against the waves of an ocean.
>
> 'Let's hope so!' it cried – small, lonely and unmoved, a stranger to the visions of hope or fear; and it flickered into disconnected words . . .
>
> 'Keep on hammering . . . builders . . . good men . . . And chance it . . . engines . . . Rout . . . good man.' [41]

Once again the literal MacWhirr functions as the antithesis of the visionary Kurtz. Thus, whereas the latter loses himself in 'the magic current of phrases' ('Heart of Darkness', 118) and kicks 'himself loose of the earth' (144) and of the works of humankind, MacWhirr is 'a stranger to visions of hope or fear'; and his 'broken shouts' are not essentially disconnected because, unlike Kurtz, he resolutely falls 'back upon' his 'own innate strength' and the 'capacity for faithfulness' ('Heart of Darkness', 116) exhibited by both his ship and the crew. Thus MacWhirr's speech, though broken by the gale ('Facing it – always facing it – that's the way to get through . . . That's enough for any man' [68]), is also wrung out by, and flung back at, it; and, therefore, it constitutes an unconscious 'moral value like the primitive acts of faith on which may be built . . . a rule of life' (2 354).

The moral value of MacWhirr's voice is reaffirmed in the second half of the story in his humane response to the desperate plight of the coolies whose howls and shrieks are linked throughout to the 'howls and shrieks' of the 'gale raging' (46). Jukes, initially, tries to evade 'the tone of deep concern' (44) in his captain's voice; but despite his heart's corruption 'by the storm' and his rebellion 'against the tyranny of training and command' (44), he descends into the 'regular little hell' of the hold, and though he 'had half a mind to scramble out again . . . the remembrance of Captain MacWhirr's voice made this impossible. His orders were to go and see' (50). After the coolies have been made secure, Jukes proudly tells his grateful captain of ' " . . . that infernal job. We did it. And it may not matter in the end." ' But to MacWhirr alone, it does matter: ' "Had to do what's fair, for all – they are only Chinamen. Give them the same chance with ourselves – hang it all. She isn't lost yet" ' (67).

'Typhoon' is unique in the Conrad canon, because it is the only story framed by letters written by the characters. This device, however, is a pure manifestation of Conrad's definition of his art as 'fluid, depending on grouping (sequence) which shifts, and on changing lights giving varied effects of perspective' (*Life and Letters*, II, 317). The last chapter, especially, is remarkable because each letter by MacWhirr, Solomon Rout and, finally, by Jukes simultaneously describes the closing events of the story and either (re)interprets or provides fresh information on the events. And because the opinions in each letter spark reactions in their readers, all of which interact with and are monitored by the omniscient narrator, we are persuaded to collaborate with the author in the production of meaning, because we are obliged 'to look back' upon the story as a whole.

MacWhirr's letter groups and interweaves two audiences within the story, his family and his nosy steward who relays details to the cook. The heavy ellipses in the letter are faithful to Mrs MacWhirr's indifferent and perfunctory reading. Because 'the only secret of her life was her abject terror of the time when her husband would come home to stay for good' (19), she misinterprets the phrase 'see you and the children again . . . ' to indicate a routine anticipation 'of coming home' (71). The narrator pointedly corrects her dismal, frigid misconstruction: 'It did not occur to her to turn back overleaf to look. She would have found it recorded there that between 4 and 6 a.m. on December 25th, Captain MacWhirr did actually think that his ship could not possibly live another hour in such a sea, and that he would never see his wife and children again' (71).

The sudden revelation of the time and date persuades the reader 'to turn back' and to look again at the 'calm that lasted over twenty minutes' which MacWhirr had spent alone in the chart-room. In the small hours of Christmas Day, when children dream of presents (unless, perhaps, like the MacWhirr women they make a religion out of shopping) and when families gather to celebrate their own continuity and (perhaps) the birth of Christ, MacWhirr is 'made to see' the ocean's capacity for 'perfidy . . . and terror'; and, faced with 'the lowest' barometer 'reading he had ever seen', with 'the worst . . . to come', and endowed with a new respect for the books on storm strategy he had ignorantly disdained, he contemplates his own mortality. (The steward's amazement at his captain's feelings testify beautifully to the confidence he inspired in his crew.) MacWhirr's actions and reflections are a brilliant blend of routine habits and illuminating realisations. Thus we watch him move from 'the feeling of dismay' induced by his scattered 'rulers . . . pencils . . . inkstand' (65) to his satisfaction that: 'If the ship had to go after all, then, at least, she wouldn't be going to the bottom with a lot of people in her fighting teeth and claw. That would have been odious. And in that feeling there was a humane intention and a vague sense of the fitness of things' (65). Now we can see why the story is set on Christmas Eve:[11] 'In this utterly un-Western, un-Christmas setting, one genuinely Christian value is affirmed – that men shall not be allowed to struggle like beasts for survival, but that they shall face their fate with charitable regard for one another as human beings' (Kolupke, 79).

Then, in a remarkable transition, more narrative attention is given to MacWhirr's obsessive concern 'to put back the matchbox in its corner of the shelf' (65) than to his realisation 'that perhaps he would never have occasion to use that box any more' (66). This brief focus on the self is, however, immediately supplanted by his concern for the ship, and in the blackness of the chart-room, during this 'awful pause', the storm 'penetrated the defences of the man and unsealed his lips': and in quick succession he says, ' "I shouldn't like to lose her" ', and after a vigorous towelling 'a murmur arose. "She may come out of it yet" ' (66). This sequence is one of the most daring and moving in the whole of Conrad's fiction, because MacWhirr neither sees the storm as a supernatural force stripping away his spirit and soul nor does he appeal on the day of his travail to the Christ who was born to save humankind from ultimate destruction. Rather, he is presented as a mere 'man' whose voice is at once involuntary and disembodied, at once unsealed by, and defiant of the gale. And unassisted by any theological faith and without any thoughts of self and home, he proceeds to face, to survive and to out-voice the storm 'in a primitive act of faith' which attests to humankind's capacity to prevail in a godless, indifferent universe.

The last chapter moves from the fragments of MacWhirr's neglected letter to Sol's which is eagerly read by his wife and transmitted to his ancient mother: 'That captain of the ship he is in – a rather simple man . . . has done something rather clever' (72). But, teasingly, Sol does not disclose the details. That task Conrad deliberately assigns to Jukes, who unwittingly undermines his own account when he rewrites the events and presents himself as full of 'light-hearted, indomitable resolution' (73) and as MacWhirr's

11 The narrator refers to 'the season of typhoons' (22), but Conrad must have known that they occur in the China seas from July to October.

intellectual and imaginative superior. His letter is an exercise in pure irony, not least because he 'reveals the secret truth of his pretences' and fails to match his creator's complex, sympathetic evaluation of his momentary funk, grit and good humour. (He is lucky that MacWhirr does not, like Falk's melancholic skipper, abandon his responsibility for his crew). Moreover, he inadvertently reveals his own run-of-the-mill racism and lack of judgement when he hastily arms the crew against an imagined revolt by those 'confounded Chinamen' (73) and then, finally, urges MacWhirr to ' "let us throw the whole lot of these dollars down to them and leave them to fight it out among themselves, while we get a rest" ' (75): a solution that would re-enact the descent into savagery that so disturbed MacWhirr's sense 'of the fitness of things' in the chart-room. Jukes, in an elegant irony, is also the unwitting contributor to one of the story's running jokes, namely 'Solomon says' (19). It originates in Mrs Rout who shares her creator's mirth with her 'trick of firing off Solomon's utterances . . . upon strangers, astonishing them easily by the unfamiliar text and the unexpectedly jocular vein of these quotations' (19); and Jukes, against the grain of his own narrative, verifies that MacWhirr's placidly astute 'Equitable Division' of the dollars among all the coolies, reserving the three remaining for 'the three most damaged . . . one to each' (77), rivals the wisdom of Solomon himself who, in his most famous case, found the true mother of the disputed child by offering to divide it equitably into two.

Unaware of the ironies he occasions, Jukes thinks he has the final word: ' "The skipper remarked to me the other day, 'There are things you find nothing about in books.' I think he got out of it very well for such a stupid man" ' (77). Jukes, clearly, misremembers and still does not know his captain. The reader's response, however, is more complex: on the one hand, we remember MacWhirr's obtuse rejection of the books on storm strategy, and on the other we are aware that this 'jocular' story revolves around the simple man, 'of literal mind and dauntless temperament', who – unloved at home, chaffed and derided by his own father and Jukes – none the less has reserves of sympathy and common sense that enable him to forge a humane morality that is responsive to, and inseparable from, the appalling, and testing circumstances that he solicited, faced and mastered.

II

Conrad first mentioned 'Falk' on 8 October 1900, as 'The [unnamed] other story and much more horrible [than 'Typhoon'] . . . I fancy I can do it in 5000 words' (**2** 295). Clearly, at this point he envisaged a mere anecdote about the taboo subject of cannibalism. On finishing 'Typhoon', in January 1901, Conrad began the story 'three times over' (**5** 92), completing it in late May. Such indecision is not surprising because in 'Falk: A Reminiscence' Conrad welds together two subjects that had always existed separately hitherto – first command and cannibalism.

The narrative of 'Falk: A Reminiscence' contains in fact (as perhaps the colon is designed to hint) two reminiscences; one of Falk by the 'more than fifty'-year-old captain, remembering, for the entertainment of a bunch of old salts, ' "an absurd episode in my life, now many years ago, when I got first the command of an iron barque, loading then in a certain Eastern seaport [Bangkok]" ' (82), and the other, long-delayed, *by* Falk to the captain, Hermann, and his niece of his 'misfortune' aboard the *Borgmester Dahl*: ' "Imagine to yourselves . . . that I have eaten man" ' (129). The captain's tale, as he insistently repeats, is absurd because in order to escape the miserable circumstances of his first command – when he followed a swindling, licentious captain and inherited a sick crew – he turns for relief to 'my friend Hermann' (82) and becomes entangled in Falk's 'extravagantly nonsensical' (125) courtship of the former's unnamed niece. Falk owns the only tugboat in the port and he wrongly views the young captain as the rival Hermann favours for the niece's hand. Driven entirely by the instinct of 'self-preservation' (117), after giving Hermann's ship precedence over the captain's, he then utterly refuses to tow the latter's barque across the sand-bar that blocks its route to the open sea. Falk acts like 'a natural force' (117) and is oblivious to the predicament of the self-conscious and immature young captain who fears that some of his enfeebled crew 'would end by dying on board if I couldn't get them out to sea soon' (110). Facing 'Horror, ruin and everlasting remorse', the captain thinks, 'I had fallen amongst a lot of unfriendly lunatics!' (111). Thus, both the potential disaster of the captain and the subsequent revelation of Falk's cannibalism are subsumed in the social comedy of the captain's exaggerated, self-mocking account of his relationship to Falk, the petty-bourgeois Hermann, and to the characters on shore who mistakenly presume, like the constable, that he is quarrelling 'with that tugboat skipper over some girl or other' (113). Then, in an elegant reversal, the release of the captain and his barque becomes a mere 'episode' in 'Falk's attempt to get married' (Author's Note, 7) to the sumptuous niece and, thereby, escape his appalling isolation. Hence the fulcrum scene in this comedy of misunderstandings is the chance conversation with Falk in Schomberg's hotel (the exact mid-point of the whole narrative) when the captain learns that 'the excellent Hermann had been making use of me . . . holding me up to Falk in the light of a rival' (119); realises that Falk is not his 'enemy' but a man who has been misled by Hermann and traduced by Schomberg and who deserves respect and pity because he is incapable of duplicity and shares Adam's inability 'to live alone . . . ' (122); and agrees 'to stand by' him when he asks permission of Hermann to propose to the niece and to tell of why I have been unfortunate once' (123). Thinking 'that was not so bad as life goes' (124), the captain is, like the reader, surprised and 'enlightened' by Falk's account of his cannibalism, which disgusts the 'squeamish' Hermann, makes the silent niece weep and ensures that the captain gets 'his sickly crew into the sea air' (115) and that Falk wins a magnificent bride.

'Falk' has never been popular with the critics. They claim that its climax is too long postponed and that the captain's urbane humour is strained and limits the tale's expectations (Watts); that his focus on Falk is blurred (Baines, Johnson) and that, unlike Marlow (say) in 'Heart of Darkness', he learns nothing. Johnson also objects that the two subjects, of the captain's initiation into the duplicity and mendacity of Hermann and Schomberg, and Falk's appalling experiences do not hang together. All these positions are tenable, but they fail, I think, to appreciate the boldness of Conrad's conception of his subject and, inseparably, the ways in which his 'highly finished' (5 275), witty design depends upon his reader '*looking back* upon my story as a whole': and, then, if my students' responses are any guide, the rich black humour, submerged below the surface on a first read, never fails to delight and amaze.

Cannibalism was, of course, a taboo subject, because for his late Victorian audience (and even for readers today) to eat another human being entails a descent into savagery and (to quote Hermann) becoming a 'Beast!' (130).[12] And as Conrad wryly remarks in his

12 'Falk', like 'Heart of Darkness', is a tale of Darwinian atavism. Griffiths contains a full account of why 'cannibalism . . . for many Victorians . . . involved the suspension of the most basic moral codes, which had formed as man advanced' and, therefore, threatened the very bases of civilised society (167–8).

Author's Note, 'Falk' 'offended the delicacy of one critic . . . by certain peculiarities of its subject' (6) and his wife Jessie recalls being 'quite physically sick when I typed those pages' (Jessie Conrad, 118).[13] Conrad slyly accredits such reactions to Hermann, who functions as the epitome of the 'squeamish' bourgeois reader who would rather such horrible subjects were not discussed in civilised company. Every facet of Conrad's 'highly finished' narrative, however, is designed to satirise such pieties; and the deliberate, protracted delay of the details of Falk's desperate deed is playfully designed to induce the reader 'to collaborate with the author' in his exposure of Hermann's 'commonplace sentimentality' as against 'the uncorrupted point of view of an almost primitive man . . . who regards the preservation of life as the supreme and moral law' (2 398).

One wonders which pages made Jessie sick, because Falk's cannibalism comes as a complete surprise to the reader, and our 'enlightenment' is the discovery that we have been duped by Conrad the cunning artificer and, as with all narrative hoaxes, much of the pleasure involves our appreciation of the ways we were misled. For Conrad, however, such '*looking back*' is not primarily a war of wits and an end in itself (as, say, in detective novels), but an illuminating process that alerts us to the ways 'the whole story' acquires 'its value and significance'. This process is evident in Conrad's subtle orchestration of the interwoven motifs of cannibalism, hunger, eating, passion, monopolism and self-preservation.

As does 'Heart of Darkness', 'Falk' uses a frame-narrator, who facetiously introduces us to a gathering of old seamen who on finishing an 'execrable' dinner imitate their 'primeval' ancestors who ate 'scorched lumps of flesh at a fire of sticks in the company of other good fellows; then gorged and happy sat . . . back among the gnawed bones to tell . . . tales of hunger and hunt – and of women, perhaps!' (81). The frame links eating and narrative as entwined communal activities; and a bad meal of burnt chops in 'a lacustrine dwelling' triggers the captain's determinedly comic story of Falk's hunting of the delicious niece and anticipates his terrible story of cannibalism that 'had to be told' (122). 'He does not feel a worse man than before' but he does feel 'unhappy', and his desire

13 The critic was, perhaps, Quiller-Couch, who fastidiously noted that 'Falk' is 'spoilt for me by a natural repugnance, which perhaps has nothing to do with criticism' (Sherry, 1973, 156). Such feelings, presumably, explain why no magazine, including *Blackwood's*, would serialise it. Conrad lamented, 'They seem to treat it as though it had the pest' (2 388).

for respectability accompanies his honest recognition that his aversion to meat 'would affect the domestic arrangements of their home' and that secrecy would sour 'companionship' (129) with his future wife. With hindsight Conrad's humour here, as throughout, is blackly comic, allowing him to posit and effect outrageous connections. Thus 'the lumps of flesh' anticipate the male gazes of the despicable Schomberg, who calls the niece ' "a fine lump of a girl" . . . He made a loud smacking noise with his thick lips' (114), and of the captain who fully shares Falk's sense that 'the girl . . . was magnificently attractive by the masterful power of flesh and blood, expressed in shape, in size, in attitude – that is, by a straight appeal to the senses' (118). The captain eagerly expresses her appeal after she has silently accepted Falk's homage in terms that invoke the delicate beauty of the butterfly, the form of a goddess of the month, and the force of a magnificent beast: 'and her very dress, stretched on her bust, seemed to palpitate like a living tissue with the strength of vitality animating her body' (129). Such reflections and associations culminate in the captain's conviction that Falk's desire 'to live' and his unadulterated, unembarrassed commitment to 'self-preservation' establish a clear link between two kinds of craving: 'He was hungry for the girl, terribly hungry, as he had been terribly hungry for food. Don't be shocked if I declare that in my belief it was the same need, the same pain, the same torture. We are in his case allowed to contemplate the foundation of all emotions – that one joy which is to live, and the one sadness at the root of the innumerable torments' (134). Hermann, of course, could neither accept nor understand the captain's invitation to the reader to share his assumption that 'the flower and the fruit, the infinite gradation in shades and in flavour of our [mature] discriminating love' (celebrated since the troubadours in Western literature) actually germinated in the soil of our 'obscure beginning' when we could not differentiate between our cravings for sex and food (134). But that is precisely Hermann's function; and, as ever in Conrad's fiction, the gap between the kind of 'civic virtue' Hermann evinces and the 'self-preservation' Falk barbarously reifies, is shown to be extremely small.[14]

14 Bertrand Russell records that after talking to Conrad: 'I felt . . . that he thought of civilised and morally tolerable human life as a dangerous walk on a thin crust of barely cooled lava which at any moment might break and let the unwary sink into fiery depths' (82).

Hermann's 'ideas' are sardonically summarised by the captain following Falk's abrupt disclosure: 'no circumstance could excuse ... such a crime. This was the opinion generally received. The duty of a human being was to starve. Falk therefore was a beast, an animal; base, low, vile, despicable, shameless, and deceitful' (132). Such responses, as the whole story demonstrates, are muddled and unexamined and the limitations of Hermann's (Herr Mann's) commonplace mind are mocked and exposed. Like MacWhirr before the typhoon, Hermann, like the *Diana*, 'seemed to know nothing of the wicked sea' (84); and at the end he cannot understand why Falk needs to tell his story and he sanctimoniously refuses to learn of the awful and attenuating circumstances. Falk, however, like MacWhirr and the captain in *The Shadow-Line* is obliged to reveal 'the fibre of his stuff' and 'the quality of his resistance'; and his harrowing tale illustrates that 'duty' is a moral concept based on a communal consensus that was destroyed when 'Everything went wrong' (135) and 'the organised life of the ship had come to an end. The solidarity of the men had gone' (139). Moreover, beasts cannot be base, vile or shameless; but both Schomberg and Hermann, and all the characters the captain encounters on shore, most certainly are. Indeed, the latter's conduct exposes him as 'the real exploiter of the book' (Tanner, 21). Thus, when he is anxious to sell up and return home and begrudges the unnecessary expense of his niece's fare, now she is no longer free labour, he tries to make Falk declare himself (and accuses him of deceit when he doesn't!) by insinuating that the captain is a rival suitor. The cannibalistic nature of his economic abuse of her labour and by analogy her body is subtly exposed in his reaction to Falk's 'I have eaten man': 'He choked, gasped, swallowed, and managed to shriek out the one word, "Beast!" ' (130). The verb sequence slyly mimics the cannibalism he squeamishly deplores, and anticipates his selfish determination to 'do his best to survive' (142), which functions as a flabby parody of Falk's will to live. Thus, though Hermann 'wouldn't like it to get about that he had been intimate with an eater of men – a common cannibal' (132) – my favourite joke in the story – he moves swiftly from hysteria to prudence when he allows his niece to marry one, as soon as her sobbing renders her (note the false display of selflessness!) 'of no help to her aunt' (143). Placed against Hermann's utilitarianism, his hollow desire to 'avenge' 'the victims of that Falk' (133), his hapless sentimentalism and his shameless inconsistencies, Falk's honesty and his determination to maintain order and morale as long as circumstances permitted, persuades both the captain and the reader to admire his 'pitiless resolution, endurance, cunning and courage – all the qualities of classic heroism' (140–1).

Admiration, however, is not endorsement, and the niece's tears over the tale of 'this appalling navigator' (142) – unlike Desdemona's for Othello – do not obscure the problems raised by Conrad's informing 'idea' of contrasting Hermann's commonplace sentimentality with Falk's uncorrupted point of view. Thus, when the captain 'with my head full of preconceived notions as to how a case of "cannibalism and suffering at sea" should be managed' (135), innocently asks, ' "You were then so lucky in the drawing of lots?" ' the astonished Falk replies:

> 'Drawing of lots? . . . Do you think I would have allowed my life to go for the drawing of lots?'
>
> Not if he could help it, I perceived, no matter what other life went.
>
> 'It was a great misfortune. Terrible. Awful,' he said. 'Many heads went wrong, but the best men would live.'
>
> 'The toughest, you mean,' I said. He considered the word. Perhaps it was strange to him, though his English was so good.
>
> 'Yes,' he asserted at last. 'The best. It was everybody for himself at last and the ship open to all.' [135]

This seminal passage, in ways Falk cannot grasp, plays on the central confusion in social Darwinism's embrace of the survival of the fittest, namely the conflation of fitness with virtue. *Falke* means hawk in German and his first name is Christian: and at both the last extremity and in his inexorable dealings with the captain, he asserts the law of the jungle and of 'a born monopolist' (141), thereby denying the Christian virtues of charity, compassion and empathy, that the captain and the niece both manifest (and the reader is persuaded to share) and that enable 'this ruthless lover of the five senses' (144) to tell his tale and re-enter the human community. From this point of view 'Falk' is 'a philosophical black comedy' (Kirschner, 18). But though we are persuaded to re-evaluate and to sympathise with Falk and to despise Hermann, much of the captain's allegorising of Falk as Hercules and the niece as Diana and of the pair as servants 'of that life that, in the midst of death, cries aloud to the senses' (142), signals Conrad's strained attempt to pump the bellows of significance.[15] Most of us, after all, are self-doubting like

15 Conrad admitted: 'I wanted him [Falk] to stand for so much that I neglected . . . to set him on his feet' (2 441) – in marked contrast to his depiction of MacWhirr who is so concretely realised.

the captain and self-interested and (even) self-unknowing like Hermann. Moreover, a world run by Falks, whose 'quality of resistance' to both the test of the sea and, subsequently, to his fellows, is monopolistic, nursing the 'law' of self-preservation 'like the only spark of a sacred fire' (117), would indeed disturb our sense of 'the fitness of things' and mark a regression to 'the night of ages' of 'primeval man', that Conrad drolly invokes at the beginning of this unsettling story.

III

In February 1915, some sixteen years after he first conceived it, Conrad began 'First Command'. He always thought of it as 'an early personal experience thing' (5 441), that returned to the events of late 1887 and early 1888, first depicted in 'Falk', when he resigned his position as first mate of the *Vidar* on 4 January and, while waiting in the Sailor's Home in Singapore for a passage home, was offered, out of the blue, his first and only command of a 346–ton iron barque, the *Otago*. Almost all we know of this crucial period in Conrad's life is derived from three sources: the separate versions of it in 'Falk' and *The Shadow-Line* and scattered references in *Lord Jim*, 'The End of the Tether', *The Mirror of the Sea* and 'The Secret Sharer'; Conrad's comments on the origins of these works; and from Norman Sherry's diligent sleuthing in the shipping records and newspapers in Bangkok and Singapore, which enabled him to check Conrad's claims as to the authenticity of *The Shadow-Line* and to reconstruct the circumstances of his first command. In *Conrad's Eastern World*, Sherry identifies the captain who dies at sea and confirms the delay of the *Otago* due to malaria among the crew (facts common to both 'Falk' and *The Shadow-Line*); and he verifies the originals of Mr Burns and Captain Ellis and the itinerary and chronology of the story. Not surprisingly, however, Sherry also shows that 'the facts of Conrad's experience at this time' (212) do not support his repeated claims that *The Shadow-Line* was 'exact autobiography' (*Life and Letters*, II, 182). Thus the original Mr Burns (Mr Born) was not crazy, the dead captain (Snadden) was not a villain, and Conrad greatly exaggerates the sickness of the crew, only five of whom needed replacing when he arrived in Singapore. Clearly, the different reasons given for the delay of the ship in Bangkok in 'Falk' (the sand-bar) and *The Shadow-Line* ('commercial complications' [204]) cannot both be 'true' and they relate to the differing concerns and moods of the two stories; but both accounts suggest (as does 'The Secret Sharer') that Conrad's chance first command stirred feelings of inadequacy and was deeply traumatic, as all three captains face 'Horror, ruin and everlasting remorse' ('Falk', 111).[16] But, whereas in 'Falk' the details of the reminiscing captain's appointment to his first command are relegated to a paragraph in order to explain his presence in Bangkok, the obtaining of it occupies the first third of *The Shadow-Line*. Then, of course, the remainder of the narrative begins where 'Falk' ends with the passage out to sea and the subsequent trials that beset the young captain and his new crew. I am less concerned, however, with the correspondences between the facts and the differing fictional versions of them, than in what Conrad called in 1915 his 'moral and intellectual condition' (Karl, 779), that led him to return to the subject of his 'First Command' only to discover that 'in consequence of my changed mental attitude to it, it became *The Shadow-Line*' (770) – differing greatly, therefore, from 'Falk' in tone, presentation, and in the value and significance that Conrad discovered in the events themselves.

Conrad's changed mental attitude, as his correspondence shows, is a complex mix of personal, familial and national conditions. When the First World War broke out in August 1914, Conrad and his family found themselves trapped in Poland during his first visit to the country of his birth for over twenty years. From the moment he returned to England in early November 1914 and throughout the composition of *The Shadow-Line* (February–December 1915) Conrad manifested 'the classic symptoms of morbid depression' (Najder, 407), compounded by debts, gout, his wife's crippled knees, his fears for Poland's future, and finally the war itself, which began badly for the Allied Forces of England, France and Russia. On 28 January 1915 Conrad even questioned his vocation: 'It seems almost criminal levity to talk at this time of books, stories, publication. This war attends my uneasy pillow like a nightmare' (2 439). None the less, within days, he began 'the old subject' of 'First Command' and barely six weeks later changed it to *The Shadow-Line* because it had 'a spiritual meaning' (5 458). During the early months of 1915 Conrad made little progress on the story. In May and June he desperately assured Pinker that the end was in sight; but by mid-October he had written less than 20,000 words, and he did not finish a first draft until mid-December. In his Author's Note

16 Such feelings, as Johnson illustrates, are more fully developed in the manuscript of 'Falk'.

(1920), Conrad admits that throughout the composition of the story, 'during this year of fire and slaughter' (5 545), he had 'an acute consciousness' that, placed against 'the supreme trial of a whole generation', the events of his own autobiographical tale were 'insignificant' and 'obscure' (152). Yet, as all the evidence shows, the spiritual meaning he found in his story arose from 'a feeling of identity, though with an enormous difference of scale' (152) between the excitements attendant upon his own chance first command and the subsequent perils encountered and survived, and that of a whole generation of young officers and men, including his son Borys. 'Everybody we know,' he wrote on 17 August 1915, 'has lost somebody . . . They all go. My boy's turn will be coming presently.' Then, in words that describe both the national tragedy and summarise the theme and the values of the story in progress, he observed: 'The shadow lies over this land. This is a time of great awe and searching of hearts and of resolute girding of loins' (5 500). 'Driven nearly mad by his own uselessness' (5 498), Conrad identified himself with Borys, who despite his bad eyesight eagerly sought 'active service' (5 497) and in September, at the tender age of seventeen, 'obtained a commission in the A.S.C. [Army Service Corps]' (5 508). Similarly, Conrad was 'proud and pleased' at the contribution of the British Merchant Service to the war-effort (5 509). He called Borys 'our young officer' (5 511) and, in words that also describe 'the systematic kindliness' (201) of the young captain in *The Shadow-Line*, claimed he 'has the temperament of a gentleman' (5 510). On 21 September Conrad accompanied his son to the ASC camp in Kent and once again fused fact with fiction when he played the part of Captain Giles: 'I wanted to be with him as long as possible on the day he had to put his boyhood definitely behind him. He dropped me opposite Bromley R[ailway] Station, I saw him wriggle between a bus and a van, and then I hobbled across the road feeling more old than I have ever felt before. But I have never seen the boy look so happy in his 17½ years of life' (5 512–13). And, as the young captain in *The Shadow-Line* 'had envisaged a command as a result of a slow course of promotion' (181) and then experienced 'a strange sense of exultation' at his sudden elevation, so Borys (fact this time following fiction) was 'incoherent with joy' on being made within a month 'second in command of a section consisting of three officers, 120 men and 25 lorries' (5 519). Borys's departure, typically sudden promotion and imminent engagement in the bloody fields of Flanders, sparked three months of sustained writing. And, once again, Conrad's feelings in mid-November that on the one hand his son 'seems to be made of the right stuff' (5 513) and his fears on the other that he could abruptly cross the final shadow-line, coincide with the young captain's anguish that 'this awful, this death-haunted command' (222) might prove 'I am no good' (229).[17]

I stress Conrad's 'changed mental attitude' towards the time and events of his own first command of the *Otago* because, in marked contrast to 'Falk' which is not intimately felt, *The Shadow-Line* is presented as an autobiography: it 'is personal experience seen in perspective with the eye of the mind and coloured by that affection one can't help feeling for such events of one's life as one has no reason to be ashamed of' (Author's Note, 152). Hence, in a radical departure from his usual fictional strategies, the authorial voice of *The Shadow-Line* is neither displaced as in (say) 'Falk' and 'Heart of Darkness' by narrators who address a fictional audience within the tale, nor skeined in a mesh of ironies as in 'Typhoon'; rather, it addresses the reader directly in a first-person, confessional voice and the reader never doubts that 'Conrad writes as a direct and full participant in the experience he records' (Leavis, 100). In marked contrast to 'Typhoon', which convinces us against the grain of several dissenting viewpoints of the moral force of MacWhirr's simple words, the reminiscing captain-narrator is self-conscious and intelligent and must, perforce, record the events and the conclusions to be drawn from them. *The Shadow-Line* from this perspective is the simplest and most direct work he ever wrote and its designs upon its readers are the most palpable.

This 'large ease of "autobiography" ', as James warned in his brilliant Preface to the New York edition of *The Ambassadors* (1909), is notoriously difficult to contain because the hero-narrator has 'the double privilege of subject and object'; and this 'single mouthful of

17 Borys's subsequent experiences uncannily follow those of his father in *The Shadow-Line*. Thus, by May 1916 'he is a Second Lieut in sole command of a section of 120 men and 15 cars, in charge of a heavy battery which is almost constantly engaged' in Flanders. He has 'no sleep for thirty hours', and 'talks affectionately of his Non-Com.[missioned] officers who are very good to him, he says, and the men are "dear fellows" . . . In reality this means that they like the boy. And that he is all right' (5 598–9). Solidarity and reciprocity are indeed intact! After the terrible slaughter of the Somme in July 1916 (the shadow-line in modern British history), Borys 'writes cheerfully (if not quite so boyishly as at first) about being "very well, very tired and very busy" ', and reminds us of Conrad's 'undying regard' for his crew, when he still 'speaks of his noncoms and men with real affection' (5 622). Borys was later gassed and shell-shocked and crossed the final shadow-line in 1978.

"method"' exposes the author to 'the terrible *fluidity* of self-revelation' and threatens the author's control of his subject, his tone, and his reader (1316). Such objections were made by an early reviewer who complained that because 'the young captain' functions as 'his own father confessor, the Homer of his own *Odyssey*', the 'preamble' is too long and marred by 'something very like priggishness'. Moreover, 'if in fiction health and triumph and the goal of the ideal are to be the outcome, somehow discussion of such matters is safest when left to some aloof narrator – safest, at any rate, when our young hero must otherwise himself refer to the "tempering and maturing" of his own character'. In works such as 'Typhoon', *Lord Jim* and *Under Western Eyes*, the reviewer argues, an 'austere, satiric, compassionate, unflinching conviction is woven through . . . the story; it is inherent in it'; whereas in *The Shadow-Line*, 'The moral overbalances the story.'[18] The reviewer's dislike of the insufferably exemplary oracle, Captain Giles, anticipates Moser's of the over-idealised portrayal of the crew who 'behave as faithfully as could be expected of men already dead from fever' and who 'never blame their captain' (139). Again, as Moser and Hawthorn among others argue, the young captain's guilt seems 'disproportionate' to the occasion and, therefore, the impulse behind his 'confession' is unconvincing, because after all the disease of the crew is exacerbated by the perfidy of the previous captain and the sympathetic doctor checked the quinine and failed to see that most of the bottles contained a substitute and useless white powder.

Conrad responds to and anticipates such criticism in his Author's Note to *The Shadow-Line* when he reflects on the problems of egotism and vanity attendant upon the autobiographical mode: 'For when we begin to meditate on the meaning of our own past it seems to fill all the world in its profundity and its magnitude.' Moreover, he acknowledges that 'the depth and the nature of the mood with which I approached it [the story] . . . is best expressed perhaps in the dedication which strikes me now as a most disproportionate thing . . . another instance of the overwhelming greatness of our own emotion to ourselves' (152). Conrad's modesty is defensive and appealing; but it is precisely his elaborate dedications that signal both his awareness of, and desire to avert, charges of egotism and disproportion and the way he wants his confession to be read. The first dedication on the title page is from the story itself – 'Worthy

18 Unsigned review, the *Times Literary Supplement*, 22 March 1917, 138.

of my undying regard' – and testifies to the supreme values of interdependence and solidarity that enabled him as a new captain to cross the shadow-line and to survive the disease and terrible calm as the ship and crew were poised 'on the brink of a slow and agonising destruction' (153). On the flyleaf appears the inscription that Conrad used to indicate that the 'experience' recorded 'is transposed into spiritual terms' (*Life and Letters*, II 183): 'TO / BORYS AND ALL OTHERS/ WHO LIKE HIMSELF HAVE CROSSED/ IN EARLY YOUTH THE SHADOW-LINE/OF THEIR GENERATION/ WITH LOVE.'[19] The writing of *The Shadow-Line* became, then, and is signalled as, an act of solidarity with his son's war-torn generation: and his choice of 'the un-English genre of the spiritual autobiography' (Guerard, 12) deliberately tested to the limit his aesthetic commitment to 'scepticism . . . the agent of truth' which preserves the artist from moralism and from favouring 'creatures made in his [own] image' (5 359).

Conrad's art in *The Shadow-Line* has, however, received sympathetic and intelligent attention from Leavis, Watt and Berthoud, and from Geddes who claims that it is 'without doubt' Conrad's 'purest and most beautiful story' (83). It has always been a favourite of mine and of my students, not least because Conrad was fully aware of, and mainly avoided, the risks of 'disproportion', self-indulgence and platitude inherent in the confessional form he adopted on his return to his own anxious first command. Conrad's tact is most evident in his handling of the narrative point of view and of the captain's psychology, and in his construction of a series of episodes that initially develop the intertwined themes of the shadow-line and the interdependence of men and then reveal the 'quality' of the crew's 'resistance' to the calamities that befall them.

The narrative point of view largely resists self-flattery, because the retrospective self views his youth with a self-directed irony. The leisurely opening scenes simultaneously reveal his callow disdain for 'the general inanity' of Captain Giles' 'discourse' and curiosity (171), and suggest that his feelings 'of life being but a waste of days' imbued with 'the menace of emptiness' (172) and of detachment 'from all earthly goings on' (170) are (like Hamlet's) exaggerated and defensive – registering his confusion following his inexplicable decision to throw up a good berth and to return home. Hence, the

19 Not surprisingly, 'this dedication', Jessie Conrad records, 'used to trouble me all the time my boy was at the front. There seemed something ominous in it' (95).

opening chapters invite the reader to participate in his volatile state of mind and by subtly exposing the younger self's fretful self-preoccupation ensure (in marked contrast to the design of 'Falk') that our 'understanding of the pattern of motives outstrips that of the narrator' (Watt, 501).[20] Thus, his irritated superiority and self-consciousness are typical of 'that twilight region between youth and maturity' (174) and, ironically, render him the potential dupe of the chief steward's 'petty intrigue'. Moreover, all his self-absorbed actions and responses alert us to his blindness to the sympathy of Captain Kent and his crew and of Captain Giles – a sympathy that establishes, despite his own callow assertions to the contrary, the value of human interdependence. As a result of Captain Giles' probings the narrator is made to feel 'that I knew very little of life . . . ' (173). Significantly, his first expression of humility coincides with the surprising entrance of the steward, whom he accosts spontaneously, and brusquely asks about the 'official communication . . . from the Harbour Office'. This 'impulse' changes the course of his life (174). It differs greatly, however, from the equivalent moment in 'Falk' – when the young captain intercepts Falk on his sudden arrival in Schomberg's dining-room – because it is not accidental; rather, it is prompted by Captain Giles' 'mysterious earnestness'. Thus, in a comic reversal, the youthful captain's dismal certainty that there are 'no opportunities to find out something about oneself' (172) yields, belatedly, to his recognition of 'the inwardness of things' (174) and he joyfully rushes to the harbour office with the 'magic word "Command" ' (176) ringing in his ears to learn of his sudden appointment, 'a gift of extraordinary potency' that makes his head swim (178). This 'sensation of dealing with mere dream-stuff', with Captain Ellis fancifully playing the part of 'deputy-Neptune', is promptly corrected by his feeling of 'the fellowship of seamen' that is 'stronger than the difference of age and station' (179). These sudden switches of mood from detachment to engagement, from dismay to exultation, from a sense of the 'miraculous' (180) that makes him feel he is 'very much like people in fairy tales' to an internalised, sober discovery of 'how much of a seaman I was, in heart and in mind' (184), from self-absorption to solidarity, are entirely characteristic of his narrative and constitute a pattern of revelations that mark his burgeoning

20 The page references are to Watt in Carabine (ed.), *Joseph Conrad: Critical Assessments*, vol 3.

self-awareness of 'a shadow-line warning one that the region of early youth . . . must be left behind' (159). From this perspective, the young captain reminds us of Jukes, who is also imaginative, fond of figures of speech, and prone to huge mood swings in his responses to the typhoon. But in his last letter Jukes fails to recognise his own psychological shifts and, therefore, in marked contrast to the seaman-author of *The Shadow-Line*, is incapable of gleaning self-knowledge from his terrifying experience of the storm.

From the moment the young captain learns of his first command, through to the end of the voyage, the narrative is built around a series of calamities. But, in marked contrast to Falk's experiences aboard the *Borgmester Dahl*, where 'Everything went wrong' and the 'solidarity' of the crew dissipates, both the captain and his men reveal 'the fibre' of their 'stuff' and affirm humankind's capacity to survive all the ocean 'may contain of perfidy, of violence, and of terror' ('Typhoon', 22). Until the end of Chapter 4, however, with the drastic discovery that there is no more quinine, the narrative follows the rhythms of the captain's psychology, veering from his self-mocking, heightened expectations to his successive disillusionments; and, therefore, the reactions of the crew are secondary. Thus, his sense when he first sits in the captain's chair of a 'dynasty' based on 'training . . . duty and . . . the blessed simplicity of its traditional point of view of life' (193) is subverted by Burns' account of his predecessor's atrocious betrayal of command. Then, the captain's beliefs that 'I won't feel really at peace till I have that ship of mine out in the Indian Ocean' (186), that 'The sea . . . was pure, safe, and friendly' (204) and 'the only remedy for all my troubles' (205), and that 'The first breeze would blow . . . away' the lingering malaria (206), all prove ungrounded. Indeed, the becalmed ocean and capricious winds suggest a 'purposeful malevolence' (215) that toys with and complements the renewed disease that wracks all save himself and Ransome and that mocks 'that special intensity of existence which is the quintessence of youthful aspirations' (213).

This pattern culminates with the shattering of the captain's illusory 'faith' in the quinine's power to 'break the spell by its medicinal virtue, make . . . the weather but a passing worry, and, like a magic powder working against mysterious malefices, secure . . . my first command against the evil powers of calms and pestilence' (216). At this moment the captain is self-absorbed and naïve and, as his incantatory imagery indicates, 'bewitched' (213). Indeed he is infected by Burns' crazed 'fixed idea' (212) that the previous captain has cast a spell on the ship. The quinine fiasco marks the nadir of the captain's fortunes and constitutes a turning point for both himself and for his relationship to his ailing crew. Thus, the very greatness of such 'a mental shock' induces 'a sort of temporary insensibility'. None the less, like Captain MacWhirr, he hastens to the deck: 'An example this of training become instinct . . . the problems of a ship at sea must be met on deck' (217). This instinctive reassertion of seamanship ensures his survival because he must now move out of himself and share the problem of the missing quinine with his stricken crew. And from this point on, though every fresh calamity heightens his sense of isolation and imbues him with despair, fear and shame, he grows increasingly aware of and thankful for the varieties of 'resistance' shown by the crew in general and by Burns and Ransome in particular.

The first figure he encounters is Burns, whose wild aspect the stunned captain completely misunderstands. He is not trying to commit suicide, but in his own mad way, as we later learn, he is preparing like the captain to face on deck the threats to the ship's survival caused by the previous captain's betrayal. At the beginning of Chapter 5 our awareness of the pattern of motives continues to outstrip the captain's because he does not realise that his 'morbid vision of her [the ship] as a floating grave' (218) coincides with the disappearance of Ransome from his side, and that his wish to be 'alone with the greatness of my trouble' (218–19) is egocentric and timid. Once again, however, he cannot avoid Burns, who surprisingly offers a rational explanation for the disappearance of the quinine and then fiercely and sensibly corrects the captain's excessive remorse ('I feel it's all my fault') with 'That's very foolish, sir' (220). The captain then determines to 'face' his crew and is astonished by their stoic acceptance that their malaria cannot be treated and by their endorsement of his proposal that the 'best chance for the ship and the men was in the efforts all of us, sick and well, must make' to get her to Singapore (221).

In a brilliant switch, the captain's appeal to the interdependence of the crew and their resolute response are followed by the first of two extracts from notes 'I wrote at the time' which record his anguished sense that humankind either 'blundered unbidden' or was 'decoyed' into an alien universe, as 'I have been decoyed into this awful, this death-haunted command . . . ' (222). The captain's desolate sense of his loss of control and his lassitude (feelings the unimaginative MacWhirr cannot experience) parallel the calm and evoke the epigraph from Baudelaire, wherein the 'flat calm' is seen as the 'grand mirror/ Of my despair' (157). Such narcissism is juxtaposed to and corrected by 'the unfailing Ransome with the uneasy heart, immune, serene, and active' (223) and by the captain's awed remembrance that the suffering of his crew highlighted 'the unsuspected nobility of some, the strength of others', manifest especially either in 'the temper of their souls or the sympathy of their imagination' (224), which ensure that they never reproach him and that they restrain his egocentric and irrational feeling that he is the victim of a malevolent plot. They are 'so worthy of my undying regard' (224), because he learns (as Conrad felt his son's generation had) that 'he could not have survived the ordeal to which he was exposed, without a full reciprocity of dependence between himself and his crew' (Berthould, 14).

'The strength of others' also includes Burns whose superstitious explanation for events misled an early reviewer to praise 'Mr. Conrad's elfin power', whereby 'all these suggestions, experiences, and episodes might be ascribed *equally* to natural or supernatural causes. The artist reserves his judgment and we reserve ours' (Sherry, 1973, 307). This posing of equal and competing causes and judgements has persisted in Conrad criticism, most recently in Erdnast-Vulcan. This view is built, I think, upon a false distinction that travesties Conrad's 'invincible conviction that whatever falls under the dominion of our senses must be in nature and, however exceptional, cannot differ in its essence from all the other effects of the visible and tangible world of which we are a self-conscious part' (Author's Note, 151). Moreover, it fails fully to engage either Burns' functions or actions in the story. Thus, initially, Burns sees himself as the captain's rival and thinks they must be enemies; but from the moment he appeals successfully to the captain from his sick-bed to be allowed to sail 'in the name of their common profession' ('He and I were sailors' [204]) he functions as the captain's double. 'The effect of a mental or moral shock on a common mind' such as Burns' takes the form of 'a mere superstitious fancy compounded of fear and animosity' (Author's Note, 151); but 'the seaman' in him, as in the captain, who feels that his 'imagination' is not 'properly under control', remains 'sufficiently sane' (224). Thus, his superstitions deeply disturb the captain and infect his discourse, and he is used (as in the shaving incident) to dramatise the captain's 'mental disorder' (217). However, he also brusquely absolves the captain of blame for the missing quinine, reinforces Captain Giles' warning about trying 'to steer west' (226) and urges him to continue heading south in order to confront and out-face 'the old ruffian' (226) whose corpse bars their way to safety. His irrational resolution is then a superstitious and, in its own way, courageous version of the captain's crossing of the shadow-line. Moreover, it is no accident that his maxims remind us of MacWhirr, another common mind, who mistakenly stands up to and then out-voices the storm. Thus, as the captain realises, though Burns 'was like a case of possession. His protest . . . was essentially quite sound' (226). And his sudden appearance on deck, when the captain feels he is 'on the edge of some violent issue, lurking in the dark', both frightens him and mocks his passive, irrational conviction that 'our helplessness' was due to 'the yet unbroken spell' of a malignant universe rather than a natural manifestation of 'the tangible world'. Nature, as ever in Conrad's fiction, is indifferent to human consciousness, yet it is precisely its oddest evolution that stamps itself on the darkness and rain. The crew survive 'the broad shadow on the horizon' (227), 'the impenetrable blackness' (229) and the 'quietness that . . . was like a foretaste of annihilation' (230), because through 'sheer spiritual strength' (230) they haul up the sail: and though Burns is too weak to assist his appearance on deck is 'a morally telling gesture' (Berthoud, 17). Burns, therefore, fully justifies his captain's tribute at the end – 'I am very proud of him' (243) – because he reaffirms the reciprocity of endeavour and resolution embodied in the captain's recognition that the crew were 'worthy of my undying regard'.

As in 'Typhoon', there is a massive ellipsis between Burns' last, anguished, professional question – 'How will you get the ship into harbour, sir, without the men to handle her?' – and the captain's report, 'Well – it did get done about forty hours afterwards' (241). Only now is the captain in a position openly to satirise his own fearful, fanciful stamping of his consciousness upon the character of the calm, the darkness, and the winds, as he laconically reviews the metaphors that the literalist Burns had unshaken faith in; and then, in a sly reversal, sardonically calls upon the metaphors of an alternative supernatural tradition – the 'fabrication' (Author's Note, 151) of Christianity: 'it did get done . . . By the exorcising virtue of Mr Burns' awful laugh, the malicious spectre had been laid, the evil spell broken, the curse removed. We were now in the hands of a kind and energetic Providence. It was rushing us on . . . ' (241).

I have left a discussion of Ransome until last because his 'serene temperament' (232) and modest purposefulness are the antithesis of Burns' deranged resolution, and because he embodies the very qualities the volatile captain struggles to attain: 'That man noticed everything, attended to everything, shed comfort around him as he moved. As he passed me he remarked in a soothing tone that the stars were coming out. They were' (238). Ransome's name of course is suggestive of Christian forgiveness and he is described, as here, in Christlike terms. But attempts to allegorise the novel along such lines are, I think, profoundly mistaken. Indeed, it is precisely Ransome's attention to actualities that ensures that, unlike his captain, he consistently disdains supernatural explanations and the metaphors that attend them. Hence, in marked contrast to Captain MacWhirr, who is fondly mocked by the figures of speech he engenders, the portrayal of Ransome's 'grace' and 'consummate seamanship', performed 'with a little smile frozen on his lips' (239), is always restrained. And, most importantly, he shares his creator's scepticism and functions to remind us that the captain's controlled satire of his own resort to the language of 'marvels and mysteries' (Author's Note, 151) drawn from fairy stories, Roman myth and other supernatural explanations for the extraordinary course of events he underwent, is newly won. Thus in response to the captain's ' "You and I seem to have been forgotten . . . by the fever-devil who has got on board this ship" . . . Ransome gave me one of his attractive, intelligent, quick glances . . . It occurred to me that I had been talking somewhat in Mr Burns' manner. It annoyed me. Yet often in darker moments I forgot myself into an attitude towards our troubles more fit for a contest against a living enemy' (226).

Such self-forgetting, of course, energises the prose, is true to the young captain's highly imaginative registering of his experiences, and it gives 'an additional turn of the racking screw' (234) to Conrad's presentation of events. Ransome, however, needs neither to dramatise nor to personify his troubles. He has had to teach himself self-restraint and his weak heart means that he incarnates the Conradian truism that Captain Giles at the end articulates, 'precious little rest in life for anybody. Better not think of it' (246). This injunction perfectly fits and anticipates a Hemingway hero. We need to recognise, however, that Ransome's necessary devotion to the task in hand and his eschewal of metaphor and of otherworldly explanations tempers the mercurial imagination of the captain and ensures that he does not funk his responsibilities both to himself and his crew. Thus immediately after the captain's anguished notation in his diary, 'I am shirking it', Ransome confirms that his captain must face the 'very black' weather 'on deck' (229).

Ransome's importance to the captain's sanity is beautifully expressed in Conrad's austere, secular play with the myth of creation.

When Ransome 'appeared quite close to me' the captain feels that he is 'stepping out of the darkness into visibility . . . as if just created with his composed face and pleasant voice' (232); but immediately afterwards, when Ransome 'stepped back two paces and vanished from my sight', the captain records: 'At once an uneasiness possessed me, as if some support had been withdrawn . . . Such must have been the darkness before creation . . . I knew I was invisible to the man at the helm. Neither could I see anything. He was alone, I was alone, every man was alone where he stood. And every form was gone too, spar, sail, fittings, rails; everything was blotted out in the dreadful smoothness of that absolute night' (233). In this moving passage the captain confronts his utter insignificance in the scheme of the universe; but 'his vivid realisation of complete human isolation in the "darkness before creation", evokes the historical dimension of the theme of solidarity; the narrator . . . is brought face to face with the long tradition of civilisation . . . and his own utter dependence on it' (Watt, 505).

At the end, Ransome begs the captain's pardon and 'with an air of anxiety' requests permission to leave the ship, so as to 'be quiet somewhere'. The captain objects, but: ' "I must go," he broke in. "I have a right!" He gasped and a look of almost savage determination passed over his face. For an instant he was another being. And I saw under the worth and comeliness of the man the humble reality of things. Life was a boon to him – this precarious hard life – and he was thoroughly alarmed about himself' (243). Ransome's 'right' unlike Falk's insistence on the right of self-preservation, attests to a consciousness of human weakness that he cannot avoid and that the captain in his last diary entry fears he may betray: 'I always suspected that I might be no good' (229). The revelation that Ransome's 'worth' is inseparable from 'this precarious hard life' it is humankind's fate to share is the rock-bed of the solidarity that the story celebrates. Ransome will never know the remission from suffering that the captain and his crew experience at the end, because he is conscious of the reality of the final shadow-line of death, 'our common enemy' (246) in every beat of his damaged heart. Ransome's grace, modesty, and scepticism inform 'the quality of his resistance' to 'the events at sea' and ensure in Berthoud's noble formulation, that he is never allowed 'to compromise that decorum of self-possession which preserves and justifies his and our existence on earth' (22). The captain's confession continually acknowledges his own struggle for such decorum: but it also affirms in full recognition of his own fears and weaknesses that 'without a full reciprocity of dependence between himself and his crew' the ship would not have survived 'this death-haunted command'. 'This lesson,' in Berthoud's fine formulation, 'may seem banal enough; yet Conrad shows that it supports the entire edifice of human life' (14).

When Conrad wrote *The Shadow-Line* in 1915, the success of the allied forces was far from assured, but he successfully mobilises his narrative to function as 'sworn witness of the qualities needed to confront the crisis' (Berthoud, 12). His elaborate dedications in the first edition of March 1917 testify to a generation that have crossed the shadow-line fighting 'for life first, for freedom of thought and development in whatever form next'.[21] His Author's Note of 1920, when the war is over and Poland has emerged as a free and independent nation after over 120 years of partition, simultaneously acknowledges 'the minute and insignificant character of my own obscure experience' and modestly celebrates his risky and unique decision to identify this version of the events of his own first command with that of 'the supreme trial of a whole generation' (152).

DR KEITH CARABINE
University of Kent, Canterbury

I am deeply indebted to Owen Knowles, a great Conradian, who critiqued a draft of this Introduction.

21 Letter to John Quinn, the American collector of his manuscripts, 6 May 1917, shortly after the United States entered the war (quoted Najder, 424).

BIBLIOGRAPHY

Jocelyn Baines, *Joseph Conrad: A Critical Biography*, Weidenfeld & Nicolson, London 1960

Cynthia Fansler Behrman, *Victorian Myths of the Sea*, Ohio University Press, Athens 1977

Jacques Berthoud, 'Introduction: Autobiography and War', *The Shadow-Line*, Penguin Books, London 1986, 7–24

T. A. Birrell, 'The Simplicity of *Typhoon*, Conrad, Flaubert and Others', *Dutch Quarterly Review*, 10/4 (1980), 272–95

William Bonney, *Thorns and Arabesques*, Johns Hopkins University Press, Baltimore 1980

Carolyn B. Brown, 'Creative Combat in 'Typhoon', *The Conradian*, 17/1 (1992), 1–16

Keith Carabine, *Joseph Conrad: Critical Assessments* (4 vols), Helm Information, Robertsbridge 1992

Sooyoung Chon, ' " Typhoon": Silver Dollars and Stars', *Conradiana*, 22/1 (1990), 25–42

Jessie Conrad, *Joseph Conrad as I Knew Him*, Heinemann, London 1926

Joseph Conrad, *The Collected Edition of the Works*, J. M. Dent, 1946–7

Joseph Conrad, *The Collected Letters*, vols **1/2/3/4/5**, Frederick R. Karl and Laurence Davies (eds), Cambridge University Press, 1983–96

Mario Curreli and Fausto Ciompi, 'A Socio-Semiotic Reading of Conrad's "Falk" ', *L'Epoque Conradienne* (1988), 35–45; reprinted in Carabine, vol 2, 543–52

Daphna Erdnast-Vulcan, *Joseph Conrad and the Modern Temper*, Clarendon Press, Oxford 1991

Ford Madox Ford, *Joseph Conrad*, Duckworth and Co., London 1924

Robert Foulke, 'Life in the Dying World of Sail, 1870–1910', *The Journal of British Studie*s, 3 (1963), 105–36

Robert Foulke, 'From the Center to the Dangerous Hemisphere: *Heart of Darkness* and *Typhoon*', in Keith Carabine, Owen Knowles and Wiesław Krajka (eds), *Conrad's Literary Career*, East European Monographs, Boulder 1992, 127–51

Gail Fraser, 'The Short Fiction', in J. H. Stape (ed.), *The Cambridge Companion to Joseph Conrad*, Cambridge University Press, 1996, 25–44

Gary Geddes, *Conrad's Later Novels*, McGill–Queens University Press, Montreal 1980

Graham Good, 'Notes on the Novella', in Charles E. May (ed.), *The New Short Story Theories*, Ohio University Press, Athens 1994, 147–64

Laurence Graver, *Conrad's Short Fiction*, University of California Press, Berkeley 1969

John W. Griffiths, *Joseph Conrad and the Anthropological Dilemma*, Clarendon Press, Oxford 1995

Albert Guerard, *Conrad the Novelist*, Harvard University Press, Cambridge, Mass. 1958

Jeremy Hawthorn, Introduction, *The Shadow-Line*, World's Classics, Oxford University Press, 1985, vii–xxv

Henry James, *French Writers and other European Writers, The Prefaces to the New York Edition*, The Library of America, New York 1984

G. Jean-Aubry, *Joseph Conrad: Life and Letters* (2 vols), Heinemann, London 1927

Bruce Johnson, 'Conrad's "Falk": Manuscript and Meaning', *Modern Language Quarterly*, 26 (1965), 267–84

F. R. Karl, *A Reader's Guide to Joseph Conrad*, Noonday Press, New York; Thames and Hudson, London; 1960

F. R. Karl, *Joseph Conrad: The Three Lives*, Farrar, Strauss and Giroux, New York; Faber and Faber, London; 1979

Joel R. Kehler, 'The Centrality of the Narrator in Conrad's "Falk" ', *Conradiana*, 6/1 (1974), 19–30

Paul Kirschner, Introduction, *Typhoon and Other Tales*, Penguin Books, London 1990, 1–31

Joseph Kolupke, 'Elephants, Empires, and Blind Men: A Reading of the Figurative Language in Conrad's "Typhoon" ', *Conradiana*, 20/1 (1988), 71–85

F. R. Leavis, 'The Shadow-Line', in *Anna Karenina and Other Essays*, Chatto and Windus, London 1967

Charles E. May (ed.), *The New Short Story Theories*, Ohio University Press, Athens 1994

William E. Messenger, 'Conrad and his "Sea Stuff" ', *Conradiana*, 6/1 (1974), 3–18

Thomas Moser, *Joseph Conrad: Achievement and Decline*, Harvard University Press, Cambridge, Mass. 1957

Zdzisław Najder, *Joseph Conrad: A Chronicle*, Cambridge University Press; Rutgers University Press, New Brunswick, New Jersey; 1983

Allan H. Pasco, 'On Defining Short Stories', in May, *The New Short Story Theories*, 114–30

Mary Louise Pratt, 'The Long and the Short of It', in May, *The New Short Story Theories*, 91–113

Dwight H. Purdy, 'Conrad at Work: The Two Serial Texts of "Typhoon" ', *Conradiana*, 19/2 (1987), 99–119

Stephen Reynolds, 'Joseph Conrad and Sea Fiction', *Quarterly Review*, 217 (1912), 159–80; reprinted in Carabine, vol 1, 493–507

Bertrand Russell, *Portraits from Memory*, London 1956

Charles I. Schuster, 'Comedy and the Limits of Language in Conrad's "Typhoon" ', *Conradiana*, 16/1 (1884), 55–71

Daniel R. Schwartz, *Conrad: From 'Almayer's Folly' to 'Under Western Eyes'*, Macmillan, London; Cornell University Press, Ithaca; 1980

Valerie Shaw, *The Short Story: A Critical Introduction*, Longman, London and New York 1983

Norman Sherry, *Conrad's Eastern World*, Cambridge University Press, 1966

Norman Sherry, *Conrad: The Critical Heritage*, Routledge & Kegan Paul, London 1973

J. I. M. Stewart, *Joseph Conrad*, Longman, London 1968

Tony Tanner, ' "Gnawed Bones" and "Artless Tales": Eating and Narrative in Conrad', in Norman Sherry (ed.), *Joseph Conrad: A Commemoration*, Macmillan, London 1976; reprinted in Carabine, vol 2, 526–42

Tony Tanner (ed.), *The Oxford Book of Sea Stories*, Oxford University Press, 1994

Ian Watt, 'Story and Idea in Conrad's *The Shadow-Line*', *Critical Quarterly*, 2/2 (1960), 133–48; reprinted in Carabine, vol 3, 659–76

Christof Wegelin, 'MacWhirr and the Testimony of the Human Voice', *Conradiana*, 7/1 (1975), 45–50

Cedric Watts, Introduction, *Typhoon and Other Tales*, World's Classics, Oxford University Press, 1986, vii–xx

A NOTE ON THE TEXT

The three stories, in keeping with Wordsworth Editions' aim to produce accessible modern texts, have undergone a 'Moderate Modernisation Programme'. Thus, for example, single quotes with double quotes within, replace double quotes with single quotes within; the old-fashioned em dash (—) is replaced with the en dash (–) with space before and after; and ellipses always have three dots (. . .). I have used as my copy texts the British first editions of 'Typhoon' and 'Falk' (*Typhoon and Other Stories*, William Heinemann, 1903) and of *The Shadow-Line* (J. M. Dent, 1917); and the Author's Notes of 1919 and 1920, respectively, are from the Kent Edition (Doubleday, Page and Company, 1925). The present volume is not a critical edition, and I have not seen any of the manuscript versions of these stories. None the less, I have checked the stories against the Heinemann Collected Edition (HC), which Conrad corrected, and the Dent Collected (DC). I also consulted and am indebted to the editions of *Typhoon and Other Tales* by Cedric Watts for World's Classics (1986) and by Paul Kirschner for Penguin Twentieth-Century Classics (1990); and, in the case of *The Shadow-Line*, the editions by Jeremy Hawthorn for World's Classics (1985) and by Jacques Berthoud for Penguin Twentieth-Century Classics (1986).

The substantive changes for 'Typhoon', following HC, are 'quaintly' for 'queerly' (68); 'has' for 'had liberated' (32); 'as though' for 'though' (46); and 'striped' for 'stripped' (51). In 'Falk', I substituted 'Plate' for 'Platte' (81); followed Conrad's changes of 'trombone' for 'trump' and 'my' for 'any escape' (88); 'ropes' ' (DC) for 'rope's' (137); and 'rather unwell' (HC) for 'unwell rather' (142). In *The Shadow-Line* three substantive changes are Conrad's: 'side' (HC) for 'lintel' (174); 'called upon' for 'called' (221); and 'masts' for 'mast' (237). I followed DC's 'those' for 'them' (183, 245). Otherwise, throughout, I followed HC incidentals only when I felt (say) that the addition or subtraction of a comma improved the sense. All hyphenated words, of which Conrad was so fond, are retained.

'Typhoon' was serialised in the *Pall Mall Gazette*, January–March 1902, and *The Critic*, New York, February–May 1902; and *The Shadow-Line* in *The English Review*, September 1916–March 1917, and the *Metropolitan Magazine*, New York, October 1916.

Typhoon

And Other Stories

By

Joseph Conrad

Author of

"The Nigger of the 'Narcissus,'" &c.

> Far as the mariner on highest mast
> Can see all around upon the calmed vast,
> So wide was Neptune's hall . . .
>
> KEATS

London

William Heinemann

1903

The title page as it appeared in the first edition

AUTHOR'S NOTE

The main characteristic of this volume consists in this, that all the stories composing it belong not only to the same period but have been written one after another in the order in which they appear in the book.

The period is that which follows on my connection with *Blackwood's Magazine*. I had just finished writing 'The End of the Tether' and was casting about for some subject which could be developed in a shorter form than the tales in the volume of 'Youth' when the instance of a steamship full of returning coolies from Singapore to some port in northern China occurred to my recollection. Years before I had heard it being talked about in the East as a recent occurrence. It was for us merely one subject of conversation amongst many others of the kind. Men earning their bread in any very specialised occupation will talk shop, not only because it is the most vital interest of their lives but also because they have not much knowledge of other subjects. They have never had the time to get acquainted with them. Life, for most of us, is not so much a hard as an exacting taskmaster.

I never met anybody personally concerned in this affair, the interest of which for us was, of course, not the bad weather but the extraordinary complication brought into the ship's life at a moment of exceptional stress by the human element below her deck. Neither was the story itself ever enlarged upon in my hearing. In that company each of us could imagine easily what the whole thing was like. The financial difficulty of it, presenting also a human problem, was solved by a mind much too simple to be perplexed by anything in the world except men's idle talk for which it was not adapted.

From the first the mere anecdote, the mere statement I might say, that such a thing had happened on the high seas, appeared to me a sufficient subject for meditation. Yet it was but a bit of a sea yarn after all. I felt that to bring out its deeper significance, which was quite apparent to me, something other, something more was required; a leading motive that would harmonise all these violent noises, and a point of view that would put all that elemental fury into its proper place.

What was needed of course was Captain MacWhirr. Directly I perceived him I could see that he was the man for the situation. I don't mean to say that I ever saw Captain MacWhirr in the flesh, or had ever come in contact with his literal mind and his dauntless temperament. MacWhirr is not an acquaintance of a few hours, or a few weeks, or a few months. He is the product of twenty years of life. My own life. Conscious invention had little to do with him. If it is true that Captain MacWhirr never walked and breathed on this earth (which I find for my part extremely difficult to believe) I can also assure my readers that he is perfectly authentic. I may venture to assert the same of every aspect of the story, while I confess that the particular typhoon of the tale was not a typhoon of my actual experience.

At its first appearance 'Typhoon', the story, was classed by some critics as a deliberately intended storm-piece. Others picked out MacWhirr, in whom they perceived a definite symbolic intention. Neither was exclusively my intention. Both the typhoon and Captain MacWhirr presented themselves to me as the necessities of the deep conviction with which I approached the subject of the story. It was their opportunity. It was also my opportunity; and it would be vain to discourse about what I made of it in a handful of pages, since the pages themselves are here, between the covers of this volume, to speak for themselves.

This is a belated reflection. If it had occurred to me before it would have perhaps done away with the existence of this Author's Note; for, indeed, the same remark applies to every story in this volume. None of them are stories of experience in the absolute sense of the word. Experience in them is but the canvas of the attempted picture. Each of them has its more than one intention. With each the question is what the writer has done with his opportunity; and each answers the question for itself in words which, if I may say so without undue solemnity, were written with a conscientious regard for the truth of my own sensations. And each of those stories, to mean something, must justify itself in its own way to the conscience of each successive reader.

'Falk' – the second story in the volume – offended the delicacy of one critic at least by certain peculiarities of its subject. But what is the subject of 'Falk'? I personally do not feel so very certain about it. He who reads must find out for himself. My intention in writing 'Falk' was not to shock anybody. As in most of my writings I insist not on the events but on their effect upon the persons in the tale. But in everything I have written there is always one invariable intention, and that is to capture the reader's attention, by securing his interest and enlisting his sympathies for the matter in hand, whatever it may be, within the limits of the visible world and within the boundaries of human emotions.

I may safely say that Falk is absolutely true to my experience of certain straightforward characters combining a perfectly natural ruthlessness with a certain amount of moral delicacy. Falk obeys the laws of self-preservation without the slightest misgivings as to his right, but at a crucial turn of that ruthlessly preserved life he will not condescend to dodge the truth. As he is presented as sensitive enough to be affected permanently by a certain unusual experience, that experience had to be set by me before the reader vividly; but it is not the subject of the tale. If we go by mere facts then the subject is Falk's attempt to get married; in which the narrator of the tale finds himself unexpectedly involved both on its ruthless and its delicate side.

'Falk' shares with one other of my stories ('The Return' in the 'Tales of Unrest' volume) the distinction of never having been serialised. I think the copy was shown to the editor of some magazine who rejected it indignantly on the sole ground that 'the girl never says anything'. This is perfectly true. From first to last Hermann's niece utters no word in the tale – and it is not because she is dumb, but for the simple reason that whenever she happens to come under the observation of the narrator she has either no occasion or is too profoundly moved to speak. The editor, who obviously had read the story, might have perceived that for himself. Apparently he did not, and I refrained from pointing out the impossibility to him because, since he did not venture to say that 'the girl' did not live, I felt no concern at his indignation . . .

J. C.
1919

TYPHOON

Chapter 1

CAPTAIN MACWHIRR, of the steamer *Nan-Shan*, had a physiognomy that, in the order of material appearances, was the exact counterpart of his mind: it presented no marked characteristics of firmness or stupidity; it had no pronounced characteristics whatever; it was simply ordinary, irresponsive, and unruffled.

The only thing his aspect might have been said to suggest, at times, was bashfulness; because he would sit, in business offices ashore, sunburnt and smiling faintly, with downcast eyes. When he raised them, they were perceived to be direct in their glance and of blue colour. His hair was fair and extremely fine, clasping from temple to temple the bald dome of his skull in a clamp as of fluffy silk. The hair of his face, on the contrary, carroty and flaming, resembled a growth of copper wire clipped short to the line of the lip; while, no matter how close he shaved, fiery metallic gleams passed, when he moved his head, over the surface of his cheeks. He was rather below the medium height, a bit round-shouldered, and so sturdy of limb that his clothes always looked a shade too tight for his arms and legs. As if unable to grasp what is due to the difference of latitudes, he wore a brown bowler hat, a complete suit of a brownish hue, and clumsy black boots. These harbour togs gave to his thick figure an air of stiff and uncouth smartness. A thin silver watch-chain looped his waistcoat, and he never left his ship for the shore without clutching in his powerful, hairy fist an elegant umbrella of the very best quality, but generally unrolled. Young Jukes, the chief mate, attending his commander to the gangway, would sometimes venture to say, with the greatest gentleness, 'Allow me, sir' – and possessing himself of the umbrella deferentially, would elevate the ferule, shake the folds, twirl a neat furl in a jiffy, and hand it back; going through the performance with a face of such portentous gravity, that Mr Solomon Rout, the chief engineer, smoking his morning cigar over the skylight, would turn away his head in order to hide a smile. 'Oh! aye! The blessed gamp . . . Thank 'ee, Jukes, thank 'ee,' would mutter Captain MacWhirr heartily, without looking up.

Having just enough imagination to carry him through each successive day, and no more, he was tranquilly sure of himself; and from the very same cause he was not in the least conceited. It is your imaginative superior who is touchy, overbearing, and difficult to please; but every ship Captain MacWhirr commanded was the floating abode of harmony and peace. It was, in truth, as impossible for him to take a flight of fancy as it would be for a watchmaker to put together a chronometer with nothing except a two-pound hammer and a whip-saw in the way of tools. Yet the uninteresting lives of men so entirely given to the actuality of the bare existence have their mysterious side. It was impossible in Captain MacWhirr's case, for instance, to understand what under heaven could have induced that perfectly satisfactory son of a petty grocer in Belfast to run away to sea. And yet he had done that very thing at the age of fifteen. It was enough, when you thought it over, to give you the idea of an immense, potent, and invisible hand thrust into the ant-heap of the earth, laying hold of shoulders, knocking heads together, and setting the unconscious faces of the multitude towards inconceivable goals and in undreamt-of directions.

His father never really forgave him for this undutiful stupidity. 'We could have got on without him,' he used to say later on, 'but there's the business. And he an only son too!' His mother wept very much after his disappearance. As it had never occurred to him to leave word behind, he was mourned over for dead till, after eight months, his first letter arrived from Talcahuano. It was short, and contained the statement: 'We had very fine weather on our passage out.' But evidently, in the writer's mind, the only important intelligence was to the effect that his captain had, on the very day of writing, entered him regularly on the ship's articles as Ordinary Seaman. 'Because I can do the work,' he explained. The mother again wept copiously, while the remark, 'Tom's an ass,' expressed the emotions of the father. He was a corpulent man, with a gift for sly chaffing, which to the end of his life he exercised in his intercourse with his son, a little pityingly, as if upon a half-witted person.

MacWhirr's visits to his home were necessarily rare, and in the course of years he despatched other letters to his parents, informing them of his successive promotions and of his movements upon the vast earth. In these missives could be found sentences like this: 'The heat here is very great.' Or: 'On Christmas day at 4 p.m. we fell in with some icebergs.' The old people ultimately became acquainted with a good many names of ships, and with the names of the skippers who commanded them – with the names of Scots and English shipowners – with the names of seas, oceans, straits, promontories – with outlandish names of lumber-ports, of rice-ports, of cotton-ports – with the names of islands – with the name of their son's young woman. She was called Lucy. It did not suggest itself to him to mention whether he thought the name pretty. And then they died.

The great day of MacWhirr's marriage came in due course, following shortly upon the great day when he got his first command.

All these events had taken place many years before the morning when, in the chart-room of the steamer *Nan-Shan*, he stood confronted by the fall of a barometer he had no reason to distrust. The fall – taking into account the excellence of the instrument, the time of the year, and the ship's position on the terrestrial globe – was of a nature ominously prophetic; but the red face of the man betrayed no sort of inward disturbance. Omens were as nothing to him, and he was unable to discover the message of a prophecy till the fulfilment had brought it home to his very door. 'That's a fall, and no mistake,' he thought. 'There must be some uncommonly dirty weather knocking about.'

The *Nan-Shan* was on her way from the southward to the treaty port of Fu-chau, with some cargo in her lower holds, and two hundred Chinese coolies returning to their village homes in the province of Fo-kien, after a few years of work in various tropical colonies. The morning was fine, the oily sea heaved without a sparkle, and there was a queer white misty patch in the sky like a halo of the sun. The fore-deck, packed with Chinamen, was full of sombre clothing, yellow faces, and pigtails, sprinkled over with a good many naked shoulders, for there was no wind, and the heat was close. The coolies lounged, talked, smoked, or stared over the rail; some, drawing water over the side, sluiced each other; a few slept on hatches, while several small parties of six sat on their heels surrounding iron trays with plates of rice and tiny teacups; and every single Celestial of them was carrying with him all he had in the world – a wooden chest with a ringing lock and brass on the corners, containing the savings of his labours: some clothes of ceremony, sticks of incense, a little opium maybe, bits of nameless rubbish of conventional value, and a small hoard of silver dollars, toiled for in coal lighters, won in gambling-houses or in petty trading, grubbed out of earth, sweated out in mines, on railway lines, in deadly jungle, under heavy burdens – amassed patiently, guarded with care, cherished fiercely.

A cross swell had set in from the direction of Formosa Channel about ten o'clock, without disturbing these passengers much, because the *Nan-Shan*, with her flat bottom, rolling chocks on bilges, and great breadth of beam, had the reputation of an exceptionally steady ship in a sea-way. Mr Jukes, in moments of expansion on shore, would proclaim loudly that the 'old girl was as good as she was pretty'. It would never have occurred to Captain MacWhirr to express his favourable opinion so loud or in terms so fanciful.

She was a good ship, undoubtedly, and not old either. She had been built in Dumbarton less than three years before, to the order of a firm of merchants in Siam – Messrs Sigg and Son. When she lay afloat, finished in every detail and ready to take up the work of her life, the builders contemplated her with pride.

'Sigg has asked us for a reliable skipper to take her out,' remarked one of the partners; and the other, after reflecting for a while, said: 'I think MacWhirr is ashore just at present.' 'Is he? Then wire him at once. He's the very man,' declared the senior, without a moment's hesitation.

Next morning MacWhirr stood before them unperturbed, having travelled from London by the midnight express after a sudden but undemonstrative parting with his wife. She was the daughter of a superior couple who had seen better days.

'We had better be going together over the ship, Captain,' said the senior partner; and the three men started to view the perfections of the *Nan-Shan* from stem to stern, and from her keelson to the trucks of her two stumpy pole-masts.

Captain MacWhirr had begun by taking off his coat, which he hung on the end of a steam windlass embodying all the latest improvements.

'My uncle wrote of you favourably by yesterday's mail to our good friends – Messrs Sigg, you know – and doubtless they'll continue you out there in command,' said the junior partner. 'You'll be able to boast of being in charge of the handiest boat of her size on the coast of China, Captain,' he added.

'Have you? Thank 'ee,' mumbled vaguely MacWhirr, to whom the view of a distant eventuality could appeal no more than the beauty of a wide landscape to a purblind tourist; and his eyes happening at the moment to be at rest upon the lock of the cabin door, he walked up to it, full of purpose, and began to rattle the handle vigorously, while he observed, in his low, earnest voice, 'You can't trust the workmen nowadays. A brand-new lock, and it won't act at all. Stuck fast. See? See?'

As soon as they found themselves alone in their office across the yard: 'You praised that fellow up to Sigg. What is it you see in him?' asked the nephew, with faint contempt.

'I admit he has nothing of your fancy skipper about him, if that's what you mean,' said the elder man curtly. 'Is the foreman of the joiners on the *Nan-Shan* outside? . . . Come in, Bates. How is it that you let Tait's people put us off with a defective lock on the cabin door? The Captain could see directly he set eye on it. Have it replaced at once. The little straws, Bates . . . the little straws . . . '

The lock was replaced accordingly, and a few days afterwards the *Nan-Shan* steamed out to the East, without MacWhirr having offered any further remark as to her fittings, or having been heard to utter a single word hinting at pride in his ship, gratitude for his appointment, or satisfaction at his prospects.

With a temperament neither loquacious nor taciturn, he found very little occasion to talk. There were matters of duty, of course – directions, orders, and so on; but the past being to his mind done with, and the future not there yet, the more general actualities of the day required no comment – because facts can speak for themselves with overwhelming precision.

Old Mr Sigg liked a man of few words, and one that 'you could be sure would not try to improve upon his instructions'. MacWhirr, satisfying these requirements, was continued in command of the *Nan-Shan*, and applied himself to the careful navigation of his ship in the China seas. She had come out on a British register, but after some time Messrs Sigg judged it expedient to transfer her to the Siamese flag.

At the news of the contemplated transfer Jukes grew restless, as if under a sense of personal affront. He went about grumbling to himself, and uttering short scornful laughs. 'Fancy having a ridiculous Noah's Ark elephant in the ensign of one's ship,' he said once at the engine-room door. 'Dash me if I can stand it: I'll throw up the billet. Don't it make *you* sick, Mr Rout?' The chief engineer only cleared his throat with the air of a man who knows the value of a good billet.

The first morning the new flag floated over the stern of the *Nan-Shan* Jukes stood looking at it bitterly from the bridge. He struggled with his feelings for a while, and then remarked, 'Queer flag for a man to sail under, sir.'

'What's the matter with the flag?' enquired Captain MacWhirr. 'Seems all right to me.' And he walked across to the end of the bridge to have a good look.

'Well, it looks queer to me,' burst out Jukes, greatly exasperated, and flung off the bridge.

Captain MacWhirr was amazed at these manners. After a while he stepped quietly into the chart-room, and opened his International Signal Code-book at the plate where the flags of all the nations are correctly figured in gaudy rows. He ran his finger over them, and when he came to Siam he contemplated with great attention the red field and the white elephant. Nothing could be more simple; but to make sure he brought the book out on the bridge for the purpose of comparing the coloured drawing with the real thing at the flag-staff astern. When next Jukes, who was carrying on the duty that day with a sort of suppressed fierceness, happened on the bridge, his commander observed: 'There's nothing amiss with that flag.'

'Isn't there?' mumbled Jukes, falling on his knees before a deck-locker and jerking therefrom viciously a spare lead-line.

'No. I looked up the book. Length twice the breadth and the elephant exactly in the middle. I thought the people ashore would know how to make the local flag. Stands to reason. You were wrong, Jukes . . . '

'Well, sir,' began Jukes, getting up excitedly, 'all I can say – ' He fumbled for the end of the coil of line with trembling hands.

'That's all right.' Captain MacWhirr soothed him, sitting heavily on a little canvas folding-stool he greatly affected. 'All you have to do is to take care they don't hoist the elephant upside-down before they get quite used to it.'

Jukes flung the new lead-line over on the fore-deck with a loud 'Here you are, bo'ss'en – don't forget to wet it thoroughly,' and turned with immense resolution towards his commander; but Captain MacWhirr spread his elbows on the bridge-rail comfortably.

'Because it would be, I suppose, understood as a signal of distress,' he went on. 'What do you think? That elephant there, I take it, stands for something in the nature of the Union Jack in the flag . . . '

'Does it!' yelled Jukes, so that every head on the *Nan-Shan*'s decks looked towards the bridge. Then he sighed, and with sudden resignation: 'It would certainly be a dam' distressful sight,' he said meekly.

Later in the day he accosted the chief engineer with a confidential 'Here, let me tell you the old man's latest.'

Mr Solomon Rout (frequently alluded to as Long Sol, Old Sol, or Father Rout), from finding himself almost invariably the tallest man on board every ship he joined, had acquired the habit of a stooping, leisurely condescension. His hair was scant and sandy, his flat cheeks were pale, his bony wrists and long scholarly hands were pale too, as though he had lived all his life in the shade.

He smiled from on high at Jukes, and went on smoking and glancing about quietly, in the manner of a kind uncle lending an ear to the tale of an excited schoolboy. Then, greatly amused but impassive, he asked: 'And did you throw up the billet?'

'No,' cried Jukes, raising a weary, discouraged voice above the harsh buzz of the *Nan-Shan*'s friction winches. All of them were hard at work, snatching slings of cargo, high up, to the end of long derricks, only, as it seemed, to let them rip down recklessly by the run. The cargo chains groaned in the gins, clinked on coamings, rattled over the side; and the whole ship quivered, with her long grey flanks smoking in wreaths of steam. 'No,' cried Jukes, 'I didn't. What's the good? I might just as well fling my resignation at this bulkhead. I don't believe you can make a man like that understand anything. He simply knocks me over.'

At that moment Captain MacWhirr, back from the shore, crossed the deck, umbrella in hand, escorted by a mournful, self-possessed Chinaman, walking behind in paper-soled silk shoes, and who also carried an umbrella.

The master of the *Nan-Shan*, speaking just audibly and gazing at his boots as his manner was, remarked that it would be necessary to call at Fu-chau this trip, and desired Mr Rout to have steam up to-morrow afternoon at one o'clock sharp. He pushed back his hat to wipe his forehead, observing at the same time that he hated going ashore anyhow; while overtopping him Mr Rout, without deigning a word, smoked austerely, nursing his right elbow in the palm of his left hand. Then Jukes was directed in the same subdued voice to keep the forward 'tween-deck clear of cargo. Two hundred coolies were going to be put down there. The Bun Hin Company were sending that lot home. Twenty-five bags of rice would be coming off in a sampan directly, for stores. All seven-years'-men they were, said Captain MacWhirr, with a camphor-wood chest to every man. The carpenter should be set to work nailing three-inch battens along the deck below, fore and aft, to keep these boxes from shifting in a sea-way. Jukes had better look to it at once. 'D'ye hear, Jukes?' This Chinaman here was coming with the ship as far as Fu-chau – a sort of interpreter he would be. Bun Hin's clerk he was, and wanted to have a look at the space. Jukes had better take him forward. 'D'ye hear, Jukes?'

Jukes took care to punctuate these instructions in proper places with the obligatory 'Yes, sir,' ejaculated without enthusiasm. His brusque 'Come along, John; make look see' set the Chinaman in motion at his heels.

'Wanchee look see, all same look see can do,' said Jukes, who having no talent for foreign languages mangled the very pidgin-English cruelly. He pointed at the open hatch. 'Catchee number one piecie place to sleep in. Eh?'

He was gruff, as became his racial superiority, but not unfriendly. The Chinaman, gazing sad and speechless into the darkness of the hatchway, seemed to stand at the head of a yawning grave.

'No catchee rain down there – savee?' pointed out Jukes. 'Suppose all'ee same fine weather, one piecie coolie-man come topside,' he pursued, warming up imaginatively. 'Make so – Phooooo!' He expanded his chest and blew out his cheeks. 'Savee, John? Breathe – fresh air. Good. Eh? Washee him piecie pants, chow-chow topside – see, John?'

With his mouth and hands he made exuberant motions of eating rice and washing clothes; and the Chinaman, who concealed his distrust of this pantomime under a collected demeanour tinged by a gentle and refined melancholy, glanced out of his almond eyes from Jukes to the hatch and back again. 'Velly good,' he murmured, in a disconsolate undertone, and hastened smoothly along the decks, dodging obstacles in his course. He disappeared, ducking low under a sling of ten dirty gunny-bags full of some costly merchandise and exhaling a repulsive smell.

Captain MacWhirr meantime had gone on the bridge, and into the chart-room, where a letter, commenced two days before, awaited termination. These long letters began with the words, 'My darling wife', and the steward, between the scrubbing of the floors and the dusting of chronometer-boxes, snatched at every opportunity to read them. They interested him much more than they possibly could the woman for whose eye they were intended; and this for the reason that they related in minute detail each successive trip of the *Nan-Shan*.

Her master, faithful to facts, which alone his consciousness reflected, would set them down with painstaking care upon many pages. The house in a northern suburb to which these pages were addressed had a bit of garden before the bow-windows, a deep porch of good appearance, coloured glass with imitation lead frame in the front door. He paid five-and-forty pounds a year for it, and did not think the rent too high, because Mrs MacWhirr (a pretentious person with a scraggy neck and a disdainful manner) was admittedly ladylike, and in the neighbourhood considered as 'quite superior'. The only secret of her life was her abject terror of the time when her husband would come home to stay for good. Under the same roof there dwelt also a daughter called Lydia and a son, Tom. These two were but slightly acquainted with their father. Mainly, they knew him as a rare but privileged visitor, who of an evening smoked his pipe in the dining-room and slept in the house. The lanky girl, upon the whole, was rather ashamed of him; the boy was frankly and utterly indifferent in a straightforward, delightful, unaffected way manly boys have.

And Captain MacWhirr wrote home from the coast of China twelve times every year, desiring quaintly to be 'remembered to the children', and subscribing himself 'your loving husband', as calmly as if the words so long used by so many men were not, apart from their shape, worn-out things, and of a faded meaning.

The China seas north and south are narrow seas. They are seas full of every-day, eloquent facts, such as islands, sand-banks, reefs, swift and changeable currents – tangled facts that nevertheless speak to a seaman in clear and definite language. Their speech appealed to Captain MacWhirr's sense of realities so forcibly that he had given up his state-room below and practically lived all his days on the bridge of his ship, often having his meals sent up, and sleeping at night in the chart-room. And he indited there his home letters. Each of them, without exception, contained the phrase, 'The weather has been very fine this trip,' or some other form of a statement to that effect. And this statement, too, in its wonderful persistence, was of the same perfect accuracy as all the others they contained.

Mr Rout likewise wrote letters; only no one on board knew how chatty he could be pen in hand, because the chief engineer had enough imagination to keep his desk locked. His wife relished his style greatly. They were a childless couple, and Mrs Rout, a big, high-bosomed, jolly woman of forty, shared with Mr Rout's toothless and venerable mother a little cottage near Teddington. She would run over her correspondence, at breakfast, with lively eyes, and scream out interesting passages in a joyous voice at the deaf old lady, prefacing each extract by the warning shout, 'Solomon says!' She had the trick of firing off Solomon's utterances also upon strangers, astonishing them easily by the unfamiliar text and the unexpectedly jocular vein of these quotations. On the day the new curate called for the first time at the cottage, she found occasion to remark, 'As Solomon says: "the engineers that go down to the sea in ships behold the wonders of sailor nature";' when a change in the visitor's countenance made her stop and stare.

'Solomon . . . Oh! . . . Mrs Rout,' stuttered the young man, very red in the face, 'I must say . . . I don't . . . '

'He's my husband,' she announced in a great shout, throwing herself back in the chair. Perceiving the joke, she laughed immoderately with a handkerchief to her eyes, while he sat wearing a forced smile, and, from his inexperience of jolly women, fully persuaded that she must be deplorably insane. They were excellent friends afterwards; for, absolving her from irreverent intention, he came to think she was a very worthy person indeed; and he learned in time to receive without flinching other scraps of Solomon's wisdom.

'For my part,' Solomon was reported by his wife to have said once, 'give me the dullest ass for a skipper before a rogue. There is a way to take a fool; but a rogue is smart and slippery.' This was an airy generalisation drawn from the particular case of Captain MacWhirr's honesty, which, in itself, had the heavy obviousness of a lump of clay. On the other hand, Mr Jukes, unable to generalise, unmarried, and unengaged, was in the habit of opening his heart after another fashion to an old chum and former shipmate, actually serving as second officer on board an Atlantic liner.

First of all he would insist upon the advantages of the Eastern trade, hinting at its superiority to the Western ocean service. He extolled the sky, the seas, the ships, and the easy life of the Far East. The *Nan-Shan*, he affirmed, was second to none as a sea-boat.

'We have no brass-bound uniforms, but then we are like brothers here,' he wrote. 'We all mess together and live like fighting-cocks . . . All the chaps of the black-squad are as decent as they make that kind, and old Sol, the Chief, is a dry stick. We are good friends. As to our old man, you could not find a quieter skipper. Sometimes you would think he hadn't sense enough to see anything wrong. And yet it isn't that. Can't be. He has been in command for a good few years now. He doesn't do anything actually foolish, and gets his ship along all right without worrying anybody. I believe he hasn't brains enough to enjoy kicking up a row. I don't take advantage of him. I would scorn it. Outside the routine of duty he doesn't seem to understand more than half of what you tell him. We get a laugh out of this at times; but it is dull, too, to be with a man like this – in the long-run. Old Sol says he hasn't much conversation. Conversation! O Lord! He never talks. The other day I had been yarning under the bridge with one of the engineers, and he must have heard us. When I came up to take my watch, he steps out of the chart-room and has a good look all round, peeps over at the sidelights, glances at the compass, squints upwards at the stars.

That's his regular performance. By and by he says: "Was that you talking just now in the port alleyway?" "Yes, sir." "With the third engineer?" "Yes, sir." He walks off to starboard, and sits under the dodger on a little campstool of his, and for half-an-hour perhaps he makes no sound, except that I heard him sneeze once. Then after a while I hear him getting up over there, and he strolls across to port, where I was. "I can't understand what you can find to talk about," says he. "Two solid hours. I am not blaming you. I see people ashore at it all day long, and then in the evening they sit down and keep at it over the drinks. Must be saying the same things over and over again. I can't understand."

'Did you ever hear anything like that? And he was so patient about it. It made me quite sorry for him. But he is exasperating too sometimes. Of course one would not do anything to vex him even if it were worth while. But it isn't. He's so jolly innocent that if you were to put your thumb to your nose and wave your fingers at him he would only wonder gravely to himself what had got into you. He told me once quite simply that he found it very difficult to make out what made people always act so queerly. He's too dense to trouble about, and that's the truth.'

Thus wrote Mr Jukes to his chum in the Western ocean trade, out of the fullness of his heart and the liveliness of his fancy.

He had expressed his honest opinion. It was not worth while trying to impress a man of that sort. If the world had been full of such men, life would have probably appeared to Jukes an unentertaining and unprofitable business. He was not alone in his opinion. The sea itself, as if sharing Mr Jukes' good-natured forbearance, had never put itself out to startle the silent man, who seldom looked up, and wandered innocently over the waters with the only visible purpose of getting food, raiment, and house-room for three people ashore. Dirty weather he had known, of course. He had been made wet, uncomfortable, tired in the usual way, felt at the time and presently forgotten. So that upon the whole he had been justified in reporting fine weather at home. But he had never been given a glimpse of immeasurable strength and of immoderate wrath, the wrath that passes exhausted but never appeased – the wrath and fury of the passionate sea. He knew it existed, as we know that crime and abominations exist; he had heard of it as a peaceable citizen in a town hears of battles, famines, and floods, and yet knows nothing of what these things mean – though, indeed, he may have been mixed up in a street row, have gone without his dinner once, or been soaked to the skin in a shower. Captain MacWhirr had sailed over the surface of the oceans as some men go skimming over the years of existence to sink gently into a placid grave, ignorant of life to the last, without ever having been made to see all it may contain of perfidy, of violence, and of terror. There are on sea and land such men thus fortunate – or thus disdained by destiny or by the sea.

Chapter 2

Observing the steady fall of the barometer, Captain MacWhirr thought, 'There's some dirty weather knocking about.' This is precisely what he thought. He had had an experience of moderately dirty weather – the term dirty as applied to the weather implying only moderate discomfort to the seaman. Had he been informed by an indisputable authority that the end of the world was to be finally accomplished by a catastrophic disturbance of the atmosphere, he would have assimilated the information under the simple idea of dirty weather, and no other, because he had no experience of cataclysms, and belief does not necessarily imply comprehension. The wisdom of his country had pronounced by means of an Act of Parliament that before he could be considered as fit to take charge of a ship he should be able to answer certain simple questions on the subject of circular storms such as hurricanes, cyclones, typhoons; and apparently he had answered them, since he was now in command of the *Nan-Shan* in the China seas during the season of typhoons. But if he had answered he remembered nothing of it. He was, however, conscious of being made uncomfortable by the clammy heat. He came out on the bridge, and found no relief to this oppression. The air seemed thick. He gasped like a fish, and began to believe himself greatly out of sorts.

The *Nan-Shan* was ploughing a vanishing furrow upon the circle of the sea that had the surface and the shimmer of an undulating piece of grey silk. The sun, pale and without rays, poured down leaden heat in a strangely indecisive light, and the Chinamen were lying prostrate about the decks. Their bloodless, pinched, yellow faces were like the faces of bilious invalids. Captain MacWhirr noticed two of them especially, stretched out on their backs below the bridge. As soon as they had closed their eyes they seemed dead.

Three others, however, were quarrelling barbarously away forward; and one big fellow, half naked, with herculean shoulders, was hanging limply over a winch; another, sitting on the deck, his knees up and his head drooping sideways in a girlish attitude, was plaiting his pigtail with infinite languor depicted in his whole person and in the very movement of his fingers. The smoke struggled with difficulty out of the funnel, and instead of streaming away spread itself out like an infernal sort of cloud, smelling of sulphur and raining soot all over the decks.

'What the devil are you doing there, Mr Jukes?' asked Captain MacWhirr.

This unusual form of address, though mumbled rather than spoken, caused the body of Mr Jukes to start as though it had been prodded under the fifth rib. He had had a low bench brought on the bridge, and sitting on it, with a length of rope curled about his feet and a piece of canvas stretched over his knees, was pushing a sail-needle vigorously. He looked up, and his surprise gave to his eyes an expression of innocence and candour.

'I am only roping some of that new set of bags we made last trip for whipping up coals,' he remonstrated gently. 'We shall want them for the next coaling, sir.'

'What became of the others?'

'Why, worn out of course, sir.'

Captain MacWhirr, after glaring down irresolutely at his chief mate, disclosed the gloomy and cynical conviction that more than half of them had been lost overboard, 'if only the truth was known', and retired to the other end of the bridge. Jukes, exasperated by this unprovoked attack, broke the needle at the second stitch, and dropping his work got up and cursed the heat in a violent undertone.

The propeller thumped, the three Chinamen forward had given up squabbling very suddenly, and the one who had been plaiting his tail clasped his legs and stared dejectedly over his knees. The lurid sunshine cast faint and sickly shadows. The swell ran higher and swifter every moment, and the ship lurched heavily in the smooth, deep hollows of the sea.

'I wonder where that beastly swell comes from,' said Jukes aloud, recovering himself after a stagger.

'North-east,' grunted the literal MacWhirr, from his side of the bridge. 'There's some dirty weather knocking about. Go and look at the glass.'

When Jukes came out of the chart-room, the cast of his

countenance had changed to thoughtfulness and concern. He caught hold of the bridge-rail and stared ahead.

The temperature in the engine-room had gone up to a hundred and seventeen degrees. Irritated voices were ascending through the skylight and through the fiddle of the stokehold in a harsh and resonant uproar, mingled with angry clangs and scrapes of metal, as if men with limbs of iron and throats of bronze had been quarrelling down there. The second engineer was falling foul of the stokers for letting the steam go down. He was a man with arms like a blacksmith, and generally feared; but that afternoon the stokers were answering him back recklessly, and slammed the furnace doors with the fury of despair. Then the noise ceased suddenly, and the second engineer appeared, emerging out of the stokehold streaked with grime and soaking wet like a chimney-sweep coming out of a well. As soon as his head was clear of the fiddle he began to scold Jukes for not trimming properly the stokehold ventilators; and in answer Jukes made with his hands deprecatory soothing signs meaning: No wind – can't be helped – you can see for yourself. But the other wouldn't hear reason. His teeth flashed angrily in his dirty face. He didn't mind, he said, the trouble of punching their blanked heads down there, blank his soul, but did the condemned sailors think you could keep steam up in the God-forsaken boilers simply by knocking the blanked stokers about? No, by George! You had to get some draught too – may he be everlastingly blanked for a swab-headed deck-hand if you didn't! And the chief, too, rampaging before the steam-gauge and carrying on like a lunatic up and down the engine-room ever since noon. What did Jukes think he was stuck up there for, if he couldn't get one of his decayed, good-for-nothing deck-cripples to turn the ventilators to the wind?

The relations of the 'engine-room' and the 'deck' of the *Nan-Shan* were, as is known, of a brotherly nature; therefore Jukes leaned over and begged the other in a restrained tone not to make a disgusting ass of himself; the skipper was on the other side of the bridge. But the second declared mutinously that he didn't care a rap who was on the other side of the bridge, and Jukes, passing in a flash from lofty disapproval into a state of exaltation, invited him in unflattering terms to come up and twist the beastly things to please himself, and catch such wind as a donkey of his sort could find. The second rushed up to the fray. He flung himself at the port ventilator as though he meant to tear it out bodily and toss it overboard. All he did was to move the cowl round a few inches, with an enormous expenditure of force, and seemed spent in the effort. He leaned against the back of the wheelhouse, and Jukes walked up to him.

'Oh, Heavens!' ejaculated the engineer in a feeble voice. He lifted his eyes to the sky, and then let his glassy stare descend to meet the horizon that, tilting up to an angle of forty degrees, seemed to hang on a slant for a while and settled down slowly. 'Heavens! Phew! What's up, anyhow?'

Jukes, straddling his long legs like a pair of compasses, put on an air of superiority. 'We're going to catch it this time,' he said. 'The barometer is tumbling down like anything, Harry. And you trying to kick up that silly row . . . '

The word 'barometer' seemed to revive the second engineer's mad animosity. Collecting afresh all his energies, he directed Jukes in a low and brutal tone to shove the unmentionable instrument down his gory throat. Who cared for his crimson barometer? It was the steam – the steam – that was going down; and what between the firemen going faint and the chief going silly, it was worse than a dog's life for him; he didn't care a tinker's curse how soon the whole show was blown out of the water. He seemed on the point of having a cry, but after regaining his breath he muttered darkly, 'I'll faint them,' and dashed off. He stopped upon the fiddle long enough to shake his fist at the unnatural daylight, and dropped into the dark hole with a whoop.

When Jukes turned, his eyes fell upon the rounded back and the big red ears of Captain MacWhirr, who had come across. He did not look at his chief officer, but said at once, 'That's a very violent man, that second engineer.'

'Jolly good second, anyhow,' grunted Jukes. 'They can't keep up steam,' he added rapidly, and made a grab at the rail against the coming lurch.

Captain MacWhirr, unprepared, took a run and brought himself up with a jerk by an awning stanchion.

'A profane man,' he said obstinately. 'If this goes on, I'll have to get rid of him the first chance.'

'It's the heat,' said Jukes. 'The weather's awful. It would make a saint swear. Even up here I feel exactly as if I had my head tied up in a woollen blanket.'

Captain MacWhirr looked up. 'D'ye mean to say, Mr Jukes, you ever had your head tied up in a blanket? What was that for?'

'It's a manner of speaking, sir,' said Jukes stolidly.

'Some of you fellows do go on! What's that about saints swearing? I wish you wouldn't talk so wild. What sort of saint would that be that would swear? No more saint than yourself, I expect. And what's a blanket got to do with it – or the weather either . . . The heat does not make me swear – does it? It's filthy bad temper. That's what it is. And what's the good of your talking like this?'

Thus Captain MacWhirr expostulated against the use of images in speech, and at the end electrified Jukes by a contemptous snort, followed by words of passion and resentment: 'Damme! I'll fire him out of the ship if he don't look out.'

And Jukes, incorrigible, thought: 'Goodness me! Somebody's put a new inside to my old man. Here's temper, if you like. Of course it's the weather; what else? It would make an angel quarrelsome – let alone a saint.'

All the Chinamen on deck appeared at their last gasp.

At its setting the sun had a diminished diameter and an expiring brown, rayless glow, as if millions of centuries elapsing since the morning had brought it near its end. A dense bank of cloud became visible to the northward; it had a sinister dark olive tint, and lay low and motionless upon the sea, resembling a solid obstacle in the path of the ship. She went floundering towards it like an exhausted creature driven to its death. The coppery twilight retired slowly, and the darkness brought out overhead a swarm of unsteady, big stars, that, as if blown upon, flickered exceedingly and seemed to hang very near the earth. At eight o'clock Jukes went into the chart-room to write up the ship's log.

He copied neatly out of the rough-book the number of miles, the course of the ship, and in the column for 'wind' scrawled the word 'calm' from top to bottom of the eight hours since noon. He was exasperated by the continuous, monotonous rolling of the ship. The heavy inkstand would slide away in a manner that suggested perverse intelligence in dodging the pen. Having written in the large space under the head of 'Remarks' 'Heat very oppressive', he stuck the end of the penholder in his teeth, pipe fashion, and mopped his face carefully.

'Ship rolling heavily in a high cross swell,' he began again, and commented to himself, 'Heavily is no word for it.' Then he wrote: 'Sunset threatening, with a low bank of clouds to N. and E. Sky clear overhead.'

Sprawling over the table with arrested pen, he glanced out of the door, and in that frame of his vision he saw all the stars flying upwards between the teakwood jambs on a black sky. The whole lot took flight together and disappeared, leaving only a blackness flecked with white flashes, for the sea was as black as the sky and speckled with foam afar. The stars that had flown to the roll came back on the return swing of the ship, rushing downwards in their glittering multitude, not of fiery points, but enlarged to tiny discs brilliant with a clear wet sheen.

Jukes watched the flying big stars for a moment, and then wrote: '8 p.m. Swell increasing. Ship labouring and taking water on her decks. Battened down the coolies for the night. Barometer still falling.' He paused, and thought to himself, 'Perhaps nothing whatever'll come of it.' And then he closed resolutely his entries: 'Every appearance of a typhoon coming on.'

On going out he had to stand aside, and Captain MacWhirr strode over the doorstep without saying a word or making a sign.

'Shut the door, Mr Jukes, will you?' he cried from within.

Jukes turned back to do so, muttering ironically: 'Afraid to catch cold, I suppose.' It was his watch below, but he yearned for communion with his kind; and he remarked cheerily to the second mate: 'Doesn't look so bad, after all – does it?'

The second mate was marching to and fro on the bridge, tripping down with small steps one moment, and the next climbing with difficulty the shifting slope of the deck. At the sound of Jukes's voice he stood still, facing forward, but made no reply.

'Hallo! That's a heavy one,' said Jukes, swaying to meet the long roll till his lowered hand touched the planks. This time the second mate made in his throat a noise of an unfriendly nature.

He was an oldish, shabby little fellow, with bad teeth and no hair on his face. He had been shipped in a hurry in Shanghai, that trip when the second officer brought from home had delayed the ship three hours in port by contriving (in some manner Captain MacWhirr could never understand) to fall overboard into an empty coal-lighter lying alongside, and had to be sent ashore to the hospital with concussion of the brain and a broken limb or two.

Jukes was not discouraged by the unsympathetic sound. 'The Chinamen must be having a lovely time of it down there,' he said. 'It's lucky for them the old girl has the easiest roll of any ship I've ever been in. There now! This one wasn't so bad.'

'You wait,' snarled the second mate.

With his sharp nose, red at the tip, and his thin pinched lips, he always looked as though he were raging inwardly; and he was concise in his speech to the point of rudeness. All his time off duty he spent in his cabin with the door shut, keeping so still in there that he was supposed to fall asleep as soon as he had disappeared; but the man who came in to wake him for his watch on deck would invariably find him with his eyes wide open, flat on his back in the bunk, and glaring irritably from a soiled pillow. He never wrote any letters, did not seem to hope for news from anywhere; and though he had been heard once to mention West Hartlepool, it was with extreme bitterness, and only in connection with the extortionate charges of a boarding-house. He was one of those men who are picked up at need in the ports of the world. They are competent enough, appear hopelessly hard up, show no evidence of any sort of vice, and carry about them all the signs of manifest failure. They come aboard on an emergency, care for no ship afloat, live in their own atmosphere of casual connection amongst their shipmates who know nothing of them, and make up their minds to leave at inconvenient times. They clear out with no words of leave-taking in some God-forsaken port other men would fear to be stranded in, and go ashore in company of a shabby sea-chest, corded like a treasure-box, and with an air of shaking the ship's dust off their feet.

'You wait,' he repeated, balanced in great swings with his back to Jukes, motionless and implacable.

'Do you mean to say we are going to catch it hot?' asked Jukes with boyish interest.

'Say? . . . I say nothing. You don't catch me,' snapped the little second mate, with a mixture of pride, scorn, and cunning, as if Jukes' question had been a trap cleverly detected. 'Oh no! None of you here shall make a fool of me if I know it,' he mumbled to himself.

Jukes reflected rapidly that this second mate was a mean little beast, and in his heart he wished poor Jack Allen had never smashed himself up in the coal-lighter. The far-off blackness ahead of the ship was like another night seen through the starry night of the earth – the starless night of the immensities beyond the created universe, revealed in its appalling stillness through a low fissure in the glittering sphere of which the earth is the kernel.

'Whatever there might be about,' said Jukes, 'we are steaming straight into it.'

'*You've* said it,' caught up the second mate, always with his back to Jukes. 'You've said it, mind – not I.'

'Oh, go to Jericho!' said Jukes frankly; and the other emitted a triumphant little chuckle.

'You've said it,' he repeated.

'And what of that?'

'I've known some real good men get into trouble with their skippers for saying a dam' sight less,' answered the second mate feverishly. 'Oh no! You don't catch me.'

'You seem deucedly anxious not to give yourself away,' said Jukes, completely soured by such absurdity. 'I wouldn't be afraid to say what I think.'

'Aye, to me! That's no great trick. I am nobody, and well I know it.'

The ship, after a pause of comparative steadiness, started upon a series of rolls, one worse than the other, and for a time Jukes, preserving his equilibrium, was too busy to open his mouth. As soon as the violent swinging had quieted down somewhat, he said: 'This is a bit too much of a good thing. Whether anything is coming or not I think she ought to be put head on to that swell. The old man is just gone in to lie down. Hang me if I don't speak to him.'

But when he opened the door of the chart-room he saw his captain reading a book. Captain MacWhirr was not lying down: he was standing up with one hand grasping the edge of the bookshelf and the other holding open before his face a thick volume. The lamp wriggled in the gimbals, the loosened books toppled from side to side on the shelf, the long barometer swung in jerky circles, the table altered its slant every moment. In the midst of all this stir and movement Captain MacWhirr, holding on, showed his eyes above the upper edge, and asked, 'What's the matter?'

'Swell getting worse, sir.'

'Noticed that in here,' muttered Captain MacWhirr. 'Anything wrong?'

Jukes, inwardly disconcerted by the seriousness of the eyes looking at him over the top of the book, produced an embarrassed grin.

'Rolling like old boots,' he said sheepishly.

'Aye! Very heavy – very heavy. What do you want?'

At this Jukes lost his footing and began to flounder.

'I was thinking of our passengers,' he said, in the manner of a man clutching at a straw.

'Passengers?' wondered the Captain gravely. 'What passengers?'

'Why, the Chinamen, sir,' explained Jukes, very sick of this conversation.

'The Chinamen! Why don't you speak plainly? Couldn't tell what you meant. Never heard a lot of coolies spoken of as passengers before. Passengers, indeed! What's come to you?'

Captain MacWhirr, closing the book on his forefinger, lowered his arm and looked completely mystified. 'Why are you thinking of the Chinamen, Mr Jukes?' he enquired.

Jukes took a plunge, like a man driven to it. 'She's rolling her decks full of water, sir. Thought you might put her head on perhaps – for a while. Till this goes down a bit – very soon, I dare say. Head to the eastward. I never knew a ship roll like this.'

He held on in the doorway, and Captain MacWhirr, feeling his grip on the shelf inadequate, made up his mind to let go in a hurry, and fell heavily on the couch.

'Head to the eastward?' he said, struggling to sit up. 'That's more than four points off her course.'

'Yes, sir. Fifty degrees . . . Would just bring her head far enough round to meet this . . . '

Captain MacWhirr was now sitting up. He had not dropped the book, and he had not lost his place.

'To the eastward?' he repeated, with dawning astonishment. 'To the . . . Where do you think we are bound to? You want me to haul a full-powered steamship four points off her course to make the Chinamen comfortable! Now, I've heard more than enough of mad things done in the world – but this . . . If I didn't know you, Jukes, I would think you were in liquor. Steer four points off . . . And what afterwards? Steer four points over the other way, I suppose, to make the course good. What put it into your head that I would start to tack a steamer as if she were a sailing-ship?'

'Jolly good thing she isn't,' threw in Jukes, with bitter readiness. 'She would have rolled every blessed stick out of her this afternoon.'

'Aye! And you just would have had to stand and see them go,' said Captain MacWhirr, showing a certain animation. 'It's a dead calm, isn't it?'

'It is, sir. But there's something out of the common coming, for sure.'

'Maybe. I suppose you have a notion I should be getting out of the way of that dirt,' said Captain MacWhirr, speaking with the utmost simplicity of manner and tone, and fixing the oilcloth on the floor with a heavy stare. Thus he noticed neither Jukes' discomfiture nor the mixture of vexation and astonished respect on his face.

'Now, here's this book,' he continued with deliberation, slapping his thigh with the closed volume. 'I've been reading the chapter on the storms there.'

This was true. He had been reading the chapter on the storms. When he had entered the chart-room, it was with no intention of taking the book down. Some influence in the air – the same influence, probably, that caused the steward to bring without orders the Captain's sea-boots and oilskin coat up to the chart-room – had as it were guided his hand to the shelf; and without taking the time to sit down he had waded with a conscious effort into the terminology of the subject. He lost himself amongst advancing semi-circles, left- and right-hand quadrants, the curves of the tracks, the probable bearing of the centre, the shifts of wind and the readings of barometer. He tried to bring all these things into a definite relation to himself, and ended by becoming contemptuously angry with such a lot of words and with so much advice, all head-work and supposition, without a glimmer of certitude.

'It's the damnedest thing, Jukes,' he said. 'If a fellow was to believe all that's in there, he would be running most of his time all over the sea trying to get behind the weather.'

Again he slapped his leg with the book; and Jukes opened his mouth, but said nothing.

'Running to get behind the weather! Do you understand that, Mr Jukes? It's the maddest thing!' ejaculated Captain MacWhirr, with pauses, gazing at the floor profoundly. 'You would think an old woman had been writing this. It passes me. If that thing means anything useful, then it means that I should at once alter the course away, away to the devil somewhere, and come booming down on Fu-chau from the northward at the tail of this dirty weather that's supposed to be knocking about in our way. From the north! Do you understand, Mr Jukes? Three hundred extra miles to the distance, and a pretty coal bill to show. I couldn't bring myself to do that if every word in there was gospel truth, Mr Jukes. Don't you expect me . . . '

And Jukes, silent, marvelled at this display of feeling and loquacity.

'But the truth is that you don't know if the fellow is right anyhow. How can you tell what a gale is made of till you get it? He isn't aboard here, is he? Very well. Here he says that the centre of them things bears eight points off the wind; but we haven't got any wind, for all the barometer falling. Where's his centre now?'

'We will get the wind presently,' mumbled Jukes.

'Let it come, then,' said Captain MacWhirr, with dignified indignation. 'It's only to let you see, Mr Jukes, that you don't find everything in books. All these rules for dodging breezes and circumventing the winds of heaven, Mr Jukes, seem to me the maddest thing, when you come to look at it sensibly.'

He raised his eyes, saw Jukes gazing at him dubiously, and tried to illustrate his meaning.

'About as queer as your extraordinary notion of dodging the ship head to sea, for I don't know how long, to make the Chinamen comfortable; whereas all we've got to do is to take them to Fu-chau, being timed to get there before noon on Friday. If the weather delays me – very well. There's your log-book to talk straight about the weather. But suppose I went swinging off my course and came in two days late, and they asked me: "Where have you been all that time, Captain?" What could I say to that? "Went around to dodge the bad weather," I would say. "It must've been dam' bad," they would say. "Don't know," I would have to say; "I've dodged clear of it." See that, Jukes? I have been thinking it all out this afternoon.'

He looked up again in his unseeing, unimaginative way. No one had ever heard him say so much at one time. Jukes, with his arms open in the doorway, was like a man invited to behold a miracle. Unbounded wonder was the intellectual meaning of his eye, while incredulity was seated in his whole countenance.

'A gale is a gale, Mr Jukes,' resumed the Captain, 'and a full-powered steam-ship has got to face it. There's just so much dirty weather knocking about the world, and the proper thing is to go through it with none of what old Captain Wilson of the *Melita* calls "storm strategy". The other day ashore I heard him hold forth about it to a lot of shipmasters who came in and sat at a table next to mine. It seemed to me the greatest nonsense. He was telling them how he – outmanoeuvred, I think he said, a terrific gale, so that it never came nearer than fifty miles to him. A neat piece of head-work he called it. How he knew there was a terrific gale fifty miles off beats me altogether. It was like listening to a crazy man. I would have thought Captain Wilson was old enough to know better.'

Captain MacWhirr ceased for a moment, then said, 'It's your watch below, Mr Jukes?'

Jukes came to himself with a start. 'Yes, sir.'

'Leave orders to call me at the slightest change,' said the Captain. He reached up to put the book away, and tucked his legs up on the couch. 'Shut the door so that it don't fly open, will you? I can't stand a door banging. They've put a lot of rubbishy locks into this ship, I must say.'

Captain MacWhirr closed his eyes.

He did so to rest himself. He was tired, and he experienced that state of mental vacuity which comes at the end of an exhaustive discussion that has liberated some belief matured in the course of meditative years. He had indeed been making his confession of faith, had he only known it; and its effect was to make Jukes, on the other side of the door, stand scratching his head for a good while.

Captain MacWhirr opened his eyes.

He thought he must have been asleep. What was that loud

noise? Wind? Why had he not been called? The lamp wriggled in its gimbals, the barometer swung in circles, the table altered its slant every moment; a pair of limp seaboots with collapsed tops went sliding past the couch. He put out his hand instantly, and captured one.

Jukes' face appeared in a crack of the door: only his face, very red, with staring eyes. The flame of the lamp leaped, a piece of paper flew up, a rush of air enveloped Captain MacWhirr. Beginning to draw on the boot, he directed an expectant gaze at Jukes' swollen, excited features.

'Came on like this,' shouted Jukes, 'five minutes ago . . . all of a sudden.'

The head disappeared with a bang, and a heavy splash and patter of drops swept past the closed door as if a pailful of melted lead had been flung against the house. A whistling could be heard now upon the deep vibrating noise outside. The stuffy chart-room seemed as full of draughts as a shed. Captain MacWhirr collared the other sea-boot on its violent passage along the floor. He was not flustered, but he could not find at once the opening for inserting his foot. The shoes he had flung off were scurrying from end to end of the cabin, gambolling playfully over each other like puppies. As soon as he stood up he kicked at them viciously, but without effect.

He threw himself into the attitude of a lunging fencer, to reach after his oilskin coat; and afterwards he staggered all over the confined space while he jerked himself into it. Very grave, straddling his legs far apart, and stretching his neck, he started to tie deliberately the strings of his sou'-wester under his chin, with thick fingers that trembled slightly. He went through all the movements of a woman putting on her bonnet before a glass, with a strained, listening attention, as though he expected every moment to hear the shout of his name in the confused clamour that had suddenly beset his ship. Its increase filled his ears while he was getting ready to go out and confront whatever it might mean. It was tumultuous and very loud – made up of the rush of the wind, the crashes of the sea, with that prolonged deep vibration of the air, like the roll of an immense and remote drum beating the charge of the gale.

He stood for a moment in the light of the lamp, thick, clumsy, shapeless in his panoply of combat, vigilant and red-faced.

'There's a lot of weight in this,' he muttered.

As soon as he attempted to open the door the wind caught it. Clinging to the handle, he was dragged out over the doorstep, and at once found himself engaged with the wind in a sort of personal scuffle whose object was the shutting of that door. At the last moment a tongue of air scurried in and licked out the flame of the lamp.

Ahead of the ship he perceived a great darkness lying upon a multitude of white flashes; on the starboard beam a few amazing stars drooped, dim and fitful, above an immense waste of broken seas, as if seen through a mad drift of smoke.

On the bridge a knot of men, indistinct and toiling, were making great efforts in the light of the wheelhouse windows that shone mistily on their heads and backs. Suddenly darkness closed upon one pane, then on another. The voices of the lost group reached him after the manner of men's voices in a gale, in shreds and fragments of forlorn shouting snatched past the ear. All at once Jukes appeared at his side, yelling, with his head down.

'Watch – put in – wheelhouse shutters – glass – afraid – blow in.'

Jukes heard his commander upbraiding.

'This – come – anything – warning – call me.'

He tried to explain, with the uproar pressing on his lips.

'Light air – remained – bridge – sudden – north-east – could turn – thought – you – sure – hear.'

They had gained the shelter of the weather-cloth, and could converse with raised voices, as people quarrel.

'I got the hands along to cover up all the ventilators. Good job I had remained on deck. I didn't think you would be asleep, and so . . . What did you say, sir? What?'

'Nothing,' cried Captain MacWhirr. 'I said – all right.'

'By all the powers! We've got it this time,' observed Jukes in a howl.

'You haven't altered her course?' enquired Captain MacWhirr, straining his voice.

'No, sir. Certainly not. Wind came out right ahead. And here comes the head sea.'

A plunge of the ship ended in a shock as if she had landed her forefoot upon something solid. After a moment of stillness a lofty flight of sprays drove hard with the wind upon their faces.

'Keep her at it as long as we can,' shouted Captain MacWhirr.

Before Jukes had squeezed the salt water out of his eyes all the stars had disappeared.

Chapter 3

JUKES WAS AS READY A MAN as any half-dozen young mates that may be caught by casting a net upon the waters; and though he had been somewhat taken aback by the startling viciousness of the first squall, he had pulled himself together on the instant, had called out the hands and had rushed them along to secure such openings about the deck as had not been already battened down earlier in the evening. Shouting in his fresh, stentorian voice, 'Jump, boys, and bear a hand!' he led in the work, telling himself the while that he had 'just expected this'.

But at the same time he was growing aware that this was rather more than he had expected. From the first stir of the air felt on his cheek the gale seemed to take upon itself the accumulated impetus of an avalanche. Heavy sprays enveloped the *Nan-Shan* from stem to stern, and instantly in the midst of her regular rolling she began to jerk and plunge as though she had gone mad with fright.

Jukes thought, 'This is no joke.' While he was exchanging explanatory yells with his captain, a sudden lowering of the darkness came upon the night, falling before their vision like something palpable. It was as if the masked lights of the world had been turned down. Jukes was uncritically glad to have his captain at hand. It relieved him as though that man had, by simply coming on deck, taken most of the gale's weight upon his shoulders. Such is the prestige, the privilege, and the burden of command.

Captain MacWhirr could expect no relief of that sort from anyone on earth. Such is the loneliness of command. He was trying to see, with that watchful manner of a seaman who stares into the wind's eye as if into the eye of an adversary, to penetrate the hidden intention and guess the aim and force of the thrust. The strong wind swept at him out of a vast obscurity; he felt under his feet the uneasiness of his ship, and he could not even discern the shadow of her shape. He wished it were not so; and very still he waited, feeling stricken by a blind man's helplessness.

To be silent was natural to him, dark or shine. Jukes, at his elbow, made himself heard yelling cheerily in the gusts, 'We must have got the worst of it at once, sir.' A faint burst of lightning quivered all round, as if flashed into a cavern – into a black and secret chamber of the sea, with a floor of foaming crests.

It unveiled for a sinister, fluttering moment a ragged mass of clouds hanging low, the lurch of the long outlines of the ship, the black figures of men caught on the bridge heads forward, as if petrified in the act of butting. The darkness palpitated down upon all this, and then the real thing came at last.

It was something formidable and swift, like the sudden smashing of a vial of wrath. It seemed to explode all round the ship with an overpowering concussion and a rush of great waters, as if an immense dam had been blown up to windward. In an instant the men lost touch of each other. This is the disintegrating power of a great wind: it isolates one from one's kind. An earthquake, a landslip, an avalanche, overtake a man incidentally, as it were – without passion. A furious gale attacks him like a personal enemy, tries to grasp his limbs, fastens upon his mind, seeks to rout his very spirit out of him.

Jukes was driven away from his commander. He fancied himself whirled a great distance through the air. Everything disappeared – even, for a moment, his power of thinking; but his hand had found one of the rail-stanchions. His distress was by no means alleviated by an inclination to disbelieve the reality of this experience. Though young, he had seen some bad weather, and had never doubted his ability to imagine the worst; but this was so much beyond his powers of fancy that it appeared incompatible with the existence of any ship whatever. He would have been incredulous about himself in the same way, perhaps, had he not been so harassed by the necessity of exerting a wrestling effort against a force trying to tear him away from his hold. Moreover, the conviction of not being utterly destroyed returned to him through the sensations of being half-drowned, bestially shaken, and partly choked.

It seemed to him he remained there precariously alone with the stanchion for a long, long time. The rain poured on him, flowed, drove in sheets. He breathed in gasps; and sometimes the water he swallowed was fresh and sometimes it was salt. For the most part he kept his eyes shut tight, as if suspecting his sight might be destroyed in the immense flurry of the elements. When he ventured to blink hastily, he derived some moral support from the green gleam of the starboard light shining feebly upon the flight of rain and sprays. He was actually looking at it when its ray fell upon the uprearing sea which put it out. He saw the head of the wave topple over, adding the mite of its crash to the tremendous uproar raging around him, and almost at the same instant the stanchion was wrenched away from his embracing arms. After a crushing thump on his back he found himself suddenly afloat and borne upwards. His first irresistible notion was that the whole China Sea had climbed on the bridge. Then, more sanely, he concluded himself gone overboard. All the time he was being tossed, flung, and rolled in great volumes of water, he kept on repeating mentally, with the utmost precipitation, the words: 'My God! My God! My God! My God!'

All at once, in a revolt of misery and despair, he formed the crazy resolution to get out of that. And he began to thresh about with his arms and legs. But as soon as he commenced his wretched struggles he discovered that he had become somehow mixed up with a face, an oilskin coat, somebody's boots. He clawed ferociously all these things in turn, lost them, found them again, lost them once more, and finally was himself caught in the firm clasp of a pair of stout arms. He returned the embrace closely round a thick solid body. He had found his captain.

They tumbled over and over, tightening their hug. Suddenly the water let them down with a brutal bang; and, stranded against the side of the wheelhouse, out of breath and bruised, they were left to stagger up in the wind and hold on where they could.

Jukes came out of it rather horrified, as though he had escaped some unparalleled outrage directed at his feelings. It weakened his faith in himself. He started shouting aimlessly to the man he could feel near him in that fiendish blackness, 'Is it you, sir? Is it you, sir?' till his temples seemed ready to burst. And he heard in answer a voice, as if crying far away, as if screaming to him fretfully from a very great distance, the one word 'Yes!' Other seas swept again over the bridge. He received them defencelessly right over his bare head, with both his hands engaged in holding.

The motion of the ship was extravagant. Her lurches had an appalling helplessness: she pitched as if taking a header into a void, and seemed to find a wall to hit every time. When she rolled she fell on her side headlong, and she would be righted back by such a demolishing blow that Jukes felt her reeling as a clubbed man reels before he collapses. The gale howled and scuffled about gigantically in the darkness as though the entire world were one black gully. At certain moments the air streamed against the ship as if sucked through a tunnel with a concentrated solid force of impact that seemed to lift her clean out of the water and keep her up for an instant with only a quiver running through her from end to end. And then she would begin her tumbling again as if dropped back into a boiling cauldron. Jukes tried hard to compose his mind and judge things coolly.

The sea, flattened down in the heavier gusts, would uprise and overwhelm both ends of the *Nan-Shan* in snowy rushes of foam, expanding wide, beyond both rails, into the night. And on this dazzling sheet, spread under the blackness of the clouds and emitting a bluish glow, Captain MacWhirr could catch a desolate glimpse of a few tiny specks black as ebony, the tops of the hatches, the battened companions, the heads of the covered winches, the foot of a mast. This was all he could see of his ship. Her middle structure, covered by the bridge which bore him, his mate, the closed wheelhouse where a man was steering shut up with the fear of being swept overboard together with the whole thing in one great crash – her middle structure was like a half-tide rock awash upon a coast. It was like an outlying rock with the water boiling up, streaming over, pouring off, beating round – like a rock in the surf to which shipwrecked people cling before they let go – only it rose, it sank, it rolled continuously, without respite and rest, like a rock that should have miraculously struck adrift from a coast and gone wallowing upon the sea.

The *Nan-Shan* was being looted by the storm with a senseless, destructive fury: trysails torn out of the extra gaskets, double-lashed awnings blown away, bridge swept clean, weather-cloths burst, rails twisted, light-screens smashed – and two of the boats had gone already. They had gone unheard and unseen, melting, as it were, in the shock and smother of the wave. It was only later, when upon the white flash of another high sea hurling itself amidships, Jukes had a vision of two pairs of davits leaping black and empty out of the solid blackness, with one overhauled fall flying and an iron-bound block capering in the air, that he became aware of what had happened within about three yards of his back.

He poked his head forward, groping for the ear of his commander. His lips touched it – big, fleshy, very wet. He cried in an agitated tone, 'Our boats are going now, sir.'

And again he heard that voice, forced and ringing feebly, but with a penetrating effect of quietness in the enormous discord of noises, as if sent out from some remote spot of peace beyond the black wastes of the gale; again he heard a man's voice – the frail and indomitable sound that can be made to carry an infinity of thought, resolution and purpose, that shall be pronouncing confident words on the last day, when heavens fall, and justice is done – again he heard it, and it was crying to him, as if from very, very far – 'All right.'

He thought he had not managed to make himself understood. 'Our boats – I say boats – the boats, sir! Two gone!'

The same voice, within a foot of him and yet so remote, yelled sensibly, 'Can't be helped.'

Captain MacWhirr had never turned his face, but Jukes caught some more words on the wind.

'What can – expect – when hammering through – such – Bound to leave – something behind – stands to reason.'

Watchfully Jukes listened for more. No more came. This was all Captain MacWhirr had to say; and Jukes could picture to himself rather than see the broad squat back before him. An impenetrable obscurity pressed down upon the ghostly glimmers of the sea. A dull conviction seized upon Jukes that there was nothing to be done.

If the steering-gear did not give way, if the immense volumes of water did not burst the deck in or smash one of the hatches, if the engines did not give up, if way could be kept on the ship against this terrific wind, and she did not bury herself in one of these awful seas, of whose white crests alone, topping high above her bows, he could now and then get a sickening glimpse – then there was a chance of her coming out of it. Something within him seemed to turn over, bringing uppermost the feeling that the *Nan-Shan* was lost.

'She's done for,' he said to himself, with a surprising mental agitation, as though he had discovered an unexpected meaning in this thought. One of these things was bound to happen. Nothing could be prevented now, and nothing could be remedied. The men on board did not count, and the ship could not last. This weather was too impossible.

Jukes felt an arm thrown heavily over his shoulders; and to this overture he responded with great intelligence by catching hold of his captain round the waist.

They stood clasped thus in the blind night, bracing each other against the wind, cheek to cheek and lip to ear, in the manner of two hulks lashed stem to stern together.

And Jukes heard the voice of his commander hardly any louder than before, but nearer, as though, starting to march athwart the prodigious rush of the hurricane, it had approached him, bearing that strange effect of quietness like the serene glow of a halo.

'D'ye know where the hands got to?' it asked, vigorous and evanescent at the same time, overcoming the strength of the wind, and swept away from Jukes instantly.

Jukes didn't know. They were all on the bridge when the real force of the hurricane struck the ship. He had no idea where they had crawled to. Under the circumstances they were nowhere, for all the use that could be made of them. Somehow the Captain's wish to know distressed Jukes.

'Want the hands, sir?' he cried apprehensively.

'Ought to know,' asserted Captain MacWhirr. 'Hold hard.'

They held hard. An outburst of unchained fury, a vicious rush of the wind absolutely steadied the ship; she rocked only, quick and light like a child's cradle, for a terrific moment of suspense, while the whole atmosphere, as it seemed, streamed furiously past her, roaring away from the tenebrous earth.

It suffocated them, and with eyes shut they tightened their grasp. What from the magnitude of the shock might have been a column of water running upright in the dark, butted against the ship, broke short, and fell on her bridge, crushingly, from on high, with a dead burying weight.

A flying fragment of that collapse, a mere splash, enveloped them in one swirl from their feet over their heads, filling violently their ears, mouths and nostrils with salt water. It knocked out their legs, wrenched in haste at their arms, seethed away swiftly under their chins; and opening their eyes, they saw the piled-up masses of foam dashing to and fro amongst what looked like the fragments of a ship. She had given way as if driven straight in. Their panting hearts yielded too before the tremendous blow; and all at once she sprang up again to her desperate plunging, as if trying to scramble out from under the ruins.

The seas in the dark seemed to rush from all sides to keep her back where she might perish. There was hate in the way she was handled, and a ferocity in the blows that fell. She was like a living creature thrown to the rage of a mob: hustled terribly, struck at, borne up, flung down, leaped upon. Captain MacWhirr and Jukes kept hold of each other, deafened by the noise, gagged by the wind; and the great physical tumult beating about their bodies, brought, like an unbridled display of passion, a profound trouble to their souls. One of these wild and appalling shrieks that are heard at times passing mysteriously overhead in the steady roar of a hurricane, swooped, as if borne on wings, upon the ship, and Jukes tried to outscream it.

'Will she live through this?'

The cry was wrenched out of his breast. It was as unintentional as the birth of a thought in the head, and he heard nothing of it himself. It all became extinct at once – thought, intention, effort – and of his cry the inaudible vibration added to the tempest waves of the air.

He expected nothing from it. Nothing at all. For indeed what answer could be made? But after a while he heard with amazement the frail and resisting voice in his ear, the dwarf sound, unconquered in the giant tumult.

'She may!'

It was a dull yell, more difficult to seize than a whisper. And presently the voice returned again, half submerged in the vast crashes, like a ship battling against the waves of an ocean.

'Let's hope so!' it cried – small, lonely and unmoved, a stranger to the visions of hope or fear; and it flickered into disconnected words: 'Ship . . . This . . . Never – Anyhow . . . for the best.' Jukes gave it up.

Then, as if it had come suddenly upon the one thing fit to withstand the power of a storm, it seemed to gain force and firmness for the last broken shouts: 'Keep on hammering . . . builders . . . good men . . . And chance it . . . engines . . . Rout . . . good man.'

Captain MacWhirr removed his arm from Jukes' shoulders, and thereby ceased to exist for his mate, so dark it was; Jukes, after a tense stiffening of every muscle, would let himself go limp all over. The gnawing of profound discomfort existed side by side with an incredible disposition to somnolence, as though he had been buffeted and worried into drowsiness. The wind would get hold of his head and try to shake it off his shoulders; his clothes, full of water, were as heavy as lead, cold and dripping like an armour of melting ice: he shivered – it lasted a long time; and with his hands closed hard on his hold, he was letting himself sink slowly into the depths of bodily misery. His mind became concentrated upon himself in an aimless, idle way, and when something pushed lightly at the back of his knees he nearly, as the saying is, jumped out of his skin.

In the start forward he bumped the back of Captain MacWhirr, who didn't move; and then a hand gripped his thigh. A lull had come, a menacing lull of the wind, the holding of a stormy breath – and he felt himself pawed all over. It was the boatswain. Jukes recognised these hands, so thick and enormous that they seemed to belong to some new species of man.

The boatswain had arrived on the bridge, crawling on all fours against the wind, and had found the chief mate's legs with the top of his head. Immediately he crouched and began to explore Jukes' person upwards, with prudent, apologetic touches, as became an inferior.

He was an ill-favoured, undersized, gruff sailor of fifty, coarsely hairy, short-legged, long-armed, resembling an elderly ape. His strength was immense; and in his great lumpy paws, bulging like brown boxing-gloves on the end of furry forearms, the heaviest objects were handled like playthings. Apart from the grizzled pelt on his chest, the menacing demeanour and the hoarse voice, he had none of the classical attributes of his rating. His good nature almost amounted to imbecility: the men did what they liked with him, and he had not an ounce of initiative in his character, which was easy-going and talkative. For these reasons Jukes disliked him; but Captain MacWhirr, to Jukes' scornful disgust, seemed to regard him as a first-rate petty officer.

He pulled himself up by Jukes' coat, taking that liberty with the greatest moderation, and only so far as it was forced upon him by the hurricane.

'What is it, boss'n, what is it?' yelled Jukes, impatiently. What could that fraud of a boss'n want on the bridge? The typhoon had got on Jukes' nerves. The husky bellowings of the other, though unintelligible, seemed to suggest a state of lively satisfaction. There could be no mistake. The old fool was pleased with something.

The boatswain's other hand had found some other body, for in a changed tone he began to enquire: 'Is it you, sir? Is it you, sir?' The wind strangled his howls.

'Yes!' cried Captain MacWhirr.

Chapter 4

All that the boatswain, out of a superabundance of yells, could make clear to Captain MacWhirr was the bizarre intelligence that 'All them Chinamen in the fore 'tween deck have fetched away, sir.'

Jukes to leeward could hear these two shouting within six inches of his face, as you may hear on a still night half a mile away two men conversing across a field. He heard Captain MacWhirr's exasperated 'What? What?' and the strained pitch of the other's hoarseness. 'In a lump . . . seen them myself . . . Awful sight, sir . . . thought . . . tell you.'

Jukes remained indifferent, as if rendered irresponsible by the force of the hurricane, which made the very thought of action utterly vain. Besides, being very young, he had found the occupation of keeping his heart completely steeled against the worst so engrossing that he had come to feel an overpowering dislike towards any other form of activity whatever. He was not scared; he knew this because, firmly believing he would never see another sunrise, he remained calm in that belief.

These are the moments of do-nothing heroics to which even good men surrender at times. Many officers of ships can no doubt recall a case in their experience when just such a trance of confounded stoicism would come all at once over a whole ship's company. Jukes, however, had no wide experience of men or storms. He conceived himself to be calm – inexorably calm; but as a matter of fact he was daunted; not abjectly, but only so far as a decent man may, without becoming loathsome to himself.

It was rather like a forced-on numbness of spirit. The long, long stress of a gale does it; the suspense of the interminably culminating catastrophe; and there is a bodily fatigue in the mere holding on to existence within the excessive tumult; a searching and insidious fatigue that penetrates deep into a man's breast to cast down and sadden his heart, which is incorrigible, and of all the gifts of the earth – even before life itself – aspires to peace.

Jukes was benumbed much more than he supposed. He held on – very wet, very cold, stiff in every limb; and in a momentary hallucination of swift visions (it is said that a drowning man thus reviews all his life) he beheld all sorts of memories altogether unconnected with his present situation. He remembered his father, for instance: a worthy businessman, who at an unfortunate crisis in his affairs went quietly to bed and died forthwith in a state of resignation. Jukes did not recall these circumstances, of course, but remaining otherwise unconcerned he seemed to see distinctly the poor man's face; a certain game of nap played when quite a boy in Table Bay on board a ship, since lost with all hands; the thick eyebrows of his first skipper; and without any emotion, as he might years ago have walked listlessly into her room and found her sitting there with a book, he remembered his mother – dead, too, now – the resolute woman, left badly off, who had been very firm in his bringing up.

It could not have lasted more than a second, perhaps not so much. A heavy arm had fallen about his shoulders; Captain MacWhirr's voice was speaking his name into his ear.

'Jukes! Jukes!'

He detected the tone of deep concern. The wind had thrown its weight on the ship, trying to pin her down amongst the seas. They made a clean breach over her, as over a deep-swimming log; and the gathered weight of crashes menaced monstrously from afar. The breakers flung out of the night with a ghostly light on their crests – the light of sea-foam that in a ferocious, boiling-up pale flash showed upon the slender body of the ship the toppling rush, the downfall, and the seething mad scurry of each wave. Never for a moment could she shake herself clear of the water; Jukes, rigid, perceived in her motion the ominous sign of haphazard floundering. She was no longer struggling intelligently. It was the beginning of the end; and the note of busy concern in Captain MacWhirr's voice sickened him like an exhibition of blind and pernicious folly.

The spell of the storm had fallen upon Jukes. He was penetrated by it, absorbed by it; he was rooted in it with a rigour of dumb attention. Captain MacWhirr persisted in his cries, but the wind got between them like a solid wedge. He hung round Jukes' neck as heavy as a millstone, and suddenly the sides of their heads knocked together.

'Jukes! Mr Jukes, I say!'

He had to answer that voice that would not be silenced. He answered in the customary manner: '. . . Yes, sir.'

And directly, his heart, corrupted by the storm that breeds a craving for peace, rebelled against the tyranny of training and command.

Captain MacWhirr had his mate's head fixed firm in the crook of his elbow, and pressed it to his yelling lips mysteriously. Sometimes Jukes would break in, admonishing hastily: 'Look out, sir!' or Captain MacWhirr would bawl an earnest exhortation to 'Hold hard, there!' and the whole black universe seemed to reel together with the ship. They paused. She floated yet. And Captain MacWhirr would resume his shouts. '. . . Says . . . whole lot . . . fetched away . . . Ought to see . . . what's the matter.'

Directly the full force of the hurricane had struck the ship, every part of her deck became untenable; and the sailors, dazed and dismayed, took shelter in the port alleyway under the bridge. It had a door aft, which they shut; it was very black, cold, and dismal. At each heavy fling of the ship they would groan all together in the dark, and tons of water could be heard scuttling about as if trying to get at them from above. The boatswain had been keeping up a gruff talk, but a more unreasonable lot of men, he said afterwards, he had never been with. They were snug enough there, out of harm's way, and not wanted to do anything, either; and yet they did nothing but grumble and complain peevishly like so many sick kids. Finally, one of them said that if there had been at least some light to see each other's noses by, it wouldn't be so bad. It was making him crazy, he declared, to lie there in the dark waiting for the blamed hooker to sink.

'Why don't you step outside, then, and be done with it at once?' the boatswain turned on him.

This called up a shout of execration. The boatswain found himself overwhelmed with reproaches of all sorts. They seemed to take it ill that a lamp was not instantly created for them out of nothing. They would whine after a light to get drowned by – anyhow! And though the unreason of their revilings was patent – since no one could hope to reach the lamp-room, which was forward – he became greatly distressed. He did not think it was decent of them to be nagging at him like this. He told them so, and was met by general contumely. He sought refuge, therefore, in an embittered silence. At the same time their grumbling and sighing and muttering worried him greatly, but by and by it occurred to him that there were six globe lamps hung in the 'tween-deck, and that there could be no harm in depriving the coolies of one of them.

The *Nan-Shan* had an athwartship coal-bunker, which, being at times used as cargo space, communicated by an iron door with the fore 'tween-deck. It was empty then, and its manhole was the foremost one in the alleyway. The boatswain could get in, therefore, without coming out on deck at all; but to his great surprise he found he could induce no one to help him in taking off the manhole cover. He groped for it all the same, but one of the crew lying in his way refused to budge.

'Why, I only want to get you that blamed light you are crying for,' he expostulated, almost pitifully.

Somebody told him to go and put his head in a bag. He regretted he could not recognise the voice, and that it was too dark to see, otherwise, as he said, he would have put a head on *that* son of a sea-cook, anyway, sink or swim. Nevertheless, he had made up his mind to show them he could get a light, if he were to die for it.

Through the violence of the ship's rolling, every movement was dangerous. To be lying down seemed labour enough. He nearly broke his neck dropping into the bunker. He fell on his back, and was sent shooting helplessly from side to side in the dangerous company of a heavy iron bar – a coal-trimmer's slice probably – left down there by somebody. This thing made him as nervous as though it had been a wild beast. He could not see it, the inside of the bunker coated with coal-dust being perfectly and impenetrably black; but he heard it sliding and clattering, and striking here and there, always in the neighbourhood of his head. It seemed to make an extraordinary noise, too – to give heavy thumps as though it had been as big as a bridge girder. This was remarkable enough for him to notice while he was flung from port to starboard and back again, and clawing desperately the smooth sides of the bunker in the endeavour to stop himself. The door into the 'tween-deck not fitting quite true, he saw a thread of dim light at the bottom.

Being a sailor, and a still active man, he did not want much of a chance to regain his feet; and as luck would have it, in scrambling up he put his hand on the iron slice, picking it up as he rose. Otherwise he would have been afraid of the thing breaking his legs, or at least knocking him down again. At first he stood still. He felt unsafe in this darkness that seemed to make the ship's motion unfamiliar, unforeseen, and difficult to counteract. He felt so much shaken for a moment that he dared not move for fear of 'taking charge again'. He had no mind to get battered to pieces in that bunker.

He had struck his head twice; he was dazed a little. He seemed to hear yet so plainly the clatter and bangs of the iron slice flying about his ears that he tightened his grip to prove to himself he had it there safely in his hand. He was vaguely amazed at the plainness with which down there he could hear the gale raging. Its howls and shrieks seemed to take on, in the emptiness of the bunker, something of the human character, of human rage and pain – being not vast but infinitely poignant. And there were, with every roll, thumps too – profound, ponderous thumps, as if a bulky object of five-ton weight or so had got play in the hold. But there was no such thing in the cargo. Something on deck? Impossible. Or alongside? Couldn't be.

He thought all this quickly, clearly, competently, like a seaman, and in the end remained puzzled. This noise, though, came deadened from outside, together with the washing and pouring of water on deck above his head. Was it the wind? Must be. It made down there a row like the shouting of a big lot of crazed men. And he discovered in himself a desire for a light too – if only to get drowned by – and a nervous anxiety to get out of that bunker as quickly as possible.

He pulled back the bolt: the heavy iron plate turned on its hinges; and it was as though he had opened the door to the sounds of the tempest. A gust of hoarse yelling met him: the air was still; and the rushing of water overhead was covered by a tumult of strangled, throaty shrieks that produced an effect of desperate confusion. He straddled his legs the whole width of the doorway and stretched his neck. And at first he perceived only what he had come to seek: six small yellow flames swinging violently on the great body of the dusk.

It was stayed like the gallery of a mine, with a row of stanchions in the middle, and cross-beams overhead, penetrating into the gloom ahead – indefinitely. And to port there loomed, like the caving in of one of the sides, a bulky mass with a slanting outline. The whole place, with the shadows and the shapes, moved all the time. The boatswain glared: the ship lurched to starboard, and a great howl came from that mass that had the slant of fallen earth.

Pieces of wood whizzed past. Planks, he thought, inexpressibly startled, and flinging back his head. At his feet a man went sliding over, open-eyed, on his back, straining with uplifted arms for nothing: and another came bounding like a detached stone with his head between his legs and his hands clenched. His pigtail whipped in the air; he made a grab at the boatswain's legs, and from his opened hand a bright white disc rolled against the boatswain's foot. He recognised a silver dollar, and yelled at it with astonishment. With a precipitated sound of trampling and shuffling of bare feet, and with guttural cries, the mound of writhing bodies piled up to port detached itself from the ship's side and shifted to starboard, sliding, inert and struggling, to a dull, brutal thump. The cries ceased. The boatswain heard a long moan through the roar and whistling of the wind; he saw an inextricable confusion of heads and shoulders, naked soles kicking upwards, fists raised, tumbling backs, legs, pigtails, faces.

'Good Lord!' he cried, horrified, and banged-to the iron door upon this vision.

This was what he had come on the bridge to tell. He could not keep it to himself; and on board ship there is only one man to whom it is worth while to unburden yourself. On his passage back the hands in the alleyway swore at him for a fool. Why didn't he bring that lamp? What the devil did the coolies matter to anybody? And when he came out, the extremity of the ship made what went on inside of her appear of little moment.

At first he thought he had left the alleyway in the very moment of her sinking. The bridge ladders had been washed away, but an enormous sea filling the after-deck floated him up. After that he had to lie on his stomach for some time, holding to a ring-bolt, getting his breath now and then, and swallowing salt water. He struggled farther on his hands and knees, too frightened and distracted to turn back. In this way he reached the after-part of the wheelhouse. In that comparatively sheltered spot he found the second mate. The boatswain was pleasantly surprised – his impression being that everybody on deck must have been washed away a long time ago. He asked eagerly where the captain was.

The second mate was lying low, like a malignant little animal under a hedge.

'Captain? Gone overboard, after getting us into this mess.' The mate, too, for all he knew or cared. Another fool. Didn't matter. Everybody was going by and by.

The boatswain crawled out again into the strength of the wind; not because he much expected to find anybody, he said, but just to get away from 'that man'. He crawled out as outcasts go to face an inclement world. Hence his great joy at finding Jukes and the Captain. But what was going on in the 'tween-deck was to him a minor matter by that time. Besides, it was difficult to make yourself heard. But he managed to convey the idea that the Chinamen had broken adrift together with their boxes, and that he had come up on purpose to report this. As to the hands, they were all right. Then, appeased, he subsided on the deck in a sitting posture, hugging with his arms and legs the stand of the engine-room telegraph – an iron casting as thick as a post. When that went, why, he expected he would go too. He gave no more thought to the coolies.

Captain MacWhirr had made Jukes understand that he wanted him to go down below – to see.

'What am I to do then, sir?' And the trembling of his whole wet body caused Jukes' voice to sound like bleating.

'See first . . . Boss'n . . . says . . . adrift.'

'That boss'n is a confounded fool,' howled Jukes shakily.

The absurdity of the demand made upon him revolted Jukes. He was as unwilling to go as if the moment he had left the deck the ship were sure to sink.

'I must know . . . can't leave . . . '

'They'll settle, sir.'

'Fight . . . boss'n says they fight . . . Why? Can't have . . . fighting . . . board ship . . . Much rather keep you here . . . case . . . I should . . . washed overboard myself . . . Stop it . . . some way. You see and tell me . . . through engine-room tube. Don't want you . . . come up here . . . too often. Dangerous . . . moving about . . . deck.'

Jukes, held with his head in chancery, had to listen to what seemed horrible suggestions.

'Don't want . . . you get lost . . . so long . . . ship isn't . . . Rout . . . Good man . . . Ship . . . may . . . through this . . . all right yet.'

All at once Jukes understood he would have to go.

'Do you think she may?' he screamed.

But the wind devoured the reply, out of which Jukes heard only the one word, pronounced with great energy ' . . . Always . . . '

Captain MacWhirr released Jukes, and bending over the boatswain, yelled 'Get back with the mate.' Jukes only knew that the arm was gone off his shoulders. He was dismissed with his orders – to do what? He was exasperated into letting go his hold carelessly, and on the instant was blown away. It seemed to him that nothing could stop him from being blown right over the stern. He flung himself down hastily, and the boatswain, who was following, fell on him.

'Don't you get up yet, sir,' cried the boatswain. 'No hurry!'

A sea swept over. Jukes understood the boatswain to splutter that the bridge ladders were gone. 'I'll lower you down, sir, by your hands,' he screamed. He shouted also something about the smokestack being as likely to go overboard as not. Jukes thought it very possible, and imagined the fires out, the ship helpless . . . The boatswain by his side kept on yelling. 'What? What is it?' Jukes cried distressfully; and the other repeated, 'What would my old woman say if she saw me now?'

In the alleyway, where a lot of water had got in and splashed in the dark, the men were still as death, till Jukes stumbled against one of them and cursed him savagely for being in the way. Two or three voices then asked, eager and weak, 'Any chance for us, sir?'

'What's the matter with you fools?' he said brutally. He felt as though he could throw himself down amongst them and never move any more. But they seemed cheered; and in the midst of obsequious warnings, 'Look out! Mind that manhole lid, sir,' they lowered him into the bunker. The boatswain tumbled down after him, and as soon as he had picked himself up he remarked, 'She would say, "Serve you right, you old fool, for going to sea." '

The boatswain had some means, and made a point of alluding to them frequently. His wife – a fat woman – and two grown-up daughters kept a greengrocer's shop in the East End of London.

In the dark, Jukes, unsteady on his legs, listened to a faint thunderous patter. A deadened screaming went on steadily at his elbow, as it were; and from above the louder tumult of the storm descended upon these near sounds. His head swam. To him, too, in that bunker, the motion of the ship seemed novel and menacing, sapping his resolution as though he had never been afloat before.

He had half a mind to scramble out again; but the remembrance of Captain MacWhirr's voice made this impossible. His orders were to go and see. What was the good of it, he wanted to know. Enraged, he told himself he would see – of course. But the boatswain, staggering clumsily, warned him to be careful how he opened that door; there was a blamed fight going on. And Jukes, as if in great bodily pain, desired irritably to know what the devil they were fighting for.

'Dollars! Dollars, sir. All their rotten chests got burst open. Blamed money skipping all over the place, and they are tumbling after it head over heels – tearing and biting like anything. A regular little hell in there.'

Jukes convulsively opened the door. The short boatswain peered under his arm.

One of the lamps had gone out, broken perhaps. Rancorous, guttural cries burst out loudly on their ears, and a strange panting sound, the working of all these straining breasts. A hard blow hit the side of the ship: water fell above with a stunning shock, and in the forefront of the gloom, where the air was reddish and thick, Jukes saw a head bang the deck violently, two thick calves waving on high, muscular arms twined round a naked body, a yellow-face, open-mouthed and with a set wild stare, look up and slide away. An empty chest clattered turning over; a man fell head first with a jump, as if lifted by a kick; and farther off, indistinct, others streamed like a mass of rolling stones down a bank, thumping the deck with their feet and flourishing their arms wildly. The hatchway ladder was loaded with coolies swarming on it like bees on a branch. They hung on the steps in a crawling, stirring cluster, beating madly with their fists the underside of the battened hatch, and the headlong rush of the water above was heard in the intervals of their yelling. The ship heeled over more, and they began to drop off: first one, then two, then all the rest went away together, falling straight off with a great cry.

Jukes was confounded. The boatswain, with gruff anxiety, begged him, 'Don't you go in there, sir.'

The whole place seemed to twist upon itself, jumping incessantly the while; and when the ship rose to a sea Jukes fancied that all these men would be shot upon him in a body. He backed out, swung the door to, and with trembling hands pushed at the bolt . . .

As soon as his mate had gone Captain MacWhirr, left alone on the bridge, sidled and staggered as far as the wheelhouse. Its door being hinged forward, he had to fight the gale for admittance, and when at last he managed to enter, it was with an instantaneous clatter and a bang, as though he had been fired through the wood. He stood within, holding on to the handle.

The steering-gear leaked steam, and in the confined space the glass of the binnacle made a shiny oval of light in a thin white fog. The wind howled, hummed, whistled, with sudden booming gusts that rattled the doors and shutters in the vicious patter of sprays. Two coils of lead-line and a small canvas bag hung on a long lanyard, swung wide off, and came back clinging to the bulkheads. The gratings underfoot were nearly afloat; with every sweeping blow of a sea, water squirted violently through the cracks all round the door, and the man at the helm had flung down his cap, his coat, and stood propped against the gear-casing in a striped cotton shirt open on his breast. The little brass wheel in his hands had the appearance of a bright and fragile toy. The cords of his neck stood hard and lean, a dark patch lay in the hollow of his throat, and his face was still and sunken as in death.

Captain MacWhirr wiped his eyes. The sea that had nearly taken him overboard had, to his great annoyance, washed his sou'-wester hat off his bald head. The fluffy, fair hair, soaked and darkened, resembled a mean skein of cotton threads festooned round his bare skull. His face, glistening with sea-water, had been made crimson with the wind, with the sting of sprays. He looked as though he had come off sweating from before a furnace.

'You here?' he muttered heavily.

The second mate had found his way into the wheelhouse some time before. He had fixed himself in a corner with his knees up, a fist pressed against each temple; and this attitude suggested rage, sorrow, resignation, surrender, with a sort of concentrated unforgiveness. He said mournfully and defiantly, 'Well, it's my watch below now: ain't it?'

The steam gear clattered, stopped, clattered again; and the helmsman's eyeballs seemed to project out of a hungry face as if the compass card behind the binnacle glass had been meat. God knows how long he had been left there to steer, as if forgotten by all his shipmates. The bells had not been struck; there had been no reliefs; the ship's routine had gone down wind; but he was trying to keep her head north-north-east. The rudder might have been gone for all he knew, the fires out, the engines broken down, the ship ready to roll over like a corpse. He was anxious not to get muddled and lose control of her head, because the compass-card swung far both ways, wriggling on the pivot, and sometimes seemed to whirl right round. He suffered from mental stress. He was horribly afraid, also, of the wheelhouse going. Mountains of water kept on tumbling against it. When the ship took one of her desperate dives the corners of his lips twitched.

Captain MacWhirr looked up at the wheelhouse clock. Screwed to the bulkhead, it had a white face on which the black hands appeared to stand quite still. It was half-past one in the morning.

'Another day,' he muttered to himself.

The second mate heard him, and lifting his head as one grieving amongst ruins, 'You won't see it break,' he exclaimed. His wrists and his knees could be seen to shake violently. 'No, by God! You won't . . . '

He took his face again between his fists.

The body of the helmsman had moved slightly, but his head didn't budge on his neck – like a stone head fixed to look one way from a column. During a roll that all but took his booted legs from under him, and in the very stagger to save himself, Captain MacWhirr said austerely, 'Don't you pay any attention to what that man says.' And then, with an indefinable change of tone, very grave, he added, 'He isn't on duty.'

The sailor said nothing.

The hurricane boomed, shaking the little place, which seemed air-tight; and the light of the binnacle flickered all the time.

'You haven't been relieved,' Captain MacWhirr went on, looking down. 'I want you to stick to the helm, though, as long as you can. You've got the hang of her. Another man coming here might make a mess of it. Wouldn't do. No child's play. And the hands are probably busy with a job down below . . . Think you can?'

The steering gear leaped into an abrupt short clatter, stopped smouldering like an ember; and the still man, with a motionless gaze, burst out, as if all the passion in him had gone into his lips: 'By Heavens, sir! I can steer for ever if nobody talks to me.'

'Oh! aye! All right . . . ' The Captain lifted his eyes for the first time to the man, ' . . . Hackett.'

And he seemed to dismiss this matter from his mind. He stooped to the engine-room speaking-tube, blew in, and bent his head. Mr Rout below answered, and at once Captain MacWhirr put his lips to the mouthpiece.

With the uproar of the gale around him he applied alternately his lips and his ear, and the engineer's voice mounted to him, harsh and as if out of the heat of an engagement. One of the stokers was disabled, the others had given in, the second engineer and the donkeyman were firing-up. The third engineer was standing by the steam-valve. The engines were being tended by hand. How was it above?

'Bad enough. It mostly rests with you,' said Captain MacWhirr. Was the mate down there yet? No? Well, he would be presently. Would Mr Rout let him talk through the speaking-tube? – through the deck speaking-tube, because he – the Captain – was going out again on the bridge directly. There was some trouble amongst the Chinamen. They were fighting, it seemed. Couldn't allow fighting anyhow . . .

Mr Rout had gone away, and Captain MacWhirr could feel against his ear the pulsation of the engines, like the beat of the ship's heart. Mr Rout's voice down there shouted something distantly. The ship pitched headlong, the pulsation leaped with a hissing tumult, and stopped dead. Captain MacWhirr's face was impassive, and his eyes were fixed aimlessly on the crouching shape of the second mate. Again Mr Rout's voice cried out in the depths, and the pulsating beats recommenced, with slow strokes – growing swifter.

Mr Rout had returned to the tube. 'It don't matter much what they do,' he said hastily; and then, with irritation, 'She takes these dives as if she never meant to come up again.'

'Awful sea,' said the Captain's voice from above.

'Don't let me drive her under,' barked Solomon Rout up the pipe.

'Dark and rain. Can't see what's coming,' uttered the voice. 'Must – keep – her – moving – enough to steer – and chance it,' it went on to state distinctly.

'I am doing as much as I dare.'

'We are – getting – smashed up – a good deal up here,' proceeded the voice mildly. 'Doing – fairly well – though. Of course, if the wheelhouse should go . . . '

Mr Rout, bending an attentive ear, muttered peevishly something under his breath.

But the deliberate voice up there became animated to ask: 'Jukes turned up yet?' Then, after a short wait, 'I wish he would bear a hand. I want him to be done and come up here in case of anything. To look after the ship. I am all alone. The second mate's lost . . . '

'What?' shouted Mr Rout into the engine-room, taking his head away. Then up the tube he cried, 'Gone overboard?' and clapped his ear to.

'Lost his nerve,' the voice from above continued in a matter-of-fact tone. 'Damned awkward circumstance.'

Mr Rout, listening with bowed neck, opened his eyes wide at this. However, he heard something like the sounds of a scuffle and broken exclamations coming down to him. He strained his hearing; and all the time Beale, the third engineer, with his arms uplifted, held between the palms of his hands the rim of a little black wheel projecting at the side of a big copper pipe. He seemed to be poising it above his head, as though it were a correct attitude in some sort of game.

To steady himself, he pressed his shoulder against the white bulkhead, one knee bent, and a sweat-rag tucked in his belt hanging on his hip. His smooth cheek was begrimed and flushed, and the coal dust on his eyelids, like the black pencilling of a make-up, enhanced the liquid brilliance of the whites, giving to his youthful face something of a feminine, exotic and fascinating aspect. When the ship pitched he would with hasty movements of his hands screw hard at the little wheel.

'Gone crazy,' began the Captain's voice suddenly in the tube. 'Rushed at me . . . Just now. Had to knock him down . . . This minute. You heard, Mr Rout?'

'The devil!' muttered Mr Rout. 'Look out, Beale!'

His shout rang out like the blast of a warning trumpet, between the iron walls of the engine-room. Painted white, they rose high into the dusk of the skylight, sloping like a roof; and the whole lofty space resembled the interior of a monument, divided by floors of iron grating, with lights flickering at different levels, and a mass of gloom lingering in the middle, within the columnar stir of machinery under the motionless swelling of the cylinders. A loud and wild resonance, made up of all the noises of the hurricane, dwelt in the still warmth of the air. There was in it the smell of hot metal, of oil, and a slight mist of steam. The blows of the sea seemed to traverse it in an unringing, stunning shock, from side to side.

Gleams, like pale long flames, trembled upon the polish of metal; from the flooring below the enormous crank-heads emerged in their turns with a flash of brass and steel – going over; while the connecting-rods, big-jointed, like skeleton limbs, seemed to thrust them down and pull them up again with an irresistible precision. And deep in the half-light other rods dodged deliberately to and fro, crossheads nodded, discs of metal rubbed smoothly against each other, slow and gentle, in a commingling of shadows and gleams.

Sometimes all those powerful and unerring movements would slow down simultaneously, as if they had been the functions of a living organism, stricken suddenly by the blight of languor; and Mr Rout's eyes would blaze darker in his long sallow face. He was fighting this fight in a pair of carpet slippers. A short shiny jacket barely covered his loins, and his white wrists protruded far out of the tight sleeves, as though the emergency had added to his stature, had lengthened his limbs, augmented his pallor, hollowed his eyes.

He moved, climbing high up, disappearing low down, with a restless, purposeful industry, and when he stood still, holding the guard-rail in front of the starting-gear, he would keep glancing to the right at the steam-gauge, at the water-gauge, fixed upon the white wall in the light of a swaying lamp. The mouths of two speaking-tubes gaped stupidly at his elbow, and the dial of the engine-room telegraph resembled a clock of large diameter, bearing on its face curt words instead of figures. The grouped letters stood out heavily black, around the pivot-head of the indicator, emphatically symbolic of loud exclamations: Ahead, Astern, Slow, Half, Stand by; and the fat black hand pointed downwards to the word Full, which, thus singled out, captured the eye as a sharp cry secures attention.

The wood-encased bulk of the low-pressure cylinder, frowning portly from above, emitted a faint wheeze at every thrust, and except for that low hiss the engines worked their steel limbs headlong or slow with a silent, determined smoothness. And all this, the white walls, the moving steel, the floor plates under Solomon Rout's feet, the floors of iron grating above his head, the dusk and the gleams, uprose and sank continuously, with one accord, upon the harsh wash of the waves against the ship's side. The whole loftiness of the place, booming hollow to the great voice of the wind, swayed at the top like a tree, would go over bodily, as if borne down this way and that by the tremendous blasts.

'You've got to hurry up,' shouted Mr Rout, as soon as he saw Jukes appear in the stokehold doorway.

Jukes' glance was wandering and tipsy; his red face was puffy, as though he had overslept himself. He had had an arduous road, and had travelled over it with immense vivacity, the agitation of his mind corresponding to the exertions of his body. He had rushed up out of the bunker, stumbling in the dark alleyway amongst a lot of bewildered men who, trod upon, asked 'What's up, sir?' in awed mutters all round him; down the stokehold ladder, missing many iron rungs in his hurry, down into a place deep as a well, black as

Tophet, tipping over back and forth like a see-saw. The water in the bilges thundered at each roll, and lumps of coal skipped to and fro, from end to end, rattling like an avalanche of pebbles on a slope of iron.

Somebody in there moaned with pain, and somebody else could be seen crouching over what seemed the prone body of a dead man; a lusty voice blasphemed; and the glow under each fire-door was like a pool of flaming blood radiating quietly in a velvety blackness.

A gust of wind struck upon the nape of Jukes' neck, and next moment he felt it streaming about his wet ankles. The stokehold ventilators hummed: in front of the six fire-doors two wild figures, stripped to the waist, staggered and stooped, wrestling with two shovels.

'Hallo! Plenty of draught now,' yelled the second engineer at once, as though he had been all the time looking out for Jukes. The donkeyman, a dapper little chap with a dazzling fair skin and a tiny, gingery moustache, worked in a sort of mute transport. They were keeping a full head of steam, and a profound rumbling, as of an empty furniture van trotting over a bridge, made a sustained bass to all the other noises of the place.

'Blowing off all the time,' went on yelling the second. With a sound as of a hundred scoured saucepans, the orifice of a ventilator spat upon his shoulder a sudden gush of salt water, and he volleyed a stream of curses upon all things on earth including his own soul, ripping and raving, and all the time attending to his business. With a sharp clash of metal the ardent pale glare of the fire opened upon his bullet head showing his spluttering lips, his insolent face, and with another clang closed like the white-hot wink of an iron eye.

'Where's the blooming ship? Can you tell me? blast my eyes! Under water – or what? It's coming down here in tons. Are the condemned cowls gone to Hades? Hey? Don't you know anything – you jolly sailor-man you . . . ?'

Jukes, after a bewildered moment, had been helped by a roll to dart through; and as soon as his eyes took in the comparative vastness, peace and brilliance of the engine-room, the ship, setting her stern heavily in the water, sent him charging head down upon Mr Rout.

The chief's arm, long like a tentacle, and straightening as if worked by a spring, went out to meet him, and deflected his rush into a spin towards the speaking-tubes. At the same time Mr Rout repeated earnestly: 'You've got to hurry up, whatever it is.'

Jukes yelled, 'Are you there, sir?' and listened. Nothing. Suddenly the roar of the wind fell straight into his ear, but presently a small voice shoved aside the shouting hurricane quietly.

'You, Jukes? – Well?'

Jukes was ready to talk: it was only time that seemed to be wanting. It was easy enough to account for everything. He could perfectly imagine the coolies battened down in the reeking 'tween-deck, lying sick and scared between the rows of chests. Then one of these chests – or perhaps several at once – breaking loose in a roll, knocking out others, sides splitting, lids flying open, and all these clumsy Chinamen rising up in a body to save their property. Afterwards every fling of the ship would hurl that tramping, yelling mob here and there, from side to side, in a whirl of smashed wood, torn clothing, rolling dollars. A struggle once started, they would be unable to stop themselves. Nothing could stop them now except main force. It was a disaster. He had seen it, and that was all he could say. Some of them must be dead, he believed. The rest would go on fighting . . .

He sent up his words, tripping over each other, crowding the narrow tube. They mounted as if into a silence of an enlightened comprehension dwelling alone up there with a storm. And Jukes wanted to be dismissed from the face of that odious trouble intruding on the great need of the ship.

Chapter 5

He waited. Before his eyes the engines turned with slow labour, that in the moment of going off into a mad fling would stop dead at Mr Rout's shout, 'Look out, Beale!' They paused in an intelligent immobility, stilled in mid-stroke, a heavy crank arrested on the cant, as if conscious of danger and the passage of time. Then, with a 'Now, then!' from the chief, and the sound of a breath expelled through clenched teeth, they would accomplish the interrupted revolution and begin another.

There was the prudent sagacity of wisdom and the deliberation of enormous strength in their movements. This was their work – this patient coaxing of a distracted ship over the fury of the waves and into the very eye of the wind. At times Mr Rout's chin would sink on his breast, and he watched them with knitted eyebrows as if lost in thought.

The voice that kept the hurricane out of Jukes' ear began: 'Take the hands with you . . . ' and left off unexpectedly.

'What could I do with them, sir?'

A harsh, abrupt, imperious clang exploded suddenly. The three pairs of eyes flew up to the telegraph dial to see the hand jump from Full to Stop, as if snatched by a devil. And then these three men in the engine-room had the intimate sensation of a check upon the ship, of a strange shrinking, as if she had gathered herself for a desperate leap.

'Stop her!' bellowed Mr Rout.

Nobody – not even Captain MacWhirr, who alone on deck had caught sight of a white line of foam coming on at such a height that he couldn't believe his eyes – nobody was to know the steepness of that sea and the awful depth of the hollow the hurricane had scooped out behind the running wall of water.

It raced to meet the ship, and, with a pause, as of girding the loins, the *Nan-Shan* lifted her bows and leaped. The flames in all the lamps sank, darkening the engine-room. One went out. With a tearing crash and a swirling, raving tumult, tons of water fell upon the deck, as though the ship had darted under the foot of a cataract.

Down there they looked at each other, stunned.

'Swept from end to end, by God!' bawled Jukes.

She dipped into the hollow straight down, as if going over the edge of the world. The engine-room toppled forward menacingly, like the inside of a tower nodding in an earthquake. An awful racket, of iron things falling, came from the stokehold. She hung on this appalling slant long enough for Beale to drop on his hands and knees and begin to crawl as if he meant to fly on all fours out of the engine-room, and for Mr Rout to turn his head slowly, rigid, cavernous, with the lower jaw dropping. Jukes had shut his eyes, and his face in a moment became hopelessly blank and gentle, like the face of a blind man.

At last she rose slowly, staggering, as if she had to lift a mountain with her bows.

Mr Rout shut his mouth; Jukes blinked; and little Beale stood up hastily.

'Another one like this, and that's the last of her,' cried the chief.

He and Jukes looked at each other, and the same thought came into their heads. The Captain! Everything must have been swept away. Steering gear gone – ship like a log. All over directly.

'Rush!' ejaculated Mr Rout thickly, glaring with enlarged, doubtful eyes at Jukes, who answered him by an irresolute glance.

The clang of the telegraph gong soothed them instantly. The black hand dropped in a flash from Stop to Full.

'Now then, Beale!' cried Mr Rout.

The steam hissed low. The piston-rods slid in and out. Jukes put his ear to the tube. The voice was ready for him. It said: 'Pick up all the money. Bear a hand now. I'll want you up here.' And that was all.

'Sir?' called up Jukes. There was no answer.

He staggered away like a defeated man from the field of battle. He had got, in some way or other, a cut above his left eyebrow – a cut to the bone. He was not aware of it in the least: quantities of the China Sea, large enough to break his neck for him, had gone over his head, had cleaned, washed, and salted that wound. It did not bleed, but only gaped red; and this gash over the eye, his dishevelled hair, the disorder of his clothes, gave him the aspect of a man worsted in a fight with fists.

'Got to pick up the dollars.' He appealed to Mr Rout, smiling pitifully at random.

'What's that?' asked Mr Rout wildly. 'Pick up . . . ? I don't care . . . ' Then, quivering in every muscle, but with an exaggeration of paternal tone, 'Go away now, for God's sake. You deck people'll drive me silly. There's that second mate been going for the old man. Don't you know? You fellows are going wrong for want of something to do . . . '

At these words Jukes discovered in himself the beginnings of anger. Want of something to do – indeed . . . Full of hot scorn against the chief, he turned to go the way he had come. In the stokehold the plump donkeyman toiled with his shovel mutely, as if his tongue had been cut out; but the second was carrying on like a noisy, undaunted maniac, who had preserved his skill in the art of stoking under a marine boiler.

'Hallo, you wandering officer! Hey! Can't you get some of your slush-slingers to wind up a few of them ashes? I am getting choked with them here. Curse it! Hallo! Hey! Remember the articles: *Sailors and firemen to assist each other*. Hey! D'ye hear?'

Jukes was climbing out frantically, and the other, lifting up his face after him, howled, 'Can't you speak? What are you poking about here for? What's your game, anyhow?'

A frenzy possessed Jukes. By the time he was back amongst the men in the darkness of the alleyway, he felt ready to wring all their necks at the slightest sign of hanging back. The very thought of it exasperated him. *He* couldn't hang back. They shouldn't.

The impetuosity with which he came amongst them carried them along. They had already been excited and startled at all his comings and goings – by the fierceness and rapidity of his movements; and more felt than seen in his rushes, he appeared formidable – busied with matters of life and death that brooked no delay. At his first word he heard them drop into the bunker one after another obediently, with heavy thumps.

They were not clear as to what would have to be done. 'What is it? What is it?' they were asking each other. The boatswain tried to explain; the sounds of a great scuffle surprised them: and the mighty shocks, reverberating awfully in the black bunker, kept them in mind of their danger. When the boatswain threw open the door it seemed that an eddy of the hurricane, stealing through the iron sides of the ship, had set all these bodies whirling like dust: there came to them a confused uproar, a tempestuous tumult, a fierce mutter, gusts of screams dying away, and the tramping of feet mingling with the blows of the sea.

For a moment they glared amazed, blocking the doorway. Jukes pushed through them brutally. He said nothing, and simply darted in. Another lot of coolies on the ladder, struggling suicidally to break through the battened hatch to a swamped deck, fell off as before, and he disappeared under them like a man overtaken by a landslide.

The boatswain yelled excitedly: 'Come along. Get the mate out. He'll be trampled to death. Come on.'

They charged in, stamping on breasts, on fingers, on faces, catching their feet in heaps of clothing, kicking broken wood; but before they could get hold of him Jukes emerged waist deep in a multitude of clawing hands. In the instant he had been lost to view, all the buttons of his jacket had gone, its back had got split up to the collar, his waistcoat had been torn open. The central struggling mass of Chinamen went over to the roll, dark, indistinct, helpless, with a wild gleam of many eyes in the dim light of the lamps.

'Leave me alone – damn you. I am all right,' screeched Jukes. 'Drive them forward. Watch your chance when she pitches. Forward with 'em. Drive them against the bulkhead. Jam 'em up.'

The rush of the sailors into the seething 'tween-deck was like a splash of cold water into a boiling cauldron. The commotion sank for a moment.

The bulk of Chinamen were locked in such a compact scrimmage that, linking their arms and aided by an appalling dive of the ship, the seamen sent it forward in one great shove, like a solid block.

Behind their backs small clusters and loose bodies tumbled from side to side.

The boatswain performed prodigious feats of strength. With his long arms open, and each great paw clutching at a stanchion, he stopped the rush of seven entwined Chinamen rolling like a boulder. His joints cracked; he said, 'Ha!' and they flew apart. But the carpenter showed the greater intelligence. Without saying a word to anybody he went back into the alleyway, to fetch several coils of cargo gear he had seen there – chain and rope. With these life-lines were rigged.

There was really no resistance. The struggle, however it began, had turned into a scramble of blind panic. If the coolies had started up after their scattered dollars they were by that time fighting only for their footing. They took each other by the throat merely to save themselves from being hurled about. Whoever got a hold anywhere would kick at the others who caught at his legs and hung on, till a roll sent them flying together across the deck.

The coming of the white devils was a terror. Had they come to kill? The individuals torn out of the ruck became very limp in the seamen's hands: some, dragged aside by the heels, were passive, like dead bodies, with open, fixed eyes. Here and there a coolie would fall on his knees as if begging for mercy; several, whom the excess of fear made unruly, were hit with hard fists between the eyes, and cowered; while those who were hurt submitted to rough handling, blinking rapidly without a plaint. Faces streamed with blood; there were raw places on the shaven heads, scratches, bruises, torn wounds, gashes. The broken porcelain out of the chests was mostly responsible for the latter. Here and there a Chinaman, wild-eyed, with his tail unplaited, nursed a bleeding sole.

They had been ranged closely, after having been shaken into submission, cuffed a little to allay excitement, addressed in gruff words of encouragement that sounded like promises of evil. They sat on the deck in ghastly, drooping rows, and at the end the carpenter, with two hands to help him, moved busily from place to place, setting taut and hitching the life-lines. The boatswain, with one leg and one arm embracing a stanchion, struggled with a lamp pressed to his breast, trying to get a light, and growling all the time like an industrious gorilla. The figures of seamen stooped repeatedly, with the movements of gleaners, and everything was being flung into the bunker: clothing, smashed wood, broken china, and the dollars too, gathered up in men's jackets. Now and then a sailor would stagger towards the doorway with his arms full of rubbish; and dolorous, slanting eyes followed his movements.

With every roll of the ship the long rows of sitting Celestials would sway forward brokenly, and her headlong dives knocked together the line of shaven polls from end to end. When the wash of water rolling on the deck died away for a moment, it seemed to Jukes, yet quivering from his exertions, that in his mad struggle down there he had overcome the wind somehow: that a silence had fallen upon the ship, a silence in which the sea struck thunderously at her sides.

Everything had been cleared out of the 'tween-deck – all the wreckage, as the men said. They stood erect and tottering above the level of heads and drooping shoulders. Here and there a coolie sobbed for his breath. Where the high light fell, Jukes could see the salient ribs of one, the yellow, wistful face of another; bowed necks; or would meet a dull stare directed at his face. He was amazed that there had been no corpses; but the lot of them seemed at their last gasp, and they appeared to him more pitiful than if they had been all dead.

Suddenly one of the coolies began to speak. The light came and went on his lean, straining face; he threw his head up like a baying hound. From the bunker came the sounds of knocking and the tinkle of some dollars rolling loose; he stretched out his arm, his mouth yawned black, and the incomprehensible guttural hooting sounds, that did not seem to belong to a human language, penetrated Jukes with a strange emotion as if a brute had tried to be eloquent.

Two more started mouthing what seemed to Jukes fierce denunciations; the others stirred with grunts and growls. Jukes ordered the hands out of the 'tween-decks hurriedly. He left last himself, backing through the door, while the grunts rose to a loud murmur and hands were extended after him as after a malefactor. The boatswain shot the bolt, and remarked uneasily, 'Seems as if the wind had dropped, sir.'

The seamen were glad to get back into the alleyway. Secretly each of them thought that at the last moment he could rush out on deck – and that was a comfort. There is something horribly repugnant in the idea of being drowned under a deck. Now they had done with the Chinamen, they again became conscious of the ship's position.

Jukes on coming out of the alleyway found himself up to the neck in the noisy water. He gained the bridge, and discovered he could detect obscure shapes as if his sight had become preternaturally acute. He saw faint outlines. They recalled not the familiar aspect of the *Nan-Shan*, but something remembered – an old dismantled steamer he had seen years ago rotting on a mudbank. She recalled that wreck.

There was no wind, not a breath, except the faint currents created by the lurches of the ship. The smoke tossed out of the funnel was settling down upon her deck. He breathed it as he passed forward. He felt the deliberate throb of the engines, and heard small sounds that seemed to have survived the great uproar: the knocking of broken fittings, the rapid tumbling of some piece of wreckage on the bridge. He perceived dimly the squat shape of his captain holding on to a twisted bridge-rail, motionless and swaying as if rooted to the planks. The unexpected stillness of the air oppressed Jukes.

'We have done it, sir,' he gasped.

'Thought you would,' said Captain MacWhirr.

'Did you?' murmured Jukes to himself.

'Wind fell all at once,' went on the Captain.

Jukes burst out: 'If you think it was an easy job – '

But his captain, clinging to the rail, paid no attention. 'According to the books the worst is not over yet.'

'If most of them hadn't been half dead with seasickness and fright, not one of us would have come out of that 'tween-deck alive,' said Jukes.

'Had to do what's fair by them,' mumbled MacWhirr stolidly. 'You don't find everything in books.'

'Why, I believe they would have risen on us if I hadn't ordered the hands out of that pretty quick,' continued Jukes with warmth.

After the whisper of their shouts, their ordinary tones, so distinct, rang out very loud to their ears in the amazing stillness of the air. It seemed to them they were talking in a dark and echoing vault.

Through a jagged aperture in the dome of clouds the light of a few stars fell upon the black sea, rising and falling confusedly. Sometimes the head of a watery cone would topple on board and mingle with the rolling flurry of foam on the swamped deck; and the *Nan-Shan* wallowed heavily at the bottom of a circular cistern of clouds. This ring of dense vapours, gyrating madly round the calm of the centre, encompassed the ship like a motionless and unbroken wall of an aspect inconceivably sinister. Within, the sea, as if agitated by an internal commotion, leaped in peaked mounds that jostled each other, slapping heavily against her sides; and a low moaning sound, the infinite plaint of the storm's fury, came from beyond the limits of the menacing calm. Captain MacWhirr remained silent, and Jukes' ready ear caught suddenly the faint, long-drawn roar of some immense wave rushing unseen under that thick blackness, which made the appalling boundary of his vision.

'Of course,' he started resentfully, 'they thought we had caught at the chance to plunder them. Of course! You said – pick up the money. Easier said than done. They couldn't tell what was in our heads. We came in, smash – right into the middle of them. Had to do it by a rush.'

'As long as it's done . . . ' mumbled the Captain, without attempting to look at Jukes. 'Had to do what's fair.'

'We shall find yet there's the devil to pay when this is over,' said Jukes, feeling very sore. 'Let them only recover a bit, and you'll see. They will fly at our throats, sir. Don't forget, sir, she isn't a British ship now. These brutes know it well, too. The damn'd Siamese flag.'

'We are on board, all the same,' remarked Captain MacWhirr.

'The trouble's not over yet,' insisted Jukes prophetically, reeling and catching on. 'She's a wreck,' he added faintly.

'The trouble's not over yet,' assented Captain MacWhirr, half aloud . . . 'Look out for her a minute.'

'Are you going off the deck, sir?' asked Jukes hurriedly, as if the storm were sure to pounce upon him as soon as he had been left alone with the ship.

He watched her, battered and solitary, labouring heavily in a wild scene of mountainous black waters lit by the gleams of distant worlds. She moved slowly, breathing into the still core of the hurricane the excess of her strength in a white cloud of steam – and the deep-toned vibration of the escape was like the defiant trumpeting of a living creature of the sea impatient for the renewal of the contest. It ceased suddenly. The still air moaned. Above Jukes' head a few stars shone into the pit of black vapours. The inky edge of the cloud-disc frowned upon the ship under the patch of glittering sky. The stars too seemed to look at her intently, as if for the last time, and the cluster of their splendour sat like a diadem on a lowering brow.

Captain MacWhirr had gone into the chart-room. There was no light there; but he could feel the disorder of that place where he used to live tidily. His armchair was upset. The books had tumbled out on the floor: he scrunched a piece of glass under his boot. He groped for the matches, and found a box on a shelf with a deep ledge. He struck one, and puckering the corners of his eyes, held out the little flame towards the barometer whose glittering top of glass and metals nodded at him continuously.

It stood very low – incredibly low, so low that Captain MacWhirr grunted. The match went out, and hurriedly he extracted another, with thick, stiff fingers.

Again a little flame flared up before the nodding glass and metal of the top. His eyes looked at it, narrowed with attention, as if expecting an imperceptible sign. With his grave face he resembled a booted and misshapen pagan burning incense before the oracle of a Joss. There was no mistake. It was the lowest reading he had ever seen in his life.

Captain MacWhirr emitted a low whistle. He forgot himself till the flame diminished to a blue spark, burnt his fingers and vanished. Perhaps something had gone wrong with the thing!

There was an aneroid glass screwed above the couch. He turned that way, struck another match, and discovered the white face of the other instrument looking at him from the bulkhead, meaningly, not to be gainsaid, as though the wisdom of men were made unerring by the indifference of matter. There was no room for doubt now. Captain MacWhirr pshawed at it, and threw the match down.

The worst was to come, then – and if the books were right this worst would be very bad. The experience of the last six hours had enlarged his conception of what heavy weather could be like. 'It'll be terrific,' he pronounced mentally. He had not consciously looked at anything by the light of the matches except at the barometer; and yet somehow he had seen that his water-bottle and the two tumblers had been flung out of their stand. It seemed to give him a more intimate knowledge of the tossing the ship had gone through. 'I wouldn't have believed it,' he thought. And his table had been cleared too; his rulers, his pencils, the inkstand – all the things that had their safe appointed places – they were gone, as if a mischievous hand had plucked them out one by one and flung them on the wet floor. The hurricane had broken in upon the orderly arrangements of his privacy. This had never happened before, and the feeling of dismay reached the very seat of his composure. And the worst was to come yet! He was glad the trouble in the 'tween-deck had been discovered in time. If the ship had to go after all, then, at least, she wouldn't be going to the bottom with a lot of people in her fighting teeth and claw. That would have been odious. And in that feeling there was a humane intention and a vague sense of the fitness of things.

These instantaneous thoughts were yet in their essence heavy and slow, partaking of the nature of the man. He extended his hand to put back the matchbox in its corner of the shelf. There were always matches there – by his order. The steward had his instructions impressed upon him long before. 'A box . . . just there, see? Not so very full . . . where I can put my hand on it, steward. Might want a light in a hurry. Can't tell on board ship *what* you might want in a hurry. Mind, now.'

And of course on his side he would be careful to put it back in its place scrupulously. He did so now, but before he removed his hand it occurred to him that perhaps he would never have occasion to use that box any more. The vividness of the thought checked him, and for an infinitesimal fraction of a second his fingers closed again on the small object as though it had been the symbol of all these little habits that chain us to the weary round of life. He released it at last, and letting himself fall on the settee, listened for the first sounds of returning wind.

Not yet. He heard only the wash of water, the heavy splashes, the dull shocks of the confused seas boarding his ship from all sides. She would never have a chance to clear her decks.

But the quietude of the air was startlingly tense and unsafe, like a slender hair holding a sword suspended over his head. By this awful pause the storm penetrated the defences of the man and unsealed his lips. He spoke out in the solitude and the pitch darkness of the cabin, as if addressing another being awakened within his breast.

'I shouldn't like to lose her,' he said half aloud.

He sat unseen, apart from the sea, from his ship, isolated, as if withdrawn from the very current of his own existence, where such freaks as talking to himself surely had no place. His palms reposed on his knees, he bowed his short neck and puffed heavily, surrendering to a strange sensation of weariness he was not enlightened enough to recognise for the fatigue of mental stress.

From where he sat he could reach the door of a washstand locker. There should have been a towel there. There was. Good . . . He took it out, wiped his face, and afterwards went on rubbing his wet head. He towelled himself with energy in the dark, and then remained motionless with the towel on his knees. A moment passed, of a stillness so profound that no one could have guessed there was a man sitting in that cabin. Then a murmur arose.

'She may come out of it yet.'

When Captain MacWhirr came out on deck, which he did brusquely, as though he had suddenly become conscious of having stayed away too long, the calm had lasted already more than fifteen minutes – long enough to make itself intolerable even to his imagination. Jukes, motionless on the forepart of the bridge, began to speak at once. His voice, blank and forced as though he were talking through hard-set teeth, seemed to flow away on all sides into the darkness, deepening again upon the sea.

'I had the wheel relieved. Hackett began to sing out that he was done. He's lying in there alongside the steering gear with a face like death. At first I couldn't get anybody to crawl out and relieve the poor devil. That boss'en's worse than no good, I always said. Thought I would have had to go myself and haul out one of them by the neck.'

'Ah, well,' muttered the Captain. He stood watchful by Jukes' side.

'The second mate's in there too, holding his head. Is he hurt, sir?'

'No – crazy,' said Captain MacWhirr, curtly.

'Looks as if he had a tumble, though.'

'I had to give him a push,' explained the Captain.

Jukes gave an impatient sigh.

'It will come very sudden,' said Captain MacWhirr, 'and from over there, I fancy. God only knows, though. These books are only good to muddle your head and make you jumpy. It will be bad, and there's an end. If we only can steam her round in time to meet it . . . '

A minute passed. Some of the stars winked rapidly and vanished.

'You left them pretty safe?' began the Captain abruptly, as though the silence were unbearable.

'Are you thinking of the coolies, sir? I rigged lifelines all ways across that 'tween-deck.'

'Did you? Good idea, Mr Jukes.'

'I didn't . . . think you cared to . . . know,' said Jukes – the lurching of the ship cut his speech as though somebody had been jerking him around while he talked – 'how I got on with . . . that infernal job. We did it. And it may not matter in the end.'

'Had to do what's fair, for all – they are only Chinamen. Give them the same chance with ourselves – hang it all. She isn't lost yet. Bad enough to be shut up below in a gale – '

'That's what I thought when you gave me the job, sir,' interjected Jukes moodily.

' – without being battered to pieces,' pursued Captain MacWhirr with rising vehemence. 'Couldn't let that go on in my ship, if I knew she hadn't five minutes to live. Couldn't bear it, Mr Jukes.'

A hollow echoing noise, like that of a shout rolling in a rocky chasm, approached the ship and went away again. The last star, blurred, enlarged, as if returning to the fiery mist of its beginning, struggled with the colossal depth of blackness hanging over the ship – and went out.

'Now for it!' muttered Captain MacWhirr. 'Mr Jukes.'

'Here, sir.'

The two men were growing indistinct to each other.

'We must trust her to go through it and come out on the other side. That's plain and straight. There's no room for Captain Wilson's storm-strategy here.'

'No, sir.'

'She will be smothered and swept again for hours,' mumbled the Captain. 'There's not much left by this time above deck for the sea to take away – unless you or me.'

'Both, sir,' whispered Jukes breathlessly.

'You are always meeting trouble half-way, Jukes,' Captain MacWhirr remonstrated quaintly. 'Though it's a fact that the second mate is no good. D'ye hear, Mr Jukes? You would be left alone if . . . '

Captain MacWhirr interrupted himself, and Jukes, glancing on all sides, remained silent.

'Don't you be put out by anything,' the Captain continued, mumbling rather fast. 'Keep her facing it. They may say what they like, but the heaviest seas run with the wind. Facing it – always facing it – that's the way to get through. You are a young sailor. Face it. That's enough for any man. Keep a cool head.'

'Yes, sir,' said Jukes, with a flutter of the heart.

In the next few seconds the Captain spoke to the engine-room and got an answer.

For some reason Jukes experienced an access of confidence, a sensation that came from outside like a warm breath, and made him feel equal to every demand. The distant muttering of the darkness stole into his ears. He noted it unmoved, out of that sudden belief in himself, as a man safe in a shirt of mail would watch a point.

The ship laboured without intermission amongst the black hills of water, paying with this hard tumbling the price of her life. She rumbled in her depths, shaking a white plummet of steam into the night, and Jukes' thought skimmed like a bird through the engine-room, where Mr Rout – good man – was ready. When the rumbling ceased it seemed to him that there was a pause of every sound, a dead pause in which Captain MacWhirr's voice rang out startingly.

'What's that? A puff of wind?' – it spoke much louder than Jukes had ever heard it before – 'On the bow. That's right. She may come out of it yet.'

The mutter of the winds drew near apace. In the forefront could be distinguished a drowsy waking plaint passing on, and far off the growth of a multiple clamour, marching and expanding. There was the throb as of many drums in it, a vicious rushing note, and like the chant of a tramping multitude.

Jukes could no longer see his captain distinctly. The darkness was absolutely piling itself upon the ship. At most he made out movements, a hint of elbows spread out, of a head thrown up.

Captain MacWhirr was trying to do up the top button of his oilskin coat with unwonted haste. The hurricane, with its power to madden the seas, to sink ships, to uproot trees, to overturn strong walls and dash the very birds of the air to the ground, had found this taciturn man in its path, and, doing its utmost, had managed to wring out a few words. Before the renewed wrath of winds swooped on his ship, Captain MacWhirr was moved to declare, in a tone of vexation, as it were: 'I wouldn't like to lose her.'

He was spared that annoyance.

Chapter 6

On a bright sunshiny day, with the breeze chasing her smoke far ahead, the *Nan-Shan* came into Fu-chau. Her arrival was at once noticed on shore, and the seamen in harbour said: 'Look! Look at that steamer. What's that? Siamese – isn't she? Just look at her!'

She seemed, indeed, to have been used as a running target for the secondary batteries of a cruiser. A hail of minor shells could not have given her upper works a more broken, torn, and devastated aspect: and she had about her the worn, weary air of ships coming from the far ends of the world – and indeed with truth, for in her short passage she had been very far; sighting, verily, even the coast of the Great Beyond, whence no ship ever returns to give up her crew to the dust of the earth. She was encrusted and grey with salt to the trucks of her masts and to the top of her funnel; as though (as some facetious seaman said) 'the crowd on board had fished her out somewhere from the bottom of the sea and brought her in here for salvage'. And further, excited by the felicity of his own wit, he offered to give five pounds for her – 'as she stands'.

Before she had been quite an hour at rest, a meagre little man, with a red-tipped nose and a face cast in an angry mould, landed from a sampan on the quay of the Foreign Concession, and incontinently turned to shake his fist at her,

A tall individual, with legs much too thin for a rotund stomach, and with watery eyes, strolled up and remarked, 'Just left her – eh? Quick work.'

He wore a soiled suit of blue flannel with a pair of dirty cricketing shoes; a dingy grey moustache drooped from his lip, and daylight could be seen in two places between the rim and the crown of his hat.

'Hallo! what are you doing here?' asked the ex-second-mate of the *Nan-Shan*, shaking hands hurriedly.

'Standing by for a job – chance worth taking – got a quiet hint,' explained the man with the broken hat, in jerky, apathetic wheezes.

The second shook his fist again at the *Nan-Shan*. 'There's a fellow there that ain't fit to have the command of a scow,' he declared, quivering with passion, while the other looked about listlessly.

'Is there?'

But he caught sight on the quay of a heavy seaman's chest, painted brown under a fringed sailcloth cover, and lashed with new manila line. He eyed it with awakened interest.

'I would talk and raise trouble if it wasn't for that damned Siamese flag. Nobody to go to – or I would make it hot for him. The fraud! Told his chief engineer – that's another fraud for you – I had lost my nerve. The greatest lot of ignorant fools that ever sailed the seas. No! You can't think . . . '

'Got your money all right?' enquired his seedy acquaintance suddenly.

'Yes. Paid me off on board,' raged the second mate. ' "Get your breakfast on shore," says he.'

'Mean skunk!' commented the tall man vaguely, and passed his tongue on his lips. 'What about having a drink of some sort?'

'He struck me,' hissed the second mate.

'No! Struck! You don't say?' The man in blue began to bustle about sympathetically. 'Can't possibly talk here. I want to know all about it. Struck – eh? Let's get a fellow to carry your chest. I know a quiet place where they have some bottled beer . . . '

Mr Jukes, who had been scanning the shore through a pair of glasses, informed the chief engineer afterwards that 'our late second mate hasn't been long in finding a friend. A chap looking uncommonly like a bummer. I saw them walk away together from the quay.'

The hammering and banging of the needful repairs did not

disturb Captain MacWhirr. The steward found in the letter he wrote, in a tidy chart-room, passages of such absorbing interest that twice he was nearly caught in the act. But Mrs MacWhirr, in the drawing-room of the forty-pound house, stifled a yawn – perhaps out of self-respect – for she was alone.

She reclined in a plush-bottomed and gilt hammock-chair near a tiled fireplace, with Japanese fans on the mantel and a glow of coals in the grate. Lifting her hands, she glanced wearily here and there into the many pages. It was not her fault they were so prosy, so completely uninteresting – from 'My darling wife' at the beginning, to 'Your loving husband' at the end. She couldn't be really expected to understand all these ship affairs. She was glad, of course, to hear from him, but she had never asked herself why, precisely.

' . . . They are called typhoons . . . The mate did not seem to like it . . . Not in books . . . Couldn't think of letting it go on . . . '

The paper rustled sharply. ' . . . A calm that lasted over twenty minutes,' she read perfunctorily; and the next words her thoughtless eyes caught, on the top of another page, were: 'see you and the children again . . . ' She had a movement of impatience. He was always thinking of coming home. He had never had such a good salary before. What was the matter now!

It did not occur to her to turn back overleaf to look. She would have found it recorded there that between 4 and 6 a.m. on December 25th, Captain MacWhirr did actually think that his ship could not possibly live another hour in such a sea, and that he would never see his wife and children again. Nobody was to know this (his letters got mislaid so quickly) – nobody whatever but the steward, who had been greatly impressed by that disclosure. So much so, that he tried to give the cook some idea of the 'narrow squeak we all had' by saying solemnly, 'The old man himself had a dam' poor opinion of our chance.'

'How do you know?' asked contemptuously the cook, an old soldier, 'He hasn't told you, maybe?'

'Well, he did give me a hint to that effect,' the steward brazened it out.

'Get along with you! He will be coming to tell *me* next,' jeered the old cook over his shoulder.

Mrs MacWhirr glanced farther, on the alert. ' . . . Do what's fair . . . Miserable objects . . . Only three, with a broken leg each, and one . . . Thought had better keep the matter quiet . . . hope to have done the fair thing . . . '

She let fall her hands. No: there was nothing more about coming home. Must have been merely expressing a pious wish. Mrs MacWhirr's mind was set at ease, and a black marble clock, priced by the local jeweller at £3 18s. *6d.*, had a discreet stealthy tick.

The door flew open, and a girl, in the long-legged, short-frocked period of existence, flung into the room. A lot of colourless, rather lanky hair was scattered over her shoulders. Seeing her mother, she stood still, and directed her pale prying eyes upon the letter.

'From father,' murmured Mrs MacWhirr. 'What have you done with your ribbon?'

The girl put her hands up to her head and pouted.

'He's well,' continued Mrs MacWhirr languidly. 'At least I think so. He never says.' She had a little laugh. The girl's face expressed a wandering indifference, and Mrs MacWhirr surveyed her with fond pride.

'Go and get your hat,' she said after a while. 'I am going out to do some shopping. There is a sale at Linom's.'

'Oh, how jolly!' uttered the child impressively, in unexpectedly grave vibrating tones, and bounded out of the room.

It was a fine afternoon, with a grey sky and dry sidewalks. Outside the draper's Mrs MacWhirr smiled upon a woman in a black mantle of generous proportions, armoured in jet and crowned with flowers blooming falsely above a bilious matronly countenance. They broke into a swift little babble of greetings and exclamations both together, very hurried, as if the street were ready to yawn open and swallow all that pleasure before it could be expressed.

Behind them the high glass doors were kept on the swing. People couldn't pass, men stood aside waiting patiently, and Lydia was absorbed in poking the end of her parasol between the stone flags. Mrs MacWhirr talked rapidly.

'Thank you very much. He's not coming home yet. Of course it's very sad to have him away, but it's such a comfort to know he keeps so well.' Mrs MacWhirr drew breath. 'The climate there agrees with him,' she added beamingly, as if poor MacWhirr had been away touring in China for the sake of his health.

Neither was the chief engineer coming home yet. Mr Rout knew too well the value of a good billet.

'Solomon says wonders will never cease,' cried Mrs Rout joyously at the old lady in her armchair by the fire. Mr Rout's mother moved slightly, her withered hands lying in black half-mittens on her lap.

The eyes of the engineer's wife fairly danced on the paper. 'That captain of the ship he is in – a rather simple man, you remember, mother? – has done something rather clever, Solomon says.'

'Yes, my dear,' said the old woman meekly, sitting with bowed silvery head, and that air of inward stillness characteristic of very old people who seem lost in watching the last flickers of life. 'I think I remember.'

Solomon Rout, Old Sol, Father Sol, The Chief, 'Rout, good man' – Mr Rout, the condescending and paternal friend of youth, had been the baby of her many children – all dead by this time. And she remembered him best as a boy of ten – long before he went away to serve his apprenticeship in some great engineering works in the North. She had seen so little of him since, she had gone through so many years, that she had now to retrace her steps very far back to recognise him plainly in the mist of time. Sometimes it seemed that her daughter-in-law was talking of some strange man.

Mrs Rout junior was disappointed. 'H'm. H'm.' She turned the page. 'How provoking! He doesn't say what it is. Says I couldn't understand how much there was in it. Fancy! What could it be so very clever? What a wretched man not to tell us!'

She read on without further remark soberly, and at last sat looking into the fire. The chief wrote just a word or two of the typhoon; but something had moved him to express an increased longing for the companionship of the jolly woman. 'If it hadn't been that mother must be looked after, I would send you your passage-money today. You could set up a small house out here. I would have a chance to see you sometimes then. We are not growing younger . . . '

'He's well, mother,' sighed Mrs Rout, rousing herself.

'He always was a strong healthy boy,' said the old woman placidly.

But Mr Jukes' account was really animated and very full. His friend in the Western Ocean trade imparted it freely to the other officers of his liner. 'A chap I know writes to me about an extraordinary affair that happened on board his ship in that typhoon – you know – that we read of in the papers two months ago. It's the funniest thing! Just see for yourself what he says. I'll show you his letter.'

There were phrases in it calculated to give the impression of light-hearted, indomitable resolution. Jukes had written them in good faith, for he felt thus when he wrote. He described with lurid effect the scenes in the 'tween-deck. ' . . . It struck me in a flash that those confounded Chinamen couldn't tell we weren't a desperate kind of robbers. 'Tisn't good to part the Chinaman from his money if he is the stronger party. We need have been desperate indeed to go thieving in such weather, but what could these beggars know of us? So, without thinking of it twice, I got the hands away in a jiffy. Our work was done – that the old man had set his heart on. We cleared out without staying to enquire how they felt. I am convinced that if they had not been so unmercifully shaken, and afraid – each individual one of them – to stand up, we would have been torn to pieces. Oh! It was pretty complete, I can tell you; and you may run to and fro across the Pond to the end of time before you find yourself with such a job on your hands.'

After this he alluded professionally to the damage done to the ship, and went on thus: 'It was when the weather quieted down that the situation became confoundedly delicate. It wasn't made any better by us having been lately transferred to the Siamese flag; though the skipper can't see that it makes any difference – "as long as *we* are on board," he says. There are feelings that this man simply hasn't got – and there's an end of it. You might just as well try to make a bedpost understand. But apart from this it is an infernally lonely state for a ship to be going about the China seas with no proper consuls, not even a gunboat of her own anywhere, nor a body to go to in case of some trouble.

'My notion was to keep these Johnnies under hatches for another fifteen hours or so; as we weren't much farther than that from Fuchau. We would find there, most likely, some sort of a man-of-war, and once under her guns we were safe enough; for surely any skipper of a man-of-war – English, French or Dutch – would see white men through as far as a row on board goes. We could get rid of them and their money afterwards by delivering them to their Mandarin or Taotai, or whatever they call these chaps in goggles you see being carried about in sedan-chairs through their stinking streets.

'The old man wouldn't see it somehow. He wanted to keep the matter quiet. He got that notion into his head, and a steam windlass couldn't drag it out of him. He wanted as little fuss made as possible, for the sake of the ship's name and for the sake of the owners – "for the sake of all concerned," says he, looking at me very hard. It made me angry hot. Of course you couldn't keep a thing like that quiet; but the chests had been secured in the usual manner and were safe enough for any earthly gale, while this had been an altogether fiendish business I couldn't give you even an idea of.

'Meantime, I could hardly keep on my feet. None of us had a spell of any sort for nearly thirty hours, and there the old man sat rubbing his chin, rubbing the top of his head, and so bothered he didn't even think of pulling his long boots off.

' "I hope, sir," says I, "you won't be letting them out on deck before we make ready for them in some shape or other." Not, mind you, that I felt very sanguine about controlling these beggars if they meant to take charge. A trouble with a cargo of Chinamen is no child's play. I was dam' tired too. "I wish," said I, "you would let us throw the whole lot of these dollars down to them and leave them to fight it out amongst themselves, while we get a rest."

' "Now you talk wild, Jukes," says he, looking up in his slow way that makes you ache all over, somehow. "We must plan out something that would be fair to all parties."

'I had no end of work on hand, as you may imagine, so I set the hands going, and then I thought I would turn in a bit. I hadn't been asleep in my bunk ten minutes when in rushes the steward and begins to pull at my leg.

' "For God's sake, Mr Jukes, come out! Come on deck quick, sir. Oh, do come out!"

'The fellow scared all the sense out of me. I didn't know what had happened: another hurricane – or what. Could hear no wind.

' "The Captain's letting them out. Oh, he is letting them out! Jump on deck, sir, and save us. The chief engineer has just run below for his revolver."

'That's what I understood the fool to say. However, Father Rout swears he went in there only to get a clean pocket-handkerchief. Anyhow, I made one jump into my trousers and flew on deck aft. There was certainly a good deal of noise going on forward of the bridge. Four of the hands with the boss'en were at work abaft. I passed up to them some of the rifles all the ships on the China coast carry in the cabin, and led them on the bridge. On the way I ran against Old Sol, looking startled and sucking at an unlighted cigar.

' "Come along," I shouted to him.

'We charged, the seven of us, up to the chart-room. All was over. There stood the old man with his sea-boots still drawn up to the hips and in shirt-sleeves – got warm thinking it out, I suppose. Bun-hin's dandy clerk at his elbow, as dirty as a sweep, was still green in the face. I could see directly I was in for something.

' "What the devil are these monkey tricks, Mr Jukes?" asks the old man, as angry as ever he could be. I tell you frankly it made me lose my tongue. "For God's sake, Mr Jukes," says he, "do take away these rifles from the men. Somebody's sure to get hurt before long if you don't. Damme, if this ship isn't worse than Bedlam! Look sharp now. I want you up here to help me and Bun-hin's Chinaman to count that money. You wouldn't mind lending a hand too, Mr Rout, now you are here. The more of us the better."

'He had settled it all in his mind while I was having a snooze. Had we been an English ship, or only going to land our cargo of coolies in an English port, like Hong-Kong, for instance, there would have been no end of enquiries and bother, claims for damages and so on. But these Chinamen know their officials better than we do.

'The hatches had been taken off already, and they were all on deck after a night and a day down below. It made you feel queer to see so many gaunt, wild faces together. The beggars stared about at the sky, at the sea, at the ship, as though they had expected the whole thing to have been blown to pieces. And no wonder! They had had a doing that would have shaken the soul out of a white man. But then they say a Chinaman has no soul. He has, though, something about him that is deuced tough. There was a fellow (amongst others of the badly hurt) who had had his eye all but knocked out. It stood out of his head the size of half a hen's egg. This would have laid out a white man on his back for a month: and yet there was that chap elbowing here and there in the crowd and talking to the others as if nothing had been the matter. They made a great hubbub amongst themselves, and whenever the old man showed his bald head on the foreside of the bridge, they would all leave off jawing and look at him from below.

'It seems that after he had done his thinking he made that Bun-hin's fellow go down and explain to them the only way they could get their money back. He told me afterwards that, all the coolies having worked in the same place and for the same length of time, he reckoned he would be doing the fair thing by them as near as possible if he shared all the cash we had picked up equally among the lot. You couldn't tell one man's dollars from another's, he said, and if you asked each man how much money he brought on board he was afraid they would lie, and he would find himself a long way short. I think he was right there. As to giving up the money to any Chinese official he could scare up in Fu-chau, he said he might just as well put the lot in his own pocket at once for all the good it would be to them. I suppose they thought so too.

'We finished the distribution before dark. It was rather a sight: the sea running high, the ship a wreck to look at, these Chinamen staggering up on the bridge one by one for their share, and the old man still booted, and in his shirt-sleeves, busy paying out at the chart-room door, perspiring like anything, and now and then coming down sharp on myself or Father Rout about one thing or another not quite to his mind. He took the share of those who were disabled himself to them on the No. 2 hatch. There were three dollars left over, and these went to the three most damaged coolies, one to each. We turned-to afterwards, and shovelled out on deck heaps of wet rags, all sorts of fragments of things without shape, and that you couldn't give a name to, and let them settle the ownership themselves.

'This certainly is coming as near as can be to keeping the thing quiet for the benefit of all concerned. What's your opinion, you pampered mail-boat swell? The old chief says that this was plainly the only thing that could be done. The skipper remarked to me the other day, "There are things you find nothing about in books." I think that he got out of it very well for such a stupid man.'

FALK

A Reminiscence

Several of us, all more or less connected with the sea, were dining in a small river-hostelry not more than thirty miles from London, and less than twenty from that shallow and dangerous puddle to which our coasting men give the grandiose name of 'German Ocean'. And through the wide windows we had a view of the Thames; an enfilading view down the Lower Hope Reach. But the dinner was execrable, and all the feast was for the eyes.

That flavour of salt-water which for so many of us had been the very water of life permeated our talk. He who hath known the bitterness of the Ocean shall have its taste for ever in his mouth. But one or two of us, pampered by the life of the land, complained of hunger. It was impossible to swallow any of that stuff. And indeed there was a strange mustiness in everything. The wooden dining-room stuck out over the mud of the shore like a lacustrine dwelling; the planks of the floor seemed rotten; a decrepid old waiter tottered pathetically to and fro before an antediluvian and worm-eaten sideboard; the chipped plates might have been disinterred from some kitchen midden near an inhabited lake; and the chops recalled times more ancient still. They brought forcibly to one's mind the night of ages when the primeval man, evolving the first rudiments of cookery from his dim consciousness, scorched lumps of flesh at a fire of sticks in the company of other good fellows; then, gorged and happy, sat him back among the gnawed bones to tell his artless tales of experience – the tales of hunger and hunt – and of women, perhaps!

But luckily the wine happened to be as old as the waiter. So, comparatively empty, but upon the whole fairly happy, we sat back and told our artless tales. We talked of the sea and all its works. The sea never changes, and its works for all the talk of men are wrapped in mystery. But we agreed that the times were changed. And we talked of old ships, of sea-accidents, of break-downs, dismastings; and of a man who brought his ship safe to Liverpool all the way from the River Plate under a jury rudder. We talked of wrecks, of short rations and of heroism – or at least of what the newspapers would have called heroism at sea – a manifestation of virtues quite different from the heroism of primitive times. And now and then falling silent all together we gazed at the sights of the river.

A P.& O. boat passed bound down. 'One gets jolly good dinners on board these ships,' remarked one of our band. A man with sharp eyes read out the name on her bows: *Arcadia*. 'What a beautiful model of a ship!' murmured some of us. She was followed by a small cargo-steamer, and the flag they hauled down aboard while we were looking showed her to be a Norwegian. She made an awful lot of smoke; and before it had quite blown away, a high-sided, short, wooden barque, in ballast and towed by a paddle-tug, appeared in front of the windows. All her hands were forward busy setting up the headgear; and aft a woman in a red hood, quite alone with the man at the wheel, paced the length of the poop back and forth, with the grey wool of some knitting work in her hands.

'German I should think,' muttered one. 'The skipper has his wife on board,' remarked another; and the light of the crimson sunset all ablaze behind the London smoke, throwing a glow of Bengal light upon the barque's spars, faded away from the Hope Reach.

Then one of us, who had not spoken before, a man of over fifty, that had commanded ships for a quarter of a century, looking after the barque now gliding far away, all black on the lustre of the river, said: This reminds me of an absurd episode in my life, now many years ago, when I got first the command of an iron barque, loading then in a certain Eastern seaport. It was also the capital of an Eastern kingdom, lying up a river as might be London lies up this old Thames of ours. No more need be said of the place; for this sort of thing might have happened anywhere where there are ships, skippers, tugboats, and orphan nieces of indescribable splendour. And the absurdity of the episode concerns only me, my enemy Falk, and my friend Hermann.

There seemed to be something like peculiar emphasis on the words 'my friend Hermann', which caused one of us (for we had just been speaking of heroism at sea) to say idly and nonchalantly: 'And was this Hermann a hero?'

Not at all, said our grizzled friend. No hero at all. He was a Schiff-führer: Ship-conductor. That's how they call a Master Mariner in Germany. I prefer our way. The alliteration is good, and there is something in the nomenclature that gives to us as a body the sense of corporate existence: Apprentice, Mate, Master, in the ancient and honourable craft of the sea. As to my friend Hermann, he might have been a consummate master of the honourable craft, but he was called officially Schiff-führer, and had the simple, heavy appearance of a well-to-do farmer, combined with the good-natured shrewdness of a small shopkeeper. With his shaven chin, round limbs, and heavy eyelids he did not look like a toiler, and even less like an adventurer of the sea. Still, he toiled upon the seas, in his own way, much as a shopkeeper works behind his counter. And his ship was the means by which he maintained his growing family.

She was a heavy, strong, blunt-bowed affair, awakening the ideas of primitive solidity, like the wooden plough of our forefathers. And there were, about her, other suggestions of a rustic and homely nature. The extraordinary timber projections which I have seen in no other vessel made her square stern resemble the tail end of a miller's wagon. But the four stern ports of her cabin, glazed with six little greenish panes each, and framed in wooden sashes painted brown, might have been the windows of a cottage in the country. The tiny white curtains and the greenery of flower-pots behind the glass completed the resemblance. On one or two occasions when passing under her stern I had detected from my boat a round arm in the act of tilting a watering-pot, and the bowed sleek head of a maiden whom I shall always call Hermann's niece, because as a matter of fact I've never heard her name, for all my intimacy with the family.

This, however, sprang up later on. Meantime in common with the rest of the shipping in that Eastern port, I was left in no doubt as to Hermann's notions of hygienic clothing. Evidently he believed in wearing good stout flannel next his skin. On most days little frocks and pinafores could be seen drying in the mizzen rigging of his ship, or a tiny row of socks fluttering on the signal halyards; but once a fortnight the family washing was exhibited in force. It covered the poop entirely. The afternoon breeze would incite to a weird and flabby activity all that crowded mass of clothing, with its vague suggestions of drowned, mutilated and flattened humanity. Trunks without heads waved at you arms without hands; legs without feet kicked fantastically with collapsible flourishes; and there were long white garments that, taking the wind fairly through their neck openings edged with lace, became for a moment violently distended as by the passage of obese and invisible bodies. On these days you could make out that ship at a great distance by the multicoloured grotesque riot going on abaft her mizzen-mast.

She had her berth just ahead of me, and her name was *Diana* – Diana not of Ephesus but of Bremen. This was proclaimed in white letters a foot long spaced widely across the stern (somewhat like the lettering of a shop-sign) under the cottage windows. This ridiculously unsuitable name struck one as an impertinence towards the memory of the most charming of goddesses; for, apart from the fact that the old craft was physically incapable of engaging in any sort of chase, there was a gang of four children belonging to her. They peeped over the rail at passing boats and occasionally dropped various objects into them. Thus, sometime before I knew Hermann to speak to, I received on my hat a horrid rag-doll belonging to Hermann's eldest daughter. However, these youngsters were upon the whole well behaved. They had fair heads, round eyes, round little knobby noses, and they resembled their father a good deal.

This *Diana* of Bremen was a most innocent old ship, and seemed to know nothing of the wicked sea, as there are on shore households that know nothing of the corrupt world. And the sentiments she suggested were unexceptionable and mainly of a domestic order. She was a home. All these dear children had learned to walk on her roomy quarter-deck. In such thoughts there is something pretty, even touching. Their teeth, I should judge, they had cut on the ends of her running gear. I have many times observed the baby Hermann (Nicholas) engaged in gnawing the whipping of the fore-royal brace. Nicholas' favourite place of residence was under the main fife-rail. Directly he was let loose he would crawl off there, and the first seaman who came along would bring him, carefully held aloft in tarry hands, back to the cabin door. I fancy there must have been a standing order to that effect. In the course of these transportations the baby, who was the only peppery person in the ship, tried to smite these stalwart young German sailors on the face.

Mrs Hermann, an engaging, stout housewife, wore on board baggy blue dresses with white dots. When, as happened once or twice, I caught her at an elegant little wash-tub rubbing hard on white collars, baby's socks, and Hermann's summer neck-ties, she would blush in girlish confusion, and raising her wet hands greet me from afar with many friendly nods. Her sleeves would be rolled up to the elbows, and the gold hoop of her wedding ring glittered among the soapsuds. Her voice was pleasant, she had a serene brow, smooth bands of very fair hair, and a good-humoured expression of the eyes. She was motherly and moderately talkative. When this simple matron smiled, youthful dimples broke out on her fresh broad cheeks. Hermann's niece on the other hand, an orphan and very silent, I never saw attempt a smile. This, however, was not gloom on her part but the restraint of youthful gravity.

They had carried her about with them for the last three years, to help with the children and be company for Mrs Hermann, as Hermann mentioned once to me. It had been very necessary while they were all little, he had added in a vexed manner. It was her arm and her sleek head that I had glimpsed one morning, through the stern-windows of the cabin, hovering over the pots of fuchsias and mignonette; but the first time I beheld her full length I surrendered to her proportions. They fix her in my mind, as great beauty, great intelligence, quickness of wit or kindness of heart might have made some other woman equally memorable.

With her it was form and size. It was her physical personality that had this imposing charm. She might have been witty, intelligent, and kind to an exceptional degree. I don't know, and this is not to the point. All I know is that she was built on a magnificent scale. Built is the only word. She was constructed, she was erected, as it were, with a regal lavishness. It staggered you to see this reckless expenditure of material upon a chit of a girl. She was youthful and also perfectly mature, as though she had been some fortunate immortal. She was heavy too, perhaps, but that's nothing. It only added to that notion of permanence. She was barely nineteen. But such shoulders! Such round arms! Such a shadowing forth of mighty limbs when with three long strides she pounced across the deck upon the overturned Nicholas – it's perfectly indescribable! She seemed a good, quiet girl, vigilant as to Lena's needs, Gustav's tumbles, the state of Carl's dear little nose – conscientious, hardworking, and all that. But what magnificent hair she had! Abundant, long, thick, of a tawny colour. It had the sheen of precious metals. She wore it plaited tightly into one single tress hanging girlishly down her back; and its end reached down to her waist. The massiveness of it surprised you. On my word it reminded one of a club. Her face was big, comely, of an unruffled expression. She had a good complexion, and her blue eyes were so pale that she appeared to look at the world with the empty white candour of a statue. You could not call her good-looking. It was something much more impressive. The simplicity of her apparel, the opulence of her form, her imposing stature, and the extraordinary sense of vigorous life that seemed to emanate from her like a perfume exhaled by a flower, made her beautiful with a beauty of a rustic and olympian order. To watch her reaching up to the clothes-line, with both arms raised high above her head, caused you to fall a-musing in a strain of pagan piety. Excellent Mrs Hermann's baggy cotton gowns had some sort of rudimentary frills at neck and bottom, but this girl's print frocks hadn't even a wrinkle; nothing but a few straight folds in the skirt falling to her feet, and these, when she stood still, had a severe and statuesque quality. She was inclined naturally to be still whether sitting or standing. However, I don't mean to say she was statuesque. She was too generously alive; but she could have stood for an allegoric statue of the Earth. I don't mean the worn-out earth of our possession, but a young Earth, a virginal planet undisturbed by the vision of a future teeming with the monstrous forms of life and death, clamorous with the cruel battles of hunger and thought.

The worthy Hermann himself was not very entertaining, though his English was fairly comprehensible. Mrs Hermann, who always let off one speech at least at me in an hospitable, cordial tone (and in Platt-Deutsch I suppose) I could not understand. As to their niece, however satisfactory to look upon (and she inspired you somehow with a hopeful view as to the prospects of mankind) she was a modest and silent presence, mostly engaged in sewing, only now and then, as I observed, falling over that work into a state of maidenly meditation. Her aunt sat opposite her, sewing also, with her feet propped on a wooden footstool. On the other side of the deck Hermann and I would get a couple of chairs out of the cabin and settle down to a smoking match, accompanied at long intervals by the pacific exchange of a few words. I came nearly every evening. Hermann I would find in his shirt sleeves. As soon as he returned from the shore on board his ship he commenced operations by taking off his coat; then he put on his head an embroidered round cap with a tassel, and changed his boots for a pair of cloth slippers. Afterwards he smoked at the cabin-door, looking at his children with an air of civic virtue, till they got caught one after another and put to bed in various state-rooms. Lastly, we would drink some beer in the cabin, which was furnished with a wooden table on cross legs, and with black straight-backed chairs – more like a farm kitchen than a ship's cuddy. The sea and all nautical affairs seemed very far removed from the hospitality of this exemplary family.

And I liked this because I had a rather worrying time on board my own ship. I had been appointed ex-officio by the British Consul to take charge of her after a man who had died suddenly, leaving for the guidance of his successor some suspiciously unreceipted bills, a few dry-dock estimates hinting at bribery, and a quantity of vouchers for three years' extravagant expenditure; all these mixed up together in a dusty old violin-case lined with ruby velvet. I found besides a large account-book, which, when opened hopefully, turned out to my infinite consternation to be filled with verses – page after page of rhymed doggerel of a jovial and improper character, written in the neatest minute hand I ever did see. In the same fiddle-case a photograph of my predecessor, taken lately in

Saigon, represented in front of a garden view, and in company of a female in strange draperies, an elderly, squat, rugged man of stern aspect in a clumsy suit of black broadcloth, and with the hair brushed forward above the temples in a manner reminding one of a boar's tusks. Of a fiddle, however, the only trace on board was the case, its empty husk as it were; but of the two last freights the ship had indubitably earned of late, there were not even the husks left. It was impossible to say where all that money had gone to. It wasn't on board. It had not been remitted home; for a letter from the owners, preserved in a desk evidently by the merest accident, complained mildly enough that they had not been favoured by a scratch of the pen for the last eighteen months. There were next to no stores on board, not an inch of spare rope or a yard of canvas The ship had been run bare, and I foresaw no end of difficulties before I could get her ready for sea.

As I was young then – not thirty yet – I took myself and my troubles very seriously. The old mate, who had acted as chief mourner at the captain's funeral, was not particularly pleased at my coming. But the fact is the fellow was not legally qualified for command, and the Consul was bound, if at all possible, to put a properly certificated man on board. As to the second mate, all I can say his name was Tottersen, or something like that. His practice was to wear on his head, in that tropical climate, a mangy fur cap. He was, without exception, the stupidest man I had ever seen on board ship. And he looked it too. He looked so confoundedly stupid that it was a matter of surprise for me when he answered to his name.

I drew no great comfort from their company, to say the least of it; while the prospect of making a long sea passage with those two fellows was depressing. And my other thoughts in solitude could not be of a gay complexion. The crew was sickly, the cargo was coming very slow; I foresaw I would have lots of trouble with the charterers, and doubted whether they would advance me enough money for the ship's expenses. Their attitude towards me was unfriendly. Altogether I was not getting on. I would discover at odd times (generally about midnight) that I was totally inexperienced, greatly ignorant of business, and hopelessly unfit for any sort of command; and when the steward had to be taken to the hospital ill with choleraic symptoms I felt bereaved of the only decent person at the after end of the ship. He was fully expected to recover, but in the meantime had to be replaced by some sort of servant. And on the recommendation of a certain Schomberg, the proprietor of the smaller of the two hotels in the place, I engaged a Chinaman. Schomberg, a brawny, hairy Alsatian, and an awful gossip, assured me that it was all right. 'First-class boy that. Came in the *suite* of his Excellency Tseng the Commissioner – you know. His Excellency Tseng lodged with me here for three weeks.'

He mouthed the Chinese Excellency at me with great unction, though the specimen of the '*suite*' did not seem very promising. At the time, however, I did not know what an untrustworthy humbug Schomberg was. The 'boy' might have been forty or a hundred and forty for all you could tell – one of those Chinamen of the death's-head type of face and completely inscrutable. Before the end of the third day he had revealed himself as a confirmed opium-smoker, a gambler, a most audacious thief, and a first-class sprinter. When he departed at the top of his speed with thirty-two golden sovereigns of my own hard-earned savings it was the last straw. I had reserved that money in case my difficulties came to the worst. Now it was gone I felt as poor and naked as a fakir. I clung to my ship, for all the bother she caused me, but what I could not bear were the long lonely evenings in her cuddy, where the atmosphere, made smelly by a leaky lamp, was agitated by the snoring of the mate. That fellow shut himself up in his stuffy cabin punctually at eight, and made gross and revolting noises like a water-logged trombone. It was odious not to be able to worry oneself in comfort on board one's own ship. Everything in this world, I reflected, even the command of a nice little barque, may be made a delusion and a snare for the unwary spirit of pride in man.

From such reflections I was glad to make my escape on board that Bremen *Diana*. There apparently no whisper of the world's iniquities had ever penetrated. And yet she lived upon the wide sea: and the sea tragic and comic, the sea with its horrors and its peculiar scandals, the sea peopled by men and ruled by iron necessity is indubitably a part of the world. But that patriarchal old tub, like some saintly retreat, echoed nothing of it. She was world-proof. Her venerable innocence apparently had put a restraint on the roaring lusts of the sea. And yet I have known the sea too long to believe in its respect for decency. An elemental force is ruthlessly frank. It may, of course, have been Hermann's skilful seamanship, but to me it looked as if the allied oceans had refrained from smashing these high bulwarks, unshipping the lumpy rudder, frightening the children, and generally opening this family's eyes out of sheer reticence. It looked like reticence. The ruthless disclosure was, in the end, left for a man to make; a man strong and elemental enough and driven to unveil some secrets of the sea by the power of a simple and elemental desire.

This, however, occurred much later, and meantime I took sanctuary in that serene old ship early every evening. The only person on board that seemed to be in trouble was little Lena, and in due course I perceived that the health of the rag-doll was more than delicate. This object led a sort of 'in extremis' existence in a wooden box placed against the starboard mooring-bitts, tended and nursed with the greatest sympathy and care by all the children, who greatly enjoyed pulling long faces and moving with hushed footsteps. Only the baby – Nicholas – looked on with a cold, ruffianly leer, as if he had belonged to another tribe altogether. Lena perpetually sorrowed over the box, and all of them were in deadly earnest. It was wonderful the way these children would work up their compassion for that bedraggled thing I wouldn't have touched with a pair of tongs. I suppose they were exercising and developing their racial sentimentalism by the means of that dummy. I was only surprised that Mrs Hermann let Lena cherish and hug that bundle of rags to that extent, it was so disreputably and completely unclean. But Mrs Hermann would raise her fine womanly eyes from her needlework to look on with amused sympathy, and did not seem to see it, somehow, that this object of affection was a disgrace to the ship's purity. Purity, not cleanliness, is the word. It was pushed so far that I seemed to detect in this too a sentimental excess, as if dirt had been removed in very love. It is impossible to give you an idea of such a meticulous neatness. It was as if every morning that ship had been arduously explored with – with toothbrushes. Her very bowsprit three times a week had its toilette made with a cake of soap and a piece of soft flannel. Arrayed – I *must* say arrayed – arrayed artlessly in dazzling white paint as to wood and dark green as to ironwork the simple-minded distribution of these colours evoked the images of simple-minded peace, of arcadian felicity; and the childish comedy of disease and sorrow struck me sometimes as an abominably real blot upon that ideal state.

I enjoyed it greatly, and on my part I brought a little mild excitement into it. Our intimacy arose from the pursuit of that thief. It was in the evening, and Hermann, who, contrary to his habits, had stayed on shore late that day, was extricating himself backwards out of a little gharry on the river bank, opposite his ship, when the hunt passed. Realising the situation as though he had eyes in his shoulder-blades, he joined us with a leap and took the lead. The Chinaman fled silent like a rapid shadow on the dust of an extremely oriental road. I followed. A long way in the rear my mate whooped like a savage. A young moon threw a bashful light on a plain like a monstrous waste ground: the architectural mass of a Buddhist temple far away projected itself in dead black on the sky. We lost the thief of course; but in my disappointment I had to admire Hermann's presence of mind. The velocity that stodgy man developed in the interests of a complete stranger earned my warm gratitude – there was something truly cordial in his exertions.

He seemed as vexed as myself at our failure, and would hardly listen to my thanks. He said it was 'nothings', and invited me on the spot to come on board his ship and drink a glass of beer with him. We poked sceptically for a while amongst the bushes, peered without conviction into a ditch or two. There was not a sound: patches of slime glimmered feebly amongst the reeds. Slowly we trudged back, drooping under the thin sickle of the moon, and I heard him mutter to himself, 'Himmel! Zwei und dreissig Pfund!' He was impressed by the figure of my loss. For a long time we had ceased to hear the mate's whoops and yells.

Then he said to me, 'Everybody has his troubles,' and as we went on remarked that he would never have known anything of mine hadn't he by an extraordinary chance been detained on shore by Captain Falk. He didn't like to stay late ashore – he added with a sigh. The something doleful in his tone I put down to his sympathy with my misfortune, of course.

On board the *Diana* Mrs Hermann's fine eyes expressed much interest and commiseration. We had found the two women sewing face to face under the open skylight in the strong glare of the lamp. Hermann walked in first, starting in the very doorway to pull off his coat, and encouraging me with loud, hospitable ejaculations: 'Come in! This way! Come in, captain!' At once, coat in hand, he began to tell his wife all about it. Mrs Hermann put the palms of her plump hands together; I smiled and bowed with a heavy heart: the niece got up from her sewing to bring Hermann's slippers and his embroidered calotte, which he assumed pontifically, talking (about me) all the time. Billows of white stuff lay between the chairs on the cabin floor; I caught the words 'Zwei und dreissig Pfund' repeated several times, and presently came the beer, which seemed delicious to my throat, parched with running and the emotions of the chase.

I didn't get away till well past midnight, long after the women had retired. Hermann had been trading in the East for three years or more, carrying freights of rice and timber mostly. His ship was well known in all the ports from Vladivostok to Singapore. She was his own property. The profits had been moderate, but the trade answered well enough while the children were small yet. In another year or so he hoped he would be able to sell the old *Diana* to a firm in Japan for a fair price. He intended to return home, to Bremen, by mail boat, second class, with Mrs Hermann and the children. He told me all this stolidly, with slow puffs at his pipe. I was sorry when knocking the ashes out he began to rub his eyes. I would have sat with him till morning. What had I to hurry on board my own ship for? To face the broken rifled drawer in my state-room. Ugh! The very thought made me feel unwell.

I became their daily guest, as you know. I think that Mrs Hermann from the first looked upon me as a romantic person. I did not, of course, tear my hair *coram populo* over my loss, and she took it for lordly indifference. Afterwards, I dare say, I did tell them some of my adventures – such as they were – and they marvelled greatly at the extent of my experience. Hermann would translate what he thought the most striking passages. Getting upon his legs, and as if delivering a lecture on a phenomenon, he addressed himself, with gestures, to the two women, who would let their sewing sink slowly on their laps. Meantime I sat before a glass of Hermann's beer, trying to look modest. Mrs Hermann would glance at me quickly, emit slight 'Ach!'s The girl never made a sound. Never. But she too would sometimes raise her pale eyes to look at me in her unseeing, gentle way. Her glance was by no means stupid; it beamed out soft and diffuse as the moon beams upon a landscape – quite differently from the scrutinising inspection of the stars. You were drowned in it, and imagined yourself to appear blurred. And yet this same glance when turned upon Christian Falk must have been as efficient as the searchlight of a battle-ship.

Falk was the other assiduous visitor on board, but from his behaviour he might have been coming to see the quarter-deck capstan. He certainly used to stare at it a good deal when keeping us company outside the cabin door, with one muscular arm thrown over the back of the chair, and his big shapely legs, in very tight white trousers, extended far out and ending in a pair of black shoes as roomy as punts. On arrival he would shake Hermann's hand with a mutter, bow to the women, and take up his careless and misanthropic attitude by our side. He departed abruptly, with a jump, going through the performance of grunts, hand-shakes, bow, as if in a panic. Sometimes, with a sort of discreet and convulsive effort, he approached the women and exchanged a few low words with them, half a dozen at most. On these occasions Hermann's usual stare became positively glassy and Mrs Hermann's kind countenance would colour up. The girl herself never turned a hair.

Falk was a Dane or perhaps a Norwegian, I can't tell now. At all events he was a Scandinavian of some sort, and a bloated monopolist to boot. It is possible he was unacquainted with the word, but he had a clear perception of the thing itself. His tariff of charges for towing ships in and out was the most brutally inconsiderate document of the sort I had ever seen. He was the commander and owner of the only tugboat on the river, a very trim white craft of 150 tons or more, as elegantly neat as a yacht, with a round wheelhouse rising like a glazed turret high above her sharp bows, and with one slender varnished pole mast forward. I dare say there are yet a few shipmasters afloat who remember Falk and his tug very well. He extracted his pound and a half of flesh from each of us merchant-skippers with an inflexible sort of indifference which made him detested and even feared. Schomberg used to remark: 'I won't talk about the fellow. I don't think he has six drinks from year's end to year's end in my place. But my advice is, gentlemen, don't you have anything to do with him, if you can help it.'

This advice, apart from unavoidable business relations, was easy to follow because Falk intruded upon no one. It seems absurd to compare a tugboat skipper to a centaur: but he reminded me somehow of an engraving in a little book I had as a boy, which represented centaurs at a stream, and there was one especially, in the foreground, prancing bow and arrows in hand, with regular severe features and an immense curled wavy beard, flowing down his breast. Falk's face reminded me of that centaur. Besides, he was a composite creature. Not a man-horse, it is true, but a man-boat. He lived on board his tug, which was always dashing up and down the river from early morn till dewy eve. In the last rays of the setting sun, you could pick out far away down the reach his beard borne high up on the white structure, foaming up stream to anchor for the night. There was the white-clad man's body, and the rich brown patch of the hair, and nothing below the waist but the 'thwart-ship white lines of the bridge-screens, that led the eye to the sharp white lines of the bows cleaving the muddy water of the river.

Separated from his boat, to me at least he seemed incomplete. The tug herself without his head and torso on the bridge looked mutilated as it were. But he left her very seldom. All the time I remained in harbour I saw him only twice on shore. On the first occasion it was at my charterers, where he came in misanthropically to get paid for towing out a French barque the day before. The second time I could hardly believe my eyes, for I beheld him reclining under his beard in a cane-bottomed chair in the billiard-room of Schomberg's hotel.

It was very funny to see Schomberg ignoring him pointedly. The artificiality of it contrasted strongly with Falk's natural unconcern. The big Alsatian talked loudly with his other customers, going from one little table to the other, and passing Falk's place of repose with his eyes fixed straight ahead. Falk sat there with an untouched glass at his elbow. He must have known by sight and name every white man in the room, but he never addressed a word to anybody. He acknowledged my presence by a drop of his eyelids, and that was all. Sprawling there in the chair, he would, now and again, draw the palms of both his hands down his face, giving at the same time a slight, almost imperceptible, shudder.

It was a habit he had, and of course I was perfectly familiar with it, since you could not remain an hour in his company without being made to wonder at such a movement breaking some long period of stillness. It was a passionate and inexplicable gesture. He used to make it at all sorts of times; as likely as not after he had been listening to little Lena's chatter about the suffering doll, for instance. The Hermann children always besieged him about his legs closely, though, in a gentle way, he shrank from them a little. He seemed, however, to feel a great affection for the whole family. For Hermann himself especially. He sought his company. In this case, for instance, he must have been waiting for him, because as soon as he appeared Falk rose hastily, and they went out together. Then Schomberg expounded in my hearing to three or four people his theory that Falk was after Captain Hermann's niece, and asserted confidently that nothing would come of it. It was the same last year when Captain Hermann was loading here, he said.

Naturally, I did not believe Schomberg, but I own that for a time I observed closely what went on. All I discovered was some impatience on Hermann's part. At the sight of Falk, stepping over the gangway, the excellent man would begin to mumble and chew between his teeth something that sounded like German swear-words. However, as we said, I'm not familiar with the language, and Hermann's soft, round-eyed countenance remained unchanged. Staring stolidly ahead he greeted him with, 'Wie geht's,' or in English, 'How are you?' with a throaty enunciation. The girl would look up for an instant and move her lips slightly: Mrs Hermann let her hands rest on her lap to talk volubly to him for a minute or so in her pleasant voice before she went on with her sewing again. Falk would throw himself into a chair, stretch his big legs, as like as not draw his hands down his face passionately. As to myself, he was not pointedly impertinent: it was rather as though he could not be bothered with such trifles as my existence; and the truth is that being a monopolist he was under no necessity to be amiable. He was sure to get his own extortionate terms out of me for towage whether he frowned or smiled. As a matter of fact, he did neither: but before many days elapsed he managed to astonish me not a little and to set Schomberg's tongue clacking more than ever.

It came about in this way. There was a shallow bar at the mouth of the river which ought to have been kept down, but the authorities of the State were piously busy gilding afresh the great Buddhist Pagoda just then, and I suppose had no money to spare for dredging operations. I don't know how it may be now, but at the time I speak of that sandbank was a great nuisance to the shipping. One of its consequences was that vessels of a certain draught of water, like Hermann's or mine, could not complete their loading in the river. After taking in as much as possible of their cargo, they had to go outside to fill up. The whole procedure was an unmitigated bore. When you thought you had as much on board as your ship could carry safely over the bar, you went and gave notice to your agents. They, in their turn, notified Falk that so-and-so was ready to go out. Then Falk (ostensibly when it fitted in with his other work, but, if the truth were known, simply when his arbitrary spirit moved him), after ascertaining carefully in the office that there was enough money to meet his bill, would come along unsympathetically, glaring at you with his yellow eyes from the bridge, and would drag you out dishevelled as to rigging, lumbered as to the decks, with unfeeling haste, as if to execution. And he would force you, too, to take the end of his own wire hawser, for the use of which there was of course an extra charge. To your shouted remonstrances against this extortion this towering trunk with one hand on the engine-room telegraph only shook its bearded head above the splash, the racket and the clouds of smoke, in which the tug, backing and filling in the smother of churning paddle-wheels behaved like a ferocious and impatient creature. He had her manned by the cheekiest gang of lascars I ever did see, whom he allowed to bawl at you insolently, and, once fast, he plucked you out of your berth as if he did not care what he smashed. Eighteen miles down the river you had to go behind him, and then three more along the coast to where a group of uninhabited rocky islets enclosed a sheltered anchorage. There you would have to lie at single anchor with your naked spars showing to seaward over these barren fragments of land scattered upon a very intensely blue sea. There was nothing to look at besides but a bare coast, the muddy edge of the brown plain with the sinuosities of the river you had left, traced in dull green, and the Great Pagoda uprising lonely and massive with shining curves and pinnacles like the gorgeous and stony efflorescence of tropical rocks. You had nothing to do but to wait fretfully for the balance of your cargo, which was sent out of the river with the greatest irregularity. And it was open to you to console yourself with the thought that, after all, this stage of bother meant that your departure from these shores was indeed approaching at last.

We both had to go through that stage, Hermann and I, and there was a sort of tacit emulation between the ships as to which should be ready first. We kept on neck and neck almost to the finish, when I won the race by going personally to give notice in the forenoon; whereas Hermann, who was very slow in making up his mind to go ashore, did not get to the agents' office till late in the day. They told him there that my ship was first on turn for next morning, and I believe he told them he was in no hurry. It suited him better to go the day after.

That evening, on board the *Diana*, he sat with his plump knees well apart, staring and puffing at the curved mouthpiece of his pipe. Presently he spoke with some impatience to his niece about putting the children to bed. Mrs Hermann, who was talking to Falk, stopped short and looked at her husband uneasily, but the girl got up at once and drove the children before her into the cabin. In a little while Mrs Hermann had to leave us to quell what, from the sounds inside, must have been a dangerous mutiny. At this Hermann grumbled to himself. For half an hour longer Falk left alone with us fidgeted on his chair, sighed lightly, then at last, after drawing his hands down his face, got up, and as if renouncing the hope of making himself understood (he hadn't opened his mouth once) he said in English: 'Well . . . Good-night, Captain Hermann.' He stopped for a moment before my chair and looked down fixedly; I may even say he glared: and he went so far as to make a deep noise in his throat. There was in all this something so marked that for the first time in our limited intercourse of nods and grunts he excited in me something like interest. But next moment he disappointed me – for he strode away hastily without a nod even.

His manner was usually odd, it is true, and I certainly did not pay much attention to it; but that sort of obscure intention, which seemed to lurk in his nonchalance like a wary old carp in a pond, had never before come so near the surface. He had distinctly aroused my expectations. I would have been unable to say what it was I expected, but at all events I did not expect the absurd developments he sprung upon me no later than the break of the very next day.

I remember only that there was, on that evening, enough point in his behaviour to make me, after he had fled, wonder audibly what he might mean. To this Hermann, crossing his legs with a swing and settling himself viciously away from me in his chair, said: 'That fellow don't know himself what he means.'

There might have been some insight in such a remark. I said nothing, and, still averted, he added: 'When I was here last year he was just the same.' An eruption of tobacco smoke enveloped his head as if his temper had exploded like gunpowder.

I had half a mind to ask him point blank whether he, at least, didn't know why Falk, a notoriously unsociable man, had taken to visiting his ship with such assiduity. After all, I reflected suddenly, it was a most remarkable thing. I wonder now what Hermann would have said. As it turned out he didn't let me ask. Forgetting all about Falk apparently, he started a monologue on his plans for the future: the selling of the ship, the going home; and falling into a reflective and calculating mood he mumbled between regular jets of smoke about the expense. The necessity of disbursing passage-money for all his tribe seemed to disturb him in a manner that was the more striking because otherwise he gave no signs of a miserly disposition. And yet he fussed over the prospect of that voyage home in a mail-boat like a sedentary grocer who has made up his mind to see the world. He was racially thrifty I suppose, and for him there must have been a great novelty in finding himself obliged to pay for travelling – for sea travelling which was the normal state of life for the family – from the very cradle for most of them. I could see he grudged prospectively every single shilling which must be spent so absurdly. It was rather funny. He would become doleful over it, and then again, with a fretful sigh, he would suppose there was nothing for it now but to take three second-class tickets – and there were the four children to pay for besides. A lot of money that to spend at once. A big lot of money.

I sat with him listening (not for the first time) to these heart-searchings till I grew thoroughly sleepy, and then I left him and turned in on board my ship. At daylight I was awakened by a yelping of shrill voices, accompanied by a great commotion in the water, and the short, bullying blasts of a steam-whistle. Falk with his tug had come for me.

I began to dress. It was remarkable that the answering noise on board my ship together with the patter of feet above my head ceased suddenly. But I heard more remote guttural cries which seemed to express surprise and annoyance. Then the voice of my mate reached me howling expostulations to somebody at a distance. Other voices joined, apparently indignant; a chorus of something that sounded like abuse replied. Now and then the steam-whistle screeched.

Altogether that unnecessary uproar was distracting, but down there in my cabin I took it calmly. In another moment, I thought, I should be going down that wretched river, and in another week at the most I should be totally quit of the odious place and all the odious people in it.

Greatly cheered by the idea, I seized the hair-brushes and looking at myself in the glass began to use them. Suddenly a hush fell upon the noise outside, and I heard (the ports of my cabin were thrown open) – I heard a deep calm voice, not on board my ship, however, hailing resolutely in English, but with a strong foreign twang, 'Go ahead!'

There may be tides in the affairs of men which taken at the flood . . . and so on. Personally I am still on the look-out for that important turn. I am, however, afraid that most of us are fated to flounder for ever in the dead water of a pool whose shores are arid indeed. But I know that there are often in men's affairs unexpectedly – even irrationally – illuminating moments when an otherwise insignificant sound, perhaps only some perfectly commonplace gesture, suffices to reveal to us all the unreason, all the fatuous unreason, of our complacency. 'Go ahead' are not particularly striking words even when pronounced with a foreign accent; yet they petrified me in the very act of smiling at myself in the glass. And then, refusing to believe my ears, but already boiling with indignation, I ran out of the cabin and up on deck.

It was incredibly true. It was perfectly true. I had no eyes for anything but the *Diana*. It was she that was being taken away. She was already out of her berth and shooting athwart the river. 'The way this loonatic plucked that ship out is a caution,' said the awed voice of my mate close to my ear. 'Hey! Hallo! Falk! Hermann! What's this infernal trick?' I yelled in a fury.

Nobody heard me. Falk certainly could not hear me. His tug was turning at full speed away under the other bank. The wire hawser between her and the *Diana*, stretched as taut as a harpstring, vibrated alarmingly.

The high black craft careened over to the awful strain. A loud crack came out of her, followed by the tearing and splintering of wood. 'There!' said the awed voice in my ear. 'He's carried away their towing chock.' And then, with enthusiasm, 'Oh! Look! Look, sir! Look at them Dutchmen skipping out of the way on the forecastle. I hope to goodness he'll break a few of their shins before he's done with 'em.'

I yelled my vain protests. The rays of the rising sun coursing level along the plain warmed my back, but I was hot enough with rage. I could not have believed that a simple towing operation could suggest so plainly the idea of abduction, of rape. Falk was simply running off with the *Diana*.

The white tug careered out into the middle of the river. The red floats of her paddle-wheels revolving with mad rapidity tore up the whole reach into foam. The *Diana* in mid-stream waltzed round with as much grace as an old barn, and flew after her ravisher. Through the ragged fog of smoke driving headlong upon the water I had a glimpse of Falk's square motionless shoulders under a white hat as big as a cart-wheel, of his red face, his yellow staring eyes, his great beard. Instead of keeping a look-out ahead, he was deliberately turning his back on the river to glare at his tow. The tall heavy craft, never so used before in her life, seemed to have lost her senses; she took a wild sheer against her helm, and for a moment came straight at us, menacing and clumsy, like a runaway mountain. She piled up a streaming, hissing, boiling wave half-way up her blunt stem, my crew let out one great howl – and then we held our breaths. It was a near thing. But Falk had her! He had her in his clutch. I fancied I could hear the steel hawser ping as it surged across the *Diana*'s forecastle, with the hands on board of her bolting away from it in all directions. It was a near thing. Hermann, with his hair rumpled, in a snuffy flannel shirt and a pair of mustard-coloured trousers, had rushed to help with the wheel. I saw his terrified round face; I saw his very teeth uncovered by a sort of ghastly fixed grin; and in a great leaping tumult of water between the two ships the *Diana* whisked past so close that I could have flung a hair-brush at his head, for, it seems, I had kept them in my hands all the time. Meanwhile Mrs Hermann sat placidly on the skylight, with a woollen shawl on her shoulders. The excellent woman in response to my indignant gesticulations fluttered a handkerchief, nodding and smiling in the kindest way imaginable. The boys, only half-dressed, were jumping about the poop in great glee, displaying their gaudy braces; and Lena in a short scarlet petticoat, with peaked elbows and thin bare arms, nursed the rag-doll with devotion. The whole family passed before my sight as if dragged across a scene of unparalleled violence. The last I saw was Hermann's niece with the baby Hermann in her arms standing apart from the others. Magnificent in her close-fitting print frock, she displayed something so commanding in the manifest perfection of her figure that the sun seemed to be rising for her alone. The flood of light brought out the opulence of her form and the vigour of her youth in a glorifying way. She went by perfectly motionless and as if lost in meditation; only the hem of her skirt stirred in the draught; the sun rays broke on her sleek tawny hair; that bald-headed ruffian, Nicholas, was whacking her on the shoulder. I saw his tiny fat arm rise and fall in a workmanlike manner. And then the four cottage windows of the *Diana* came into view retreating swiftly down the river. The sashes were up, and one of the white calico curtains fluttered straight out like a streamer above the agitated water of the wake.

To be thus tricked out of one's turn was an unheard-of occurrence. In my agent's office, where I went to complain at once, they protested with apologies they couldn't understand how the mistake arose: but Schomberg, when I dropped in later to get some tiffin, though surprised to see me, was perfectly ready with an explanation. I found him seated at the end of a long narrow table, facing his wife – a scraggy little woman, with long ringlets and a blue tooth, who smiled abroad stupidly and looked frightened when you spoke to her. Between them a waggling punkah fanned twenty vacant cane-bottomed chairs and two rows of shiny plates. Three Chinamen in white jackets loafed with napkins in their hands around that desolation. Schomberg's pet *table-d'hôte* was not much of a success that day. He was feeding himself furiously and seemed to overflow with bitterness.

He began by ordering in a brutal voice the chops to be brought back for me, and turning in his chair: 'Mistake they told you? Not a bit of it! Don't you believe it for a moment, captain! Falk isn't a man to make mistakes unless on purpose.' His firm conviction was that Falk had been trying all along to curry favour on the cheap with Hermann. 'On the cheap – mind you! It doesn't cost him a cent to put that insult upon you, and Captain Hermann gets in a day ahead of your ship. Time's money! Eh? You are very friendly with Captain Hermann I believe, but a man is bound to be pleased at any little advantage he may get. Captain Hermann is a good businessman, and there's no such thing as a friend in business. Is there?' He leaned forward and began to cast stealthy glances as usual. 'But Falk is, and always was, a miserable fellow. I would despise him.'

I muttered, grumpily, that I had no particular respect for Falk.

'I would despise him,' he insisted, with an appearance of anxiety which would have amused me if I had not been fathoms deep in discontent. To a young man fairly conscientious and as well-meaning as only the young man can be, the current ill-usage of life comes with a peculiar cruelty. Youth that is fresh enough to believe in guilt, in innocence, and in itself, will always doubt whether it have not perchance deserved its fate. Sombre of mind and without appetite, I struggled with the chop while Mrs Schomberg sat with her everlasting stupid grin and Schomberg's talk gathered way like a slide of rubbish.

'Let me tell you. It's all about that girl. I don't know what Captain Hermann expects, but if he asked me I could tell him something about Falk. He's a miserable fellow. That man is a perfect slave. That's what I call him. A slave. Last year I started this *table d'hôte*, and sent cards out – you know. You think he had one meal in the house? Give the thing a trial? Not once. He has got hold now of a Madras cook – a blamed fraud that I hunted out of my cookhouse with a rattan. He was not fit to cook for white men. No, not for the white men's dogs either; but, see, any damned native that can boil a pot of rice is good enough for Mr Falk. Rice and a little fish he buys for a few cents from the fishing-boats outside is what he lives on. You would hardly credit it – eh? A white man, too . . .'

He wiped his lips, using the napkin with indignation, and looking at me. It flashed through my mind in the midst of my depression that if all the meat in the town was like these *table-d'hôte* chops, Falk wasn't so far wrong. I was on the point of saying this, but Schomberg's stare was intimidating. 'He's a vegetarian, perhaps,' I murmured instead.

'He's a miser. A miserable miser,' affirmed the hotel-keeper with great force. 'The meat here is not so good as at home – of course. And dear too. But look at me. I only charge a dollar for the tiffin, and one dollar and fifty cents for the dinner. Show me anything cheaper. Why am I doing it? There's little profit in this game. Falk wouldn't look at it. I do it for the sake of a lot of young white fellows here that hadn't a place where they could get a decent meal and eat it decently in good company. There's first-rate company always at my table.'

The convinced way he surveyed the empty chairs made me feel as if I had intruded upon a tiffin of ghostly Presences.

'A white man should eat like a white man, dash it all,' he burst out impetuously. 'Ought to eat meat, must eat meat. I manage to get meat for my patrons all the year round. Don't I? I am not catering for a dam' lot of coolies: Have another chop, captain . . . No? You, boy – take away!'

He threw himself back and waited grimly for the curry. The half-closed jalousies darkened the room pervaded by the smell of fresh whitewash: a swarm of flies buzzed and settled in turns, and poor Mrs Schomberg's smile seemed to express the quintessence of all the imbecility that had ever spoken, had ever breathed, had ever been fed on infamous buffalo meat within these bare walls. Schomberg did not open his lips till he was ready to thrust therein a spoonful of greasy rice. He rolled his eyes ridiculously before he swallowed the hot stuff, and only then broke out afresh.

'It is the most degrading thing. They take the dish up to the wheelhouse for him with a cover on it, and he shuts both the doors before he begins to eat. Fact! Must be ashamed of himself. Ask the engineer. He can't do without an engineer – don't you see – and as no respectable man can be expected to put up with such a table, he allows them fifteen dollars a month extra mess money. I assure you it is so! You just ask Mr Ferdinand da Costa. That's the engineer he has now. You may have seen him about my place, a delicate dark young man, with very fine eyes and a little moustache. He arrived here a year ago from Calcutta. Between you and me, I guess the money-lenders there must have been after him. He rushes here for a meal every chance he can get, for just please tell me what satisfaction is that for a well-educated young fellow to feed all alone in his cabin – like a wild beast? That's what Falk expects his engineers to put up with for fifteen dollars extra. And the rows on board every time a little smell of cooking gets about the deck! You wouldn't believe! The other day da Costa got the cook to fry a steak for him – a turtle steak it was too, not beef at all – and the fat caught or something. Young da Costa himself was telling me of it here in this room. "Mr Schomberg" – says he – "if I had let a cylinder cover blow off through the skylight by my negligence Captain Falk couldn't have been more savage. He frightened the cook so that he won't put anything on the fire for me now." Poor da Costa had tears in his eyes. Only try to put yourself in his place, captain: a sensitive, gentlemanly young fellow. Is he expected to eat his food raw? But that's your Falk all over. Ask anyone you like. I suppose the fifteen dollars extra he has to give keep on rankling – in there.'

And Schomberg tapped his manly breast. I sat half stunned by his irrelevant babble. Suddenly he gripped my forearm in an impressive and cautious manner, as if to lead me into a very cavern of confidence.

'It's nothing but enviousness,' he said in a lowered tone, which had a stimulating effect upon my wearied hearing. 'I don't suppose there is one person in this town that he isn't envious of. I tell you he's dangerous. Even I myself am not safe from him. I know for certain he tried to poison . . . '

'Oh, come now,' I cried, revolted.

'But I know for certain. The people themselves came and told me of it. He went about saying everywhere I was a worse pest to this town than the cholera. He had been talking against me ever since I opened this hotel. And he poisoned Captain Hermann's mind too. Last time the *Diana* was loading here Captain Hermann used to come in every day for a drink or a cigar. This time he hasn't been here twice in a week. How do you account for that?'

He squeezed my arm till he extorted from me some sort of mumble.

'He makes ten times the money I do. I've another hotel to fight against, and there is no other tug on the river. I am not in his way, am I? He wouldn't be fit to run an hotel if he tried. But that's just his nature. He can't bear to think I am making a living. I only hope it makes him properly wretched. He's like that in everything. He would like to keep a decent table well enough. But no – for the sake of a few cents. Can't do it. It's too much for him. That's what I call being a slave to it. But he's mean enough to kick up a row when his nose gets tickled a bit. See that? That just paints him. Miserly and envious. You can't account for it any other way. Can you? I have been studying him these three years.'

He was anxious I should assent to his theory. And indeed on thinking it over it would have been plausible enough if there hadn't been always the essential falseness of irresponsibility in Schomberg's chatter. However, I was not disposed to investigate the psychology of Falk. I was engaged just then in eating despondently a piece of stale Dutch cheese, being too much crushed to care what I swallowed myself, let alone bothering my head about Falk's ideas of gastronomy. I could expect from their study no clue to his conduct in matters of business, which seemed to me totally unrestrained by morality or even by the commonest sort of decency. How insignificant and contemptible I must appear, for the fellow to dare treat me like this – I reflected suddenly, writhing in silent agony. And I consigned Falk and all his peculiarities to the devil with so much mental fervour as to forget Schomberg's existence, till he grabbed my arm urgently. 'Well, you may think and think till every hair of your head falls off, captain; but you can't explain it in any other way.'

For the sake of peace and quietness I admitted hurriedly that I couldn't; persuaded that now he would leave off. But the only result was to make his moist face shine with the pride of cunning. He removed his hand for a moment to scare a black mass of flies off the sugar-basin, and caught hold of my arm again.

'To be sure. And in the same way everybody is aware he would like to get married. Only he can't. Let me quote you an instance. Well, two years ago a Miss Vanlo, a very ladylike girl, came from home to keep house for her brother, Fred, who had an engineering shop for small repairs by the water side. Suddenly Falk takes to going up to their bungalow after dinner and sitting for hours in the verandah saying nothing. The poor girl couldn't tell for the life of her what to do with such a man, so she would keep on playing the piano and singing to him evening after evening till she was ready to drop. And it wasn't as if she had been a strong young woman either. She was thirty, and the climate had been playing the deuce with her. Then – don't you know – Fred had to sit up with them for propriety, and during whole weeks on end never got a single chance to get to bed before midnight. That was not pleasant for a tired man – was it? And besides Fred had worries then because his shop didn't pay and he was dropping money fast. He just longed to get away from here and try his luck somewhere else, but for the sake of his sister he hung on and on till he ran himself into debt over his ears – I can tell you. I, myself, could show a handful of his chits for meals and drinks in my drawer. I could never find out tho' where he found all the money at last. Can't be but he must have got something out of that brother of his, a coal merchant in Port Said. Anyhow he paid everybody before he left, but the girl nearly broke her heart. Disappointment, of course, and at her age, don't you know . . . Mrs Schomberg here was very friendly with her, and she could tell you. Awful despair. Fainting fits. It was a scandal. A notorious scandal. To that extent that old Mr Siegers – not your present charterer, but Mr Siegers the father, the old gentleman who retired from business on a fortune and got buried at sea going home, *he* had to interview Falk in his private office. He was a man who could speak like a Dutch Uncle, and, besides, Messrs Siegers had been helping Falk with a good bit of money from the start. In fact you may say they made him as far as that goes. It so happened that just at the time he turned up here, their firm was chartering a lot of sailing-ships every year, and it suited their business that there should be good towing facilities on the river. See? . . . Well – there's always an ear at the keyhole – isn't there? In fact,' he lowered his tone confidentially, 'in this case it was a good friend of mine; a man you can see here any evening; only they conversed rather low. Anyhow my friend's certain that Falk was trying to make all sorts of excuses, and old Mr Siegers was coughing a lot. And yet Falk wanted all the time to be married too. Why! It's notorious the man has been longing for years to make a home for himself. Only he can't face the expense. When it comes to putting his hand in his pocket – it chokes him off. That's the truth and no other. I've always said so, and everybody agrees with me by this time. What do you think of that – eh?'

He appealed confidently to my indignation, but having a mind to annoy him I remarked, 'that it seemed to me very pitiful – if true'.

He bounced in his chair as if I had run a pin into him. I don't know what he might have said, only at that moment we heard through the half-open door of the billiard-room the footsteps of two men entering from the verandah, a murmur of two voices; at the sharp tapping of a coin on a table Mrs Schomberg half rose irresolutely. 'Sit still,' he hissed at her, and then, in an hospitable, jovial tone, contrasting amazingly with the angry glance that had made his wife sink in her chair, he cried very loud: 'Tiffin still going on in here, gentlemen.'

There was no answer, but the voices dropped suddenly. The head Chinaman went out. We heard the clink of ice in the glasses, pouring sounds, the shuffling of feet, the scraping of chairs. Schomberg, after wondering in a low mutter who the devil could be there at this time of the day, got up napkin in hand to peep through the doorway cautiously. He retreated rapidly on tip-toe, and whispering behind his hand informed me that it was Falk, Falk himself who was in there, and, what's more, he had Captain Hermann with him.

The return of the tug from the outer Roads was unexpected but possible, for Falk had taken away the *Diana* at half-past five, and it was now two o'clock. Schomberg wished me to observe that neither of these men would spend a dollar on a tiffin, which they must have wanted. But by the time I was ready to leave the dining-room Falk had gone. I heard the last of his big boots on the planks of the verandah. Hermann was sitting quite alone in the large, wooden room with the two lifeless billiard tables shrouded in striped covers, mopping his face diligently. He wore his best go-ashore clothes, a stiff collar, black coat, large white waistcoat, grey trousers. A white cotton sunshade with a cane handle reposed between his legs, his side whiskers were neatly brushed, his chin had been freshly shaved; and he only distantly resembled the dishevelled and terrified man in a snuffy night shirt and ignoble old trousers I had seen in the morning hanging on to the wheel of the *Diana*.

He gave a start at my entrance, and addressed me at once in some confusion, but with genuine eagerness. He was anxious to make it clear he had nothing to do with what he called the 'tam' pizness' of the morning. It was most inconvenient. He had reckoned upon another day up in town to settle his bills and sign certain papers. There were also some few stores to come, and sundry pieces of 'my ironwork', as he called it quaintly, landed for repairs, had been left behind. Now he would have to hire a native boat to take all this out to the ship. It would cost five or six dollars perhaps. He had had no warning from Falk. Nothing . . . He hit the table with his dumpy fist . . . Der verfluchte Kerl came in the morning like a 'tam' ropper', making a great noise, and took him away. His mate was not prepared, his ship was moored fast – he protested it was shameful to come upon a man in that way. Shameful! Yet such was the power Falk had on the river that when I suggested in a chilling tone that he might have simply refused to have his ship moved, Hermann was quite startled at the idea. I never realised so well before that this is an age of steam. The exclusive possession of a marine boiler had given Falk the whip hand of us all. Hermann recovering, put it to me appealingly that I knew very well how unsafe it was to contradict that fellow. At this I only smiled distantly.

'Der Kerl!' he cried. He was sorry he had not refused. He was indeed. The damage! The damage! What for all that damage! There was no occasion for damage. Did I know how much damage he had done? It gave me a certain satisfaction to tell him that I had heard his old wagon of a ship crack fore and aft as she went by. 'You passed close enough to me,' I added significantly.

He threw both his hands up to heaven at the recollection. One of them grasped by the middle the white parasol, and he resembled curiously a caricature of a shopkeeping citizen in one of his own German comic papers. 'Ach! That was dangerous,' he cried. I was amused. But directly he added with an appearance of simplicity, 'The side of your iron ship would have been crushed in like – like this matchbox.'

'Would it?' I growled, much less amused now; but by the time I had decided that this remark was not meant for a dig at me he had worked himself into a high state of resentfulness against Falk. The inconvenience, the damage, the expense! Gottferdam! Devil take the fellow. Behind the bar Schomberg with a cigar in his teeth, pretended to be writing with a pencil on a large sheet of paper; and as Hermann's excitement increased it made me comfortingly aware of my own calmness and superiority. But it occurred to me while I listened to his revilings, that after all the good man had come up in the tug. There perhaps – since he must come to town – he had no option. But evidently he had had a drink with Falk, either accepted or offered. How was that? So I checked him by saying loftily that I hoped he would make Falk pay for every penny of the damage.

'That's it! That's it! Go for him,' called out Schomberg from the bar, flinging his pencil down and rubbing his hands.

We ignored his noise. But Hermann's excitement suddenly went off the boil as when you remove a saucepan from the fire. I urged on his consideration that he had done now with Falk and Falk's confounded tug. He, Hermann, would not, perhaps, turn up again in this part of the world for years to come, since he was going to sell the *Diana* at the end of this very trip ('Go home passenger in a mail boat,' he murmured mechanically). He was therefore safe from Falk's malice. All he had to do was to race off to his consignees and stop payment of the towage bill before Falk had the time to get in and lift the money.

Nothing could have been less in the spirit of my advice than the thoughtful way in which he set about to make his parasol stay propped against the edge of the table.

While I watched his concentrated efforts with astonishment he threw at me one or two perplexed, half-shy glances. Then he sat down. 'That's all very well,' he said reflectively.

It cannot be doubted that the man had been thrown off his balance by being hauled out of the harbour against his wish. His stolidity had been profoundly stirred, else he would never have made up his mind to ask me unexpectedly whether I had not remarked that Falk had been casting eyes upon his niece. 'No more than myself,' I answered with literal truth. The girl was of the sort one necessarily casts eyes at in a sense. She made no noise, but she filled most satisfactorily a good bit of space.

'But you, captain, are not the same kind of man,' observed Hermann.

I was not, I am happy to say, in a position to deny this. 'What about the lady?' I could not help asking. At this he gazed for a time into my face, earnestly, and made as if to change the subject. I heard him beginning to mutter something unexpected, about his children growing old enough to require schooling. He would have to leave them ashore with their grandmother when he took up that new command he expected to get in Germany.

This constant harping on his domestic arrangements was funny. I suppose it must have been like the prospect of a complete alteration in his life. An epoch. He was going, too, to part with the *Diana*! He had served in her for years. He had inherited her. From an uncle, if I remember rightly. And the future loomed big before him, occupying his thought exclusively with all its aspects as on the eve of a venturesome enterprise. He sat there frowning and biting his lip, and suddenly he began to fume and fret.

I discovered to my momentary amusement that he seemed to imagine I could, should or ought, have caused Falk in some way to pronounce himself. Such a hope was incomprehensible, but funny. Then the contact with all this foolishness irritated me. I said crossly that I had seen no symptoms, but if there were any – since he, Hermann, was so sure – then it was still worse. What pleasure Falk found in humbugging people in just that way I couldn't say. It was, however, my solemn duty to warn him. It had lately, I said, come to my knowledge that there was a man (not a very long time ago either) who had been taken in just like this.

All this passed in undertones, and at this point Schomberg, exasperated at our secrecy, went out of the room slamming the door with a crash that positively lifted us in our chairs. This, or else what I had said, huffed my Hermann. He supposed, with a contemptuous toss of his head towards the door which trembled yet, that I had got hold of some of that man's silly tales. It looked, indeed, as though his mind had been thoroughly poisoned against Schomberg. 'His tales were – they were,' he repeated, seeking for the word – 'trash.' They were trash, he reiterated and moreover I was young yet . . .

This horrid aspersion (I regret I am no longer exposed to that sort of insult) made me huffy too. I felt ready in my own mind to back up every assertion of Schomberg's and on any subject. In a moment, devil only knows why, Hermann and I were looking at each other most inimically. He caught up his hat without more ado and I gave myself the pleasure of calling after him: 'Take my advice and make Falk pay for breaking up your ship. You aren't likely to get anything else out of him.'

When I got on board my ship later on, the old mate, who was very full of the events of the morning, remarked: 'I saw the tug coming back from the outer Roads just before two p.m.' (He never by any chance used the words morning or afternoon. Always p.m. or a.m., log-book style.) 'Smart work that. Man's always in a state of hurry. He's a regular chucker-out, ain't he, sir? There's a few pubs I know of in the East End of London that would be all the better for one of his sort around the bar.' He chuckled at his joke. 'A regular chucker-out. Now he has fired out that Dutchman head over heels, I suppose our turn's coming tomorrow morning.'

We were all on deck at break of day (even the sick – poor devils – had crawled out) ready to cast off in the twinkling of an eye. Nothing came. Falk did not come. At last, when I began to think that probably something had gone wrong in his engine-room, we perceived the tug going by, full pelt, down the river, as if we hadn't existed. For a moment I entertained the wild notion that he was going to turn round in the next reach. Afterwards I watched his smoke appear above the plain, now here, now there, according to the windings of the river. It disappeared. Then without a word I went down to breakfast. I just simply went down to breakfast.

Not one of us uttered a sound till the mate, after imbibing – by means of suction out of a saucer – his second cup of tea, exclaimed: 'Where the devil is the man gone to?'

'Courting!' I shouted, with such a fiendish laugh that the old chap didn't venture to open his lips any more.

I started to the office perfectly calm. Calm with excessive rage. Evidently they knew all about it already, and they treated me to a show of consternation. The manager, a soft-footed, immensely obese man, breathing short, got up to meet me, while all round the room the young clerks, bending over the papers on their desks, cast upward glances in my direction. The fat man, without waiting for my complaint, wheezing heavily and in a tone as if he himself were incredulous, conveyed to me the news that Falk – Captain Falk – had declined – had absolutely declined – to tow my ship – to have anything to do with my ship – this day or any other day. Never!

I did my best to preserve a cool appearance, but, all the same, I must have shown how much taken aback I was. We were talking in the middle of the room. Suddenly behind my back some ass blew his nose with great force, and at the same time another quill-driver jumped up and went out on the landing hastily. It occurred to me I was cutting a foolish figure there. I demanded angrily to see the principal in his private room.

The skin of Mr Siegers' head showed dead white between the iron-grey streaks of hair lying plastered cross-wise from ear to ear over the top of his skull in the manner of a bandage. His narrow sunken face was of a uniform and permanent terra-cotta colour, like a piece of pottery. He was sickly, thin, and short, with wrists like a boy of ten. But from that debile body there issued a bullying voice, tremendously loud, harsh and resonant, as if produced by some powerful mechanical contrivance in the nature of a fog-horn. I do not know what he did with it in the private life of his home, but in the larger sphere of business it presented the advantage of overcoming arguments without the slightest mental effort, by the mere volume of sound. We had had several passages of arms. It took me all I knew to guard the interests of my owners – whom, *nota bene*, I had never seen – while Siegers (who had made their acquaintance some years before, during a business tour in Australia) pretended to the knowledge of their innermost minds, and, in the character of 'our very good friends', threw them perpetually at my head.

He looked at me with a jaundiced eye (there was no love lost between us), and declared at once that it was strange, very strange. His pronunciation of English was so extravagant that I can't even attempt to reproduce it. For instance, he said 'Fferie strantch'. Combined with the bellowing intonation it made the language of one's childhood sound weirdly startling, and even if considered purely as a kind of unmeaning noise it filled you with astonishment at first. 'They had,' he continued, 'been acquainted with Captain Falk for very many years, and never had any reason . . . '

'That's why I come to you, of course,' I interrupted. 'I've the right to know the meaning of this infernal nonsense.' In the half-light of the room, which was greenish, because of the tree-tops screening the window, I saw him writhe his meagre shoulders. It came into my head, as disconnected ideas will come at all sorts of times into one's head, that this, most likely, was the very room where, if the tale were true, Falk had been lectured by Mr Siegers, the father. Mr Siegers' (the son's) overwhelming voice, in brassy blasts, as though he had been trying to articulate his words through a trombone, was expressing his great regret at conduct characterised by a very marked want of discretion . . . As I lived I was being lectured too! His deafening gibberish was difficult to follow, but it was *my* conduct – mine! – that . . . Damn! I wasn't going to stand this.

'What on earth are you driving at?' I asked in a passion. I put my hat on my head (he never offered a seat to anybody), and as he seemed for the moment struck dumb by my irreverence, I turned my back on him and marched out. His vocal arrangements blared after me a few threats of coming down on the ship for the demurrage of the lighters, and all the other expenses consequent upon the delays arising from my frivolity.

Once outside in the sunshine my head swam. It was no longer a question of mere delay. I perceived myself involved in hopeless and humiliating absurdities that were leading me to something very like a disaster. 'Let us be calm,' I muttered to myself, and ran into the shade of a leprous wall. From that short side-street I could see the broad main thoroughfare, ruinous and gay, running away, away between stretches of decaying masonry, bamboo fences, ranges of arcades of brick and plaster, hovels of lath and mud, lofty temple gates of carved timber, huts of rotten mats – an immensely wide thoroughfare, loosely packed as far as the eye could reach with a barefooted and brown multitude paddling ankle deep in the dust. For a moment I felt myself about to go out of my mind with worry and desperation.

Some allowance must be made for the feelings of a young man new to responsibility. I thought of my crew. Half of them were ill, and I really began to think that some of them would end by dying on board if I couldn't get them out to sea soon. Obviously I should have to take my ship down the river, either working under canvas or dredging with the anchor down; operations which, in common with many modern sailors, I only knew theoretically. And I almost shrank from undertaking them shorthanded and without local knowledge of the river bed, which is so necessary for the confident handling of the ship. There were no pilots, no beacons, no buoys of any sort; but there was a very devil of a current for anybody to see, no end of shoal places, and at least two obviously awkward turns of the channel between me and the sea. But how dangerous these turns were I could not tell. I didn't even know what my ship was capable of! I had never handled her in my life. A misunderstanding between a man and his ship, in a difficult river with no room to make it up, is bound to end in trouble for the man. On the other hand, it must be owned I had not much reason to count upon a general run of good luck. And suppose I had the misfortune to pile her up high and dry on some beastly shoal? That would have been the final undoing of that voyage. It was plain that if Falk refused to tow me out he would also refuse to pull me off. This meant – what? A day lost at the very best; but more likely a whole fortnight of frizzling on some pestilential mudflat, of desperate work, of discharging cargo; more than likely it meant borrowing money at an exorbitant rate of interest – from the Siegers' gang too at that. They were a power in the port. And that elderly seaman of mine, Gambril, had looked pretty ghastly when I went forward to dose him with quinine that morning. *He* would certainly die – not to speak of two or three others that seemed nearly as bad, and of the rest of them just ready to catch any tropical disease going. Horror, ruin and everlasting remorse. And no help. None. I had fallen amongst a lot of unfriendly lunatics!

At any rate, if I must take my ship down myself it was my duty to procure if possible some local knowledge. But that was not easy. The only person I could think of for that service was a certain Johnson, formerly captain of a country ship, but now spliced to a country wife and gone utterly to the bad. I had only heard of him in the vaguest way, as living concealed in the thick of two hundred thousand natives, and only emerging into the light of day for the purpose of hunting up some brandy. I had a notion that if I could lay my hands on him I would sober him on board my ship and use him for a pilot. Better than nothing. Once a sailor always a sailor – and he had known the river for years. But in our Consulate (where I arrived dripping after a sharp walk) they could tell me nothing. The excellent young men on the staff, though willing to help me, belonged to a sphere of the white colony for which that sort of Johnson does not exist. Their suggestion was that I should hunt the man up myself with the help of the Consulate's constable – an ex-sergeant-major of a regiment of Hussars.

This man, whose usual duty apparently consisted in sitting behind a little table in an outer room of Consular offices, when ordered to assist me in my search for Johnson displayed lots of energy and a marvellous amount of local knowledge of a sort. But he did not conceal an immense and sceptical contempt for the whole business. We explored together on that afternoon an infinity of infamous grog shops, gambling dens, opium dens. We walked up narrow lanes where our gharry – a tiny box of a thing on wheels, attached to a jibbing Burmah pony – could by no means have passed. The constable seemed to be on terms of scornful intimacy with Maltese, with Eurasians, with Chinamen, with Klings, and with the sweepers attached to a temple, with whom he talked at the gate. We interviewed also through a grating in a mud wall closing a blind alley an immensely corpulent Italian, who, the ex-sergeant-major remarked to me perfunctorily, had 'killed another man last year'. Thereupon he addressed him as 'Antonio' and 'Old Buck', though that bloated carcase, apparently more than half filling the sort of cell wherein it sat, recalled rather a fat pig in a stye. Familiar and never unbending, the sergeant chucked – absolutely chucked – under the chin a horribly wrinkled and shrivelled old hag propped on a stick, who had volunteered some sort of information: and with the same stolid face he kept up an animated conversation with the groups of swathed brown women, who sat smoking cheroots on the doorsteps of a long range of clay hovels. We got out of the gharry and clambered into dwellings airy like packing crates, or descended into places sinister like cellars. We got in, we drove on, we got out again for the sole purpose, as it seemed, of looking behind a heap of rubble. The sun declined; my companion was curt and sardonic in his answers, but it appears we were just missing Johnson all along. At last our conveyance stopped once more with a jerk, and the driver jumping down opened the door.

A black mudhole blocked the lane. A mound of garbage crowned with the dead body of a dog arrested us not. An empty Australian beef tin bounded cheerily before the toe of my boot. Suddenly we clambered through a gap in a prickly fence . . .

It was a very clean native compound: and the big native woman, with bare brown legs as thick as bedposts, pursuing on all fours a silver dollar that came rolling out from somewhere, was Mrs Johnson herself. 'Your man's at home,' said the ex-sergeant, and stepped aside in complete and marked indifference to anything that might follow. Johnson – at home – stood with his back to a native house built on posts and with its walls made of mats. In his left hand he held a banana. Out of the right he dealt another dollar into space. The woman captured this one on the wing, and there and then plumped down on the ground to look at us with greater comfort.

'My man' was sallow of face, grizzled, unshaven, muddy on elbows and back; where the seams of his serge coat yawned you could see his white nakedness. The vestiges of a paper collar encircled his neck. He looked at us with a grave, swaying surprise. 'Where do you come from?' he asked. My heart sank. How could I have been stupid enough to waste energy and time for this?

But having already gone so far I approached a little nearer and declared the purpose of my visit. He would have to come at once with me, sleep on board my ship, and tomorrow, with the first of the ebb, he would give me his assistance in getting my ship down to the sea, without steam. A six-hundred-ton barque, drawing nine feet aft. I proposed to give him eighteen dollars for his local knowledge; and all the time I was speaking he kept on considering attentively the various aspects of the banana, holding first one side up to his eye, then the other.

'You've forgotten to apologise,' he said at last with extreme precision. 'Not being a gentleman yourself, you don't know apparently when you intrude upon a gentleman. I am one. I wish you to understand that when I am in funds I don't work, and now . . .'

I would have pronounced him perfectly sober had he not paused in great concern to try and brush a hole off the knee of his trousers.

'I have money – and friends. Every gentleman has. Perhaps you would like to know my friend? His name is Falk. You could borrow some money. Try to remember. F–A–L–K. Falk.' Abruptly his tone changed. 'A noble heart,' he said muzzily.

'Has Falk been giving you some money?' I asked, appalled by the detailed finish of the dark plot.

'Lent me, my good man, not given me,' he corrected suavely. 'Met me taking the air last evening, and being as usual anxious to oblige – Hadn't you better go to the devil out of my compound?'

And upon this, without other warning, he let fly with the banana, which missed my head and took the constable just under the left eye. He rushed at the miserable Johnson, stammering with fury. They fell . . . But why dwell on the wretchedness, the breathlessness, the degradation, the senselessness, the weariness, the ridicule and humiliation and – and – the perspiration, of these moments? I dragged the ex-hussar off. He was like a wild beast. It seems he had been greatly annoyed at losing his free afternoon on my account. The garden of his bungalow required his personal attention, and at the slight blow of the banana the brute in him had broken loose. We left Johnson on his back still black in the face, but beginning to kick feebly. Meantime, the big woman had remained sitting on the ground, apparently paralysed with extreme terror.

For half an hour we jolted inside our rolling box, side by side, in profound silence. The ex-sergeant was busy staunching the blood of a long scratch on his cheek. 'I hope you're satisfied,' he said suddenly. 'That's what comes of all that tomfool business. If you hadn't quarrelled with that tugboat skipper over some girl or other, all this wouldn't have happened.'

'You heard *that* story?' I said.

'Of course I heard. And I shouldn't wonder if the Consul-General himself doesn't come to hear of it. How am I to go before him tomorrow with that thing on my cheek – I want to know. It's *you* who ought to have got this!'

After that, till the gharry stopped and he jumped out without leave-taking, he swore to himself steadily, horribly; muttering great, purposeful, trooper oaths, to which the worst a sailor can do is like the prattle of a child. For my part I had just the strength to crawl into Schomberg's coffee-room, where I wrote at a little table a note to the mate instructing him to get everything ready for dropping down the river next day. I couldn't face my ship. Well! she had a clever sort of skipper and no mistake – poor thing! What a horrid mess! I took my head between my hands. At times the obviousness of my innocence would reduce me to despair. What had I done? If I had done something to bring about the situation I should at least have learned not to do it again. But I felt guiltless to the point of imbecility. The room was empty yet; only Schomberg prowled round me goggle-eyed and with a sort of awed respectful curiosity. No doubt he had set the story going himself; but he was a good-hearted chap, and I am really persuaded he participated in all my troubles. He did what he could for me. He ranged aside the heavy matchstand, set a chair straight, pushed a spittoon slightly with his foot – as you show small attentions to a friend under a great sorrow – sighed, and at last, unable to hold his tongue: 'Well! I warned you, captain. That's what comes of running your head against Mr Falk. Man'll stick at nothing.'

I sat without stirring, and after surveying me with a sort of commiseration in his eyes, he burst out in a hoarse whisper: 'But for a fine lump of a girl, she's a fine lump of a girl.' He made a loud smacking noise with his thick lips. 'The finest lump of a girl that I ever . . . ' he was going on with great unction, but for some reason or other broke off. I fancied myself throwing something at his head. 'I don't blame you, captain. Hang me if I do,' he said with a patronising air.

'Thank you,' I said resignedly. It was no use fighting against this false fate. I don't know even if I was sure myself where the truth of the matter began. The conviction that it would end disastrously had been driven into me by all the successive shocks my sense of security had received. I began to ascribe an extraordinary potency to agents in themselves powerless. It was as if Schomberg's baseless gossip had the power to bring about the thing itself or the abstract enmity of Falk could put my ship ashore.

I have already explained how fatal this last would have been. For my further action, my youth, my inexperience, my very real concern for the health of my crew must be my excuse. The action itself, when it came, was purely impulsive. It was set in movement quite undiplomatically and simply by Falk's appearance in the doorway of the coffee-room.

The room was full by then and buzzing with voices. I had been looked at with curiosity by everyone, but how am I to describe the sensation produced by the appearance of Falk himself blocking the doorway? The tension of expectation could be measured by the profundity of the silence that fell upon the very click of the billiard balls. As to Schomberg, he looked extremely frightened; he hated mortally any sort of row (*fracas* he called it) in his establishment. *Fracas* was bad for business, he affirmed; but, in truth, this specimen of portly, middle-aged manhood was of a timid disposition. I don't know what, considering my presence in the place, they all hoped would come of it. A sort of stag fight, perhaps. Or they may have supposed Falk had come in only to annihilate me completely. As a matter of fact, Falk had come in because Hermann had asked him to enquire after the precious white cotton parasol which, in the worry and excitement of the previous day, he had forgotten at the table where we had held our little discussion.

It was this that gave me my opportunity. I don't think I would have gone to seek Falk out. No. I don't think so. There are limits. But there was an opportunity and I seized it – I have already tried to explain why. Now I will merely state that, in my opinion, to get his sickly crew into the sea air and secure a quick despatch for his ship a skipper would be justified in going to any length, short of absolute crime. He should put his pride in his pocket; he may accept confidences; he must explain his innocence as if it were a sin; he may take advantage of misconceptions, of desires and of weaknesses; he ought to conceal his horror and other emotions, and, if the fate of a human being, and that human being a magnificent young girl, is strangely involved – why, he should contemplate that fate (whatever it might seem to be) without turning a hair. And all these things I have done: the explaining, the listening, the pretending – even to the discretion – and nobody, not even Hermann's niece, I believe, need throw stones at me now. Schomberg at all events needn't, since from first to last, I am happy to say, there was not the slightest '*fracas*'.

Overcoming a nervous contraction of the windpipe, I had managed to exclaim 'Captain Falk!' His start of surprise was perfectly genuine, but afterwards he neither smiled nor scowled. He simply waited. Then, when I had said, 'I must have a talk with you,' and had pointed to a chair at my table, he moved up to me, though he didn't sit down. Schomberg, however, with a long tumbler in his hand, was making towards us prudently, and I discovered then the only sign of weakness in Falk. He had for Schomberg a repulsion resembling that sort of physical fear some people experience at the sight of a toad. Perhaps to a man so essentially and silently concentrated upon himself (though he could talk well enough, as I was to find out presently) the other's irrepressible loquacity, embracing every human being within range of the tongue, might have appeared unnatural, disgusting, and monstrous. He suddenly gave signs of restiveness – positively like a horse about to rear, and, muttering hurriedly as if in great pain, 'No. I can't stand that fellow,' seemed ready to bolt. This weakness of his gave me the advantage at the very start. 'Verandah,' I suggested, as if rendering him a service, and walked him out by the arm. We stumbled over a few chairs; we had the feeling of open space before us, and felt the fresh breath of the river – fresh, but tainted. The Chinese theatres across the water made, in the sparsely twinkling masses of gloom an Eastern town presents at night, blazing centres of light, and of a distant and howling uproar. I felt him become suddenly tractable again like an animal, like a good-tempered horse when the object that scares him is removed. Yes. I felt in the darkness there how tractable he was, without my conviction of his inflexibility – tenacity, rather, perhaps – being in the least weakened. His very arm abandoning itself to my grasp was as hard as marble – like a limb of iron. But I heard a tumultuous scuffling of boot-soles within. The unspeakable idiots inside were crowding to the windows, climbing over each other's backs behind the blinds, billiard cues and all. Somebody broke a window-pane, and with the sound of falling glass, so suggestive of riot and devastation, Schomberg reeled out after us in a state of funk which had prevented his parting with his brandy and soda. He must have trembled like an aspen leaf. The piece of ice in the long tumbler he held in his hand tinkled with an effect of chattering teeth. 'I beg you, gentlemen,' he expostulated thickly. 'Come! Really, now, I must insist . . . '

How proud I am of my presence of mind! 'Hallo,' I said instantly in a loud and naïve tone, 'somebody's breaking your windows, Schomberg. Would you please tell one of your boys to bring out here a pack of cards and a couple of lights? And two long drinks. Will you?'

To receive an order soothed him at once. It was business. 'Certainly,' he said in an immensely relieved tone. The night was rainy, with wandering gusts of wind, and while we waited for the candles Falk said, as if to justify his panic, 'I don't interfere in anybody's business. I don't give any occasion for talk. I am a respectable man. But this fellow is always making out something wrong, and can never rest till he gets somebody to believe him.'

This was the first of my knowledge of Falk. This desire of respectability, of being like everybody else, was the only recognition he vouchsafed to the organisation of mankind. For the rest he might have been the member of a herd, not of a society. Self-preservation was his only concern. Not selfishness, but mere self-preservation. Selfishness presupposes consciousness, choice, the presence of other men; but his instinct acted as though he were the last of mankind nursing that law like the only spark of a sacred fire. I don't mean to say that living naked in a cavern would have satisfied him. Obviously he was the creature of the conditions to which he was born. No doubt self-preservation meant also the preservation of these conditions. But essentially it meant something much more simple, natural, and powerful. How shall I express it? It meant the preservation of the five senses of his body – let us say – taking it in its narrowest as well as in its widest meaning. I think you will admit before long the justice of this judgement. However, as we stood there together in the dark verandah I had judged nothing as yet – and I had no desire to judge – which is an idle practice anyhow. The light was long in coming.

'Of course,' I said in a tone of mutual understanding, 'it isn't exactly a game of cards I want with you.'

I saw him draw his hands down his face – the vague stir of the passionate and meaningless gesture; but he waited in silent patience. It was only when the lights had been brought out that he opened his lips. I understood his mumble to mean that 'he didn't know any game'.

'Like this, Schomberg and all the other fools will have to keep off,' I said tearing open the pack. 'Have you heard that we are universally supposed to be quarrelling about a girl? You know who – of course. I am really ashamed to ask, but is it possible that you do me the honour to think me dangerous?'

As I said these words I felt how absurd it was and also I felt flattered – for, really, what else could it be? His answer, spoken in his usual dispassionate undertone, made it clear that it was so, but not precisely as flattering as I supposed. He thought me dangerous with Hermann, more than with the girl herself; but, as to quarrelling, I saw at once how inappropriate the word was. We had no quarrel. Natural forces are not quarrelsome. You can't quarrel with the wind that inconveniences and humiliates you by blowing off your hat in a street full of people. He had no quarrel with me. Neither would a boulder, falling on my head, have had. He fell upon me in accordance with the law by which he was moved – not of gravitation, like a detached stone, but of self-preservation. Of course this is giving it a rather wide interpretation. Strictly speaking, he had existed and could have existed without being married.

Yet he told me that he had found it more and more difficult to live alone. Yes. He told me this in his low, careless voice, to such a pitch of confidence had we arrived at the end of half an hour.

It took me just about that time to convince him that I had never dreamed of marrying Hermann's niece. Could any necessity have been more extravagant? And the difficulty was the greater because he was so hard hit that he couldn't imagine anybody being able to remain in a state of indifference. Any man with eyes in his head, he seemed to think, could not help coveting so much bodily magnificence. This profound belief was conveyed by the manner he listened sitting sideways to the table and playing absently with a few cards I had dealt to him at random. And the more I saw into him the more I saw of him. The wind swayed the lights so that his sunburnt face, whiskered to the eyes, seemed to successively flicker crimson at me and to go out. I saw the extraordinary breadth of the high cheekbones, the perpendicular style of the features, the massive forehead, steep like a cliff, denuded at the top, largely uncovered at the temples. The fact is I had never before seen him without his hat; but now, as if my fervour had made him hot, he had taken it off and laid it gently on the floor. Something peculiar in the shape and setting of his yellow eyes gave them the provoking silent intensity which characterised his glance. But the face was thin, furrowed, worn; I discovered that through the bush of his hair, as you may detect the gnarled shape of a tree trunk lost in a dense undergrowth. These overgrown cheeks were sunken. It was an anchorite's bony head fitted with a Capuchin's beard and adjusted to a herculean body. I don't mean athletic. Hercules, I take it, was not an athlete. He was a strong man, susceptible to female charms, and not afraid of dirt. And thus with Falk, who was a strong man. He was extremely strong, just as the girl (since I must think of them together) was magnificently attractive by the masterful power of flesh and blood, expressed in shape, in size, in attitude – that is, by a straight appeal to the senses. His mind meantime, preoccupied with respectability, quailed before Schomberg's tongue and seemed absolutely impervious to my protestations; and I went so far as to protest that I would just as soon think of marrying my mother's (dear old lady!) faithful female cook as Hermann's niece. Sooner, I protested, in my desperation, much sooner; but it did not appear that he saw anything outrageous in the proposition, and in his sceptical immobility he seemed to nurse the argument that at all events the cook was very, very far away. It must be said that, just before, I had gone wrong by appealing to the evidence of my manner whenever I called on board the *Diana*. I had never attempted to approach the girl, or to speak to her, or even to look at her in any marked way. Nothing could be clearer. But, as his own idea of – let us say – courting, seemed to consist precisely in sitting silently for hours in the vicinity of the beloved object, that line of argument inspired him with distrust. Staring down his extended legs he let out a grunt – as much as to say, 'That's all very fine, but you can't throw dust in *my* eyes.'

At last I was exasperated into saying, 'Why don't you put the matter at rest by talking to Hermann?' and I added sneeringly: 'You don't expect me perhaps to speak for you?'

To this he said, very loud for him, 'Would you?'

And for the first time he lifted his head to look at me with wonder and incredulity. He lifted his head so sharply that there could be no mistake. I had touched a spring. I saw the whole extent of my opportunity, and could hardly believe in it.

'Why. Speak to . . . Well, of course,' I proceeded very slowly, watching him with great attention, for, on my word, I feared a joke. 'Not, perhaps, to the young lady herself. I can't speak German, you know. But . . . '

He interrupted me with the earnest assurance that Hermann had the highest opinion of me; and at once I felt the need for the greatest possible diplomacy at this juncture. So I demurred just enough to draw him on. Falk sat up, but except for a very noticeable enlargement of the pupils, till the irises of his eyes were reduced to two narrow yellow rings, his face, I should judge, was incapable of expressing excitement. 'Oh, yes! Hermann did have the greatest . . . '

'Take up your cards. Here's Schomberg peeping at us through the blind!' I said.

We went through the motions of what might have been a game of écarté. Presently the intolerable scandalmonger withdrew, probably to inform the people in the billiard-room that we two were gambling on the verandah like mad.

We were not gambling, but it was a game; a game in which I felt I held the winning cards. The stake, roughly speaking, was the success of the voyage – for me; and he, I apprehended, had nothing to lose. Our intimacy matured rapidly, and before many words had been exchanged I perceived that the excellent Hermann had been making use of me. That simple and astute Teuton had been, it seems, holding me up to Falk in the light of a rival. I was young enough to be shocked at so much duplicity. 'Did he tell you that in so many words?' I asked with indignation.

Hermann had not. He had given hints only; and of course it had not taken very much to alarm Falk; but, instead of declaring himself, he had taken steps to remove the family from under my influence. He was perfectly straightforward about it – as straightforward as a tile falling on your head. There was no duplicity in that man; and when I congratulated him on the perfection of his arrangements – even to the bribing of the wretched Johnson against me – he had a genuine movement of protest. Never bribed. He knew the man wouldn't work as long as he had a few cents in his pocket to get drunk on, and, naturally (he said – '*naturally*') he let him have a dollar or two. He was himself a sailor, he said, and anticipated the view another sailor, like myself, was bound to take. On the other hand, he was sure that I should have to come to grief. He hadn't been knocking about for the last seven years up and down that river for nothing. It would have been no disgrace to me – but he asserted confidently I would have had my ship very awkwardly ashore at a spot two miles below the Great Pagoda . . .

And with all that he had no ill-will. That was evident. This was a crisis in which his only object had been to gain time – I fancy. And presently he mentioned that he had written for some jewellery, real good jewellery – had written to Hong-Kong for it. It would arrive in a day or two.

'Well, then,' I said cheerily, 'everything is all right. All you've got to do is to present it to the lady together with your heart, and live happy ever after.'

Upon the whole he seemed to accept that view as far as the girl was concerned, but his eyelids drooped. There was still something in the way. For one thing Hermann disliked him so much. As to me, on the contrary, it seemed as though he could not praise me enough. Mrs Hermann too. He didn't know why they disliked him so. It made everything most difficult.

I listened impassive, feeling more and more diplomatic. His speech was not transparently clear. He was one of those men who seem to live, feel, suffer in a sort of mental twilight. But as to being fascinated by the girl and possessed by the desire of home life with her – it was as clear as daylight. So much being at stake, he was afraid of putting it to the hazard of the declaration. Besides, there was something else. And with Hermann being so set against him . . .

'I see,' I said thoughtfully, while my heart beat fast with the excitement of my diplomacy. 'I don't mind sounding Hermann. In fact, to show you how mistaken you were, I am ready to do all I can for you in that way.'

A light sigh escaped him. He drew his hands down his face, and it emerged, bony, unchanged of expression, as if all the tissues had been ossified. All the passion was in those big brown hands. He was satisfied. Then there was that other matter. If there were anybody on earth it was I who could persuade Hermann to take a reasonable view! I had a knowledge of the world and lots of experience. Hermann admitted this himself. And then I was a sailor too. Falk thought that a sailor would be able to understand certain things best . . .

He talked as if the Hermanns had been living all their life in a rural hamlet, and I alone had been capable, with my practice in life, of a large and indulgent view of certain occurrences. That was what my diplomacy was leading me to. I began suddenly to dislike it.

'I say, Falk,' I asked quite brusquely, 'you haven't already a wife put away somewhere?' The pain and disgust of his denial were very striking.

Couldn't I understand that he was as respectable as any white man hereabouts; earning his living honestly. He was suffering from my suspicion, and the low undertone of his voice made his protestations sound very pathetic. For a moment he shamed me, but, my diplomacy notwithstanding, I seemed to develop a conscience, as if in very truth it were in my power to decide the success of this matrimonial enterprise. By pretending hard enough we come to believe anything – anything to our advantage. And I had been pretending very hard, because I meant yet to be towed safely down the river. But, through conscience or stupidity, I couldn't help alluding to the Vanlo affair. 'You acted rather badly there. Didn't you?' was what I ventured actually to say – for the logic of our conduct is always at the mercy of obscure and unforeseen impulses.

His dilated pupils swerved from my face, glancing at the window with a sort of scared fury. We heard behind the blinds the continuous and sudden clicking of ivory, a jovial murmur of many voices, and Schomberg's deep manly laugh.

'That confounded old woman of a hotel-keeper then would never, never let it rest!' Falk exclaimed. Well, yes! It had happened two years ago. When it came to the point he owned he couldn't make up his mind to trust Fred Vanlo – no sailor, a bit of a fool too. He could not trust him, but, to stop his row, he had lent him enough money to pay all his debts before he left. I was greatly surprised to hear this. Then Falk could not be such a miser after all. So much the better for the girl. For a time he sat silent; then he picked up a card, and while looking at it he said: 'You need not think of anything bad. It was an accident. I've been unfortunate once.'

'Then in heaven's name say nothing about it.'

As soon as these words were out of my mouth I fancied I had said something immoral. He shook his head negatively. It had to be told. He considered it proper that the relations of the lady should know. No doubt – I thought to myself – had Miss Vanlo not been thirty and damaged by the climate he would have found it possible to entrust Fred Vanlo with this confidence. And then the figure of Hermann's niece appeared before my mind's eye, with the wealth of her opulent form, her rich youth, her lavish strength. With that powerful and immaculate vitality, her girlish form must have shouted aloud of life to that man, whereas poor Miss Vanlo could only sing sentimental songs to the strumming of a piano.

'And that Hermann hates me, I know it!' he cried in his undertone, with a sudden recrudescence of anxiety. 'I must tell them. It is proper that they should know. You would say so yourself.'

He then murmured an utterly mysterious allusion to the necessity for peculiar domestic arrangements. Though my curiosity was excited I did not want to hear any of his confidences. I feared he might give me a piece of information that would make my assumed role of match-maker odious – however unreal it was. I was aware that he could have the girl for the asking; and keeping down a desire to laugh in his face, I expressed a confident belief in my ability to argue away Hermann's dislike for him. 'I am sure I can make it all right,' I said. He looked very pleased.

And when we rose not a word had been said about towage! Not a word! The game was won and the honour was safe. Oh! blessed white cotton umbrella! We shook hands, and I was holding myself with difficulty from breaking into a step dance of joy when he came back, striding all the length of the verandah, and said doubtfully: 'I say, captain, I have your word? You – you – won't turn round?'

Heavens! The fright he gave me. Behind his tone of doubt there was something desperate and menacing. The infatuated ass. But I was equal to the situation.

'My dear Falk,' I said, beginning to lie with a glibness and effrontery that amazed me even at the time – 'confidence for confidence.' (He had made no confidences.) 'I will tell you that I am already engaged to an extremely charming girl at home, and so you understand . . . '

He caught my hand and wrung it in a crushing grip.

'Pardon me. I feel it every day more difficult to live alone . . . '

'On rice and fish,' I interrupted smartly, giggling with the sheer nervousness of a danger escaped.

He dropped my hand as if it had become suddenly red hot. A moment of profound silence ensued, as though something extraordinary had happened.

'I promise you to obtain Hermann's consent,' I faltered out at last, and it seemed to me that he could not help seeing through that humbugging promise. 'If there's anything else to get over I shall endeavour to stand by you,' I conceded further, feeling somehow defeated and overborne; 'but you must do your best yourself.'

'I have been unfortunate once,' he muttered unemotionally, and turning his back on me he went away, thumping slowly the plank floor as if his feet had been shod with iron.

Next morning, however, he was lively enough as man-boat, a combination of splashing and shouting; of the insolent commotion below with the steady overbearing glare of the silent head-piece above. He turned us out most unnecessarily at an ungodly hour, but it was nearly eleven in the morning before he brought me up a cable's length from Hermann's ship. And he did it very badly too, in a hurry, and nearly contriving to miss altogether the patch of good holding ground, because, forsooth, he had caught sight of Hermann's niece on the poop. And so did I; and probably as soon as he had seen her himself. I saw the modest, sleek glory of the tawny head, and the full, grey shape of the girlish print frock she filled so perfectly, so satisfactorily, with the seduction of unfaltering curves – a very nymph of *Diana* the Huntress. And *Diana* the ship sat, high-walled and as solid as an institution, on the smooth level of the water, the most uninspiring and respectable craft upon the seas, useful and ugly, devoted to the support of domestic virtues like any grocer's shop on shore. At once Falk steamed away; for there was some work for him to do. He would return in the evening.

He ranged close by us, passing out dead slow, without a hail. The beat of the paddle-wheels reverberating amongst the stony islets, as if from the ruined walls of a vast arena, filled the anchorage confusedly with the clapping sounds of a mighty and leisurely applause. Abreast of Hermann's ship he stopped the engines; and a profound silence reigned over the rocks, the shore and the sea, for the time it took him to raise his hat aloft before the nymph of the grey print frock. I had snatched up my binoculars, and I can answer for it she didn't stir a limb, standing by the rail shapely and erect, with one of her hands grasping a rope at the height of her head, while the way of the tug carried slowly past her the lingering and profound homage of the man. There was for me an enormous significance in the scene, the sense of having witnessed a solemn declaration. The die was cast. After such a manifestation he couldn't back out. And I reflected that it was nothing whatever to me now. With a rush of black smoke belching suddenly out of the funnel, and a mad swirl of paddle-wheels provoking a burst of weird and precipitated clapping, the tug shot out of the desolate arena. The rocky islets lay on the sea like the heaps of a cyclopean ruin on a plain; the centipedes and scorpions lurked under the stones; there was not a single blade of grass in sight anywhere, not a single lizard sunning himself on a boulder by the shore. When I looked again at Hermann's ship the girl had disappeared. I could not detect the smallest dot of a bird on the immense sky, and the flatness of the land continued the flatness of the sea to the naked line of the horizon.

This is the setting now inseparably connected with my knowledge of Falk's misfortune. My diplomacy had brought me there, and now I had only to wait the time for taking up the role of an ambassador. My diplomacy was a success; my ship was safe; old Gambril would probably live; a feeble sound of a tapping hammer came intermittently from the *Diana*. During the afternoon I looked at times at the old homely ship, the faithful nurse of Hermann's progeny, or yawned towards the distant temple of Buddha, like a lonely hillock on the plain, where shaven priests cherish the thoughts of that Annihilation which is the worthy reward of us all. Unfortunate! He had been unfortunate once. Well, that was not so bad as life goes. And what the devil could be the nature of that misfortune? I remembered that I had known a man before who had declared himself to have fallen, years ago, a victim to misfortune; but this misfortune, whose effects appeared permanent (he looked desperately hard up) when considered dispassionately, seemed indistinguishable from a breach of trust. Could it be something of that nature? Apart, however, from the utter improbability that he would offer to talk of it even to his future uncle-in-law I had a strange feeling that Falk's physique unfitted him for that sort of delinquency. As the person of Hermann's niece exhaled the profound physical charm of feminine form, so her adorer's big frame embodied to my senses the hard, straight masculinity that would conceivably kill but would not condescend to cheat. The thing was obvious. I might just as well have suspected the girl of a curvature of the spine. And I perceived that the sun was about to set.

The smoke of Falk's tug hove in sight, far away at the mouth of the river. It was time for me to assume the character of an ambassador, and the negotiation would not be difficult except in the matter of keeping my countenance. It was all too extravagantly nonsensical, and I conceived that it would be best to compose for myself a grave demeanour. I practised this in my boat as I went along, but the bashfulness that came secretly upon me the moment I stepped on the deck of the *Diana* is inexplicable. As soon as we had exchanged greetings Hermann asked me eagerly if I knew whether Falk had found his white parasol.

'He's going to bring it to you himself directly,' I said with great solemnity. 'Meantime I am charged with an important message for which he begs your favourable consideration. He is in love with your niece . . .'

'*Ach So!*' he hissed with an animosity that made my assumed gravity change into the most genuine concern. What meant this tone? And I hurried on.

'He wishes, with your consent of course, to ask her to marry him at once – before you leave here, that is. He would speak to his Consul.'

Hermann sat down and smoked violently. Five minutes passed in that furious meditation, and then, taking the long pipe out of his mouth, he burst into a hot diatribe against Falk – against his cupidity, his stupidity (a fellow that can hardly be got to say 'yes' or 'no' to the simplest question) – against his outrageous treatment of the shipping in port (because he saw they were at his mercy) – and against his manner of walking, which to his (Hermann's) mind showed a conceit positively unbearable. The damage to the old *Diana* was not forgotten, of course, and there was nothing of any nature said or done by Falk (even to the last offer of refreshment in the hotel) that did not seem to have been a cause of offence. 'Had the cheek' to drag him (Hermann) into that coffee-room; as though a drink from him could make up for forty-seven dollars and fifty cents of damage in the cost of wood alone – not counting two days' work for the carpenter. Of course he would not stand in the girl's way. He was going home to Germany. There were plenty of poor girls walking about in Germany.

'He's very much in love,' was all I found to say.

'Yes,' he cried. 'And it is time, too, after making himself and me talked about ashore the last voyage I was here, and then now again; coming on board every evening unsettling the girl's mind, and saying nothing. What sort of conduct is that?'

The seven thousand dollars the fellow was always talking about did not, in his opinion, justify such behaviour. Moreover, nobody had seen them. He (Hermann) seriously doubted if there were seven thousand cents, and the tug, no doubt, was mortgaged up to the top of the funnel to the firm of Siegers. But let that pass. He wouldn't stand in the girl's way. Her head was so turned that she had become no good to them of late. Quite unable even to put the children to bed without her aunt. It was bad for the children; they got unruly; and yesterday he had actually had to give Gustav a thrashing.

For that, too, Falk was made responsible apparently. And looking at my Hermann's heavy, puffy, good-natured face, I knew he would not exert himself till greatly exasperated, and, therefore, would thrash very hard, and being fat would resent the necessity. How Falk had managed to turn the girl's head was more difficult to understand. I supposed Hermann would know. And then hadn't there been Miss Vanlo? It could not be his silvery tongue, or the subtle seduction of his manner; he had no more of what is called 'manner' than an animal – which, however, on the other hand, is never, and can never be called vulgar. Therefore it must have been his bodily appearance, exhibiting a virility of nature as exaggerated as his beard, and resembling a sort of constant ruthlessness. It was seen in the very manner he lolled in the chair. He meant no offence, but his intercourse was characterised by that sort of frank disregard of susceptibilities a man of seven foot six, living in a world of dwarfs, would naturally assume, without in the least wishing to be unkind. But amongst men of his own stature, or nearly, this frank use of his advantages, in such matters as the awful towage bills for instance, caused much impotent gnashing of teeth. When attentively considered it seemed appalling at times. He was a strange beast. But maybe women liked it. Seen in that light he was well worth taming, and I suppose every woman at the bottom of her heart considers herself as a tamer of strange beasts. But Hermann arose with precipitation to carry the news to his wife. I had barely the time, as he made for the cabin door, to grab him by the seat of his inexpressibles. I begged him to wait till Falk in person had spoken with him. There remained some small matter to talk over, as I understood.

He sat down again at once, full of suspicion.

'What matter?' he said surlily. 'I have had enough of his nonsense. There's no matter at all, as he knows very well; the girl has nothing in the world. She came to us in one thin dress when my brother died, and I have a growing family.'

'It can't be anything of that kind,' I opined. 'He's desperately enamoured of your niece. I don't know why he did not say so before. Upon my word, I believe it is because he was afraid to lose, perhaps, the felicity of sitting near her on your quarter-deck.'

I intimated my conviction that his love was so great as to be in a sense cowardly. The effects of a great passion are unaccountable. It has been known to make a man timid. But Hermann looked at me as if I had foolishly raved; and the twilight was dying out rapidly.

'You don't believe in passion, do you, Hermann?' I said cheerily. 'The passion of fear will make a cornered rat courageous. Falk's in a corner. He will take her off your hands in one thin frock just as she came to you. And after ten years' service it isn't a bad bargain,' I added.

Far from taking offence, he resumed his air of civic virtue. The sudden night came upon him while he stared placidly along the deck, bringing in contact with his thick lips, and taking away again after a jet of smoke, the curved mouthpiece fitted to the stem of his pipe. The night came upon him and buried in haste his whiskers, his globular eyes, his puffy pale face, his fat knees and the vast flat slippers on his fatherly feet. Only his short arms in respectable white shirt-sleeves remained very visible, propped up like the flippers of a seal reposing on the strand.

'Falk wouldn't settle anything about repairs. Told me to find out first how much wood I should require and he would see,' he remarked; and after he had spat peacefully in the dusk we heard over the water the beat of the tug's floats. There is, on a calm night, nothing more suggestive of fierce and headlong haste than the rapid sound made by the paddle-wheels of a boat threshing her way through a quiet sea; and the approach of Falk towards his fate seemed to be urged by an impatient and passionate desire. The engines must have been driven to the very utmost of their revolutions. We heard them slow down at last, and, vaguely, the white hull of the tug appeared moving against the black islets, whilst a slow and rhythmical clapping as of thousands of hands rose on all sides. It ceased all at once, just before Falk brought her up. A single brusque splash was followed by the long-drawn rumbling of iron links running through the hawse pipe. Then a solemn silence fell upon the Roadstead.

'He will soon be here,' I murmured, and after that we waited for him without a word. Meantime, raising my eyes, I beheld the glitter of a lofty sky above the *Diana*'s mastheads. The multitude of stars gathered into clusters, in rows, in lines, in masses, in groups, shone all together, unanimously – and the few isolated ones, blazing by themselves in the midst of dark patches, seemed to be of a superior kind and of an inextinguishable nature. But long striding footsteps were heard hastening along the deck; the high bulwarks of the

Diana made a deeper darkness. We rose from our chairs quickly, and Falk, appearing before us, all in white, stood still.

Nobody spoke at first, as though we had been covered with confusion. His arrival was fiery, but his white bulk, of indefinite shape and without features, made him loom up like a man of snow.

'The captain here has been telling me . . . ' Hermann began in a homely and amicable voice; and Falk had a low, nervous laugh. His cool, negligent undertone had no inflexions, but the strength of a powerful emotion made him ramble in his speech. He had always desired a home. It was difficult to live alone, though he was not answerable. He was domestic; there had been difficulties; but since he had seen Hermann's niece he found that it had become at last impossible to live by himself. 'I mean – impossible,' he repeated with no sort of emphasis and only with the slightest of pauses, but the word fell into my mind with the force of a new idea.

'I have not said anything to her yet,' Hermann observed quietly. And Falk dismissed this by a 'That's all right. Certainly. Very proper.' There was a necessity for perfect frankness – in marrying, especially. Hermann seemed attentive, but he seized the first opportunity to ask us into the cabin. 'And by the by, Falk,' he said innocently, as we passed in, 'the timber came to no less than forty-seven dollars and fifty cents.'

Falk, uncovering his head, lingered in the passage. 'Some other time,' he said; and Hermann nudged me angrily – I don't know why. The girl alone in the cabin sat sewing at some distance from the table. Falk stopped short in the doorway. Without a word, without a sign, without the slightest inclination of his bony head, by the silent intensity of his look alone, he seemed to lay his herculean frame at her feet. Her hands sank slowly on her lap, and raising her clear eyes, she let her soft, beaming glance enfold him from head to foot like a slow and pale caress. He was very hot when he sat down; she, with bowed head, went on with her sewing; her neck was very white under the light of the lamp; but Falk, hiding his face in the palms of his hands, shuddered faintly. He drew them down, even to his beard, and his uncovered eyes astonished me by their tense and irrational expression – as though he had just swallowed a heavy gulp of alcohol. It passed away while he was binding us to secrecy. Not that he cared, but he did not like to be spoken about; and I looked at the girl's marvellous, at her wonderful, at her regal hair, plaited tight into that one astonishing and maidenly tress. Whenever she moved her well-shaped head it would stir stiffly to and fro on her back. The thin cotton sleeve fitted the irreproachable roundness of her arm like a skin; and her very dress, stretched on her bust, seemed to palpitate like a living tissue with the strength of vitality animating her body. How good her complexion was, the outline of her soft cheek and the small convoluted conch of her rosy ear! To pull her needle she kept the little finger apart from the others; it seemed a waste of power to see her sewing – eternally sewing – with that industrious and precise movement of her arm, going on eternally upon all the oceans, under all the skies, in innumerable harbours. And suddenly I heard Falk's voice declare that he could not marry a woman unless she knew of something in his life that had happened ten years ago. It was an accident. An unfortunate accident. It would affect the domestic arrangements of their home, but, once told, it need not be alluded to again for the rest of their lives. 'I should want my wife to feel for me,' he said. 'It has made me unhappy.' And how could he keep the knowledge of it to himself – he asked us – perhaps through years and years of companionship? What sort of companionship would that be? He had thought it over. A wife must know. Then why not at once? He counted on Hermann's kindness for presenting the affair in the best possible light. And Hermann's countenance, mystified before, became very sour. He stole an inquisitive glance at me. I shook my head blankly. Some people thought, Falk went on, that such an experience changed a man for the rest of his life. He couldn't say. It was hard, awful, and not to be forgotten, but he did not think himself a worse man than before. Only he talked in his sleep now, he believed . . . At last I began to think he had accidentally killed someone; perhaps a friend – his own father maybe; when he went on to say that probably we were aware he never touched meat. Throughout he spoke English, of course, on my account.

He swayed forward heavily.

The girl, with her hands raised before her pale eyes, was threading her needle. He glanced at her, and his mighty trunk overshadowed the table, bringing nearer to us the breadth of his shoulders, the thickness of his neck, and that incongruous, anchorite head, burnt in the desert, hollowed and lean as if by excesses of vigils and fasting. His beard flowed imposingly downwards, out of sight, between the two brown hands gripping the edge of the table, and his persistent glance, made sombre by the wide dilations of the pupils, fascinated.

'Imagine to yourselves,' he said in his ordinary voice, 'that I have eaten man.'

I could only ejaculate a faint 'Ah!' of complete enlightenment.

But Hermann, dazed by the excessive shock, actually murmured, 'Himmel! What for?'

'It was my terrible misfortune to do so,' said Falk in a measured undertone. The girl, unconscious, sewed on. Mrs Hermann was absent in one of the state-rooms, sitting up with Lena, who was feverish; but Hermann suddenly put both his hands up with a jerk. The embroidered calotte fell, and, in the twinkling of an eye, he had rumpled his hair all ends up in a most extravagant manner. In this state he strove to speak; with every effort his eyes seemed to start further out of their sockets; his head looked like a mop. He choked, gasped, swallowed, and managed to shriek out the one word, 'Beast!'

From that moment till Falk went out of the cabin the girl, with her hands folded on the work lying in her lap, never took her eyes off him. His own, in the blindness of his heart, darted all over the cabin, only seeking to avoid the sight of Hermann's raving. It was ridiculous, and was made almost terrible by the stillness of every other person present. It was contemptible, and was made appalling by the man's overmastering horror of this awful sincerity, coming to him suddenly, with the confession of such a fact. He walked with great strides; he gasped. He wanted to know from Falk how dared he to come and tell him this? Did he think himself a proper person to be sitting in this cabin where his wife and children lived? Tell his niece! Expected him to tell his niece! His own brother's daughter! Shameless! Did I ever hear tell of such impudence? – he appealed to me. 'This man here ought to have gone and hidden himself out of sight instead of . . . '

'But it's a great misfortune for me. But it's a great misfortune for me,' Falk would ejaculate from time to time.

However, Hermann kept on running frequently against the corners of the table. At last he lost a slipper, and crossing his arms on his breast, walked up with one stocking foot very close to Falk, in order to ask him whether he did think there was anywhere on earth a woman abandoned enough to mate with such a monster. 'Did he? Did he? Did he?' I tried to restrain him. He tore himself out of my hands; he found his slipper, and, endeavouring to put it on, stormed standing on one leg – and Falk, with a face unmoved and averted eyes, grasped all his mighty beard in one vast palm.

'Was it right then for me to die myself?' he asked thoughtfully. I laid my hand on his shoulder.

'Go away,' I whispered imperiously, without any clear reason for this advice, except that I wished to put an end to Hermann's odious noise. 'Go away.'

He looked searchingly for a moment at Hermann before he made a move. I left the cabin, too, to see him out of the ship. But he hung about the quarter-deck.

'It is my misfortune,' he said in a steady voice.

'You were stupid to blurt it out in such a manner. After all, we don't hear such confidences every day.'

'What does the man mean?' he mused in deep undertones. 'Somebody had to die – but why me?'

He remained still for a time in the dark – silent; almost invisible. All at once he pinned my elbows to my sides. I felt utterly powerless in his grip, and his voice, whispering in my ear, vibrated.

'It's worse than hunger. Captain, do you know what that means? And I could kill then – or be killed. I wish the crowbar had smashed my skull ten years ago. And I've got to live now. Without her. Do you understand? Perhaps many years. But how? What can be done? If I had allowed myself to look at her once I would have carried her off before that man in my hands – like this.'

I felt myself snatched off the deck, then suddenly dropped – and I staggered backwards, feeling bewildered and bruised. What a man! All was still; he was gone. I heard Hermann's voice declaiming in the cabin, and I went in.

I could not at first make out a single word, but Mrs Hermann, who, attracted by the noise, had come in some time before, with an expression of surprise and mild disapproval depicted broadly on her face, was giving now all the signs of profound, helpless agitation. Her husband shot a string of guttural words at her, and instantly putting out one hand to the bulkhead as if to save herself from falling, she clutched the loose bosom of her dress with the other. He harangued the two women extraordinarily, with much of his shirt hanging out of his waistbelt, stamping his foot, turning from one to the other, sometimes throwing both his arms together, straight up above his rumpled hair, and keeping them in that position while he uttered a passage of loud denunciation; at others folding them tight across his breast – and then he hissed with indignation, elevating his shoulders and protruding his head. The girl was crying.

She had not changed her attitude. From her steady eyes that, following Falk in his retreat, had remained fixed wistfully on the cabin door, the tears fell rapid, thick, on her hands, on the work in her lap, warm and gentle like a shower in spring. She wept without grimacing, without noise – very touching, very quiet, with something more of pity than of pain in her face, as one weeps in compassion rather than in grief – and Hermann, before her, declaimed. I caught several times the word 'Mensch', man; and also 'Fressen', which last I looked up afterwards in my dictionary. It means 'Devour'. Hermann seemed to be requesting an answer of some sort from her; his whole body swayed. She remained mute and perfectly still; at last his agitation gained her; she put the palms of her hands together, her full lips parted, no sound came. His voice scolded shrilly, his arms went like a windmill – suddenly he shook a thick fist at her. She burst out into loud sobs. He seemed stupefied.

Mrs Hermann rushed forward babbling rapidly. The two women fell on each other's necks, and, with an arm round her niece's waist, she led her away. Her own eyes were simply streaming, her face was flooded. She shook her head back at me negatively, I wonder why to this day. The girl's head dropped heavily on her shoulder. They disappeared together.

Then Hermann sat down and stared at the cabin floor.

'We don't know all the circumstances,' I ventured to break the silence. He retorted tartly that he didn't want to know of any. According to his ideas no circumstances could excuse a crime – and certainly not such a crime. This was the opinion generally received. The duty of a human being was to starve. Falk therefore was a beast, an animal; base, low, vile, despicable, shameless, and deceitful. He had been deceiving him since last year. He was, however, inclined to think that Falk must have gone mad quite recently; for no sane person, without necessity, uselessly, for no earthly reason, and regardless of another's self-respect and peace of mind, would own to having devoured human flesh. 'Why tell?' he cried. 'Who was asking him?' It showed Falk's brutality because after all he had selfishly caused him (Hermann) much pain. He would have preferred not to know that such an unclean creature had been in the habit of caressing his children. He hoped I would say nothing of all this ashore, though. He wouldn't like it to get about that he had been intimate with an eater of men – a common cannibal. As to the scene he had made (which I judged quite unnecessary) he was not going to inconvenience and restrain himself for a fellow that went about courting and upsetting girls' heads, while he knew all the time that no decent housewifely girl could think of marrying him. At least he (Hermann) could not conceive how any girl could. 'Fancy Lena! . . . No, it was impossible. The thoughts that would come into their heads every time they sat down to a meal. Horrible! Horrible!'

'You are too squeamish, Hermann,' I said.

He seemed to think it was eminently proper to be squeamish if the word meant disgust at Falk's conduct; and turning up his eyes sentimentally he drew my attention to the horrible fate of the victims – the victims of that Falk. I said that I knew nothing about them. He seemed surprised. Could not anybody imagine without knowing? He – for instance – felt he would like to avenge them. But what if – said I – there had not been any? They might have died as it were, naturally – of starvation. He shuddered. But to be eaten – after death! To be devoured! He gave another deep shudder, and asked suddenly, 'Do you think it is true?'

His indignation and his personality together would have been enough to spoil the reality of the most authentic thing. When I looked at him I doubted the story – but the remembrance of Falk's words, looks, gestures, invested it not only with an air of reality but with the absolute truth of primitive passion.

'It is true just as much as you are able to make it; and exactly in the way you like to make it. For my part, when I hear you clamouring about it, I don't believe it is true at all.'

And I left him pondering. The men in my boat, lying at the foot of *Diana*'s side-ladder, told me that the captain of the tug had gone away in his gig some time ago.

I let my fellows pull an easy stroke; because of the heavy dew the clear sparkle of the stars seemed to fall on me cold and wetting. There was a sense of lurking gruesome horror somewhere in my mind, and it was mingled with clear and grotesque images. Schomberg's gastronomic tittle-tattle was responsible for these; and I half hoped I should never see Falk again. But the first thing my anchor-watchman told me was that the captain of the tug was on board. He had sent his boat away and was now waiting for me in the cuddy.

He was lying full length on the stern settee, his face buried in the cushions. I had expected to see it discomposed, contorted, despairing. It was nothing of the kind; it was just as I had seen it twenty times, steady and glaring from the bridge of the tug. It was immovably set and hungry, dominated like the whole man by the singleness of one instinct.

He wanted to live. He had always wanted to live. So we all do – but in us the instinct serves a complex conception, and in him this instinct existed alone. There is in such simple development a gigantic force, and like the pathos of a child's naïve and uncontrolled desire. He wanted that girl, and the utmost that can be said for him was that he wanted that particular girl alone. I think I saw then the obscure beginning, the seed germinating in the soil of an unconscious need, the first shoot of that tree bearing now for a mature mankind the flower and the fruit, the infinite gradation in shades and in flavour of our discriminating love. He was a child. He was as frank as a child too. He was hungry for the girl, terribly hungry, as he had been terribly hungry for food.

Don't be shocked if I declare that in my belief it was the same need, the same pain, the same torture. We are in his case allowed to contemplate the foundation of all the emotions – that one joy which is to live, and the one sadness at the root of the innumerable torments. It was made plain by the way he talked. He had never suffered so. It was gnawing, it was fire; it was there, like this! And after pointing below his breastbone, he made a hard wringing motion with his hands. And I assure you that, seen as I saw it with my bodily eyes, it was anything but laughable. And again, as he was presently to tell me (alluding to an early incident of the disastrous voyage when some damaged meat had been flung overboard), he said that a time soon came when his heart ached (that was the expression he used), and he was ready to tear his hair out at the thought of all that rotten beef thrown away.

I had heard all this; I witnessed his physical struggles, seeing the working of the rack and hearing the true voice of pain. I witnessed it all patiently, because the moment I came into the cuddy he had called upon me to stand by him – and this, it seems, I had diplomatically promised.

His agitation was impressive and alarming in the little cabin, like the floundering of a great whale driven into a shallow cove in a coast. He stood up; he flung himself down headlong; he tried to tear the cushion with his teeth; and again hugging it fiercely to his face he let himself fall on the couch. The whole ship seemed to feel the shock of his despair; and I contemplated with wonder the lofty forehead, the noble touch of time on the uncovered temples, the unchanged hungry character of the face – so strangely ascetic and so incapable of portraying emotion.

What should he do? He had lived by being near her. He had sat – in the evening – I knew? – all his life! She sewed. Her head was bent – so. Her head – like this – and her arms. Ah! Had I seen? Like this.

He dropped on a stool, bowed his powerful neck whose nape was red, and with his hands stitched the air, ludicrous, sublimely imbecile and comprehensible.

And now he couldn't have her? No! That was too much. After

thinking too that . . . What had he done? What was my advice? Take her by force? No? Mustn't he? Who was there then to kill him? For the first time I saw one of his features move: a fighting teeth-baring curl of the lip . . . 'Not Hermann, perhaps.' He lost himself in thought as though he had fallen out of the world.

I may note that the idea of suicide apparently did not enter his head for a single moment. It occurred to me to ask: 'Where was it that this shipwreck of yours took place?'

'Down south,' he said vaguely with a start.

'You are not down south now,' I said. 'Violence won't do. They would take her away from you in no time. And what was the name of the ship?'

'*Borgmester Dahl*,' he said. 'It was no shipwreck.'

He seemed to be waking up by degrees from that trance, and waking up calmed.

'Not a shipwreck? What was it?'

'Break-down,' he answered, looking more like himself every moment. By this only I learned that it was a steamer. I had till then supposed they had been starving in boats or on a raft – or perhaps on a barren rock.

'She did not sink then?' I asked in surprise. He nodded. 'We sighted the southern ice,' he pronounced dreamily.

'And you alone survived?'

He sat down. 'Yes. It was a terrible misfortune for me. Everything went wrong. All the men went wrong. I survived.'

Remembering the things one reads of it was difficult to realise the true meaning of his answers. I ought to have seen at once – but I did not; so difficult is it for our minds, remembering so much, instructed so much, informed of so much, to get in touch with the real actuality at our elbow. And with my head full of preconceived notions as to how a case of 'cannibalism and suffering at sea' should be managed I said – 'You were then so lucky in the drawing of lots?'

'Drawing of lots?' he said. 'What lots? Do you think I would have allowed my life to go for the drawing of lots?'

Not if he could help it, I perceived, no matter what other life went.

'It was a great misfortune. Terrible. Awful,' he said. 'Many heads went wrong, but the best men would live.'

'The toughest, you mean,' I said. He considered the word. Perhaps it was strange to him, though his English was so good.

'Yes,' he asserted at last. 'The best. It was everybody for himself at last and the ship open to all.'

Thus from question to question I got the whole story. I fancy it was the only way I could that night have stood by him. Outwardly at least he was himself again; the first sign of it was the return of that incongruous trick he had of drawing both his hands down his face – and it had its meaning now, with that slight shudder of the frame and the passionate anguish of these hands uncovering a hungry immovable face, the wide pupils of the intent, silent, fascinating eyes.

It was an iron steamer of a most respectable origin. The burgomaster of Falk's native town had built her. She was the first steamer ever launched there. The burgomaster's daughter had christened her. Country people drove in carts from miles around to see her. He told me all this. He got the berth as, what we should call, a chief mate. He seemed to think it had been a feather in his cap; and, in his own corner of the world, this lover of life was of good parentage.

The burgomaster had advanced ideas in the ship-owning line. At that time not everyone would have known enough to think of despatching a cargo steamer to the Pacific. But he loaded her with pitch-pine deals and sent her off to hunt for her luck. Wellington was to be the first port, I fancy. It doesn't matter, because in latitude 44° south and somewhere half-way between Good Hope and New Zealand the tail-shaft broke and the propeller dropped off.

They were steaming then with a fresh gale on the quarter and all their canvas set, to help the engines. But by itself the sail power was not enough to keep way on her. When the propeller went the ship broached-to at once, and the masts got whipped overboard.

The disadvantage of being dismasted consisted in this, that they had nothing to hoist flags on to make themselves visible at a distance. In the course of the first few days several ships failed to sight them; and the gale was drifting them out of the usual track. The voyage had been, from the first, neither very successful nor very harmonious. There had been quarrels on board. The captain was a clever, melancholic man, who had no unusual grip on his crew. The ship had been amply provisioned for the passage, but, somehow or other, several barrels of meat were found spoiled on opening, and had been thrown overboard soon after leaving home, as a sanitary measure. Afterwards the crew of the *Borgmester Dahl* thought of that rotten carrion with tears of regret, covetousness and despair.

She drove south. To begin with, there had been an appearance of organisation, but soon the bonds of discipline became relaxed. A sombre idleness succeeded. They looked with sullen eyes at the horizon. The gales increased: she lay in the trough, the seas made a clean breach over her. On one frightful night, when they expected their hulk to turn over with them every moment, a heavy sea broke on board, deluged the store-rooms and spoiled the best part of the remaining provisions. It seems the hatch had not been properly secured. This instance of neglect is characteristic of utter discouragement. Falk tried to inspire some energy into his captain, but failed. From that time he retired more into himself, always trying to do his utmost in the situation. It grew worse. Gale succeeded gale, with black mountains of water hurling themselves on the *Borgmester Dahl.* Some of the men never left their bunks; many became quarrelsome. The chief-engineer, an old man, refused to speak at all to anybody. Others shut themselves up in their berths to cry. On calm days the inert steamer rolled on a leaden sea under a murky sky, or showed, in sunshine, the squalor of sea waifs, the dried white salt, the rust, the jagged broken places. Then the gales came again. They kept body and soul together on short rations. Once, an English ship, scudding in a storm, tried to stand by them, heaving-to pluckily under their lee. The seas swept her decks; the men in oilskins clinging to her rigging looked at them, and they made desperate signs over their shattered bulwarks. Suddenly her main-topsail went, yard and all, in a terrific squall; she had to bear up under bare poles and disappeared.

Other ships had spoken them before, but at first they had refused to be taken off, expecting the assistance of some steamer. There were very few steamers in those latitudes then; and when they desired to leave this dead and drifting carcase, no ship came in sight. They had drifted south out of men's knowledge. They failed to attract the attention of a lonely whaler: and very soon the edge of the polar ice-cap rose from the sea and closed the southern horizon like a wall. One morning they were alarmed by finding themselves floating amongst detached pieces of ice. But the fear of sinking passed away like their vigour, like their hopes; the shocks of the floes knocking against the ship's side could not rouse them from their apathy: and the *Borgmester Dahl* drifted out again, unharmed, into open water. They hardly noticed the change.

The funnel had gone overboard in one of the heavy rolls; two of their three boats had disappeared, washed away in bad weather, and the davits swung to and fro, unsecured, with chafed ropes' ends waggling to the roll. Nothing was done on board, and Falk told me how he had often listened to the water washing about the dark engine-room where the engines, stilled for ever, were decaying slowly into a mass of rust, as the stilled heart decays within the lifeless body. At first, after the loss of the motive power, the tiller had been thoroughly secured by lashings. But in course of time these had rotted, chafed, rusted, parting one by one: and the rudder, freed, banged heavily to and fro night and day, sending dull shocks through the whole frame of the vessel. This was dangerous. Nobody cared enough to lift a little finger. He told me that even now sometimes waking up at night, he fancied he could hear the dull vibrating thuds. The pintles carried away, and it dropped off at last.

The final catastrophe came with the sending off of their one remaining boat. It was Falk who had managed to preserve her intact, and now it was agreed that some of the hands should sail away into the track of the shipping to procure assistance. She was provisioned with all the food they could spare for the six who were to go. They waited for a fine day. It was long in coming. At last one morning they lowered her into the water.

Directly, in that demoralised crowd, trouble broke out. Two men who had no business there had jumped into the boat under the pretence of unhooking the tackles, while some sort of squabble arose on the deck amongst these weak, tottering spectres of a ship's company. The captain, who had been for days living secluded and unapproachable in the chart-room, came to the rail. He ordered the two men to come up on board and menaced them with his revolver. They pretended to obey, but suddenly cutting the boat's painter, gave a shove against the ship's side and made ready to hoist the sail.

'Shoot, sir! Shoot them down!' cried Falk – 'and I will jump overboard to regain the boat.' But the captain, after taking aim with an irresolute arm, turned suddenly away.

A howl of rage arose. Falk dashed into his cabin for his own pistol. When he returned it was too late. Two more men had leaped into the water, but the fellows in the boat beat them off with the oars, hoisted the boat's lug and sailed away. They were never heard of again.

Consternation and despair possessed the remaining ship's company, till the apathy of utter hopelessness re-asserted its sway. That day a fireman committed suicide, running up on deck with his throat cut from ear to ear, to the horror of all hands. He was thrown overboard. The captain had locked himself in the chart-room, and Falk, knocking vainly for admittance, heard him reciting over and over again the names of his wife and children, not as if calling upon them or commending them to God, but in a mechanical voice like an exercise of memory. Next day the doors of the chart-room were swinging open to the roll of the ship, and the captain had disappeared. He must during the night have jumped into the sea. Falk locked both the doors and kept the keys.

The organised life of the ship had come to an end. The solidarity of the men had gone. They became indifferent to each other. It was Falk who took in hand the distribution of such food as remained. They boiled their boots for soup to eke out the rations, which only made their hunger more intolerable. Sometimes whispers of hate were heard passing between the languid skeletons that drifted endlessly to and fro, north and south, east and west, upon that carcase of a ship.

And in this lies the grotesque horror of this sombre story. The last extremity of sailors, overtaking a small boat or a frail craft, seems easier to bear, because of the direct danger of the seas. The confined space, the close contact, the imminent menace of the waves, seem to draw men together, in spite of madness, suffering and despair. But there was a ship – safe, convenient, roomy: a ship with beds, bedding, knives, forks, comfortable cabins, glass and china, and a complete cook's galley, pervaded, ruled and possessed by the pitiless spectre of starvation. The lamp oil had been drunk, the wicks cut up for food, the candles eaten. At night she floated dark in all her recesses and full of fears. One day Falk came upon a man gnawing a splinter of pine wood. Suddenly he threw the piece of wood away, tottered to the rail, and fell over. Falk, too late to prevent the act, saw him claw the ship's side desperately before he went down. Next day another man did the same thing, after uttering horrible imprecations. But this one somehow managed to get hold of the broken rudder chains and hung on there, silently. Falk set about trying to save him, and all the time the man, holding with both hands, looked at him anxiously with his sunken eyes. Then, just as Falk was ready to put his hand on him, the man let go his hold and sank like a stone. Falk reflected on these sights. His heart revolted against the horror of death, and he said to himself that he would struggle for every precious minute of his life.

One afternoon – as the survivors lay about on the after deck – the carpenter, a tall man with a black beard, spoke of the last sacrifice. There was nothing eatable left on board. Nobody said a word to this; but that company separated quickly, these listless feeble spectres slunk off one by one to hide in fear of each other. Falk and the carpenter remained on deck together. Falk liked the big carpenter. He had been the best man of the lot, helpful and ready as long as there was anything to do, the longest hopeful, and had preserved to the last some vigour and decision of mind.

They did not speak to each other. Henceforth no voices were to be heard conversing sadly on board that ship. After a time the carpenter tottered away forward; but later on Falk, going to drink at the fresh-water pump, had the inspiration to turn his head. The carpenter had stolen upon him from behind, and, summoning all his strength, was aiming with a crowbar a blow at the back of his skull.

Dodging just in time, Falk made his escape and ran into his cabin. While he was loading his revolver there, he heard the sound of heavy blows struck upon the bridge. The locks of the chart-room doors were slight, they flew open, and the carpenter, possessing himself of the captain's revolver, fired a shot of defiance.

Falk was about to go on deck and have it out at once, when he remarked that one of the ports of his cabin commanded the approaches to the fresh water-pump. Instead of going out he remained in and secured the door. 'The best man shall survive,' he said to himself – and the other, he reasoned, must at sometime or other come there to drink. These starving men would drink often to cheat the pangs of their hunger. But the carpenter too must have noticed the position of the port. They were the two best men in the ship, and the game was with them. All the rest of the day Falk saw no one and heard no sound. At night he strained his eyes. It was dark – he heard a rustling noise once, but he was certain that no one could have come near the pump. It was to the left of his deck port, and he could not have failed to see a man, for the night was clear and starry. He saw nothing; towards morning another faint noise made him suspicious. Deliberately and quietly he unlocked his door. He had not slept, and had not given way to the horror of the situation. He wanted to live.

But during the night the carpenter, without at all trying to approach the pump, had managed to creep quietly along the starboard bulwark, and, unseen, had crouched down right under Falk's deck port. When daylight came he rose up suddenly, looked in, and putting his arm through the round brass-framed opening, fired at Falk within a foot. He missed – and Falk, instead of attempting to seize the arm holding the weapon, opened his door unexpectedly, and with the muzzle of his long revolver nearly touching the other's side, shot him dead.

The best man had survived. Both of them had at the beginning just strength enough to stand on their feet, and both had displayed pitiless resolution, endurance, cunning and courage – all the qualities of classic heroism. At once Falk threw overboard the captain's revolver. He was a born monopolist. Then after the report of the two shots, followed by a profound silence, there crept out into the cold, cruel dawn of Antarctic regions, from various hiding-places, over the deck of that dismantled corpse of a ship floating on a grey sea ruled by iron necessity and with a heart of ice – there crept into view one by one, cautious, slow, eager, glaring, and unclean, a band of hungry and livid skeletons. Falk faced them, the possessor of the only fire-arm on board, and the second best man – the carpenter – was lying dead between him and them.

'He was eaten, of course,' I said.

He bent his head slowly, shuddered a little, drawing his hands over his face, and said, 'I had never any quarrel with that man. But there were our lives between him and me.'

Why continue the story of that ship, that story before which, with its fresh-water pump like a spring of death, its man with the weapon, the sea ruled by iron necessity, its spectral band swayed by terror and hope, its mute and unhearing heaven? – the fable of the *Flying Dutchman* with its convention of crime and its sentimental retribution fades like a graceful wreath, like a wisp of white mist. What is there to say that every one of us cannot guess for himself? I believe Falk began by going through the ship, revolver in hand, to annex all the matches. Those starving wretches had plenty of matches! He had no mind to have the ship set on fire under his feet, either from hate or from despair. He lived in the open, camping on the bridge, commanding all the after deck and the only approach to the pump. He lived! Some of the others lived too – concealed, anxious, coming out one by one from their hiding-places at the seductive sound of a shot. And he was not selfish. They shared, but only three of them all were alive when a whaler, returning from her cruising-ground, nearly ran over the waterlogged hull of the *Borgmester Dahl*, which, it seems, in the end had in some way sprung a leak in both her holds, but being loaded with deals could not sink.

'They all died,' Falk said. 'These three too, afterwards. But I would not die. All died, all! under this terrible misfortune. But was I, too, to throw away my life? Could I? Tell me, captain? I was alone there, quite alone, just like the others. Each man was alone. Was I to give up my revolver? Who to? Or was I to throw it into the sea? What would have been the good? Only the best man would survive. It was a great, terrible, and cruel misfortune.'

He had survived! I saw him before me as though preserved for a witness to the mighty truth of an unerring and eternal principle. Great beads of perspiration stood on his forehead. And suddenly it struck the table with a heavy blow, as he fell forward throwing his hands out.

'And this is worse,' he cried. 'This is a worse pain! This is more terrible.'

He made my heart thump with the profound conviction of his cry. And after he had left me alone I called up before my mental eye the image of the girl weeping silently, abundantly, patiently, and as if irresistibly. I thought of her tawny hair. I thought how, if unplaited, it would have covered her all round as low as the hips, like the hair of a siren. And she had bewitched him. Fancy a man who would guard his own life with the inflexibility of a pitiless and immovable fate, being brought to lament that once a crowbar had missed his skull! The sirens sing and lure to death, but this one had been weeping silently as if for the pity of his life. She was the tender and voiceless siren of this appalling navigator. He evidently wanted to live his whole conception of life. Nothing else would do. And she too was a servant of that life that, in the midst of death, cries aloud to our senses. She was eminently fitted to interpret for him its feminine side. And in her own way, and with her own profusion of sensuous charms, she also seemed to illustrate the eternal truth of an unerring principle. I don't know though what sort of principle Hermann illustrated when he turned up early on board my ship with a most perplexed air. It struck me, however, that he too would do his best to survive. He seemed greatly calmed on the subject of Falk, but still very full of it.

'What is it you said I was last night? You know,' he asked after some preliminary talk. 'Too – too – I don't know. A very funny word.'

'Squeamish?' I suggested.

'Yes. What does it mean?'

'That you exaggerate things – to yourself. Without enquiry, and so on.'

He seemed to turn it over in his mind. We went on talking. This Falk was the plague of his life. Upsetting everybody like this! Mrs Hermann was rather unwell this morning. His niece was crying still. There was nobody to look after the children. He struck his umbrella on the deck. She would be like that for months. Fancy carrying all the way home, second class, a perfectly useless girl who is crying all the time. It was bad for Lena too, he observed; but on what grounds I could not guess. Perhaps of the bad example. That child was already sorrowing and crying enough over the rag doll. Nicholas was really the least sentimental person of the family.

'Why does she weep?' I asked.

'From pity,' cried Hermann.

It was impossible to make out women. Mrs Hermann was the only one he pretended to understand. She was very, very upset and doubtful.

'Doubtful about what?' I asked.

He averted his eyes and did not answer this. It was impossible to make them out. For instance, his niece was weeping for Falk. Now he (Hermann) would like to wring his neck – but then . . . He supposed he had too tender a heart. 'Frankly,' he asked at last, 'what do you think of what we heard last night, captain?'

'In all these tales,' I observed, 'there is always a good deal of exaggeration.'

And not letting him recover from his surprise I assured him that I knew all the details. He begged me not to repeat them. His heart was too tender. They made him feel unwell. Then, looking at his feet and speaking very slowly, he supposed that he need not see much of them after they were married. For, indeed, he could not bear the sight of Falk. On the other hand it was ridiculous to take home a girl with her head turned. A girl that weeps all the time and is of no help to her aunt.

'Now you will be able to do with one cabin only on your passage home,' I said.

'Yes, I had thought of that,' he said brightly, almost. 'Yes! Himself, his wife, four children – one cabin might do. Whereas if his niece went . . . '

'And what does Mrs Hermann say to it?' I enquired.

Mrs Hermann did not know whether a man of that sort could make a girl happy – she had been greatly deceived in Captain Falk. She had been very upset last night.

Those good people did not seem to be able to retain an impression for a whole twelve hours. I assured him on my own personal knowledge that Falk possessed in himself all the qualities to make his niece's future prosperous. He said he was glad to hear this, and that he would tell his wife. Then the object of the visit came out. He wished me to help him to resume relations with Falk. His niece, he said, had expressed the hope I would do so in my kindness. He was evidently anxious that I should, for though he seemed to have forgotten nine-tenths of his last night's opinions and the whole of his indignation, yet he evidently feared to be sent to the right-about. 'You told me he was very much in love,' he concluded slyly, and leered in a sort of bucolic way.

As soon as he had left my ship I called Falk on board by signal – the tug still lying at the anchorage. He took the news with calm gravity, as though he had all along expected the stars to fight for him in their courses.

I saw them once more together, and only once – on the quarter-deck of the *Diana*. Hermann sat smoking with a shirt-sleeved elbow hooked over the back of his chair. Mrs Hermann was sewing alone. As Falk stepped over the gangway, Hermann's niece, with a slight swish of the skirt and a swift friendly nod to me, glided past my chair.

They met in sunshine abreast of the mainmast. He held her hands and looked down at them, and she looked up at him with her candid and unseeing glance. It seemed to me they had come together as if attracted, drawn and guided to each other by a mysterious influence. They were a complete couple. In her grey frock, palpitating with life, generous of form, olympian and simple, she was indeed the siren to fascinate that dark navigator, this ruthless lover of the five senses. From afar I seemed to feel the masculine strength with which he grasped those hands she had extended to him with a womanly swiftness. Lena, a little pale, nursing her beloved lump of dirty rags, ran towards her big friend; and then in the drowsy silence of the good old ship Mrs Hermann's voice rang out so changed that it made me spin round in my chair to see what was the matter.

'Lena, come here!' she screamed. And this good-natured matron gave me a wavering glance, dark and full of fearsome distrust. The child ran back, surprised, to her knee. But the two, standing before each other in sunlight with clasped hands, had heard nothing, had seen nothing and no one. Three feet away from them in the shade a seaman sat on a spar, very busy splicing a strop, and dipping his fingers into a tar-pot, as if utterly unaware of their existence.

When I returned in command of another ship, some five years afterwards, Mr and Mrs Falk had left the place. I should not wonder if Schomberg's tongue had succeeded at last in scaring Falk away for good; and, indubitably, there was a tale still going about the town of a certain Falk, owner of a tug, who had won his wife at cards from the captain of an English ship.

JOSEPH CONRAD

THE SHADOW-LINE

A CONFESSION

"Worthy of my undying regard"

LONDON & TORONTO
J. M. DENT & SONS LTD.
PARIS: J. M. DENT ET FILS

The title page as it appeared in the first edition

TO

BORYS AND ALL OTHERS

WHO LIKE HIMSELF HAVE CROSSED
IN EARLY YOUTH THE SHADOW-LINE
OF THEIR GENERATION

WITH LOVE

AUTHOR'S NOTE

This story, which I admit to be in its brevity a fairly complex piece of work, was not intended to touch on the supernatural. Yet more than one critic has been inclined to take it in that way, seeing in it an attempt on my part to give the fullest scope to my imagination by taking it beyond the confines of the world of living, suffering humanity. But as a matter of fact my imagination is not made of stuff so elastic as all that. I believe that if I attempted to put the strain of the supernatural on it it would fail deplorably and exhibit an unlovely gap. But I could never have attempted such a thing, because all my moral and intellectual being is penetrated by an invincible conviction that whatever falls under the dominion of our senses must be in nature and, however exceptional, cannot differ in its essence from all the other effects of the visible and tangible world of which we are a self-conscious part. The world of the living contains enough marvels and mysteries as it is; marvels and mysteries acting upon our emotions and intelligence in ways so inexplicable that it would almost justify the conception of life as an enchanted state. No, I am too firm in my consciousness of the marvellous to be ever fascinated by the mere supernatural, which (take it any way you like) is but a manufactured article, the fabrication of minds insensitive to the intimate delicacies of our relation to the dead and to the living, in their countless multitudes; a desecration of our tenderest memories; an outrage on our dignity.

Whatever my native modesty may be it will never condescend so low as to seek help for my imagination within those vain imaginings common to all ages and that in themselves are enough to fill all lovers of mankind with unutterable sadness. As to the effect of a mental or moral shock on a common mind, it is quite a legitimate subject for study and description. Mr Burns' moral being receives a severe shock in his relations with his late captain, and this in his diseased state turns into a mere superstitious fancy compounded of fear and animosity. This fact is one of the elements of the story, but there is nothing supernatural in it, nothing so to speak from beyond the confines of this world which in all conscience holds enough mystery and terror in itself.

Perhaps if I had published this tale, which I have had for a long time in my mind, under the title of 'First Command' no suggestion of the supernatural would have been found in it by any impartial reader, critical or otherwise. I will not consider here the origins of the feeling in which its actual title, 'The Shadow-Line', occurred to my mind. Primarily the aim of this piece of writing was the presentation of certain facts which certainly were associated with the change from youth, care-free and fervent, to the more self-conscious and more poignant period of maturer life. Nobody can doubt that before the supreme trial of a whole generation I had an acute consciousness of the minute and insignificant character of my own obscure experience. There could be no question here of any parallelism. That notion never entered my head. But there was a feeling of identity, though with an enormous difference of scale – as of one single drop measured against the bitter and stormy immensity of an ocean. And this was very natural too. For when we begin to meditate on the meaning of our own past it seems to fill all the world in its profundity and its magnitude. This book was written in the last three months of the year 1916. Of all the subjects of which a writer of tales is more or less conscious within himself this is the only one I found it possible to attempt at the time. The depth and the nature of the mood with which I approached it is best expressed perhaps in the dedication which strikes me now as a most disproportionate thing – as but another instance of the overwhelming greatness of our own emotion to ourselves.

This much having been said, I may pass on now to a few remarks about the mere material of the story. As to locality it belongs to that part of the Eastern Seas from which I have carried away into my writing life the greatest number of suggestions. From my statement that I thought of this story for a long time under the title of 'First Command' the reader may guess that it is concerned with my personal experience. And as a matter of fact it *is* personal experience seen in perspective with the eye of the mind and coloured by that affection one can't help feeling for such events of one's life as one has no reason to be ashamed of. And that affection is as intense (I appeal here to universal experience) as the shame, and almost the anguish with which one remembers some unfortunate occurrences, down to mere mistakes in speech, that have been perpetrated by one in the past. The effect of perspective in memory is to make things loom large because the essentials stand out isolated from their surroundings of insignificant daily facts which have naturally faded out of one's mind. I remember that period of my sea-life with pleasure because begun inauspiciously it turned out in the end a success from a personal point of view, leaving a tangible proof in the terms of the letter the owners of the ship wrote to me two years afterwards when I resigned my command in order to come home. This resignation marked the beginning of another phase of my seaman's life, its terminal phase, if I may say so, which in its own way has coloured another portion of my writings. I didn't know then how near its end my sea-life was, and therefore I felt no sorrow except at parting with the ship. I was sorry also to break my connection with the firm who owned her and who were pleased to receive with friendly kindness and give their confidence to a man who had entered their service in an accidental manner and in very adverse circumstances. Without disparaging the earnestness of my purpose I suspect now that luck had no small part in the success of the trust reposed in me. And one cannot help remembering with pleasure the time when one's best efforts were seconded by a run of luck.

The words '*Worthy of my undying regard*' selected by me for the motto on the title page are quoted from the text of the book itself; and, though one of my critics surmised that they applied to the ship, it is evident from the place where they stand that they refer to the men of that ship's company: complete strangers to their new captain and who yet stood by him so well during those twenty days that seemed to have been passed on the brink of a slow and agonising destruction. And *that* is the greatest memory of all! For surely it is a great thing to have commanded a handful of men worthy of one's undying regard.

J. C.
1920

– D'autre fois, calme plat, grand miroir
De mon désespoir.

BAUDELAIRE

Chapter 1

ONLY THE YOUNG have such moments. I don't mean the very young. No. The very young have, properly speaking, no moments. It is the privilege of early youth to live in advance of its days in all the beautiful continuity of hope which knows no pauses and no introspection.

One closes behind one the little gate of mere boyishness – and enters an enchanted garden. Its very shades glow with promise. Every turn of the path has its seduction. And it isn't because it is an undiscovered country. One knows well enough that all mankind had streamed that way. It is the charm of universal experience from which one expects an uncommon or personal sensation – a bit of one's own.

One goes on recognising the landmarks of the predecessors, excited, amused, taking the hard luck and the good luck together – the kicks and the halfpence, as the saying is – the picturesque common lot that holds so many possibilities for the deserving or perhaps for the lucky. Yes. One goes on. And the time, too, goes on – till one perceives ahead a shadow-line warning one that the region of early youth, too, must be left behind.

This is the period of life in which such moments of which I have spoken are likely to come. What moments? Why, the moments of boredom, of weariness, of dissatisfaction. Rash moments. I mean moments when the still young are inclined to commit rash actions, such as getting married suddenly or else throwing up a job for no reason.

This is not a marriage story. It wasn't so bad as that with me. My action, rash as it was, had more the character of divorce – almost of desertion. For no reason on which a sensible person could put a finger I threw up my job – chucked my berth – left the ship of which the worst that could be said was that she was a steamship and therefore, perhaps, not entitled to that blind loyalty which . . . However, it's no use trying to put a gloss on what even at the time I myself half suspected to be a caprice.

It was in an Eastern port. She was an Eastern ship, inasmuch as then she belonged to that port. She traded among dark islands on a blue reef-scarred sea, with the Red Ensign over the taffrail and at her masthead a house-flag, also red, but with a green border and with a white crescent in it. For an Arab owned her, and a Syed at that. Hence the green border on the flag. He was the head of a great House of Straits Arabs, but as loyal a subject of the complex British Empire as you could find east of the Suez Canal. World politics did not trouble him at all, but he had a great occult power amongst his own people.

It was all one to us who owned the ship. He had to employ white men in the shipping part of his business, and many of those he so employed had never set eyes on him from the first to the last day. I myself saw him but once, quite accidentally on a wharf – an old, dark little man, blind in one eye, in a snowy robe and yellow slippers. He was having his hand severely kissed by a crowd of Malay pilgrims to whom he had done some favour, in the way of food and money. His alms-giving, I have heard, was most extensive, covering almost the whole Archipelago. For isn't it said that 'The charitable man is the friend of Allah'?

Excellent (and picturesque) Arab owner, about whom one needed not to trouble one's head, a most excellent Scottish ship – for she was that from the keel up – excellent sea-boat, easy to keep clean, most handy in every way, and if it had not been for her internal propulsion, worthy of any man's love, I cherish to this day a profound respect for her memory. As to the kind of trade she was engaged in and the character of my shipmates, I could not have been happier if I had had the life and the men made to my order by a benevolent Enchanter.

And suddenly I left all this. I left it in that, to us, inconsequential manner in which a bird flies away from a comfortable branch. It was as though all unknowing I had heard a whisper or seen something. Well – perhaps! One day I was perfectly right and the next everything was gone – glamour, flavour, interest, contentment – everything. It was one of these moments, you know. The green sickness of late youth descended on me and carried me off. Carried me off that ship, I mean.

We were only four white men on board, with a large crew of Kalashes and two Malay petty officers. The Captain stared hard as if wondering what ailed me. But he was a sailor, and he, too, had been young at one time. Presently a smile came to lurk under his thick iron-grey moustache, and he observed that, of course, if I felt I must go he couldn't keep me by main force. And it was arranged that I should be paid off the next morning. As I was going out of the chart-room he added suddenly, in a peculiar wistful tone, that he hoped I would find what I was so anxious to go and look for. A soft, cryptic utterance which seemed to reach deeper than any diamond-hard tool could have done. I do believe he understood my case.

But the second engineer attacked me differently. He was a sturdy young Scot, with a smooth face and light eyes. His honest red countenance emerged out of the engine-room companion and then the whole robust man, with shirt sleeves turned up, wiping slowly the massive fore-arms with a lump of cotton-waste. And his light eyes expressed bitter distaste, as though our friendship had turned to ashes. He said weightily: 'Oh! Aye! I've been thinking it was about time for you to run away home and get married to some silly girl.'

It was tacitly understood in the port that John Nieven was a fierce mysogynist; and the absurd character of the sally convinced me that he meant to be nasty – very nasty – had meant to say the most crushing thing he could think of. My laugh sounded deprecatory. Nobody but a friend could be so angry as that. I became a little crestfallen. Our chief engineer also took a characteristic view of my action, but in a kindlier spirit.

He was young, too, but very thin, and with a mist of fluffy brown beard all round his haggard face. All day long, at sea or in harbour, he could be seen walking hastily up and down the after-deck, wearing an intense, spiritually rapt expression, which was caused by a perpetual consciousness of unpleasant physical sensations in his internal economy. For he was a confirmed dyspeptic. His view of my case was very simple. He said it was nothing but deranged liver. Of course! He suggested I should stay for another trip and mean-time dose myself with a certain patent medicine in which his own belief was absolute. 'I'll tell you what I'll do. I'll buy you two bottles, out of my own pocket. There. I can't say fairer than that, can I?'

I believe he would have perpetrated the atrocity (or generosity) at the merest sign of weakening on my part. By that time, however, I was more discontented, disgusted, and dogged than ever. The past eighteen months, so full of new and varied experience, appeared a dreary, prosaic waste of days. I felt – how shall I express it? – that there was no truth to be got out of them.

What truth? I should have been hard put to it to explain. Probably, if pressed, I would have burst into tears simply. I was young enough for that.

Next day the Captain and I transacted our business in the harbour office. It was a lofty, big, cool, white room, where the screened light of day glowed serenely. Everybody in it – the officials, the public – were in white. Only the heavy polished desks gleamed darkly in a central avenue, and some papers lying on them were blue. Enormous punkahs sent from on high a gentle draught through that immaculate interior and upon our perspiring heads.

The official behind the desk we approached grinned amiably and kept it up till, in answer to his perfunctory question, 'Sign off and on again?' my Captain answered, 'No! Signing off for good.' And then his grin vanished in sudden solemnity. He did not look at me again till he handed me my papers with a sorrowful expression, as if they had been my passports for Hades.

While I was putting them away he murmured some question to the Captain, and I heard the latter answer good-humouredly: 'No. He leaves us to go home.'

'Oh!' the other exclaimed, nodding mournfully over my sad condition.

I didn't know him outside the official building, but he leaned forward over the desk to shake hands with me, compassionately, as one would with some poor devil going out to be hanged; and I am afraid I performed my part ungraciously, in the hardened manner of an impenitent criminal.

No homeward-bound mail-boat was due for three or four days. Being now a man without a ship, and having for a time broken my connection with the sea – become, in fact, a mere potential passenger – it would have been more appropriate perhaps if I had gone to stay at an hotel. There it was, too, within a stone's throw of the harbour office, low, but somehow palatial, displaying its white, pillared pavilions surrounded by trim grass plots. I would have felt a passenger indeed in there! I gave it a hostile glance and directed my steps towards the Officers' Sailors' Home.

I walked in the sunshine, disregarding it, and in the shade of the big trees on the esplanade without enjoying it. The heat of the tropical East descended through the leafy boughs, enveloping my thinly-clad body, clinging to my rebellious discontent, as if to rob it of its freedom.

The Officers' Home was a large bungalow with a wide verandah and a curiously suburban-looking little garden of bushes and a few trees between it and the street. That institution partook somewhat of the character of a residential club, but with a slightly Governmental flavour about it, because it was administered by the Harbour

Office. Its manager was officially styled Chief Steward. He was an unhappy, wizened little man, who if put into a jockey's rig would have looked the part to perfection. But it was obvious that at sometime or other in his life, in some capacity or other, he had been connected with the sea. Possibly in the comprehensive capacity of a failure.

I should have thought his employment a very easy one, but he used to affirm for some reason or other that his job would be the death of him someday. It was rather mysterious. Perhaps everything naturally was too much trouble for him. He certainly seemed to hate having people in the house.

On entering it I thought he must be feeling pleased. It was as still as a tomb. I could see no one in the living rooms; and the verandah, too, was empty, except for a man at the far end dozing prone in a long chair. At the noise of my footsteps he opened one horribly fish-like eye. He was a stranger to me. I retreated from there, and, crossing the dining-room – a very bare apartment with a motionless punkah hanging over the centre table – I knocked at a door labelled in black letters: 'Chief Steward'.

The answer to my knock being a vexed and doleful plaint: 'Oh, dear! Oh, dear! What is it now?' I went in at once.

It was a strange room to find in the tropics. Twilight and stuffiness reigned in there. The fellow had hung enormously ample, dusty, cheap lace curtains over his windows, which were shut. Piles of cardboard boxes, such as milliners and dressmakers use in Europe, cumbered the corners; and by some means he had procured for himself the sort of furniture that might have come out of a respectable parlour in the East End of London – a horsehair sofa, armchairs of the same. I glimpsed grimy antimacassars scattered over that horrid upholstery, which was awe-inspiring, insomuch that one could not guess what mysterious accident, need, or fancy had collected it there. Its owner had taken off his tunic, and in white trousers and a thin short-sleeved singlet prowled behind the chair-backs nursing his meagre elbows.

An exclamation of dismay escaped him when he heard that I had come for a stay; but he could not deny that there were plenty of vacant rooms.

'Very well. Can you give me the one I had before?'

He emitted a faint moan from behind a pile of cardboard boxes on the table, which might have contained gloves or handkerchiefs or neckties. I wonder what the fellow did keep in them? There was a smell of decaying coral, or Oriental dust, of zoological specimens in that den of his. I could only see the top of his head and his unhappy eyes levelled at me over the barrier.

'It's only for a couple of days,' I said, intending to cheer him up.

'Perhaps you would like to pay in advance?' he suggested eagerly.

'Certainly not!' I burst out directly I could speak. 'Never heard of such a thing! This is the most infernal cheek . . . '

He had seized his head in both hands – a gesture of despair which checked my indignation.

'Oh, dear! Oh, dear! Don't fly out like this. I am asking everybody.'

'I don't believe it,' I said bluntly.

'Well, I am going to. And if you gentlemen all agreed to pay in advance I could make Hamilton pay up too. He's always turning up ashore dead broke, and even when he has some money he won't settle his bills. I don't know what to do with him. He swears at me and tells me I can't chuck a white man out into the street here. So if you only would . . . '

I was amazed. Incredulous too. I suspected the fellow of gratuitous impertinence. I told him with marked emphasis that I would see him and Hamilton hanged first, and requested him to conduct me to my room with no more of his nonsense. He produced then a key from somewhere and led the way out of his lair, giving me a vicious sidelong look in passing.

'Anyone I know staying here?' I asked him before he left my room.

He had recovered his usual pained impatient tone, and said that Captain Giles was there, back from a Solo Sea trip. Two other guests were staying also. He paused. And, of course, Hamilton, he added.

'Oh, yes! Hamilton,' I said, and the miserable creature took himself off with a final groan.

His impudence still rankled when I came into the dining-room at tiffin time. He was there on duty overlooking the Chinamen servants. The tiffin was laid on one end only of the long table, and the punkah was stirring the hot air lazily – mostly above a barren waste of polished wood.

We were four around the cloth. The dozing stranger from the chair was one. Both his eyes were partly opened now, but they did not seem to see anything. He was supine. The dignified person next him, with short side whiskers and a carefully scraped chin, was, of course, Hamilton. I have never seen anyone so full of dignity for the station in life Providence had been pleased to place him in. I had been told that he regarded me as a rank outsider. He raised not only his eyes, but his eyebrows as well, at the sound I made pulling back my chair.

Captain Giles was at the head of the table. I exchanged a few words of greeting with him and sat down on his left. Stout and pale, with a great shiny dome of a bald forehead and prominent brown eyes, he might have been anything but a seaman. You would not have been surprised to learn that he was an architect. To me (I know how absurd it is) to me he looked like a churchwarden. He had the appearance of a man from whom you would expect sound advice, moral sentiments, with perhaps a platitude or two thrown in on occasion, not from a desire to dazzle, but from honest conviction.

Though very well known and appreciated in the shipping world, he had no regular employment. He did not want it. He had his own peculiar position. He was an expert. An expert in – how shall I say it? – in intricate navigation. He was supposed to know more about remote and imperfectly charted parts of the Archipelago than any man living. His brain must have been a perfect warehouse of reefs, positions, bearings, images of headlands, shapes of obscure coasts, aspects of innumerable islands, desert and otherwise. Any ship, for instance, bound on a trip to Palawan or somewhere that way would have Captain Giles on board, either in temporary command or 'to assist the master'. It was said that he had a retaining fee from a wealthy firm of Chinese steamship owners, in view of such services. Besides, he was always ready to relieve any man who wished to take a spell ashore for a time. No owner was ever known to object to an arrangement of that sort. For it seemed to be the established opinion at the port that Captain Giles was as good as the best, if not a little better. But in Hamilton's view he was an 'outsider'. I believe that for Hamilton the generalisation 'outsider' covered the whole lot of us; though I suppose that he made some distinctions in his mind.

I didn't try to make conversation with Captain Giles, whom I had not seen more than twice in my life. But, of course, he knew who I was. After a while, inclining his big shiny head my way, he addressed me first in his friendly fashion. He presumed from seeing me there, he said, that I had come ashore for a couple of days' leave.

He was a low-voiced man. I spoke a little louder, saying that: No – I had left the ship for good.

'A free man for a bit,' was his comment.

'I suppose I may call myself that – since eleven o'clock,' I said.

Hamilton had stopped eating at the sound of our voices. He laid down his knife and fork gently, got up, and muttering something about 'this infernal heat cutting one's appetite', went out of the room. Almost immediately we heard him leave the house down the verandah steps.

On this Captain Giles remarked easily that the fellow had no doubt gone off to look after my old job. The Chief Steward, who had been leaning against the wall, brought his face of an unhappy goat nearer to the table and addressed us dolefully. His object was to unburden himself of his eternal grievance against Hamilton. The man kept him in hot water with the Harbour Office as to the state of his accounts. He wished to goodness he would get my job, though in truth what would it be? Temporary relief at best.

I said: 'You needn't worry. He won't get my job. My successor is on board already.'

He was surprised, and I believe his face fell a little at the news. Captain Giles gave a soft laugh. We got up and went out on the verandah, leaving the supine stranger to be dealt with by the Chinamen. The last thing I saw they had put a plate with a slice of pine-apple on it before him and stood back to watch what would happen. But the experiment seemed a failure. He sat insensible.

It was imparted to me in a low voice by Captain Giles that this was an officer of some Rajah's yacht which had come into our port to be dry-docked. Must have been 'seeing life' last night, he added, wrinkling his nose in an intimate, confidential way which pleased me vastly. For Captain Giles had prestige. He was credited with wonderful adventures and with some mysterious tragedy in his life. And no man had a word to say against him. He continued: 'I remember him first coming ashore here some years ago. Seems only the other day. He was a nice boy. Oh! these nice boys!'

I could not help laughing aloud. He looked startled, then joined in the laugh. 'No! No! I didn't mean that,' he cried. 'What I meant is that some of them do go soft mighty quick out here.'

Jocularly I suggested the beastly heat as the first cause. But Captain Giles disclosed himself possessed of a deeper philosophy. Things out East were made easy for white men. That was all right. The difficulty was to go on keeping white, and some of these nice boys did not know how. He gave me a searching look, and in a benevolent, heavy-uncle manner asked point blank: 'Why did you throw up your berth?'

I became angry all of a sudden; for you can understand how exasperating such a question was to a man who didn't know. I said to myself that I ought to shut up that moralist; and to him aloud I said with challenging politeness: 'Why . . . ? Do you disapprove?'

He was too disconcerted to do more than mutter confusedly: 'I! . . . In a general way . . . ' and then gave me up. But he retired in good order, under the cover of a heavily humorous remark that he, too, was getting soft, and that this was his time for taking his little siesta – when he was on shore. 'Very bad habit. Very bad habit.'

The simplicity of the man would have disarmed a touchiness even more youthful than mine. So when next day at tiffin he bent his head towards me and said that he had met my late Captain last evening, adding in an undertone: 'He's very sorry you left. He had never had a mate that suited him so well,' I answered him earnestly, without any affectation, that I certainly hadn't been so comfortable in any ship or with any commander in all my sea-going days.

'Well – then,' he murmured.

'Haven't you heard, Captain Giles, that I intend to go home?'

'Yes,' he said benevolently. 'I have heard that sort of thing so often before.'

'What of that?' I cried. I thought he was the most dull, unimaginative man I had ever met. I don't know what more I would have said, but the much-belated Hamilton came in just then and took his usual seat. So I dropped into a mumble.

'Anyhow, you shall see it done this time.'

Hamilton, beautifully shaved, gave Captain Giles a curt nod, but didn't even condescend to raise his eyebrows at me; and when he spoke it was only to tell the Chief Steward that the food on his plate wasn't fit to be set before a gentleman. The individual addressed seemed much too unhappy to groan. He only cast his eyes up to the punkah and that was all.

Captain Giles and I got up from the table, and the stranger next to Hamilton followed our example, manoeuvring himself to his feet with difficulty. He, poor fellow, not because he was hungry but I verily believe only to recover his self-respect, had tried to put some of that unworthy food into his mouth. But after dropping his fork twice and generally making a failure of it, he had sat still with an air of intense mortification combined with a ghastly glazed stare. Both Giles and I had avoided looking his way at table.

On the verandah he stopped short on purpose to address to us anxiously a long remark which I failed to understand completely. It sounded like some horrible unknown language. But when Captain Giles, after only an instant for reflection, answered him with homely friendliness, 'Aye, to be sure. You are right there,' he appeared very much gratified indeed, and went away (pretty straight too) to seek a distant long chair.

'What was he trying to say?' I asked with disgust.

'I don't know. Mustn't be down too much on a fellow. He's feeling pretty wretched, you may be sure; and tomorrow he'll feel worse yet.'

Judging by the man's appearance it seemed impossible. I wondered what sort of complicated debauch had reduced him to that unspeakable condition. Captain Giles' benevolence was spoiled by a curious air of complacency which I disliked. I said with a little laugh: 'Well, he will have you to look after him.'

He made a deprecatory gesture, sat down, and took up a paper. I did the same. The papers were old and uninteresting, filled up mostly with dreary stereotyped descriptions of Queen Victoria's first jubilee celebrations. Probably we should have quickly fallen into a tropical afternoon doze if it had not been for Hamilton's voice raised in the dining-room. He was finishing his tiffin there. The big double doors stood wide open permanently, and he could not have had any idea how near to the doorway our chairs were placed. He was heard in a loud, supercilious tone answering some statement ventured by the Chief Steward.

'I am not going to be rushed into anything. They will be glad enough to get a gentleman I imagine. There is no hurry.'

A loud whispering from the steward succeeded and then again Hamilton was heard with even intenser scorn.

'What? That young ass who fancies himself for having been chief mate with Kent so long? . . . Preposterous.'

Giles and I looked at each other. Kent being the name of my late commander, Captain Giles' whisper, 'He's talking of you,' seemed to me sheer waste of breath. The Chief Steward must have stuck to his point whatever it was, because Hamilton was heard again more supercilious, if possible, and also very emphatic: 'Rubbish, my good man! One doesn't *compete* with a rank outsider like that. There's plenty of time.'

Then there was pushing of chairs, footsteps in the next room, and plaintive expostulations from the Steward, who was pursuing Hamilton, even out of doors through the main entrance.

'That's a very insulting sort of man,' remarked Captain Giles – superfluously, I thought. 'Very insulting. You haven't offended him in some way, have you?'

'Never spoke to him in my life,' I said grumpily. 'Can't imagine what he means by competing. He has been trying for my job after I left – and didn't get it. But that isn't exactly competition.'

Captain Giles balanced his big, benevolent head thoughtfully.

'He didn't get it,' he repeated very slowly. 'No, not likely either, with Kent. Kent is no end sorry you left him. He gives you the name of a good seaman too.'

I flung away the paper I was still holding. I sat up, I slapped the table with my open palm. I wanted to know why he would keep harping on that, my absolutely private affair. It was exasperating, really.

Captain Giles silenced me by the perfect equanimity of his gaze. 'Nothing to be annoyed about,' he murmured reasonably, with an evident desire to soothe the childish irritation he had aroused. And he was really a man of an appearance so inoffensive that I tried to explain myself as much as I could. I told him that I did not want to hear any more about what was past and gone. It had been very nice while it lasted, but now it was done with I preferred not to talk about it or even think about it. I had made up my mind to go home.

He listened to the whole tirade in a particular, lending-the-ear attitude, as if trying to detect a false note in it somewhere; then straightened himself up and appeared to ponder sagaciously over the matter.

'Yes. You told me you meant to go home. Anything in view there?'

Instead of telling him that it was none of his business I said sullenly: 'Nothing that I know of.'

I had indeed considered that rather blank side of the situation I had created for myself by leaving suddenly my very satisfactory employment. And I was not very pleased with it. I had it on the tip of my tongue to say that common sense had nothing to do with my action, and that therefore it didn't deserve the interest Captain Giles seemed to be taking in it. But he was puffing at a short wooden pipe now, and looked so guileless, dense, and commonplace, that it seemed hardly worth while to puzzle him either with truth or sarcasm.

He blew a cloud of smoke, then surprised me by a very abrupt: 'Paid your passage money yet?'

Overcome by the shameless pertinacity of a man to whom it was rather difficult to be rude, I replied with exaggerated meekness that I had not done so yet. I thought there would be plenty of time to do that tomorrow.

And I was about to turn away, withdrawing my privacy from his fatuous, objectless attempts to test what sort of stuff it was made of, when he laid down his pipe in an extremely significant manner, you know, as if a critical moment had come, and leaned sideways over the table between us.

'Oh! You haven't yet!' He dropped his voice mysteriously. 'Well, then I think you ought to know that there's something going on here.'

I had never in my life felt more detached from all earthly goings on. Freed from the sea for a time, I preserved the sailor's consciousness of complete independence from all land affairs. How could they concern me? I gazed at Captain Giles' animation with scorn rather than with curiosity.

To his obviously preparatory question whether our Steward had spoken to me that day I said he hadn't. And what's more he would have had precious little encouragement if he had tried to. I didn't want the fellow to speak to me at all.

Unrebuked by my petulance, Captain Giles, with an air of immense sagacity, began to tell me a minute tale about a Harbour Office peon. It was absolutely pointless. A peon was seen walking that morning on the verandah with a letter in his hand. It was in an official envelope. As the habit of these fellows is, he had shown it to the first white man he came across. That man was our friend in the armchair. He, as I knew, was not in a state to interest himself in any sublunary matters. He could only wave the peon away. The peon then wandered on along the verandah and came upon Captain Giles, who was there by an extraordinary chance . . .

At this point he stopped with a profound look. The letter, he continued, was addressed to the Chief Steward. Now what could Captain Ellis, the Master Attendant, want to write to the Steward for? The fellow went every morning, anyhow, to the Harbour Office with his report, for orders or what not. He hadn't been back more than an hour before there was an office peon chasing him with a note. Now what was that for?

And he began to speculate. It was not for this – and it could not be for that. As to that other thing it was unthinkable.

The fatuousness of all this made me stare. If the man had not been somehow a sympathetic personality I would have resented it like an insult. As it was, I felt only sorry for him. Something remarkably earnest in his gaze prevented me from laughing in his face. Neither did I yawn at him. I just stared.

His tone became a shade more mysterious. Directly the fellow (meaning the Steward) got that note he rushed for his hat and bolted out of the house. But it wasn't because the note called him to the Harbour Office. He didn't go there. He was not absent long enough for that. He came darting back in no time, flung his hat away, and raced about the dining-room moaning and slapping his forehead. All these exciting facts and manifestations had been observed by Captain Giles. He had, it seems, been meditating upon them ever since.

I began to pity him profoundly. And in a tone which I tried to make as little sarcastic as possible I said that I was glad he had found something to occupy his morning hours.

With his disarming simplicity he made me observe, as if it were a matter of some consequence, how strange it was that he should have spent the morning indoors at all. He generally was out before tiffin, visiting various offices, seeing his friends in the harbour, and so on. He had felt out of sorts somewhat on rising. Nothing much. Just enough to make him feel lazy.

All this with a sustained, holding stare which, in conjunction with the general inanity of the discourse, conveyed the impression of mild, dreary lunacy. And when he hitched his chair a little and dropped his voice to the low note of mystery, it flashed upon me that high professional reputation was not necessarily a guarantee of sound mind.

It never occurred to me then that I didn't know in what soundness of mind exactly consisted and what a delicate and, upon the whole, unimportant matter it was. With some idea of not hurting his feelings I blinked at him in an interested manner. But when he proceeded to ask me mysteriously whether I remembered what had passed just now between that Steward of ours and 'that man Hamilton', I only grunted sour assent and turned away my head.

'Aye. But do you remember every word?' he insisted tactfully.

'I don't know. It's none of my business,' I snapped out, consigning, moreover, the Steward and Hamilton aloud to eternal perdition.

I meant to be very energetic and final, but Captain Giles continued to gaze at me thoughtfully. Nothing could stop him. He went on to point out that my personality was involved in that conversation. When I tried to preserve the semblance of unconcern he became positively cruel. I heard what the man had said? Yes? What did I think of it then? – he wanted to know.

Captain Giles' appearance excluding the suspicion of mere sly malice, I came to the conclusion that he was simply the most tactless idiot on earth. I almost despised myself for the weakness of attempting to enlighten his common understanding. I started to explain that I did not think anything whatever. Hamilton was not worth a thought. What such an offensive loafer . . . – 'Aye! that he is,' interjected Captain Giles – . . . thought or said was below any decent man's contempt, and I did not propose to take the slightest notice of it.

This attitude seemed to me so simple and obvious that I was really astonished at Giles giving no sign of assent. Such perfect stupidity was almost interesting.

'What would you like me to do?' I asked, laughing. 'I can't start a row with him because of the opinion he has formed of me. Of course, I've heard of the contemptuous way he alludes to me. But he doesn't intrude his contempt on my notice. He has never expressed it in my hearing. For even just now he didn't know we could hear him. I should only make myself ridiculous.'

That hopeless Giles went on puffing at his pipe moodily. All at once his face cleared, and he spoke.

'You missed my point.'

'Have I? I am very glad to hear it,' I said.

With increasing animation he stated again that I had missed his point. Entirely. And in a tone of growing self-conscious complacency he told me that few things escaped his attention, and he was rather used to think them out, and generally from his experience of life and men arrived at the right conclusion.

This bit of self-praise, of course, fitted excellently the laborious inanity of the whole conversation. The whole thing strengthened in me that obscure feeling of life being but a waste of days, which, half-unconsciously, had driven me out of a comfortable berth, away from men I liked, to flee from the menace of emptiness . . . and to find inanity at the first turn. Here was a man of recognised character and achievement disclosed as an absurd and dreary chatterer. And it was probably like this everywhere – from east to west, from the bottom to the top of the social scale.

A great discouragement fell on me. A spiritual drowsiness. Giles' voice was going on complacently; the very voice of the universal hollow conceit. And I was no longer angry with it. There was nothing original, nothing new, startling, informing to expect from the world: no opportunities to find out something about oneself, no wisdom to acquire, no fun to enjoy. Everything was stupid and overrated, even as Captain Giles was. So be it.

The name of Hamilton suddenly caught my ear and roused me up.

'I thought we had done with him,' I said, with the greatest possible distaste.

'Yes. But considering what we happened to hear just now I think you ought to do it.'

'Ought to do it?' I sat up bewildered. 'Do what?'

Captain Giles confronted me very much surprised.

'Why! Do what I have been advising you to try. You go and ask the Steward what was there in that letter from the Harbour Office. Ask him straight out.'

I remained speechless for a time. Here was something unexpected and original enough to be altogether incomprehensible. I murmured, astounded, 'But I thought it was Hamilton that you . . . '

'Exactly. Don't you let him. You do what I tell you. You tackle that Steward. You'll make him jump, I bet,' insisted Captain Giles, waving his smouldering pipe impressively at me. Then he took three rapid puffs at it.

His aspect of triumphant acuteness was indescribable. Yet the man remained a strangely sympathetic creature. Benevolence radiated from him ridiculously, mildly, impressively. It was irritating, too. But I pointed out coldly, as one who deals with the incomprehensible, that I didn't see any reason to expose myself to a snub from the fellow. He was a very unsatisfactory steward and a miserable wretch besides, but I would just as soon think of tweaking his nose.

'Tweaking his nose,' said Captain Giles in a scandalised tone. 'Much use it would be to you.'

That remark was so irrelevant that one could make no answer to it. But the sense of the absurdity was beginning at last to exercise its well-known fascination. I felt I must not let the man talk to me any more. I got up, observing curtly that he was too much for me – that I couldn't make him out.

Before I had time to move away he spoke again in a changed tone of obstinacy and puffing nervously at his pipe.

'Well – he's a – no account cuss – anyhow. You just ask him. That's all.'

That new manner impressed me – or rather made me pause. But sanity asserting its sway at once, I left the verandah after giving him a mirthless smile. In a few strides I found myself in the dining-room, now cleared and empty. But during that short time various thoughts occurred to me, such as: that Giles had been making fun of me, expecting some amusement at my expense; that I probably looked silly and gullible; that I knew very little of life . . .

The door facing me across the dining-room flew open, to my extreme surprise. It was the door inscribed with the word 'Steward' and the man himself ran out of his stuffy Philistinish lair, in his absurd hunted-animal manner, making for the garden door.

To this day I don't know what made me call after him: 'I say!

Wait a minute.' Perhaps it was the sidelong glance he gave me; or possibly I was yet under the influence of Captain Giles' mysterious earnestness. Well, it was an impulse of some sort; an effect of that force somewhere within our lives which shapes them this way or that. For if these words had not escaped from my lips (my will had nothing to do with that) my existence would, to be sure, have been still a seaman's existence, but directed on now to me utterly inconceivable lines.

No. My will had nothing to do with it. Indeed, no sooner had I made that fateful noise than I became extremely sorry for it. Had the man stopped and faced me I would have had to retire in disorder. For I had no notion to carry out Captain Giles' idiotic joke, either at my own expense or at the expense of the Steward.

But here the old human instinct of the chase came into play. He pretended to be deaf, and I, without thinking a second about it, dashed along my own side of the dining table and cut him off at the very door.

'Why can't you answer when you are spoken to?' I asked roughly.

He leaned against the side of the door. He looked extremely wretched. Human nature is, I fear, not very nice right through. There are ugly spots in it. I found myself growing angry, and that, I believe, only because my quarry looked so woe-begone. Miserable beggar!

I went for him without more ado. 'I understand there was an official communication to the Home from the Harbour Office this morning. Is that so?'

Instead of telling me to mind my own business, as he might have done, he began to whine with an undertone of impudence. He couldn't see me anywhere this morning. He couldn't be expected to run all over the town after me.

'Who wants you to?' I cried. And then my eyes became opened to the inwardness of things and speeches, the triviality of which had been so baffling and tiresome.

I told him I wanted to know what was in that letter. My sternness of tone and behaviour was only half assumed. Curiosity can be a very fierce sentiment – at times.

He took refuge in a silly, muttering sulkiness. It was nothing to me, he mumbled. I had told him I was going home. And since I was going home he didn't see why he should . . .

That was the line of his argument, and it was irrelevant enough to be almost insulting. Insulting to one's intelligence, I mean.

In that twilight region between youth and maturity, in which I had my being then, one is peculiarly sensitive to that kind of insult. I am afraid my behaviour to the Steward became very rough indeed. But it wasn't in him to face out anything or anybody. Drug habit or solitary tippling, perhaps. And when I forgot myself so far as to swear at him he broke down and began to shriek.

I don't mean to say that he made a great outcry. It was a cynical shrieking confession, only faint – piteously faint. It wasn't very coherent either, but sufficiently so to strike me dumb at first. I turned my eyes from him in righteous indignation, and perceived Captain Giles in the verandah doorway surveying quietly the scene, his own handiwork, if I may express it in that way. His smouldering black pipe was very noticeable in his big, paternal fist. So, too, was the glitter of his heavy gold watch-chain across the breast of his white tunic. He exhaled an atmosphere of virtuous sagacity thick enough for any innocent soul to fly to confidently. I flew to him.

'You would never believe it,' I cried. 'It was a notification that a master is wanted for some ship. There's a command apparently going about and this fellow puts the thing in his pocket.'

The Steward screamed out in accents of loud despair, 'You will be the death of me!'

The mighty slap he gave his wretched forehead was very loud, too. But when I turned to look at him he was no longer there. He had rushed away somewhere out of sight. This sudden disappearance made me laugh.

This was the end of the incident – for me. Captain Giles, however, staring at the place where the Steward had been, began to haul at his gorgeous gold chain till at last the watch came up from the deep pocket like solid truth from a well. Solemnly he lowered it down again and only then said: 'Just three o'clock. You will be in time – if you don't lose any, that is.'

'In time for what?' I asked.

'Good Lord! For the Harbour Office. This must be looked into.'

Strictly speaking, he was right. But I've never had much taste for investigation, for showing people up and all that, no doubt, ethically meritorious kind of work. And my view of the episode was purely ethical. If anyone had to be the death of the Steward I didn't see why it shouldn't be Captain Giles himself, a man of age and standing, and a permanent resident. Whereas I, in comparison, felt myself a mere bird of passage in that port. In fact, it might have been said that I had already broken off my connection. I muttered that I didn't think – it was nothing to me . . .

'Nothing?' repeated Captain Giles, giving some signs of quiet, deliberate indignation. 'Kent warned me you were a peculiar young fellow. You will tell me next that a command is nothing to you – and after all the trouble I've taken, too!'

'The trouble!' I murmured, uncomprehending. What trouble? All I could remember was being mystified and bored by his conversation for a solid hour after tiffin. And he called that taking a lot of trouble.

He was looking at me with a self-complacency which would have been odious in any other man. All at once, as if a page of a book had been turned over disclosing a word which made plain all that had gone before, I perceived that this matter had also another than an ethical aspect.

And still I did not move. Captain Giles lost his patience a little. With an angry puff at his pipe he turned his back on my hesitation.

But it was not hesitation on my part. I had been, if I may express myself so, put out of gear mentally. But as soon as I had convinced myself that this stale, unprofitable world of my discontent contained such a thing as a command to be seized, I recovered my powers of locomotion.

It's a good step from the Officers' Home to the Harbour Office; but with the magic word 'Command' in my head I found myself suddenly on the quay as if transported there in the twinkling of an eye, before a portal of dressed white stone above a flight of shallow white steps.

All this seemed to glide towards me swiftly. The whole great roadstead to the right was just a mere flicker of blue, and the dim cool hall swallowed me up out of the heat and glare of which I had not been aware till the very moment I passed in from it.

The broad inner staircase insinuated itself under my feet somehow. Command is a strong magic. The first human beings I perceived distinctly since I had parted with the indignant back of Captain Giles were the crew of the harbour steam-launch lounging on the spacious landing about the curtained archway of the shipping office.

It was there that my buoyancy abandoned me. The atmosphere of officialdom would kill anything that breathes the air of human endeavour, would extinguish hope and fear alike in the supremacy of paper and ink. I passed heavily under the curtain which the Malay coxswain of the harbour launch raised for me. There was nobody in the office except the clerks, writing in two industrious rows. But the head shipping-master hopped down from his elevation and hurried along on the thick mats to meet me in the broad central passage.

He had a Scottish name, but his complexion was of a rich olive hue, his short beard was jet black, and his eyes, also black, had a languishing expression. He asked confidentially: 'You want to see Him?'

All lightness of spirit and body having departed from me at the touch of officialdom, I looked at the scribe without animation and asked in my turn wearily: 'What do you think? Is it any use?'

'My goodness! He has asked for you twice today.'

This emphatic He was the supreme authority, the Marine Superintendent, the Harbour-Master – a very great person in the eyes of every single quill-driver in the room. But that was nothing to the opinion he had of his own greatness.

Captain Ellis looked upon himself as a sort of divine (pagan) emanation, the deputy-Neptune for the circumambient seas. If he did not actually rule the waves, he pretended to rule the fate of the mortals whose lives were cast upon the waters.

This uplifting illusion made him inquisitorial and peremptory. And as his temperament was choleric there were fellows who were actually afraid of him. He was redoubtable, not in virtue of his office, but because of his unwarrantable assumptions. I had never had anything to do with him before.

I said: 'Oh! He has asked for me twice. Then perhaps I had better go in.'

'You must! You must!'

The shipping-master led the way with a mincing gait round the whole system of desks to a tall and important-looking door, which he opened with a deferential action of the arm.

He stepped right in (but without letting go of the handle) and, after gazing reverently down the room for a while, beckoned me in by a silent jerk of the head. Then he slipped out at once and shut the door after me most delicately.

Three lofty windows gave on the harbour. There was nothing in them but the dark-blue sparkling sea and the paler luminous blue of the sky. My eye caught in the depths and distances of these blue tones the white speck of some big ship just arrived and about to anchor in the outer roadstead. A ship from home – after perhaps ninety days at sea. There is something touching about a ship coming in from sea and folding her white wings for a rest.

The next thing I saw was the top-knot of silver hair surmounting Captain Ellis's smooth red face, which would have been apoplectic if it hadn't had such a fresh appearance.

Our deputy-Neptune had no beard on his chin, and there was no trident to be seen standing in a corner anywhere, like an umbrella. But his hand was holding a pen – the official pen, far mightier than the sword in making or marring the fortune of simple toiling men. He was looking over his shoulder at my advance.

When I had come well within range he saluted me by a nerve-shattering: 'Where have you been all this time?'

As it was no concern of his I did not take the slightest notice of the shot. I said simply that I had heard there was a master needed for some vessel, and being a sailing-ship man I thought I would apply . . .

He interrupted me. 'Why! Hang it! *You* are the right man for that job – if there had been twenty others after it. But no fear of that. They are all afraid to catch hold. That's what's the matter.'

He was very irritated. I said innocently: 'Are they, sir. I wonder why?'

'Why!' he fumed. 'Afraid of the sails. Afraid of a white crew. Too much trouble. Too much work. Too long out here. Easy life and deck-chairs more their mark. Here I sit with the Consul-General's cable before me, and the only man fit for the job not to be found anywhere. I began to think you were funking it too . . . '

'I haven't been long getting to the office,' I remarked calmly.

'You have a good name out here, though,' he growled savagely without looking at me.

'I am very glad to hear it from you, sir,' I said.

'Yes. But you are not on the spot when you are wanted. You know you weren't. That steward of yours wouldn't dare to neglect a message from this office. Where the devil did you hide yourself for the best part of the day?'

I only smiled kindly down on him, and he seemed to recollect himself, and asked me to take a seat. He explained that the master of a British ship having died in Bankok the Consul-General had cabled to him a request for a competent man to be sent out to take command.

Apparently, in his mind, I was the man from the first, though for the looks of the thing the notification addressed to the Sailors' Home was general. An agreement had already been prepared. He gave it to me to read, and when I handed it back to him with the remark that I accepted its terms, the deputy-Neptune signed it, stamped it with his own exalted hand, folded it in four (it was a sheet of blue foolscap), and presented it to me – a gift of extraordinary potency, for, as I put it in my pocket, my head swam a little.

'This is your appointment to the command,' he said with a certain gravity. 'An official appointment binding the owners to conditions which you have accepted. Now – when will you be ready to go?'

I said I would be ready that very day if necessary. He caught me at my word with great readiness. The steamer *Melita* was leaving for Bankok that evening about seven. He would request her captain officially to give me a passage and wait for me till ten o'clock.

Then he rose from his office chair, and I got up too. My head swam, there was no doubt about it, and I felt a heaviness of limbs as if they had grown bigger since I had sat down on that chair. I made my bow.

A subtle change in Captain Ellis's manner became perceptible as though he had laid aside the trident of deputy-Neptune. In reality, it was only his official pen that he had dropped on getting up.

Chapter 2

HE SHOOK HANDS with me: 'Well, there you are, on your own, appointed officially under my responsibility.'

He was actually walking with me to the door. What a distance off it seemed! I moved like a man in bonds. But we reached it at last. I opened it with the sensation of dealing with mere dream-stuff, and then at the last moment the fellowship of seamen asserted itself, stronger than the difference of age and station. It asserted itself in Captain Ellis's voice.

'Goodbye – and good luck to you,' he said so heartily that I could only give him a grateful glance. Then I turned and went out, never to see him again in my life. I had not made three steps into the outer office when I heard behind my back a gruff, loud, authoritative voice, the voice of our deputy-Neptune.

It was addressing the head shipping-master, who, having let me in, had, apparently, remained hovering in the middle distance ever since.

'Mr R., let the harbour launch have steam up to take the captain here on board the *Melita* at half-past nine tonight.'

I was amazed at the startled assent of R.'s 'Yes, sir.' He ran before me out on the landing. My new dignity sat yet so lightly on me that I was not aware that it was I, the Captain, the object of this last graciousness. It seemed as if all of a sudden a pair of wings had grown on my shoulders. I merely skimmed along the polished floor.

But R. was impressed.

'I say!' he exclaimed on the landing, while the Malay crew of the steam-launch standing by looked stonily at the man for whom they were going to be kept on duty so late, away from their gambling, from their girls, or their pure domestic joys. 'I say! His own launch. What have you done to him?'

His stare was full of respectful curiosity. I was quite confounded.

'Was it for me? I hadn't the slightest notion,' I stammered out.

He nodded many times. 'Yes. And the last person who had it before you was a Duke. So, there!'

I think he expected me to faint on the spot. But I was in too much of a hurry for emotional displays. My feelings were already in such a whirl that this staggering information did not seem to make the slightest difference. It fell into the seething cauldron of my brain, and I carried it off with me after a short but effusive passage of leave-taking with R.

The favour of the great throws an aureole round the fortunate object of its selection. That excellent man enquired whether he could do anything for me. He had known me only by sight, and he was well aware he would never see me again; I was, in common with the other seamen of the port, merely a subject for official writing, filling up of forms with all the artificial superiority of a man of pen and ink to the men who grapple with realities outside the consecrated walls of official buildings. What ghosts we must have been to him! Mere symbols to juggle with in books and heavy registers, without brains and muscles and perplexities; something hardly useful and decidedly inferior.

And he – the office hours being over – wanted to know if he could be of any use to me!

I ought, properly speaking – I ought to have been moved to tears. But I did not even think of it. It was only another miraculous manifestation of that day of miracles. I parted from him as if he had been a mere symbol. I floated down the staircase. I floated out of the official and imposing portal. I went on floating along.

I use that word rather than the word 'flew', because I have a distinct impression that, though uplifted by my aroused youth, my movements were deliberate enough. To that mixed white, brown, and yellow portion of mankind, out abroad on their own affairs, I presented the appearance of a man walking rather sedately. And nothing in the way of abstraction could have equalled my deep detachment from the forms and colours of this world. It was, as it were, absolute.

And yet, suddenly, I recognised Hamilton. I recognised him without effort, without a shock, without a start. There he was, strolling towards the Harbour Office with his stiff, arrogant dignity. His red face made him noticeable at a distance. It flamed, over there, on the shady side of the street.

He had perceived me too. Something (unconscious exuberance of spirits, perhaps) moved me to wave my hand to him elaborately. This lapse from good taste happened before I was aware that I was capable of it.

The impact of my impudence stopped him short, much as a bullet might have done. I verily believe he staggered, though as far as I could see he didn't actually fall. I had gone past in a moment and did not turn my head. I had forgotten his existence.

The next ten minutes might have been ten seconds or ten centuries for all my consciousness had to do with it. People might have been falling dead around me, houses crumbling, guns firing, I wouldn't have known. I was thinking: 'By Jove! I have got it.' *It* being the command. It had come about in a way utterly unforeseen in my modest day-dreams.

I perceived that my imagination had been running in conventional channels and that my hopes had always been drab stuff. I had envisaged a command as a result of a slow course of promotion in the employ of some highly respectable firm. The reward of faithful service. Well, faithful service was all right. One would naturally give that for one's own sake, for the sake of the ship, for the love of the life of one's choice; not for the sake of the reward.

There is something distasteful in the notion of a reward.

And now here I had my command, absolutely in my pocket, in a way undeniable indeed, but most unexpected; beyond my imaginings, outside all reasonable expectations, and even notwithstanding the existence of some sort of obscure intrigue to keep it away from me. It is true that the intrigue was feeble, but it helped the feeling of wonder – as if I had been specially destined for that ship I did not know, by some power higher than the prosaic agencies of the commercial world.

A strange sense of exultation began to creep into me. If I had worked for that command ten years or more there would have been nothing of the kind. I was a little frightened.

'Let us be calm,' I said to myself.

Outside the door of the Officers' Home the wretched Steward

seemed to be waiting for me. There was a broad flight of a few steps, and he ran to and fro on the top of it as if chained there. A distressed cur. He looked as though his throat were too dry for him to bark.

I regret to say I stopped before going in. There had been a revolution in my moral nature. He waited open-mouthed, breathless, while I looked at him for half a minute.

'And you thought you could keep me out of it,' I said scathingly.

'You said you were going home,' he squeaked miserably. 'You said so. You said so.'

'I wonder what Captain Ellis will have to say to that excuse,' I uttered slowly with a sinister meaning.

His lower jaw had been trembling all the time and his voice was like the bleating of a sick goat. 'You have given me away? You have done for me?'

Neither his distress nor yet the sheer absurdity of it was able to disarm me. It was the first instance of harm being attempted to be done to me – at any rate, the first I had ever found out. And I was still young enough, still too much on this side of the shadow-line, not to be surprised and indignant at such things.

I gazed at him inflexibly. Let the beggar suffer. He slapped his forehead and I passed in, pursued, into the dining-room, by his screech: 'I always said you'd be the death of me.'

This clamour not only overtook me, but went ahead, as it were, on to the verandah and brought out Captain Giles.

He stood before me in the doorway in all the commonplace solidity of his wisdom. The gold chain glittered on his breast. He clutched a smouldering pipe.

I extended my hand to him warmly and he seemed surprised, but did respond heartily enough in the end, with a faint smile of superior knowledge which cut my thanks short as if with a knife. I don't think that more than one word came out. And even for that one, judging by the temperature of my face, I had blushed as if for a bad action. Assuming a detached tone, I wondered how on earth he had managed to spot the little underhand game that had been going on.

He murmured complacently that there were but few things done in the town that he could not see the inside of. And as to this house, he had been using it off and on for nearly ten years. Nothing that went on in it could escape his great experience. It had been no trouble to him. No trouble at all.

Then in his quiet, thick tone he wanted to know if I had complained formally of the Steward's action.

I said that I hadn't – though, indeed, it was not for want of opportunity. Captain Ellis had gone for me bald-headed in a most ridiculous fashion for being out of the way when wanted.

'Funny old gentleman,' interjected Captain Giles. 'What did you say to that?'

'I said simply that I came along the very moment I heard of his message. Nothing more. I didn't want to hurt the Steward. I would scorn to harm such an object. No. I made no complaint, but I believe he thinks I've done so. Let him think. He's got a fright that he won't forget in a hurry, for Captain Ellis would kick him out into the middle of Asia . . . '

'Wait a moment,' said Captain Giles, leaving me suddenly. I sat down feeling very tired, mostly in my head. Before I could start a train of thought he stood again before me, murmuring the excuse that he had to go and put the fellow's mind at ease.

I looked up with surprise. But in reality I was indifferent. He explained that he had found the Steward lying face downwards on the horsehair sofa. He was all right now.

'He would not have died of fright,' I said contemptuously.

'No. But he might have taken an overdose out of one of those little bottles he keeps in his room,' Captain Giles argued seriously. 'The confounded fool has tried to poison himself once – a couple of years ago.'

'Really,' I said without emotion. 'He doesn't seem very fit to live, anyhow.'

'As to that, it may be said of a good many.'

'Don't exaggerate like this!' I protested, laughing irritably. 'But I wonder what this part of the world would do if you were to leave off looking after it, Captain Giles? Here you have got me a command and saved the Steward's life in one afternoon. Though why you should have taken all that interest in either of us is more than I can understand.'

Captain Giles remained silent for a minute. Then gravely: 'He's not a bad steward really. He can find a good cook, at any rate. And, what's more, he can keep him when found. I remember the cooks we had here before his time . . . '

I must have made a movement of impatience, because he interrupted himself with an apology for keeping me yarning there, while no doubt I needed all my time to get ready.

What I really needed was to be alone for a bit. I seized this opening hastily. My bedroom was a quiet refuge in an apparently uninhabited wing of the building. Having absolutely nothing to do (for I had not unpacked my things), I sat down on the bed and abandoned myself to the influences of the hour. To the unexpected influences . . .

And first I wondered at my state of mind. Why was I not more surprised? Why? Here I was, invested with a command in the twinkling of an eye, not in the common course of human affairs, but more as if by enchantment. I ought to have been lost in astonishment. But I wasn't. I was very much like people in fairy tales. Nothing ever astonishes them. When a fully appointed gala coach is produced out of a pumpkin to take her to a ball Cinderella does not exclaim. She gets in quietly and drives away to her high fortune.

Captain Ellis (a fierce sort of fairy) had produced a command out of a drawer almost as unexpectedly as in a fairy tale. But a command is an abstract idea, and it seemed a sort of 'lesser marvel' till it flashed upon me that it involved the concrete existence of a ship.

A ship! My ship! She was mine, more absolutely mine for possession and care than anything in the world; an object of responsibility and devotion. She was there waiting for me, spell-bound, unable to move, to live, to get out into the world (till I came), like an enchanted princess. Her call had come to me as if from the clouds. I had never suspected her existence. I didn't know how she looked, I had barely heard her name, and yet we were indissolubly united for a certain portion of our future, to sink or swim together!

A sudden passion of anxious impatience rushed through my veins and gave me such a sense of the intensity of existence as I have never felt before or since. I discovered how much of a seaman I was, in heart, in mind, and, as it were, physically – a man exclusively of sea and ships; the sea the only world that counted, and the ships the test of manliness, of temperament, of courage and fidelity – and of love.

I had an exquisite moment. It was unique also. Jumping up from my seat, I paced up and down my room for a long time. But when I came into the dining-room I behaved with sufficient composure. I only couldn't eat anything at dinner.

Having declared my intention not to drive but to walk down to the quay, I must render the wretched Steward justice that he bestirred himself to find me some coolies for the luggage. They departed, carrying all my worldly possessions (except a little money I had in my pocket) slung from a long pole. Captain Giles volunteered to walk down with me.

We followed the sombre, shaded alley across the Esplanade. It was moderately cool there under the trees. Captain Giles remarked, with a sudden laugh: 'I know who's jolly thankful at having seen the last of you.'

I guessed that he meant the Steward. The fellow had borne himself to me in a sulkily frightened manner at the last. I expressed my wonder that he should have tried to do me a bad turn for no reason at all.

'Don't you see that what he wanted was to get rid of our friend Hamilton by dodging him in front of you for that job? That would have removed him for good, see?'

'Heavens!' I exclaimed, feeling humiliated somehow. 'Can it be possible? What a fool he must be! That overbearing, impudent loafer! Why! He couldn't . . . And yet he's nearly done it, I believe; for the Harbour Office was bound to send somebody.'

'Aye. A fool like our Steward can be dangerous sometimes,' declared Captain Giles sententiously. 'Just because he is a fool,' he added, imparting further instruction in his complacent low tones. 'For,' he continued in the manner of a set demonstration, 'no sensible person would risk being kicked out of the only berth between himself and starvation just to get rid of a simple annoyance – a small worry. Would he now?'

'Well, no,' I conceded, restraining a desire to laugh at that something mysteriously earnest in delivering the conclusions of his wisdom as though they were the product of prohibited operations. 'But that fellow looks as if he were rather crazy. He must be.'

'As to that, I believe everybody in the world is a little mad,' he announced quietly.

'You make no exceptions?' I enquired, just to hear his answer.

He kept silent for a little while, then got home in an effective manner.

'Why! Kent says that even of you.'

'Does he?' I retorted, extremely embittered all at once against my former captain. 'There's nothing of that in the written character from him which I've got in my pocket. Has he given you any instances of my lunacy?'

Captain Giles explained in a conciliating tone that it had been only a friendly remark in reference to my abrupt leaving of the ship for no apparent reason.

I muttered grumpily: 'Oh! leaving his ship,' and mended my pace. He kept up by my side in the deep gloom of the avenue as if it were his conscientious duty to see me out of the colony as an undesirable character. He panted a little, which was rather pathetic in a way.

But I was not moved. On the contrary. His discomfort gave me a sort of malicious pleasure.

Presently I relented, slowed down, and said: 'What I really wanted was to get a fresh grip. I felt it was time. Is that so very mad?'

He made no answer. We were issuing from the avenue. On the bridge over the canal a dark, irresolute figure seemed to be awaiting something or somebody.

It was a Malay policeman, barefooted, in his blue uniform. The silver band on his little round cap shone dimly in the light of the street lamp. He peered in our direction timidly.

Before we could come up to him he turned about and walked in front of us in the direction of the jetty. The distance was some hundred yards; and then I found my coolies squatting on their heels. They had kept the pole on their shoulders, and all my worldly goods, still tied to the pole, were resting on the ground between them. As far as the eye could reach along the quay there was not another soul abroad except the police peon, who saluted us.

It seems he had detained the coolies as suspicious characters, and had forbidden them the jetty. But at a sign from me he took off the embargo with alacrity. The two patient fellows, rising together with a faint grunt, trotted off along the planks, and I prepared to take my leave of Captain Giles, who stood there with an air as though his mission were drawing to a close. It could not be denied that he had done it all. And while I hesitated about an appropriate sentence he made himself heard: 'I expect you'll have your hands pretty full of tangled-up business.'

I asked him what made him think so; and he answered that it was his general experience of the world. Ship a long time away from her port, owners inaccessible by cable, and the only man who could explain matters dead and buried.

'And you yourself new to the business in a way,' he concluded in a sort of unanswerable tone.

'Don't insist,' I said. 'I know it only too well. I only wish you could impart to me some small portion of your experience before I go. As it can't be done in ten minutes I had better not begin to ask you. There's that harbour launch waiting for me too. But I won't feel really at peace till I have that ship of mine out in the Indian Ocean.'

He remarked casually that from Bankok to the Indian Ocean was a pretty long step. And this murmur, like a dim flash from a dark lantern, showed me for a moment the broad belt of islands and reefs between that unknown ship, which was mine, and the freedom of the great waters of the globe.

But I felt no apprehension. I was familiar enough with the Archipelago by that time. Extreme patience and extreme care would see me through the region of broken land, of faint airs and of dead water to where I would feel at last my command swing on the great swell and list over to the great breath of regular winds, that would give her the feeling of a large, more intense life. The road would be long. All roads are long that lead towards one's heart's desire. But this road my mind's eye could see on a chart, professionally, with all its complications and difficulties, yet simple enough in a way. One is a seaman or one is not. And I had no doubt of being one.

The only part I was a stranger to was the Gulf of Siam. And I mentioned this to Captain Giles. Not that I was concerned very much. It belonged to the same region the nature of which I knew, into whose very soul I seemed to have looked during the last months of that existence with which I had broken now, suddenly, as one parts with some enchanting company.

'The gulf . . . Ay! A funny piece of water – that,' said Captain Giles.

Funny, in this connection, was a vague word. The whole thing sounded like an opinion uttered by a cautious person mindful of actions for slander.

I didn't enquire as to the nature of that funniness. There was really no time. But at the very last he volunteered a warning.

'Whatever you do keep to the east side of it. The west side is dangerous at this time of the year. Don't let anything tempt you over. You'll find nothing but trouble there.'

Though I could hardly imagine what could tempt me to involve my ship amongst the currents and reefs of the Malay shore, I thanked him for the advice.

He gripped my extended arm warmly, and the end of our acquaintance came suddenly in the words: 'Good-night.'

That was all he said: 'Good-night.' Nothing more. I don't know what I intended to say, but surprise made me swallow it, whatever it was. I choked slightly, and then exclaimed with a sort of nervous haste: 'Oh! Good-night, Captain Giles, good-night.'

His movements were always deliberate, but his back had receded some distance along the deserted quay before I collected myself enough to follow his example and made a half turn in the direction of the jetty.

Only my movements were not deliberate. I hurried down to the steps and leaped into the launch. Before I had fairly landed in her stern-sheets the slim little craft darted away from the jetty with a sudden swirl of her propeller and the hard rapid puffing of the exhaust in her vaguely gleaming brass funnel amidships.

The misty churning at her stern was the only sound in the world. The shore lay plunged in the silence of the deepest slumber. I watched the town recede still and soundless in the hot night, till the abrupt hail, 'Steam-launch, ahoy!' made me spin round face forward. We were close to a white, ghostly steamer. Lights shone on her decks, in her port-holes. And the same voice shouted from her: 'Is that our passenger?'

'It is,' I yelled.

Her crew had been obviously on the jump. I could hear them running about. The modern spirit of haste was loudly vocal in the orders to 'Heave away on the cable' – to 'Lower the side-ladder', and in urgent requests to me to 'Come along, sir! We have been delayed three hours for you . . . Our time is seven o'clock, you know!'

I stepped on the deck. I said 'No! I don't know.' The spirit of modern hurry was embodied in a thin, long-armed, long-legged man, with a closely-clipped grey beard. His meagre hand was hot and dry. He declared feverishly: 'I am hanged if I would have waited another five minutes – harbour-master or no harbour-master.'

'That's your own business,' I said. 'I didn't ask you to wait for me.'

'I hope you don't expect any supper,' he burst out. 'This isn't a boarding-house afloat. You are the first passenger I ever had in my life and I hope to goodness you will be the last.'

I made no answer to this hospitable communication; and, indeed, he didn't wait for any, bolting away on to his bridge to get his ship under way.

For the four days he had me on board he did not depart from that half-hostile attitude. His ship having been delayed three hours on my account he couldn't forgive me for not being a more distinguished person. He was not exactly outspoken about it, but that feeling of annoyed wonder was peeping out perpetually in his talk.

He was absurd.

He was also a man of much experience, which he liked to trot out; but no greater contrast with Captain Giles could have been imagined. He would have amused me if I had wanted to be amused. But I did not want to be amused. I was like a lover looking forward to a meeting. Human hostility was nothing to me. I thought of my unknown ship. It was amusement enough, torment enough, occupation enough.

He perceived my state, for his wits were sufficiently sharp for that, and he poked sly fun at my preoccupation in the manner some nasty, cynical old men assume towards the dreams and illusions of youth. I, on my side, refrained from questioning him as to the appearance of my ship, though I knew that being in Bankok every month or so he must have known her by sight. I was not going to expose the ship, my ship! to some slighting reference.

He was the first really unsympathetic man I had ever come in contact with. My education was far from being finished, though I didn't know it. No! I didn't know it.

All I knew was that he disliked me and had some contempt for my person. Why? Apparently because his ship had been delayed three hours on my account. Who was I to have such a thing done for me? Such a thing had never been done for him. It was a sort of jealous indignation.

My expectation, mingled with fear, was wrought to its highest pitch. How slow had been the days of the passage and how soon they were over. One morning, early, we crossed the bar, and while the sun was rising splendidly over the flat spaces of the land we steamed up the innumerable bends, passed under the shadow of the great gilt pagoda, and reached the outskirts of the town.

There it was, spread largely on both banks, the Oriental capital which had as yet suffered no white conqueror; an expanse of brown houses of bamboo, of mats, of leaves, of a vegetable-matter style of architecture, sprung out of the brown soil on the banks of the muddy river. It was amazing to think that in those miles of human habitations there was not probably half a dozen pounds of nails. Some of those houses of sticks and grass, like the nests of an aquatic race, clung to the low shores. Others seemed to grow out of the water; others again floated in long anchored rows in the very middle of the stream. Here and there in the distance, above the crowded mob of low, brown roof ridges, towered great piles of masonry, King's Palace, temples, gorgeous and dilapidated, crumbling under the vertical sunlight, tremendous, overpowering, almost palpable, which seemed to enter one's breast with the breath of one's nostrils and soak into one's limbs through every pore of one's skin.

The ridiculous victim of jealousy had for some reason or other to stop his engines just then. The steamer drifted slowly up with the tide. Oblivious of my new surroundings I walked the deck, in anxious, deadened abstraction, a commingling of romantic reverie with a very practical survey of my qualifications. For the time was approaching for me to behold my command and to prove my worth in the ultimate test of my profession.

Suddenly I heard myself called by that imbecile. He was beckoning me to come up on his bridge.

I didn't care very much for that, but as it seemed that he had something particular to say I went up the ladder.

He laid his hand on my shoulder and gave me a slight turn, pointing with his other arm at the same time.

'There! That's your ship, Captain,' he said.

I felt a thump in my breast – only one, as if my heart had then ceased to beat. There were ten or more ships moored along the bank, and the one he meant was partly hidden from my sight by her next astern. He said: 'We'll drift abreast her in a moment.'

What was his tone? Mocking? Threatening? Or only indifferent? I could not tell. I suspected some malice in this unexpected manifestation of interest.

He left me, and I leaned over the rail of the bridge looking over the side. I dared not raise my eyes. Yet it had to be done – and, indeed, I could not have helped myself. I believe I trembled.

But directly my eyes had rested on my ship all my fear vanished. It went off swiftly, like a bad dream. Only that a dream leaves no shame behind it, and that I felt a momentary shame at my unworthy suspicions.

Yes, there she was. Her hull, her rigging filled my eye with a great content. That feeling of life-emptiness which had made me so restless for the last few months lost its bitter plausibility, its evil influence, dissolved in a flow of joyous emotion.

At the first glance I saw that she was a high-class vessel, a harmonious creature in the lines of her fine body, in the proportioned tallness of her spars. Whatever her age and her history, she had preserved the stamp of her origin. She was one of those craft that, in virtue of their design and complete finish, will never look old. Amongst her companions moored to the bank, and all bigger than herself, she looked like a creature of high breed – an Arab steed in a string of carthorses.

A voice behind me said in a nasty equivocal tone: 'I hope you are satisfied with her, Captain.' I did not even turn my head. It was the master of the steamer, and whatever he meant, whatever he thought of her, I knew that, like some rare women, she was one of those creatures whose mere existence is enough to awaken an unselfish delight. One feels that it is good to be in the world in which she has her being.

That illusion of life and character which charms one in men's finest handiwork radiated from her. An enormous baulk of teak-wood timber swung over her hatchway; lifeless matter, looking heavier and bigger than anything aboard of her. When they started lowering it the surge of the tackle sent a quiver through her from water-line to the trucks up the fine nerves of her rigging, as though she had shuddered at the weight. It seemed cruel to load her so . . .

Half an hour later, putting my foot on her deck for the first time, I received the feeling of deep physical satisfaction. Nothing could equal the fullness of that moment, the ideal completeness of that emotional experience which had come to me without the preliminary toil and disenchantments of an obscure career.

My rapid glance ran over her, enveloped, appropriated the form concreting the abstract sentiment of my command. A lot of details perceptible to a seaman struck my eye vividly in that instant. For the rest, I saw her disengaged from the material conditions of her being. The shore to which she was moored was as if it did not exist. What were to me all the countries of the globe? In all the parts of the world washed by navigable waters our relation to each other would be the same – and more intimate than there are words to express in the language. Apart from that, every scene and episode would be a mere passing show. The very gang of yellow coolies busy about the main hatch was less substantial than the stuff dreams are made of. For who on earth would dream of Chinamen? . . .

I went aft, ascended the poop, where, under the awning, gleamed the brasses of the yacht-like fittings, the polished surfaces of the rails, the glass of the skylights. Right aft two seamen, busy cleaning the steering gear, with the reflected ripples of light running playfully up their bent backs, went on with their work, unaware of me and of the almost affectionate glance I threw at them in passing towards the companion-way of the cabin.

The doors stood wide open, the slide was pushed right back. The half-turn of the staircase cut off the view of the lobby. A low humming ascended from below, but it stopped abruptly at the sound of my descending footsteps.

Chapter 3

THE FIRST THING I saw down there was the upper part of a man's body projecting backwards, as it were, from one of the doors at the foot of the stairs. His eyes looked at me very wide and still. In one hand he held a dinner plate, in the other a cloth.

'I am your new captain,' I said quietly.

In a moment, in the twinkling of an eye, he had got rid of the plate and the cloth and jumped to open the cabin door. As soon as I passed into the saloon he vanished, but only to reappear instantly, buttoning up a jacket he had put on with the swiftness of a 'quick-change' artist.

'Where's the chief mate?' I asked.

'In the hold, I think, sir. I saw him go down the after-hatch ten minutes ago.'

'Tell him I am on board.'

The mahogany table under the skylight shone in the twilight like a dark pool of water. The sideboard, surmounted by a wide looking-glass in an ormolu frame, had a marble top. It bore a pair of silver-plated lamps and some other pieces – obviously a harbour display. The saloon itself was panelled in two kinds of wood in the excellent, simple taste prevailing when the ship was built.

I sat down in the armchair at the head of the table – the captain's chair, with a small tell-tale compass swung above it – a mute reminder of unremitting vigilance.

A succession of men had sat in that chair. I became aware of that thought suddenly, vividly, as though each had left a little of himself between the four walls of these ornate bulkheads; as if a sort of composite soul, the soul of command, had whispered suddenly to mine of long days at sea and of anxious moments.

'You, too!' it seemed to say, 'you, too, shall taste of that peace and that unrest in a searching intimacy with your own self – obscure as we were and as supreme in the face of all the winds and all the seas, in an immensity that receives no impress, preserves no memories, and keeps no reckoning of lives.'

Deep within the tarnished ormolu frame, in the hot half-light sifted through the awning, I saw my own face propped between my hands. And I stared back at myself with the perfect detachment of distance, rather with curiosity than with any other feeling, except of some sympathy for this latest representative of what for all intents and purposes was a dynasty; continuous not in blood, indeed, but in its experience, in its training, in its conception of duty, and in the blessed simplicity of its traditional point of view of life.

It struck me that this quietly staring man whom I was watching, both as if he were myself and somebody else, was not exactly a lonely figure. He had his place in a line of men whom he did not know, of whom he had never heard; but who were fashioned by the same influences, whose souls in relation to their humble life's work had no secrets for him.

Suddenly I perceived that there was another man in the saloon, standing a little on one side and looking intently at me. The chief mate. His long, red moustache determined the character of his physiognomy, which struck me as pugnacious in (strange to say) a ghastly sort of way.

How long had he been there looking at me, appraising me in my unguarded day-dreaming state? I would have been more disconcerted if, having the clock set in the top of the mirror-frame right in front of me, I had not noticed that its long hand had hardly moved at all.

I could not have been in that cabin more than two minutes altogether. Say three . . . So he could not have been watching me more than a mere fraction of a minute, luckily. Still, I regretted the occurrence.

But I showed nothing of it as I rose leisurely (it had to be leisurely) and greeted him with perfect friendliness.

There was something reluctant and at the same time attentive in his bearing. His name was Burns. We left the cabin and went round the ship together. His face in the full light of day appeared very worn, meagre, even haggard. Somehow I had a delicacy as to looking too often at him; his eyes, on the contrary, remained fairly glued on my face. They were greenish and had an expectant expression.

He answered all my questions readily enough, but my ear seemed to catch a tone of unwillingness. The second officer, with three or four hands, was busy forward. The mate mentioned his name and I nodded to him in passing. He was very young. He struck me as rather a cub.

When we returned below I sat down on one end of a deep, semicircular, or, rather, semi-oval settee, upholstered in red plush. It extended right across the whole after-end of the cabin. Mr Burns, motioned to sit down, dropped into one of the swivel-chairs round the table, and kept his eyes on me as persistently as ever, and with that strange air as if all this were make-believe and he expected me to get up, burst into a laugh, slap him on the back, and vanish from the cabin.

There was an odd stress in the situation which began to make me uncomfortable. I tried to react against this vague feeling.

'It's only my inexperience,' I thought.

In the face of that man, several years, I judged, older than myself, I became aware of what I had left already behind me – my youth. And that was indeed poor comfort. Youth is a fine thing, a mighty power – as long as one does not think of it. I felt I was becoming self-conscious. Almost against my will I assumed a moody gravity. I said: 'I see you have kept her in very good order, Mr Burns.'

Directly I had uttered these words I asked myself angrily why the deuce did I want to say that? Mr Burns in answer had only blinked at me. What on earth did he mean?

I fell back on a question which had been in my thoughts for a long time – the most natural question on the lips of any seaman whatever joining a ship. I voiced it (confound this self-consciousness) in a *dégagé* cheerful tone: 'I suppose she can travel – what?'

Now a question like this might have been answered normally, either in accents of apologetic sorrow or with a visibly suppressed pride, in a 'I don't want to boast, but you shall see' sort of tone. There are sailors, too, who would have been roughly outspoken: 'Lazy brute,' or openly delighted: 'She's a flyer.' Two ways, if four manners.

But Mr Burns found another way, a way of his own which had, at all events, the merit of saving his breath, if no other.

Again he did not say anything. He only frowned. And it was an angry frown. I waited. Nothing more came.

'What's the matter? . . . Can't you tell after being nearly two years in the ship?' I addressed him sharply.

He looked as startled for a moment as though he had discovered my presence only that very moment. But this passed off almost at once. He put on an air of indifference. But I suppose he thought it better to say something. He said that a ship needed, just like a man, the chance to show the best she could do, and that this ship had never had a chance since he had been on board of her. Not that he could remember. The last captain . . . He paused.

'Has he been so very unlucky?' I asked with frank incredulity. Mr Burns turned his eyes away from me. No, the late captain was not an unlucky man. One couldn't say that. But he had not seemed to want to make use of his luck.

Mr Burns – man of enigmatic moods – made this statement with an inanimate face and staring wilfully at the rudder casing. The statement itself was obscurely suggestive. I asked quietly: 'Where did he die?'

'In this saloon. Just where you are sitting now,' answered Mr Burns.

I repressed a silly impulse to jump up; but upon the whole I was relieved to hear that he had not died in the bed which was now to be mine. I pointed out to the chief mate that what I really wanted to know was where he had buried his late captain.

Mr Burns said that it was at the entrance to the gulf. A roomy grave; a sufficient answer. But the mate, overcoming visibly something within him – something like a curious reluctance to believe in my advent (as an irrevocable fact, at any rate), did not stop at that – though, indeed, he may have wished to do so.

As a compromise with his feelings, I believe, he addressed himself persistently to the rudder-casing, so that to me he had the appearance of a man talking in solitude, a little unconsciously, however.

His tale was that at seven bells in the forenoon watch he had all hands mustered on the quarter-deck and told them that they had better go down to say goodbye to the captain.

Those words, as if grudged to an intruding personage, were enough for me to evoke vividly that strange ceremony: the barefooted, bareheaded seamen crowding shyly into that cabin, a small mob pressed against that sideboard, uncomfortable rather than moved, shirts open on sunburnt chests, weather-beaten faces, and all staring at the dying man with the same grave and expectant expression.

'Was he conscious?' I asked.

'He didn't speak, but he moved his eyes to look at them,' said the mate.

After waiting a moment Mr Burns motioned the crew to leave the cabin, but he detained the two eldest men to stay with the captain while he went on deck with his sextant to 'take the sun'. It was getting towards noon and he was anxious to obtain a good observation for latitude. When he returned below to put his sextant away he found that the two men had retreated out into the lobby. Through the open door he had a view of the captain lying easy against the pillows. He had 'passed away' while Mr Burns was taking his observation. As near noon as possible. He had hardly changed his position.

Mr Burns sighed, glanced at me inquisitively, as much as to say, 'Aren't you going yet?' and then turned his thoughts from his new captain back to the old, who, being dead, had no authority, was not in anybody's way, and was much easier to deal with.

Mr Burns dealt with him at some length. He was a peculiar man – of sixty-five about – iron grey, hard-faced, obstinate, and uncommunicative. He used to keep the ship loafing at sea for inscrutable reasons. Would come on deck at night sometimes, take some sail off her, God only knows why or wherefore, then go below, shut himself up in his cabin, and play on the violin for hours – till daybreak perhaps. In fact, he spent most of his time day or night playing the violin. That was when the fit took him. Very loud, too.

It came to this, that Mr Burns mustered his courage one day and remonstrated earnestly with the captain. Neither he nor the second mate could get a wink of sleep in their watches below for the noise . . . And how could they be expected to keep awake while on duty? he pleaded. The answer of that stern man was that if he and the second mate didn't like the noise, they were welcome to pack up their traps and walk over the side. When this alternative was offered the ship happened to be six hundred miles from the nearest land.

Mr Burns at this point looked at me with an air of curiosity. I began to think that my predecessor was a remarkably peculiar old man.

But I had to hear stranger things yet. It came out that this stern, grim, wind-tanned, rough, sea-salted, taciturn sailor of sixty-five was not only an artist, but a lover as well. In Haiphong, when they got there after a course of most unprofitable peregrinations (during which the ship was nearly lost twice), he got himself, in Mr Burns' own words, 'mixed up' with some woman. Mr Burns had had no personal knowledge of that affair, but positive evidence of it existed in the shape of a photograph taken in Haiphong. Mr Burns found it in one of the drawers in the captain's room.

In due course I, too, saw that amazing human document (I even threw it overboard later). There he sat, with his hands reposing on his knees, bald, squat, grey, bristly, recalling a wild boar somehow; and by his side towered an awful, mature, white female with rapacious nostrils and a cheaply ill-omened stare in her enormous eyes. She was disguised in some semi-oriental, vulgar, fancy costume.

She resembled a low-class medium or one of those women who tell fortunes by cards for half-a-crown. And yet she was striking. A professional sorceress from the slums. It was incomprehensible. There was something awful in the thought that she was the last reflection of the world of passion for the fierce soul which seemed to look at one out of the sardonically savage face of that old seaman. However, I noticed that she was holding some musical instrument – guitar or mandoline – in her hand. Perhaps that was the secret of her sortilege.

For Mr Burns that photograph explained why the unloaded ship was kept sweltering at anchor for three weeks in a pestilential hot harbour without air. They lay there and gasped. The captain, appearing now and then on short visits, mumbled to Mr Burns unlikely tales about some letters he was waiting for.

Suddenly, after vanishing for a week, he came on board in the middle of the night and took the ship out to sea with the first break of dawn. Daylight showed him looking wild and ill. The mere getting clear of the land took two days, and somehow or other they bumped slightly on a reef. However, no leak developed, and the captain, growling, 'No matter,' informed Mr Burns that he had made up his mind to take the ship to Hong-Kong and dry-dock her there.

At this Mr Burns was plunged into despair. For indeed, to beat up to Hong-Kong against a fierce monsoon, with a ship not sufficiently ballasted and with her supply of water not completed, was an insane project.

But the captain growled peremptorily, 'Stick her at it,' and Mr Burns, dismayed and enraged, stuck her at it, and kept her at it, blowing away sails, straining the spars, exhausting the crew – nearly maddened by the absolute conviction that the attempt was impossible and was bound to end in some catastrophe.

Meantime the captain, shut up in his cabin and wedged in a corner of his settee against the crazy bounding of the ship, played the violin – or, at any rate, made continuous noise on it.

When he appeared on deck he would not speak and not always answer when spoken to. It was obvious that he was ill in some mysterious manner, and beginning to break up.

As the days went by the sounds of the violin became less and less loud, till at last only a feeble scratching would meet Mr Burns' ear as he stood in the saloon listening outside the door of the captain's state-room.

One afternoon in perfect desperation he burst into that room and made such a scene, tearing his hair and shouting such horrid imprecations that he cowed the contemptuous spirit of the sick man. The water-tanks were low, they had not gained fifty miles in a fortnight. She would never reach Hong-Kong.

It was like fighting desperately towards destruction for the ship and the men. This was evident without argument. Mr Burns, losing all restraint, put his face close to his captain's and fairly yelled: 'You, sir, are going out of the world. But I can't wait till you are dead before I put the helm up. You must do it yourself. You must do it now!'

The man on the couch snarled in contempt: 'So I am going out of the world – am I?'

'Yes, sir – you haven't many days left in it,' said Mr Burns, calming down. 'One can see it by your face.'

'My face, eh? . . . Well, put the helm up and be damned to you.'

Burns flew on deck, got the ship before the wind, then came down again, composed but resolute.

'I've shaped a course for Pulo Condor, sir,' he said. 'When we make it, if you are still with us, you'll tell me into what port you wish me to take the ship and I'll do it.'

The old man gave him a look of savage spite, and said these atrocious words in deadly, slow tones: 'If I had my wish, neither the ship nor any of you would ever reach a port. And I hope you won't.'

Mr Burns was profoundly shocked. I believe he was positively frightened at the time. It seems, however, that he managed to produce such an effective laugh that it was the old man's turn to be frightened. He shrank within himself and turned his back on him.

'And his head was not gone then,' Mr Burns assured me excitedly. 'He meant every word of it.'

Such was practically the late captain's last speech. No connected sentence passed his lips afterwards. That night he used the last of his strength to throw his fiddle over the side. No one had actually seen him in the act, but after his death Mr Burns couldn't find the thing anywhere. The empty case was very much in evidence, but the fiddle was clearly not in the ship. And where else could it have gone to but overboard?

'Threw his violin overboard!' I exclaimed.

'He did,' cried Mr Burns excitedly. 'And it's my belief he would have tried to take the ship down with him if it had been in human power. He never meant her to see home again. He wouldn't write to his owners, he never wrote to his old wife either – he wasn't going to. He had made up his mind to cut adrift from everything. That's what it was. He didn't care for business, or freights, or for making a passage – or anything. He meant to have gone wandering about the world till he lost her with all hands.'

Mr Burns looked like a man who had escaped great danger. For a little he would have exclaimed: 'If it hadn't been for me!' And the transparent innocence of his indignant eyes was underlined quaintly by the arrogant pair of moustaches which he proceeded to twist, and as if extend, horizontally.

I might have smiled if I had not been busy with my own sensations, which were not those of Mr Burns. I was already the man in command. My sensations could not be like those of any other man on board. In that community I stood, like a king in his country, in a class all by myself. I mean an hereditary king, not a mere elected head of a state. I was brought there to rule by an agency as remote from the people and as inscrutable almost to them as the Grace of God.

And like a member of a dynasty, feeling a semi-mystical bond with the dead, I was profoundly shocked by my immediate predecessor.

That man had been in all essentials but his age just such another man as myself. Yet the end of his life was a complete act of treason, the betrayal of a tradition which seemed to me as imperative as any guide on earth could be. It appeared that even at sea a man could become the victim of evil spirits. I felt on my face the breath of unknown powers that shape our destinies.

Not to let the silence last too long I asked Mr Burns if he had written to his captain's wife. He shook his head. He had written to nobody.

In a moment he became sombre. He never thought of writing. It took him all his time to watch incessantly the loading of the ship by a rascally Chinese stevedore. In this Mr Burns gave me the first glimpse of the real chief mate's soul which dwelt uneasily in his body.

He mused, then hastened on with gloomy force.

'Yes! The captain died as near noon as possible. I looked through his papers in the afternoon. I read the service over him at sunset and then I stuck the ship's head north and brought her in here. I – brought – her – in.'

He struck the table with his fist.

'She would hardly have come in by herself,' I observed. 'But why didn't you make for Singapore instead?'

His eyes wavered. 'The nearest port,' he muttered sullenly.

I had framed the question in perfect innocence, but this answer (the difference in distance was insignificant) and his manner offered me a clue to the simple truth. He took the ship to a port where he expected to be confirmed in his temporary command from lack of a qualified master to put over his head; whereas Singapore, he surmised justly, would be full of qualified men. But his naïve reasoning forgot to take into account the telegraph cable reposing on the bottom of the very Gulf up which he had turned that ship which he imagined himself to have saved from destruction. Hence the bitter flavour of our interview. I tasted it more and more distinctly – and it was less and less to my taste.

'Look here, Mr Burns,' I began, very firmly. 'You may as well understand that I did not run after this command. It was pushed in my way. I've accepted it. I am here to take the ship home first of all, and you may be sure that I shall see to it that every one of you on board here does his duty to that end. This is all I have to say – for the present.'

He was on his feet by this time, but instead of taking his dismissal he remained with trembling, indignant lips, and looking at me hard as though, really, after this, there was nothing for me to do in common decency but to vanish from his outraged sight. Like all very simple emotional states this was moving. I felt sorry for him – almost sympathetic, till (seeing that I did not vanish) he spoke in a tone of forced restraint.

'If I hadn't a wife and a child at home you may be sure, sir, I would have asked you to let me go the very minute you came on board.'

I answered him with a matter-of-course calmness as though some remote third person were in question.

'And I, Mr Burns, would not have let you go. You have signed the ship's articles as chief officer, and till they are terminated at the final port of discharge I shall expect you to attend to your duty and give me the benefit of your experience to the best of your ability.'

Stony incredulity lingered in his eyes; but it broke down before my friendly attitude. With a slight upward toss of his arms (I got to know that gesture well afterwards) he bolted out of the cabin.

We might have saved ourselves that little passage of harmless sparring. Before many days had elapsed it was Mr Burns who was pleading with me anxiously not to leave him behind; while I could only return him but doubtful answers. The whole thing took on a somewhat tragic complexion.

And this horrible problem was only an extraneous episode, a mere complication in the general problem of how to get that ship – which was mine with her appurtenances and her men, with her body and her spirit now slumbering in that pestilential river – how to get her out to sea.

Mr Burns, while still acting captain, had hastened to sign a charter-party which in an ideal world without guile would have been an excellent document. Directly I ran my eye over it I foresaw trouble ahead unless the people of the other part were quite exceptionally fair-minded and open to argument.

Mr Burns, to whom I imparted my fears, chose to take great umbrage at them. He looked at me with that usual incredulous stare, and said bitterly: 'I suppose, sir, you want to make out I've acted like a fool?'

I told him, with my systematic kindliness which always seemed to augment his surprise, that I did not want to make out anything. I would leave that to the future.

And, sure enough, the future brought in a lot of trouble. There were days when I used to remember Captain Giles with nothing short of abhorrence. His confounded acuteness had let me in for this job; while his prophecy that I 'would have my hands full' coming true, made it appear as if done on purpose to play an evil joke on my young innocence.

Yes. I had my hands full of complications which were most valuable as 'experience'. People have a great opinion of the advantages of experience. But in that connection experience means always something disagreeable as opposed to the charm and innocence of illusions.

I must say I was losing mine rapidly. But on these instructive complications I must not enlarge more than to say that they could all be resumed in the one word: delay.

A mankind which has invented the proverb, 'Time is money,' will understand my vexation. The word 'Delay' entered the secret chamber of my brain, resounded there like a tolling bell which maddens the ear, affected all my senses, took on a black colouring, a bitter taste, a deadly meaning.

'I am really sorry to see you worried like this. Indeed, I am . . . '

It was the only humane speech I used to hear at that time. And it came from a doctor, appropriately enough.

A doctor is humane by definition. But that man was so in reality. His speech was not professional. I was not ill. But other people were, and that was the reason of his visiting the ship.

He was the doctor of our Legation and, of course, of the Consulate too. He looked after the ship's health, which generally was poor, and trembling, as it were, on the verge of a break-up.

Yes. The men ailed. And thus time was not only money, but life as well.

I had never seen such a steady ship's company. As the doctor remarked to me: 'You seem to have a most respectable lot of seamen.' Not only were they consistently sober, but they did not even want to go ashore. Care was taken to expose them as little as possible to the sun. They were employed on light work under the awnings. And the humane doctor commended me.

'Your arrangements appear to me to be very judicious, my dear captain.'

It is difficult to express how much that pronouncement comforted me. The doctor's round full face framed in a light-coloured whisker was the perfection of a dignified amenity. He was the only human being in the world who seemed to take the slightest interest in me. He would generally sit in the cabin for half an hour or so at every visit.

I said to him one day: 'I suppose the only thing now is to take care of them as you are doing, till I can get the ship to sea?'

He inclined his head, shutting his eyes under the large spectacles, and murmured: 'The sea . . . undoubtedly.'

The first member of the crew fairly knocked over was the steward – the first man to whom I had spoken on board. He was taken ashore (with choleraic symptoms) and died there at the end of a week. Then, while I was still under the startling impression of this first home-thrust of the climate, Mr Burns gave up and went to bed in a raging fever without saying a word to anybody.

I believe he had partly fretted himself into that illness; the climate did the rest with the swiftness of an invisible monster ambushed in the air, in the water, in the mud of the river-bank. Mr Burns was a predestined victim.

I discovered him lying on his back, glaring sullenly and radiating heat on one like a small furnace. He would hardly answer my questions, and only grumbled: couldn't a man take an afternoon off duty with a bad headache – for once?

That evening, as I sat in the saloon after dinner, I could hear him muttering continuously in his room. Ransome, who was clearing the table, said to me: 'I am afraid, sir, I won't be able to give the mate all the attention he's likely to need. I will have to be forward in the galley a great part of my time.'

Ransome was the cook. The mate had pointed him out to me the first day, standing on the deck, his arms crossed on his broad chest, gazing on the river.

Even at a distance his well-proportioned figure, something thoroughly sailor-like in his poise, made him noticeable. On nearer view the intelligent, quiet eyes, a well-bred face, the disciplined independence of his manner made up an attractive personality. When, in addition, Mr Burns told me that he was the best seaman in the ship, I expressed my surprise that in his earliest prime and of such appearance he should sign on as cook on board a ship.

'It's his heart,' Mr Burns had said. 'There's something wrong with it. He mustn't exert himself too much or he may drop dead suddenly.'

And he was the only one the climate had not touched – perhaps because, carrying a deadly enemy in his breast, he had schooled himself into a systematic control of feelings and movements. When one was in the secret this was apparent in his manner. After the poor steward died, and as he could not be replaced by a white man in this Oriental port, Ransome had volunteered to do the double work.

'I can do it all right, sir, as long as I go about it quietly,' he had assured me.

But obviously he couldn't be expected to take up sick-nursing in addition. Moreover, the doctor peremptorily ordered Mr Burns ashore.

With a seaman on each side holding him up under the arms, the mate went over the gangway more sullen than ever. We built him up with pillows in the gharry, and he made an effort to say brokenly: 'Now – you've got – what you wanted – got me out of – the ship.'

'You were never more mistaken in your life, Mr Burns,' I said quietly, duly smiling at him; and the trap drove off to a sort of sanatorium, a pavilion of bricks which the doctor had in the grounds of his residence.

I visited Mr Burns regularly. After the first few days, when he didn't know anybody, he received me as if I had come either to gloat over a crushed enemy or else to curry favour with a deeply-wronged person. It was either one or the other, just as it happened according to his fantastic sick-room moods. Whichever it was, he managed to convey it to me even during the period when he appeared almost too weak to talk. I treated him to my invariable kindliness.

Then one day, suddenly, a surge of downright panic burst through all this craziness.

If I left him behind in this deadly place he would die. He felt it, he was certain of it. But I wouldn't have the heart to leave him ashore. He had a wife and child in Sydney.

He produced his wasted fore-arms from under the sheet which covered him and clasped his fleshless claws. He would die! He would die here . . .

He absolutely managed to sit up, but only for a moment, and when he fell back I really thought that he would die there and then. I called to the Bengali dispenser, and hastened away from the room.

Next day he upset me thoroughly by renewing his entreaties. I returned an evasive answer, and left him the picture of ghastly despair. The day after I went in with reluctance, and he attacked me at once in a much stronger voice and with an abundance of argument which was quite startling. He presented his case with a sort of crazy vigour, and asked me finally how would I like to have a man's death on my conscience? He wanted me to promise that I would not sail without him.

I said that I really must consult the doctor first. He cried out at that. The doctor! Never! That would be a death sentence.

The effort had exhausted him. He closed his eyes, but went on rambling in a low voice. I had hated him from the start. The late captain had hated him too. Had wished him dead. Had wished all hands dead . . .

'What do you want to stand in with that wicked corpse for, sir? He'll have you too,' he ended, blinking his glazed eyes vacantly.

'Mr Burns,' I cried, very much discomposed, 'what on earth are you talking about?'

He seemed to come to himself, though he was too weak to start.

'I don't know,' he said languidly. 'But don't ask that doctor, sir. You and I are sailors. Don't ask him, sir. Someday perhaps you will have a wife and child yourself.'

And again he pleaded for the promise that I would not leave him behind. I had the firmness of mind not to give it to him. Afterwards this sternness seemed criminal; for my mind was made up. That prostrated man, with hardly strength enough to breathe and ravaged by a passion of fear, was irresistible. And, besides, he had happened to hit on the right words. He and I were sailors. That was a claim, for I had no other family. As to the wife-and-child (someday) argument, it had no force. It sounded merely bizarre.

I could imagine no claim that would be stronger and more absorbing than the claim of that ship, of these men snared in the river by silly commercial complications, as if in some poisonous trap.

However, I had nearly fought my way out. Out to sea. The sea – which was pure, safe, and friendly. Three days more.

That thought sustained and carried me on my way back to the

ship. In the saloon the doctor's voice greeted me, and his large form followed his voice, issuing out of the starboard spare cabin where the ship's medicine chest was kept securely lashed in the bed-place.

Finding that I was not on board he had gone in there, he said, to inspect the supply of drugs, bandages, and so on. Everything was completed and in order.

I thanked him; I had just been thinking of asking him to do that very thing, as in a couple of days, as he knew, we were going to sea, where all our troubles of every sort would be over at last.

He listened gravely and made no answer. But when I opened to him my mind as to Mr Burns, he sat down by my side, and, laying his hand on my knee amicably, begged me to think what it was I was exposing myself to.

The man was just strong enough to bear being moved and no more. But he couldn't stand a return of the fever. I had before me a passage of sixty days perhaps, beginning with intricate navigation and ending probably with a lot of bad weather. Could I run the risk of having to go through it single-handed, with no chief officer and with a second quite a youth? . . .

He might have added that it was my first command too. He did probably think of that fact, for he checked himself. It was very present to my mind.

He advised me earnestly to cable to Singapore for a chief officer, even if I had to delay my sailing for a week.

'Not a day,' I said. The very thought gave me the shivers. The hands seemed fairly fit, all of them, and this was the time to get them away. Once at sea I was not afraid of facing anything. The sea was now the only remedy for all my troubles.

The doctor's glasses were directed at me like two lamps searching the genuineness of my resolution. He opened his lips as if to argue further, but shut them again without saying anything. I had a vision of poor Burns so vivid in his exhaustion, helplessness, and anguish, that it moved me more than the reality I had come away from only an hour before. It was purged from the drawbacks of his personality, and I could not resist it.

'Look here,' I said. 'Unless you tell me officially that the man must not be moved I'll make arrangements to have him brought on board tomorrow, and shall take the ship out of the river next morning, even if I have to anchor outside the bar for a couple of days to get her ready for sea.'

'Oh! I'll make all the arrangements myself,' said the doctor at once. 'I spoke as I did only as a friend – as a well-wisher, and that sort of thing.'

He rose in his dignified simplicity and gave me a warm handshake, rather solemnly, I thought. But he was as good as his word. When Mr Burns appeared at the gangway carried on a stretcher, the doctor himself walked by its side. The programme had been altered in so far that this transportation had been left to the last moment, on the very morning of our departure.

It was barely an hour after sunrise. The doctor waved his big arm to me from the shore and walked back at once to his trap, which had followed him empty to the river-side. Mr Burns, carried across the quarter-deck, had the appearance of being absolutely lifeless. Ransome went down to settle him in his cabin. I had to remain on deck to look after the ship, for the tug had got hold of our tow-rope already.

The splash of our shore-fasts falling in the water produced a complete change of feeling in me. It was like the imperfect relief of awakening from a nightmare. But when the ship's head swung down the river away from that town, Oriental and squalid, I missed the expected elation of that striven-for moment. What there was, undoubtedly, was a relaxation of tension which translated itself into a sense of weariness after an inglorious fight.

About midday we anchored a mile outside the bar. The afternoon was busy for all hands. Watching the work from the poop, where I remained all the time, I detected in it some of the languor of the six weeks spent in the steaming heat of the river. The first breeze would blow that away. Now the calm was complete. I judged that the second officer – a callow youth with an unpromising face – was not, to put it mildly, of that invaluable stuff from which a commander's right hand is made. But I was glad to catch along the main deck a few smiles on those seamen's faces at which I had hardly had time to have a good look as yet. Having thrown off the mortal coil of shore affairs, I felt myself familiar with them and yet a little strange, like a long-lost wanderer among his kin.

Ransome flitted continually to and fro between the galley and the cabin. It was a pleasure to look at him. The man positively had grace. He alone of all the crew had not had a day's illness in port. But with the knowledge of that uneasy heart within his breast I could detect the restraint he put on the natural sailor-like agility of his movements. It was as though he had something very fragile or very explosive to carry about his person and was all the time aware of it.

I had occasion to address him once or twice. He answered me in his pleasant quiet voice and with a faint, slightly wistful smile. Mr Burns appeared to be resting. He seemed fairly comfortable.

After sunset I came out on deck again to meet only a still void. The thin, featureless crust of the coast could not be distinguished. The darkness had risen around the ship like a mysterious emanation from the dumb and lonely waters. I leaned on the rail and turned my ear to the shadows of the night. Not a sound. My command might have been a planet flying vertiginously on its appointed path in a space of infinite silence. I clung to the rail as if my sense of balance were leaving me for good. How absurd. I hailed nervously.

'On deck there!'

The immediate answer, 'Yes, sir,' broke the spell. The anchor-watch man ran up the poop ladder smartly. I told him to report at once the slightest sign of a breeze coming.

Going below I looked in on Mr Burns. In fact, I could not avoid seeing him, for his door stood open. The man was so wasted that, in that white cabin, under a white sheet, and with his diminished head sunk in the white pillow, his red moustaches captured one's eyes exclusively, like something artificial – a pair of moustaches from a shop exhibited there in the harsh light of the bulkhead-lamp without a shade.

While I stared with a sort of wonder he asserted himself by opening his eyes and even moving them in my direction. A minute stir.

'Dead calm, Mr Burns,' I said resignedly.

In an unexpectedly distinct voice Mr Burns began a rambling speech. Its tone was very strange, not as if affected by his illness, but as if of a different nature. It sounded unearthly. As to the matter, I seemed to make out that it was the fault of the 'old man' – the late captain – ambushed down there under the sea with some evil intention. It was a weird story.

I listened to the end; then stepping into the cabin I laid my hand on the mate's forehead. It was cool. He was light-headed only from extreme weakness. Suddenly he seemed to become aware of me, and in his own voice – of course, very feeble – he asked regretfully: 'Is there no chance at all to get under way, sir?'

'What's the good of letting go our hold of the ground only to drift, Mr Burns?' I answered.

He sighed, and I left him to his immobility. His hold on life was as slender as his hold on sanity. I was oppressed by my lonely responsibilities. I went into my cabin to seek relief in a few hours' sleep, but almost before I closed my eyes the man on deck came down reporting a light breeze. Enough to get under way with, he said.

And it was no more than just enough. I ordered the windlass manned, the sails loosed, and the topsails set. But by the time I had cast the ship I could hardly feel any breath of wind. Nevertheless, I trimmed the yards and put everything on her. I was not going to give up the attempt.

Chapter 4

WITH HER ANCHOR at the bow and clothed in canvas to her very trucks, my command seemed to stand as motionless as a model ship set on the gleams and shadows of polished marble. It was impossible to distinguish land from water in the enigmatical tranquillity of the immense forces of the world. A sudden impatience possessed me.

'Won't she answer the helm at all?' I said irritably to the man whose strong brown hands grasping the spokes of the wheel stood out lighted on the darkness; like a symbol of mankind's claim to the direction of its own fate.

He answered me: 'Yes, sir. She's coming-to slowly.'

'Let her head come up to south.'

'Aye, aye, sir.'

I paced the poop. There was not a sound but that of my footsteps, till the man spoke again.

'She is at south now, sir.'

I felt a slight tightness of the chest before I gave out the first course of my first command to the silent night, heavy with dew and sparkling with stars. There was a finality in the act committing me to the endless vigilance of my lonely task.

'Steady her head at that,' I said at last. 'The course is south.'

'South, sir,' echoed the man.

I sent below the second mate and his watch and remained in charge, walking the deck through the chill, somnolent hours that precede the dawn.

Slight puffs came and went, and whenever they were strong enough to wake up the black water the murmur alongside ran through my very heart in a delicate crescendo of delight and died away swiftly. I was bitterly tired. The very stars seemed weary of waiting for daybreak. It came at last with a mother-of-pearl sheen at the zenith, such as I had never seen before in the tropics, unglowing, almost grey, with a strange reminder of high latitudes.

The voice of the look-out man hailed from forward: 'Land on the port bow, sir.'

'All right.'

Leaning on the rail I never even raised my eyes. The motion of the ship was imperceptible. Presently Ransome brought me the cup of morning coffee. After I had drunk it I looked ahead, and in the still streak of very bright pale orange light I saw the land profiled flatly as if cut out of black paper and seeming to float on the water as light as cork. But the rising sun turned it into mere dark vapour, a doubtful, massive shadow trembling in the hot glare.

The watch finished washing decks. I went below and stopped at Mr Burns' door (he could not bear to have it shut), but hesitated to speak to him till he moved his eyes. I gave him the news.

'Sighted Cape Liant at daylight. About fifteen miles.'

He moved his lips then, but I heard no sound till I put my ear down, and caught the peevish comment: 'This is crawling . . . No luck.'

'Better luck than standing still, anyhow,' I pointed out resignedly, and left him to whatever thoughts or fancies haunted his hopeless prostration.

Later that morning, when relieved by my second officer, I threw myself on my couch and for some three hours or so I really found oblivion. It was so perfect that on waking up I wondered where I was. Then came the immense relief of the thought: on board my ship! At sea! At sea!

Through the port-holes I beheld an unruffled, sun-smitten horizon. The horizon of a windless day. But its spaciousness alone was enough to give me a sense of a fortunate escape, a momentary exultation of freedom.

I stepped out into the saloon with my heart lighter than it had been for days. Ransome was at the sideboard preparing to lay the table for the first sea dinner of the passage. He turned his head, and something in his eyes checked my modest elation.

Instinctively I asked: 'What is it now?' not expecting in the least the answer I got. It was given with that sort of contained serenity which was characteristic of the man.

'I am afraid we haven't left all sickness behind us, sir.'

'We haven't! What's the matter?'

He told me then that two of our men had been taken bad with fever in the night. One of them was burning and the other was shivering, but he thought that it was pretty much the same thing. I thought so too. I felt shocked by the news. 'One burning, the other shivering, you say? No. We haven't left the sickness behind. Do they look very ill?'

'Middling bad, sir.' Ransome's eyes gazed steadily into mine. We exchanged smiles. Ransome's a little wistful, as usual, mine no doubt grim enough, to correspond with my secret exasperation.

I asked: 'Was there any wind at all this morning?'

'Can hardly say that, sir. We've moved all the time though. The land ahead seems a little nearer.'

That was it. A little nearer. Whereas if we had only had a little more wind, only a very little more, we might, we should, have been abreast of Liant by this time and increasing our distance from that contaminated shore. And it was not only the distance. It seemed to me that a stronger breeze would have blown away the infection which clung to the ship. It obviously did cling to the ship. Two men. One burning, one shivering. I felt a distinct reluctance to go and look at them. What was the good? Poison is poison. Tropical fever is tropical fever. But that it should have stretched its claw after us over the sea seemed to me an extraordinary and unfair licence. I could hardly believe that it could be anything worse than the last desperate pluck of the evil from which we were escaping into the clean breath of the sea. If only that breath had been a little stronger. However, there was the quinine against the fever. I went into the spare cabin where the medicine chest was kept to prepare two doses. I opened it full of faith as a man opens a miraculous shrine. The upper part was inhabited by a collection of bottles, all square-shouldered and as like each other as peas. Under that orderly array there were two drawers, stuffed as full of things as one could imagine – paper packages, bandages, cardboard boxes officially labelled. The lower of the two, in one of its compartments, contained our provision of quinine.

There were five bottles, all round and all of a size. One was about a third full. The other four remained still wrapped up in paper and sealed. But I did not expect to see an envelope lying on top of them. A square envelope, belonging, in fact, to the ship's stationery.

It lay so that I could see it was not closed down, and on picking it up and turning it over I perceived that it was addressed to myself. It contained a half-sheet of notepaper, which I unfolded with a queer sense of dealing with the uncanny, but without any excitement as people meet and do extraordinary things in a dream.

'My dear Captain,' it began, but I ran to the signature. The writer was the doctor. The date was that of the day on which, returning from my visit to Mr Burns in the hospital, I had found the excellent doctor waiting for me in the cabin; and when he told me that he had been putting in time inspecting the medicine chest for me. How bizarre! While expecting me to come in at any moment he had been amusing himself by writing me a letter, and then as I came in had hastened to stuff it into the medicine-chest drawer. A rather incredible proceeding. I turned to the text in wonder.

In a large, hurried, but legible hand the good, sympathetic man for some reason, either of kindness or more likely impelled by the irresistible desire to express his opinion, with which he didn't want to damp my hopes before, was warning me not to put my trust in the beneficial effects of a change from land to sea. 'I didn't want to add to your worries by discouraging your hopes,' he wrote. 'I am afraid that, medically speaking, the end of your troubles is not yet.' In short, he expected me to have to fight a probable return of tropical illness. Fortunately I had a good provision of quinine. I should put my trust in that, and administer it steadily, when the ship's health would certainly improve.

I crumpled up the letter and rammed it into my pocket. Ransome carried off two big doses to the men forward. As to myself, I did not go on deck as yet. I went instead to the door of Mr Burns' room, and gave him that news, too.

It was impossible to say the effect it had on him. At first I thought that he was speechless. His head lay sunk in the pillow. He moved his lips enough, however, to assure me that he was getting much stronger; a statement shockingly untrue on the face of it.

That afternoon I took my watch as a matter of course. A great over-heated stillness enveloped the ship and seemed to hold her motionless in a flaming ambience composed in two shades of blue. Faint, hot puffs eddied nervelessly from her sails. And yet she moved. She must have. For, as the sun was setting, we had drawn abreast of Cape Liant and dropped it behind us: an ominous retreating shadow in the last gleams of twilight.

In the evening, under the crude glare of his lamp, Mr Burns seemed to have come more to the surface of his bedding. It was as if a depressing hand had been lifted off him. He answered my few words by a comparatively long, connected speech. He asserted himself strongly. If he escaped being smothered by this stagnant heat, he said, he was confident that in a very few days he would be able to come up on deck and help me.

While he was speaking I trembled lest this effort of energy should leave him lifeless before my eyes. But I cannot deny that there was something comforting in his willingness. I made a suitable reply, but pointed out to him that the only thing that could really help us was wind – a fair wind.

He rolled his head impatiently on the pillow. And it was not comforting in the least to hear him begin to mutter crazily about the late captain, that old man buried in latitude 8° 20', right in our way – ambushed at the entrance of the Gulf.

'Are you still thinking of your late captain, Mr Burns?' I said. 'I imagine the dead feel no animosity against the living. They care nothing for them.'

'You don't know that one,' he breathed out feebly.

'No. I didn't know him, and he didn't know me. And so he can't have any grievance against me, anyway.'

'Yes. But there's all the rest of us on board,' he insisted.

I felt the inexpungible strength of common sense being insidiously menaced by this gruesome, by this insane delusion. And I said: 'You mustn't talk so much. You will tire yourself.'

'And there is the ship herself,' he persisted in a whisper.

'Now, not a word more,' I said, stepping in and laying my hand on his cool forehead. It proved to me that this atrocious absurdity was rooted in the man himself and not in the disease, which, apparently, had emptied him of every power, mental and physical, except that one fixed idea.

I avoided giving Mr Burns any opening for conversation for the next few days. I merely used to throw him a hasty, cheery word when passing his door. I believe that if he had had the strength he would have called out after me more than once. But he hadn't the strength. Ransome, however, observed to me one afternoon that the mate 'seemed to be picking up wonderfully'.

'Did he talk any nonsense to you of late?' I asked casually.

'No, sir.' Ransome was startled by the direct question; but, after a pause, he added equably: 'He told me this morning, sir, that he was sorry he had to bury our late captain right in the ship's way, as one may say, out of the Gulf.'

'Isn't this nonsense enough for you?' I asked, looking confidently at the intelligent, quiet face on which the secret uneasiness in the man's breast had thrown a transparent veil of care.

Ransome didn't know. He had not given a thought to the matter. And with a faint smile he flitted away from me on his never-ending duties, with his usual guarded activity.

Two more days passed. We had advanced a little way – a very little way – into the larger space of the Gulf of Siam. Seizing eagerly upon the elation of the first command thrown into my lap, by the agency of Captain Giles, I had yet an uneasy feeling that such luck as this has got perhaps to be paid for in some way. I had held, professionally, a review of my chances. I was competent enough for that. At least, I thought so. I had a general sense of my preparedness which only a man pursuing a calling he loves can know. That feeling seemed to me the most natural thing in the world. As natural as breathing. I imagined I could not have lived without it.

I don't know what I expected. Perhaps nothing else than that special intensity of existence which is the quintessence of youthful aspirations. Whatever I expected I did not expect to be beset by hurricanes. I knew better than that. In the Gulf of Siam there are no hurricanes. But neither did I expect to find myself bound hand and foot to the hopeless extent which was revealed to me as the days went on.

Not that the evil spell held us always motionless. Mysterious currents drifted us here and there, with a stealthy power made manifest by the changing vistas of the islands fringing the east shore of the Gulf. And there were winds too, fitful and deceitful. They raised hopes only to dash them into the bitterest disappointment, promises of advance ending in lost ground, expiring in sighs, dying into dumb stillness in which the currents had it all their own way – their own inimical way.

The Island of Koh-ring, a great, black, upheaved ridge amongst a lot of tiny islets, lying upon the glassy water like a triton amongst minnows, seemed to be the centre of the fatal circle. It seemed impossible to get away from it. Day after day it remained in sight. More than once, in a favourable breeze, I would take its bearing in the fast ebbing twilight, thinking that it was for the last time. Vain hope. A night of fitful airs would undo the gains of temporary favour, and the rising sun would throw out the black relief of Koh-ring, looking more barren, inhospitable, and grim than ever.

'It's like being bewitched, upon my word,' I said once to Mr Burns, from my usual position in the doorway.

He was sitting up in his bed-place. He was progressing towards the world of living men, if he could hardly have been said to have rejoined it yet. He nodded to me his frail and bony head in a wisely mysterious assent.

'Oh, yes, I know what you mean,' I said. 'But you cannot expect me to believe that a dead man has the power to put out of joint the meteorology of this part of the world. Though indeed it seems to have gone utterly wrong. The land and sea breezes have got broken up into small pieces. We cannot depend upon them for five minutes together.'

'It won't be very long now before I can come up on deck,' muttered Mr Burns, 'and then we shall see.'

Whether he meant this for a promise to grapple with supernatural evil I couldn't tell. At any rate, it wasn't the kind of assistance I needed. On the other hand, I had been living on deck practically night and day so as to take advantage of every chance to get my ship a little more to the southward. The mate, I could see, was extremely weak yet, and not quite rid of his delusion, which to me appeared but a symptom of his disease. At all events, the hopefulness of an invalid was not to be discouraged. I said: 'You will be most welcome there, I am sure, Mr Burns. If you go on improving at this rate you'll be presently one of the healthiest men in the ship.'

This pleased him, but his extreme emaciation converted his self-satisfied smile into a ghastly exhibition of long teeth under the red moustache.

'Aren't the fellows improving, sir?' he asked soberly, with an extremely sensible expression of anxiety on his face.

I answered him only with a vague gesture and went away from the door. The fact was that disease played with us capriciously very much as the winds did. It would go from one man to another with a lighter or heavier touch, which always left its mark behind, staggering some, knocking others over for a time, leaving this one, returning to another, so that all of them had now an invalidish aspect and a hunted, apprehensive look in their eyes; while Ransome and I, the only two completely untouched, went amongst them assiduously distributing quinine. It was a double fight. The adverse weather held us in front and the disease pressed on our rear. I must say that the men were very good. The constant toil of trimming the yards they faced willingly. But all spring was out of their limbs, and as I looked at them from the poop I could not keep from my mind the dreadful impression that they were moving in poisoned air.

Down below, in his cabin, Mr Burns had advanced so far as not only to be able to sit up, but even to draw up his legs. Clasping them with bony arms, like an animated skeleton, he emitted deep, impatient sighs.

'The great thing to do, sir,' he would tell me on every occasion, when I gave him the chance, 'the great thing is to get the ship past 8° 20' of latitude. Once she's past that we're all right.'

At first I used only to smile at him, though, God knows, I had not much heart left for smiles. But at last I lost my patience.

'Oh, yes. The latitude 8° 20'. That's where you buried your late captain, isn't it?' Then with severity: 'Don't you think, Mr Burns, it's about time you dropped all that nonsense?'

He rolled at me his deep-sunken eyes in a glance of invincible obstinacy. But for the rest, he only muttered, just loud enough for me to hear, something about 'Not surprised . . . find . . . play us some beastly trick yet . . . '

Such passages as this were not exactly wholesome for my resolution. The stress of adversity was beginning to tell on me. At the same time I felt a contempt for that obscure weakness of my soul. I said to myself disdainfully that it should take much more than that to affect in the smallest degree my fortitude.

I didn't know then how soon and from what unexpected direction it would be attacked.

It was the very next day. The sun had risen clear of the southern shoulder of Koh-ring, which still hung, like an evil attendant, on our port quarter. It was intensely hateful to my sight. During the night we had been heading all round the compass, trimming the yards again and again, to what I fear must have been for the most part imaginary puffs of air. Then just about sunrise we got for an hour an inexplicable, steady breeze, right in our teeth. There was no sense in it. It fitted neither with the season of the year, nor with the secular experience of seamen as recorded in books, nor with the aspect of the sky. Only purposeful malevolence could account for it. It sent us travelling at a great pace away from our proper course; and if we had been out on pleasure sailing bent it would have been a delightful breeze, with the awakened sparkle of the sea, with the sense of motion and a feeling of unwonted freshness. Then all at once, as if disdaining to carry farther the sorry jest, it dropped and died out completely in less than five minutes. The ship's head swung where it listed; the stilled sea took on the polish of a steel plate in the calm.

I went below, not because I meant to take some rest, but simply because I couldn't bear to look at it just then. The indefatigable Ransome was busy in the saloon. It had become a regular practice with him to give me an informal health report in the morning. He turned away from the sideboard with his usual pleasant, quiet gaze. No shadow rested on his intelligent forehead.

'There are a good many of them middling bad this morning, sir,' he said in a calm tone.

'What? All knocked out?'

'Only two actually in their bunks, sir, but . . . '

'It's last night that has done for them. We have had to pull and haul all the blessed time.'

'I heard, sir. I had a mind to come out and help, only, you know . . . '

'Certainly not. You mustn't . . . The fellows lie at night about the decks, too. It isn't good for them.'

Ransome assented. But men couldn't be looked after like children. Moreover, one could hardly blame them for trying for such coolness and such air as there was to be found on deck. He himself, of course, knew better.

He was, indeed, a reasonable man. Yet it would have been hard to say that the others were not. The last few days had been for us like the ordeal of the fiery furnace. One really couldn't quarrel with their common, imprudent humanity making the best of the moments of relief, when the night brought in the illusion of coolness and the starlight twinkled through the heavy, dew-laden air. Moreover, most of them were so weakened that hardly anything could be done without everybody that could totter mustering on the braces. No, it was no use remonstrating with them. But I fully believed that quinine was of very great use indeed.

I believed in it. I pinned my faith to it. It would save the men, the ship, break the spell by its medicinal virtue, make time of no account, the weather but a passing worry, and, like a magic powder working against mysterious malefices, secure the first passage of my first command against the evil powers of calms and pestilence. I looked upon it as more precious than gold, and unlike gold, of which there hardly ever seems to be enough anywhere, the ship had a sufficient store of it. I went in to get it with the purpose of weighing out doses. I stretched my hand with the feeling of a man reaching for an unfailing panacea, took up a fresh bottle and unrolled the wrapper, noticing as I did so that the ends, both top and bottom, had come unsealed . . .

But why record all the swift steps of the appalling discovery? You have guessed the truth already. There was the wrapper, the bottle, and the white powder inside, some sort of powder! But it wasn't quinine. One look at it was quite enough. I remember that at the very moment of picking up the bottle, before I even dealt with the wrapper, the weight of the object I had in my hand gave me an instant of premonition. Quinine is as light as feathers; and my nerves must have been exasperated into an extraordinary sensibility.

I let the bottle smash itself on the floor. The stuff, whatever it was, felt gritty under the sole of my shoe. I snatched up the next bottle and then the next. The weight alone told the tale. One after another they fell, breaking at my feet, not because I threw them down in my dismay, but slipping through my fingers as if this disclosure were too much for my strength.

It is a fact that the very greatness of a mental shock helps one to bear up against it, by producing a sort of temporary insensibility. I came out of the state-room stunned, as if something heavy had dropped on my head. From the other side of the saloon, across the table, Ransome, with a duster in his hand, stared open-mouthed. I don't think that I looked wild. It is quite possible that I appeared to be in a hurry because I was instinctively hastening up on deck. An example this of training become instinct. The difficulties, the dangers, the problems of a ship at sea must be met on deck.

To this fact, as it were of nature, I responded instinctively; which may bė taken as a proof that for a moment I must have been robbed of my reason.

I was certainly off my balance, a prey to impulse, for at the bottom of the stairs I turned and flung myself at the doorway of Mr Burns' cabin. The wildness of his aspect checked my mental disorder. He was sitting up in his bunk, his body looking immensely long, his head drooping a little sideways, with affected complacency. He flourished, in his trembling hand, on the end of a fore-arm no thicker than a stout walking-stick, a shining pair of scissors which he tried before my very eyes to jab at his throat.

I was to a certain extent horrified; but it was rather a secondary sort of effect, not really strong enough to make me yell at him in some such manner as: 'Stop!' . . . 'Heavens!' 'What are you doing?'

In reality he was simply overtaxing his returning strength in a shaky attempt to clip off the thick growth of his red beard. A large towel was spread over his lap, and a shower of stiff hairs, like bits of copper wire, was descending on it at every snip of the scissors.

He turned to me his face grotesque beyond the fantasies of mad dreams, one cheek all bushy as if with a swollen flame, the other denuded and sunken, with the untouched long moustache on that side asserting itself, lonely and fierce. And while he stared thunder-struck, with the gaping scissors on his fingers, I shouted my discovery at him fiendishly, in six words, without comment.

Chapter 5

I HEARD THE CLATTER of the scissors escaping from his hand, noted the perilous heave of his whole person over the edge of the bunk after them, and then, returning to my first purpose, pursued my course on to the deck. The sparkle of the sea filled my eyes. It was gorgeous and barren, monotonous and without hope under the empty curve of the sky. The sails hung motionless and slack, the very folds of their sagging surfaces moved no more than carved granite. The impetuosity of my advent made the man at the helm start slightly. A block aloft squeaked incomprehensibly, for what on earth could have made it do so? It was a whistling note like a bird's. For a long, long time I faced an empty world, steeped in an infinity of silence, through which the sunshine poured and flowed for some mysterious purpose. Then I heard Ransome's voice at my elbow.

'I have put Mr Burns back to bed, sir.'

'You have.'

'Well, sir, he got out, all of a sudden, but when he let go of the edge of his bunk he fell down. He isn't light-headed, though, it seems to me.'

'No,' I said dully, without looking at Ransome. He waited for a moment, then, cautiously as if not to give offence: 'I don't think we need lose much of that stuff, sir,' he said, 'I can sweep it up, every bit of it almost, and then we could sift the glass out. I will go about it at once. It will not make the breakfast late, not ten minutes.'

'Oh, yes,' I said bitterly. 'Let the breakfast wait, sweep up every bit of it, and then throw the damned lot overboard!'

The profound silence returned, and when I looked over my shoulder Ransome – the intelligent, serene Ransome – had vanished from my side. The intense loneliness of the sea acted like poison on my brain. When I turned my eyes to the ship, I had a morbid vision of her as a floating grave. Who hasn't heard of ships found drifting, haphazard, with their crews all dead? I looked at the seaman at the helm, I had an impulse to speak to him, and, indeed, his face took on an expectant cast as if he had guessed my intention. But in the end I went below, thinking I would be alone with the greatness of my trouble for a little while. But through his open door Mr Burns saw me come down, and addressed me grumpily: 'Well, sir?'

I went in. 'It isn't well at all,' I said.

Mr Burns, re-established in his bed-place, was concealing his hirsute cheek in the palm of his hand.

'That confounded fellow has taken away the scissors from me,' were the next words he said.

The tension I was suffering from was so great that it was perhaps just as well that Mr Burns had started on this grievance. He seemed very sore about it and grumbled, 'Does he think I am mad, or what?'

'I don't think so, Mr Burns,' I said. I looked upon him at that moment as a model of self-possession. I even conceived on that account a sort of admiration for that man, who had (apart from the intense materiality of what was left of his beard) come as near to being a disembodied spirit as any man can do and live. I noticed the preternatural sharpness of the ridge of his nose, the deep cavities of his temples, and I envied him. He was so reduced that he would probably die very soon. Enviable man! So near extinction – while I had to bear within me a tumult of suffering vitality, doubt, confusion, self-reproach, and an indefinite reluctance to meet the horrid logic of the situation. I could not help muttering: 'I feel as if I were going mad myself.'

Mr Burns glared spectrally, but otherwise wonderfully composed.

'I always thought he would play us some deadly trick,' he said, with a peculiar emphasis on the *he*.

It gave me a mental shock, but I had neither the mind, nor the heart, nor the spirit to argue with him. My form of sickness was indifference. The creeping paralysis of a hopeless outlook. So I only gazed at him. Mr Burns broke into further speech.

'Eh? What? No! You won't believe it? Well, how do you account for this? How do you think it could have happened?'

'Happened?' I repeated dully. 'Why, yes, how in the name of the infernal powers did this thing happen?'

Indeed, on thinking it out, it seemed incomprehensible that it should just be like this: the bottles emptied, refilled, rewrapped, and replaced. A sort of plot, a sinister attempt to deceive, a thing resembling sly vengeance – but for what? – or else a fiendish joke. But Mr Burns was in possession of a theory. It was simple, and he uttered it solemnly in a hollow voice.

'I suppose they have given him about fifteen pounds in Haiphong for that little lot.'

'Mr Burns!' I cried.

He nodded grotesquely over his raised legs, like two broomsticks in the pyjamas, with enormous bare feet at the end.

'Why not? The stuff is pretty expensive in this part of the world, and they were very short of it in Tonkin. And what did he care? You have not known him. I have, and I have defied him. He feared neither God, nor devil, nor man, nor wind, nor sea, nor his own conscience. And I believe he hated everybody and everything. But I think he was afraid to die. I believe I am the only man who ever stood up to him. I faced him in that cabin where you live now, when he was sick, and I cowed him then. He thought I was going to twist his neck for him. If he had had his way we would have been beating up against the north-east monsoon, as long as he lived and afterwards too, for ages and ages. Acting the Flying Dutchman in the China Sea! Ha! Ha!'

'But why should he replace the bottles like this?' . . . I began.

'Why shouldn't he? Why should he want to throw the bottles away? They fit the drawer. They belong to the medicine chest.'

'And they were wrapped up,' I cried.

'Well, the wrappers were there. Did it from habit, I suppose, and as to refilling, there is always a lot of stuff they send in paper parcels that burst after a time. And then, who can tell? I suppose you didn't taste it, sir? But, of course, you are sure . . . '

'No,' I said. 'I didn't taste it. It is all overboard now.'

Behind me, a soft, cultivated voice said: 'I have tasted it. It seemed a mixture of all sorts, sweetish, saltish, very horrible.'

Ransome, stepping out of the pantry, had been listening for some time, as it was very excusable in him to do.

'A dirty trick,' said Mr Burns. 'I always said he would.'

The magnitude of my indignation was unbounded. And the kind, sympathetic doctor too. The only sympathetic man I ever knew . . . instead of writing that warning letter, the very refinement of sympathy, why didn't the man make a proper inspection? But, as a matter of fact, it was hardly fair to blame the doctor. The fittings were in order and the medicine chest is an officially arranged affair. There was nothing really to arouse the slightest suspicion. The person I could never forgive was myself. Nothing should ever be taken for granted. The seed of everlasting remorse was sown in my breast.

'I feel it's all my fault,' I exclaimed, 'mine, and nobody else's. That's how I feel. I shall never forgive myself.'

'That's very foolish, sir,' said Mr Burns fiercely.

And after this effort he fell back exhausted on his bed. He closed his eyes, he panted; this affair, this abominable surprise had shaken him up, too. As I turned away I perceived Ransome looking at me blankly. He appreciated what it meant, but he managed to produce his pleasant, wistful smile. Then he stepped back into his pantry, and I rushed up on deck again to see whether there was any wind, any breath under the sky, any stir of the air, any sign of hope. The deadly stillness met me again. Nothing was changed except that there was a different man at the wheel. He looked ill. His whole figure drooped, and he seemed rather to cling to the spokes than hold them with a controlling grip. I said to him: 'You are not fit to be here.'

'I can manage, sir,' he said feebly.

As a matter of fact, there was nothing for him to do. The ship had no steerage way. She lay with her head to the westward, the everlasting Koh-ring visible over the stern, with a few small islets, black spots in the great blaze, swimming before my troubled eyes. And but for those bits of land there was no speck on the sky, no speck on the water, no shape of vapour, no wisp of smoke, no sail, no boat, no stir of humanity, no sign of life, nothing!

The first question was, what to do? What could one do? The first thing to do obviously was to tell the men. I did it that very day. I wasn't going to let the knowledge simply get about. I would face them. They were assembled on the quarter-deck for the purpose. Just before I stepped out to speak to them I discovered that life could hold terrible moments. No confessed criminal had ever been so oppressed by his sense of guilt. This is why, perhaps, my face was set hard and my voice curt and unemotional while I made my declaration that I could do nothing more for the sick, in the way of drugs. As to such care as could be given them they knew they had had it.

I would have held them justified in tearing me limb from limb. The silence which followed upon my words was almost harder to bear than the angriest uproar. I was crushed by the infinite depth of its reproach. But, as a matter of fact, I was mistaken. In a voice which I had great difficulty in keeping firm, I went on: 'I suppose, men, you have understood what I said, and you know what it means.'

A voice or two were heard: 'Yes, sir . . . We understand.'

They had kept silent simply because they thought that they were not called upon to say anything; and when I told them that I intended to run into Singapore and that the best chance for the ship and the men was in the efforts all of us, sick and well, must make to get her along out of this, I received the encouragement of a low, assenting murmur and of a louder voice exclaiming: 'Surely there is a way out of this blamed hole.'

Here is an extract from the notes I wrote at the time.

> We have lost Koh-ring at last. For many days now I don't think I have been two hours below altogether. I remain on deck, of course, night and day, and the nights and the days wheel over us in succession, whether long or short, who can say? All sense of time is lost in the monotony of expectation, of hope, and of desire – which is only one: Get the ship to the southward! Get the ship to the southward! The effect is curiously mechanical; the sun climbs and descends, the night swings over our heads as if somebody below the horizon were turning a crank. It is the pettiest, the most aimless! . . . and all through that miserable performance I go on, tramping, tramping the deck. How many miles have I walked on the poop of that ship! A stubborn pilgrimage of sheer restlessness, diversified by short excursions below to look upon Mr Burns. I don't know whether it is an illusion, but he seems to become more substantial from day to day. He doesn't say much, for, indeed, the situation doesn't lend itself to idle remarks. I notice this even with the men as I watch them moving or sitting about the decks. They don't talk to each other. It strikes me that if there exist an invisible ear catching the whispers of the earth, it will find this ship the most silent spot on it . . .
>
> No, Mr Burns has not much to say to me. He sits in his bunk with his beard gone, his moustaches flaming, and with an air of silent determination on his chalky physiognomy. Ransome tells me he devours all the food that is given him to the last scrap, but that, apparently, he sleeps very little. Even at night, when I go below to fill my pipe, I notice that, though dozing flat on his back, he still looks very determined. From the side glance he gives me when awake it seems as though he were annoyed at being interrupted in some arduous mental operation; and as I emerge on deck the ordered arrangement of the stars meets my eye, unclouded, infinitely wearisome. There they are: stars, sun, sea, light, darkness, space, great waters; the formidable Work of the Seven Days, into which mankind seems to have blundered unbidden. Or else decoyed. Even as I have been decoyed into this awful, this death-haunted command . . .

The only spot of light in the ship at night was that of the compass-lamps, lighting up the faces of the succeeding helmsmen; for the rest we were lost in the darkness, I walking the poop and the men lying about the decks. They were all so reduced by sickness that no watches could be kept. Those who were able to walk remained all the time on duty, lying about in the shadows of the main deck, till my voice raised for an order would bring them to their enfeebled feet, a tottering little group, moving patiently about the ship, with hardly a murmur, a whisper amongst them all. And every time I had to raise my voice it was with a pang of remorse and pity.

Then about four o'clock in the morning a light would gleam forward in the galley. The unfailing Ransome with the uneasy heart, immune, serene, and active, was getting ready the early coffee for the men. Presently he would bring me a cup up on the poop, and it was then that I allowed myself to drop into my deck-chair for a couple of hours of real sleep. No doubt I must have been snatching short dozes when leaning against the rail for a moment in sheer exhaustion; but, honestly, I was not aware of them, except in the painful form of convulsive starts that seemed to come on me even while I walked. From about five, however, until after seven I would sleep openly under the fading stars.

I would say to the helmsman: 'Call me at need,' and drop into that chair and close my eyes, feeling that there was no more sleep for me on earth. And then I would know nothing till, some time between seven and eight, I would feel a touch on my shoulder and look up at Ransome's face, with its faint, wistful smile and friendly, grey eyes, as though he were tenderly amused at my slumbers. Occasionally the second mate would come up and relieve me at early coffee time. But it didn't really matter. Generally it was a dead calm, or else faint airs so changing and fugitive that it really wasn't worth while to touch a brace for them. If the air steadied at all the seaman at the helm could be trusted for a warning shout: 'Ship's all aback, sir!' which like a trumpet-call would make me spring a foot above the deck. Those were the words which it seemed to me would have made me spring up from eternal sleep. But this was not often. I have never met since such breathless sunrises. And if the second mate happened to be there (he had generally one day in three free of fever) I would find him sitting on the skylight half-senseless, as it were, and with an idiotic gaze fastened on some object near by – a rope, a cleat, a belaying pin, a ringbolt.

That young man was rather troublesome. He remained cubbish in his sufferings. He seemed to have become completely imbecile;

and when the return of fever drove him to his cabin below the next thing would be that we would miss him from there. The first time it happened Ransome and I were very much alarmed. We started a quiet search and ultimately Ransome discovered him curled up in the sail-locker, which opened into the lobby by a sliding-door. When remonstrated with, he muttered sulkily, 'It's cool in there.' That wasn't true. It was only dark there.

The fundamental defects of his face were not improved by its uniform livid hue. It was not so with many of the men. The wastage of ill-health seemed to idealise the general character of the features, bringing out the unsuspected nobility of some, the strength of others, and in one case revealing an essentially comic aspect. He was a short, gingery, active man with a nose and chin of the Punch type, and whom his shipmates called 'Frenchy'. I don't know why. He may have been a Frenchman, but I never heard him utter a single word in French.

To see him coming aft to the wheel comforted one. The blue dungaree trousers turned up the calf, one leg a little higher than the other, the clean check shirt, the white canvas cap, evidently made by himself, made up a whole of peculiar smartness, and the persistent jauntiness of his gait, even, poor fellow, when he couldn't help tottering, told of his invincible spirit. There was also a man called Gambril. He was the only grizzled person in the ship. His face was of an austere type. But if I remember all their faces, wasting tragically before my eyes, most of their names have vanished from my memory.

The words that passed between us were few and puerile in regard of the situation. I had to force myself to look them in the face. I expected to meet reproachful glances. There were none. The expression of suffering in their eyes was indeed hard enough to bear. But that they couldn't help. For the rest, I ask myself whether it was the temper of their souls or the sympathy of their imagination that made them so wonderful, so worthy of my undying regard.

For myself, neither was my soul highly tempered, nor my imagination properly under control. There were moments when I felt, not only that I would go mad, but that I had gone mad already; so that I dared not open my lips for fear of betraying myself by some insane shriek. Luckily I had only orders to give, and an order has a steadying influence upon him who has to give it. Moreover, the seaman, the officer of the watch, in me was sufficiently sane. I was like a mad carpenter making a box. Were he ever so convinced that he was King of Jerusalem, the box he would make would be a sane box. What I feared was a shrill note escaping me involuntarily and upsetting my balance. Luckily, again, there was no necessity to raise one's voice. The brooding stillness of the world seemed sensitive to the slightest sound like a whispering gallery. The conversational tone would almost carry a word from one end of the ship to the other. The terrible thing was that the only voice that I ever heard was my own. At night especially it reverberated very lonely amongst the planes of the unstirring sails.

Mr Burns, still keeping to his bed with that air of secret determination, was moved to grumble at many things. Our interviews were short five-minute affairs, but fairly frequent. I was everlastingly diving down below to get a light, though I did not consume much tobacco at that time. The pipe was always going out; for in truth my mind was not composed enough to enable me to get a decent smoke. Likewise, for most of the time during the twenty-four hours I could have struck matches on deck and held them aloft till the flame burnt my fingers. But I always used to run below. It was a change. It was the only break in the incessant strain; and, of course, Mr Burns through the open door could see me come in and go out every time.

With his knees gathered up under his chin and staring with his greenish eyes over them, he was a weird figure, and with my knowledge of the crazy notion in his head, not a very attractive one for me. Still, I had to speak to him now and then, and one day he complained that the ship was very silent. For hours and hours, he said, he was lying there, not hearing a sound, till he did not know what to do with himself.

'When Ransome happens to be forward in his galley everything's so still that one might think everybody in the ship was dead,' he grumbled. 'The only voice I do hear sometimes is yours, sir, and that isn't enough to cheer me up. What's the matter with the men? Isn't there one left that can sing out at the ropes?'

'Not one, Mr Burns,' I said. 'There is no breath to spare on board this ship for that. Are you aware that there are times when I can't muster more than three hands to do anything?'

He asked swiftly but fearfully: 'Nobody dead yet, sir?'

'No.'

'It wouldn't do,' Mr Burns declared forcibly. 'Mustn't let him. If he gets hold of one he will get them all.'

I cried out angrily at this. I believe I even swore at the disturbing effect of these words. They attacked all the self-possession that was left to me. In my endless vigil in the face of the enemy I had been haunted by gruesome images enough. I had had visions of a ship drifting in calms and swinging in light airs, with all her crew dying slowly about her decks. Such things had been known to happen.

Mr Burns met my outburst by a mysterious silence.

'Look here,' I said. 'You don't believe yourself what you say. You can't. It's impossible. It isn't the sort of thing I have a right to expect from you. My position's bad enough without being worried with your silly fancies.'

He remained unmoved. On account of the way in which the light fell on his head I could not be sure whether he had smiled faintly or not. I changed my tone.

'Listen,' I said. 'It's getting so desperate that I had thought for a moment, since we can't make our way south, whether I wouldn't try to steer west and make an attempt to reach the mail-boat track. We could always get some quinine from her, at least. What do you think?'

He cried out: 'No, no, no. Don't do that, sir. You mustn't for a moment give up facing that old ruffian. If you do he will get the upper hand of us.'

I left him. He was impossible. It was like a case of possession. His protest, however, was essentially quite sound. As a matter of fact, my notion of heading out west on the chance of sighting a problematical steamer could not bear calm examination. On the side where we were we had enough wind, at least from time to time, to struggle on towards the south. Enough, at least, to keep hope alive. But suppose that I had used those capricious gusts of wind to sail away to the westward, into some region where there was not a breath of air for days on end, what then? Perhaps my appalling vision of a ship floating with a dead crew would become a reality for the discovery weeks afterwards by some horror-stricken mariners.

That afternoon Ransome brought me up a cup of tea, and while waiting there, tray in hand, he remarked in the exactly right tone of sympathy: 'You are holding out well, sir.'

'Yes,' I said. 'You and I seem to have been forgotten.'

'Forgotten, sir?'

'Yes, by the fever-devil who has got on board this ship,' I said.

Ransome gave me one of his attractive, intelligent, quick glances and went away with the tray. It occurred to me that I had been talking somewhat in Mr Burns' manner. It annoyed me. Yet often in darker moments I forgot myself into an attitude towards our troubles more fit for a contest against a living enemy.

Yes. The fever-devil had not laid his hand yet either on Ransome or on me. But he might at any time. It was one of those thoughts one had to fight down, keep at arm's length at any cost. It was unbearable to contemplate the possibility of Ransome, the housekeeper of the ship, being laid low. And what would happen to my command if I got knocked over, with Mr Burns too weak to stand without holding on to his bed-place and the second mate reduced to a state of permanent imbecility? It was impossible to imagine, or, rather, it was only too easy to imagine.

I was alone on the poop. The ship having no steerage way, I had sent the helmsman away to sit down or lie down somewhere in the shade. The men's strength was so reduced that all unnecessary calls on it had to be avoided. It was the austere Gambril with the grizzly beard. He went away readily enough, but he was so weakened by repeated bouts of fever, poor fellow, that in order to get down the poop ladder he had to turn sideways and hang on with both hands to the brass rail. It was just simply heartbreaking to watch. Yet he was neither very much worse nor much better than most of the half-dozen miserable victims I could muster up on deck.

It was a terribly lifeless afternoon. For several days in succession low clouds had appeared in the distance, white masses with dark convolutions resting on the water, motionless, almost solid, and yet all the time changing their aspects subtly. Towards evening they vanished as a rule. But this day they awaited the setting sun, which glowed and smouldered sulkily amongst them before it sank down. The punctual and wearisome stars reappeared over our mastheads, but the air remained stagnant and oppressive.

The unfailing Ransome lighted the binnacle lamps and glided, all shadowy, up to me.

'Will you go down and try to eat something, sir?' he suggested.

His low voice startled me. I had been standing looking out over the rail, saying nothing, feeling nothing, not even the weariness of my limbs, overcome by the evil spell.

'Ransome,' I asked abruptly, 'how long have I been on deck? I am losing the notion of time.'

'Fourteen days, sir,' he said. 'It was a fortnight last Monday since we left the anchorage.'

His equable voice sounded mournful somehow. He waited a bit, then added: 'It's the first time that it looks as if we were to have some rain.'

I noticed then the broad shadow on the horizon extinguishing the low stars completely, while those overhead, when I looked up, seemed to shine down on us through a veil of smoke.

How it got there, how it had crept up so high, I couldn't say. It had an ominous appearance. The air did not stir. At a renewed invitation from Ransome I did go down into the cabin to – in his words – 'try to eat something'. I don't know that the trial was very successful. I suppose at that period I did exist on food in the usual way; but the memory is now that in those days life was sustained on invincible anguish, as a sort of infernal stimulant exciting and consuming at the same time.

It's the only period of my life in which I attempted to keep a diary. No, not the only one. Years later, in conditions of moral isolation, I did put down on paper the thoughts and events of a score of days. But this was the first time. I don't remember how it came about or how the pocket-book and the pencil came into my hands. It's inconceivable that I should have looked for them on purpose. I suppose they saved me from the crazy trick of talking to myself.

Strangely enough, in both cases I took to that sort of thing in circumstances in which I did not expect, in colloquial phrase, 'to come out of it'. Neither could I expect the record to outlast me. This shows that it was purely a personal need for intimate relief and not a call of egotism.

Here I must give another sample of it, a few detached lines, now looking very ghostly to my own eyes, out of the part scribbled that very evening –

> There is something going on in the sky like a decomposition, like a corruption of the air, which remains as still as ever. After all, mere clouds, which may or may not hold wind or rain. Strange that it should trouble me so. I feel as if all my sins had found me out. But I suppose the trouble is that the ship is still lying motionless, not under command; and that I have nothing to do to keep my imagination from running wild amongst the disastrous images of the worst that may befall us. What's going to happen? Probably nothing. Or anything. It may be a furious squall coming, butt-end foremost. And on deck there are five men with the vitality and the strength of, say, two. We may have all our sails blown away. Every stitch of canvas has been on her since we broke ground at the mouth of the Mei-nam, fifteen days ago . . . or fifteen centuries. It seems to me that all my life before that momentous day is infinitely remote, a fading memory of light-hearted youth, something on the other side of a shadow. Yes, sails may very well be blown away. And that would be like a death sentence on the men. We haven't strength enough on

board to bend another suit; incredible thought, but it is true. Or we may even get dismasted. Ships have been dismasted in squalls simply because they weren't handled quick enough, and we have no power to whirl the yards around. It's like being bound hand and foot preparatory to having one's throat cut. And what appals me most of all is that I shrink from going on deck to face it. It's due to the ship, it's due to the men who are there on deck – some of them, ready to put out the last remnant of their strength at a word from me. And I am shrinking from it. From the mere vision. My first command. Now I understand that strange sense of insecurity in my past. I always suspected that I might be no good. And here is proof positive. I am shirking it. I am no good.

At that moment, or, perhaps, the moment after, I became aware of Ransome standing in the cabin. Something in his expression startled me. It had a meaning which I could not make out. I exclaimed: 'Somebody's dead!'

It was his turn then to look startled.

'Dead? Not that I know of, sir. I have been in the forecastle only ten minutes ago and there was no dead man there then.'

'You did give me a scare,' I said.

His voice was extremely pleasant to listen to. He explained that he had come down below to close Mr Burns' port in case it should come on to rain. He did not know that I was in the cabin, he added.

'How does it look outside?' I asked him.

'Very black indeed, sir. There is something in it for certain.'

'In what quarter?'

'All round, sir.'

I repeated idly: 'All round. For certain,' with my elbows on the table.

Ransome lingered in the cabin as if he had something to do there, but hesitated about doing it. I said suddenly: 'You think I ought to be on deck?'

He answered at once but without any particular emphasis or accent: 'I do, sir.'

I got to my feet briskly, and he made way for me to go out. As I passed through the lobby I heard Mr Burns' voice saying: 'Shut the door of my room, will you, steward?' And Ransome's rather surprised: 'Certainly, sir.'

I thought that all my feelings had been dulled into complete indifference. But I found it as trying as ever to be on deck. The impenetrable blackness beset the ship so close that it seemed that by thrusting one's hand over the side one could touch some unearthly substance. There was in it an effect of inconceivable terror and of inexpressible mystery. The few stars overhead shed a dim light upon the ship alone, with no gleams of any kind upon the water, in detached shafts piercing an atmosphere which had turned to soot. It was something I had never seen before, giving no hint of the direction from which any change would come, the closing in of a menace from all sides.

There was still no man at the helm. The immobility of all things was perfect. If the air had turned black, the sea, for all I knew, might have turned solid. It was no good looking in any direction, watching for any sign, speculating upon the nearness of the moment. When the time came the blackness would overwhelm silently the bit of starlight falling upon the ship, and the end of all things would come without a sigh, stir, or murmur of any kind, and all our hearts would cease to beat, like run-down clocks.

It was impossible to shake off that sense of finality. The quietness that came over me was like a foretaste of annihilation. It gave me a sort of comfort, as though my soul had become suddenly reconciled to an eternity of blind stillness.

The seaman's instinct alone survived whole in my moral dissolution. I descended the ladder to the quarter-deck. The starlight seemed to die out before reaching that spot, but when I asked quietly: 'Are you there, men?' my eyes made out shadowy forms starting up around me, very few, very indistinct; and a voice spoke: 'All here, sir.' Another amended anxiously: 'All that are any good for anything, sir.'

Both voices were very quiet and unringing; without any special character of readiness or discouragement. Very matter-of-fact voices.

'We must try to haul this mainsail close up,' I said.

The shadows swayed away from me without a word. Those men were the ghosts of themselves, and their weight on a rope could be no more than the weight of a bunch of ghosts. Indeed, if ever a sail was hauled up by sheer spiritual strength it must have been that sail, for, properly speaking, there was not muscle enough for the task in the whole ship, let alone the miserable lot of us on deck. Of course, I took the lead in the work myself. They wandered feebly after me from rope to rope, stumbling and panting. They toiled like Titans. We were an hour at it at least, and all the time the black universe made no sound. When the last leech-line was made fast, my eyes, accustomed to the darkness, made out the shapes of exhausted men drooping over the rails, collapsed on hatches. One hung over the after-capstan, sobbing for breath; and I stood amongst them like a tower of strength, impervious to disease and feeling only the sickness of my soul. I waited for some time, fighting against the weight of my sins, against my sense of unworthiness, and then I said: 'Now, men, we'll go aft and square the mainyard. That's about all we can do for the ship; and for the rest she must take her chance.'

Chapter 6

As WE ALL WENT UP it occurred to me that there ought to be a man at the helm. I raised my voice not much above a whisper, and, noiselessly, an uncomplaining spirit in a fever-wasted body appeared in the light aft, the head with hollow eyes illuminated against the blackness which had swallowed up our world – and the universe. The bared fore-arm extended over the upper spokes seemed to shine with a light of its own.

I murmured to that luminous appearance: 'Keep the helm right amidships.'

It answered in a tone of patient suffering: 'Right amidships, sir.'

Then I descended to the quarter-deck. It was impossible to tell whence the blow would come. To look round the ship was to look into a bottomless, black pit. The eye lost itself in inconceivable depths.

I wanted to ascertain whether the ropes had been picked up off the deck. One could only do that by feeling with one's feet. In my cautious progress I came against a man in whom I recognised Ransome. He possessed an unimpaired physical solidity which was manifest to me at the contact. He was leaning against the quarter-deck capstan and kept silent. It was like a revelation. He was the collapsed figure sobbing for breath I had noticed before we went on the poop.

'You have been helping with the mainsail!' I exclaimed in a low tone.

'Yes, sir,' sounded his quiet voice.

'Man! What were you thinking of? You mustn't do that sort of thing.'

After a pause he assented. 'I suppose I mustn't.' Then after another short silence he added: 'I am all right now,' quickly, between the tell-tale gasps.

I could neither hear nor see anybody else; but when I spoke up, answering sad murmurs filled the quarter-deck, and its shadows seemed to shift here and there. I ordered all the halyards laid down on deck clear for running.

'I'll see to that, sir,' volunteered Ransome in his natural, pleasant tone, which comforted one and aroused one's compassion too, somehow.

That man ought to have been in his bed, resting, and my plain duty was to send him there. But perhaps he would not have obeyed me. I had not the strength of mind to try. All I said was: 'Go about it quietly, Ransome.'

Returning on the poop I approached Gambril. His face, set with hollow shadows in the light, looked awful, finally silenced. I asked him how he felt, but hardly expected an answer. Therefore I was astonished at his comparative loquacity.

'Them shakes leaves me as weak as a kitten, sir,' he said, preserving finely that air of unconsciousness as to anything but his business a helmsman should never lose. 'And before I can pick up my strength that there hot fit comes along and knocks me over again.'

He sighed. There was no complaint in his tone, but the bare words were enough to give me a horrible pang of self-reproach. It held me dumb for a time. When the tormenting sensation had passed off I asked: 'Do you feel strong enough to prevent the rudder taking charge if she gets sternway on her? It wouldn't do to get something smashed about the steering-gear now. We've enough difficulties to cope with as it is.'

He answered with just a shade of weariness that he was strong enough to hang on. He could promise me that she shouldn't take the wheel out of his hands. More he couldn't say.

At that moment Ransome appeared quite close to me, stepping out of the darkness into visibility suddenly, as if just created with his composed face and pleasant voice.

Every rope on deck, he said, was laid down clear for running, as far as one could make certain by feeling. It was impossible to see anything. Frenchy had stationed himself forward. He said he had a jump or two left in him yet.

Here a faint smile altered for an instant the clear, firm design of Ransome's lips. With his serious clear, grey eyes, his serene temperament, he was a priceless man altogether. Soul as firm as the muscles of his body.

He was the only man on board (except me, but I had to preserve my liberty of movement) who had a sufficiency of muscular strength to trust to. For a moment I thought I had better ask him to take the wheel. But the dreadful knowledge of the enemy he had to carry about him made me hesitate. In my ignorance of physiology it occurred to me that he might die suddenly, from excitement, at a critical moment.

While this gruesome fear restrained the ready words on the tip of my tongue, Ransome stepped back two paces and vanished from my sight.

At once an uneasiness possessed me, as if some support had been withdrawn. I moved forward too, outside the circle of light, into the darkness that stood in front of me like a wall. In one stride I penetrated it. Such must have been the darkness before creation. It had closed behind me. I knew I was invisible to the man at the helm. Neither could I see anything. He was alone, I was alone, every man was alone where he stood. And every form was gone too, spar, sail, fittings, rails; everything was blotted out in the dreadful smoothness of that absolute night.

A flash of lightning would have been a relief – I mean physically. I would have prayed for it if it hadn't been for my shrinking apprehension of the thunder. In the tension of silence I was suffering from it seemed to me that the first crash must turn me into dust.

And thunder was, most likely, what would happen next. Stiff all over and hardly breathing, I waited with a horribly strained expectation. Nothing happened. It was maddening. But a dull, growing ache in the lower part of my face made me aware that I had been grinding my teeth madly enough, for God knows how long.

It's extraordinary I should not have heard myself doing it; but I hadn't. By an effort which absorbed all my faculties I managed to keep my jaw still. It required much attention, and while thus engaged I became bothered by curious, irregular sounds of faint tapping on the deck. They could be heard single, in pairs, in groups. While I wondered at this mysterious devilry, I received a slight blow under the left eye and felt an enormous tear run down my cheek. Raindrops. Enormous. Forerunners of something. Tap. Tap. Tap . . .

I turned about, and, addressing Gambril earnestly, entreated him to 'hang on to the wheel'. But I could hardly speak from emotion. The fatal moment had come. I held my breath. The tapping had stopped as unexpectedly as it had begun, and there was a renewed moment of intolerable suspense; something like an additional turn of the racking screw. I don't suppose I would have ever screamed, but I remember my conviction that there was nothing else for it but to scream.

Suddenly – how am I to convey it? Well, suddenly the darkness turned into water. This is the only suitable figure. A heavy shower, a downpour, comes along, making a noise. You hear its approach on the sea, in the air too, I verily believe. But this was different. With no preliminary whisper or rustle, without a splash, and even without the ghost of impact, I became instantaneously soaked to the skin. Not a very difficult matter, since I was wearing only my sleeping-suit. My hair got full of water in an instant, water streamed on my skin, it filled my nose, my ears, my eyes. In a fraction of a second I swallowed quite a lot of it.

As to Gambril, he was fairly choked. He coughed pitifully, the broken cough of a sick man; and I beheld him as one sees a fish in an aquarium by the light of an electric bulb, an elusive, phosphorescent shape. Only he did not glide away. But something else happened. Both binnacle lamps went out. I suppose the water forced itself into them, though I wouldn't have thought that possible, for they fitted into the cowl perfectly.

The last gleam of light in the universe had gone, pursued by a low exclamation of dismay from Gambril. I groped for him and seized his arm. How startlingly wasted it was.

'Never mind,' I said. 'You don't want the light. All you need to do is to keep the wind, when it comes, at the back of your head. You understand?'

'Aye, aye, sir . . . But I should like to have a light,' he added nervously.

All that time the ship lay as steady as a rock. The noise of the water pouring off the sails and spars, flowing over the break of the poop, had stopped short. The poop scuppers gurgled and sobbed for a little while longer, and then perfect silence, joined to perfect immobility, proclaimed the yet unbroken spell of our helplessness, poised on the edge of some violent issue, lurking in the dark.

I started forward restlessly. I did not need my sight to pace the poop of my ill-starred first command with perfect assurance. Every square foot of her decks was impressed indelibly on my brain, to the very grain and knots of the planks. Yet, all of a sudden, I fell clean over something, landing full length on my hands and face.

It was something big and alive. Not a dog – more like a sheep, rather. But there were no animals in the ship. How could an animal . . . It was an added and fantastic horror which I could not resist. The hair of my head stirred even as I picked myself up, awfully scared; not as a man is scared while his judgement, his reason still try to resist, but completely, boundlessly, and, as it were, innocently scared – like a little child.

I could see It – that Thing! The darkness, of which so much had just turned into water, had thinned down a little. There It was! But I did not hit upon the notion of Mr Burns issuing out of the companion on all fours till he attempted to stand up, and even then the idea of a bear crossed my mind first.

He growled like one when I seized him round the body. He had buttoned himself up into an enormous winter overcoat of some woolly material, the weight of which was too much for his reduced state. I could hardly feel the incredibly thin lath of his body, lost within the thick stuff, but his growl had depth and substance: Confounded dumb ship with a craven, tip-toeing crowd. Why couldn't they stamp and go with a brace? Wasn't there one God-forsaken lubber in the lot fit to raise a yell on a rope?

'Skulking's no good, sir,' he attacked me directly. 'You can't slink past the old murderous ruffian. It isn't the way. You must go for him boldly – as I did. Boldness is what you want. Show him that you don't care for any of his damned tricks. Kick up a jolly old row.'

'Good God, Mr Burns,' I said angrily. 'What on earth are you up to? What do you mean by coming up on deck in this state?'

'Just that! Boldness. The only way to scare the old bullying rascal.'

I pushed him, still growling, against the rail. 'Hold on to it,' I said roughly. I did not know what to do with him. I left him in a hurry, to go to Gambril, who had called faintly that he believed there was some wind aloft. Indeed, my own ears had caught a feeble flutter of wet canvas, high up overhead, the jingle of a slack chain sheet . . .

These were eerie, disturbing, alarming sounds in the dead stillness of the air around me. All the instances I had heard of topmasts being whipped out of a ship while there was not wind enough on her deck to blow out a match rushed into my memory.

'I can't see the upper sails, sir,' declared Gambril shakily.

'Don't move the helm. You'll be all right,' I said confidently.

The poor man's nerve was gone. I was not in much better case. It was the moment of breaking strain and was relieved by the abrupt sensation of the ship moving forward as if of herself under my feet. I heard plainly the soughing of the wind aloft, the low cracks of the upper spars taking the strain, long before I could feel the least draught on my face turned aft, anxious and sightless like the face of a blind man.

Suddenly a louder sounding note filled our ears, the darkness started streaming against our bodies, chilling them exceedingly. Both of us, Gambril and I, shivered violently in our clinging, soaked garments of thin cotton. I said to him: 'You are all right now, my man. All you've got to do is to keep the wind at the back of your head. Surely you are up to that. A child could steer this ship in smooth water.'

He muttered: 'Aye! A healthy child.' And I felt ashamed of having been passed over by the fever which had been preying on every man's strength but mine, in order that my remorse might be the more bitter, the feeling of unworthiness more poignant, and the sense of responsibility heavier to bear.

The ship had gathered great way on her almost at once on the calm water. I felt her slipping through it with no other noise but a mysterious rustle alongside. Otherwise she had no motion at all, neither lift nor roll. It was a disheartening steadiness which had lasted for eighteen days now; for never, never had we had wind enough in that time to raise the slightest run of the sea. The breeze freshened suddenly. I thought it was high time to get Mr Burns off the deck. He worried me. I looked upon him as a lunatic who would be very likely to start roaming over the ship and break a limb or fall overboard.

I was truly glad to find he had remained holding on where I had left him, sensibly enough. He was, however, muttering to himself ominously.

This was discouraging. I remarked in a matter-of-fact tone: 'We have never had so much wind as this since we left the roads.'

'There's some heart in it too,' he growled judiciously. It was a remark of a perfectly sane seaman. But he added immediately: 'It was about time I should come on deck. I've been nursing my strength for this – just for this. Do you see it, sir?'

I said I did, and proceeded to hint that it would be advisable for him to go below now and take a rest.

His answer was an indignant: 'Go below! Not if I know it, sir.'

Very cheerful! He was a horrible nuisance. And all at once he started to argue. I could feel his crazy excitement in the dark.

'You don't know how to go about it, sir. How could you? All this whispering and tip-toeing is no good. You can't hope to slink past a cunning, wide-awake, evil brute like he was. You never heard him talk. Enough to make your hair stand on end. No! No! He wasn't mad. He was no more mad than I am. He was just downright wicked. Wicked so as to frighten most people. I will tell you what he was. He was nothing less than a thief and a murderer at heart. And do you think he's any different now because he's dead? Not he! His carcass lies a hundred fathom under, but he's just the same . . . in latitude 8° 20' North.'

He snorted defiantly. I noted with weary resignation that the breeze had got lighter while he raved. He was at it again.

'I ought to have thrown the beggar out of the ship over the rail like a dog. It was only on account of the men . . . Fancy having to read the Burial Service over a brute like that! . . . "Our departed brother" . . . I could have laughed. That was what he couldn't bear. I suppose I am the only man that ever stood up to laugh at him. When he got sick it used to scare that . . . brother . . . Brother . . . Departed . . . Sooner call a shark brother.'

The breeze had let go so suddenly that the way of the ship brought the wet sails heavily against the masts. The spell of deadly stillness had caught us up again. There seemed to be no escape.

'Hallo!' exclaimed Mr Burns in a startled voice. 'Calm again!'

I addressed him as though he had been sane.

'This is the sort of thing we've been having for seventeen days, Mr Burns,' I said with intense bitterness. 'A puff, then a calm, and in a moment, you'll see, she'll be swinging on her heel with her head away from her course to the devil somewhere.'

He caught at the word. 'The old dodging Devil,' he screamed piercingly, and burst into such a loud laugh as I had never heard before. It was a provoking, mocking peal, with a hair-raising, screeching over-note of defiance. I stepped back utterly confounded.

Instantly there was a stir on the quarter-deck, murmurs of dismay. A distressed voice cried out in the dark below us: 'Who's that gone crazy, now?'

Perhaps they thought it was their captain! Rush is not the word that could be applied to the utmost speed the poor fellows were up to; but in an amazing short time every man in the ship able to walk upright had found his way on to that poop.

I shouted to them: 'It's the mate. Lay hold of him a couple of you . . . '

I expected this performance to end in a ghastly sort of fight. But Mr Burns cut his derisive screeching dead short and turned upon them fiercely, yelling: 'Aha! Dog-gone ye! You've found your tongues – have ye? I thought you were dumb. Well, then – laugh!

Laugh – I tell you. Now then – all together. One, two, three – laugh!'

A moment of silence ensued, of silence so profound that you could have heard a pin drop on the deck. Then Ransome's unperturbed voice uttered pleasantly the words: 'I think he has fainted, sir – ' The little motionless knot of men stirred, with low murmurs of relief. 'I've got him under the arms. Get hold of his legs, someone.'

Yes. It was a relief. He was silenced for a time – for a time. I could not have stood another peal of that insane screeching. I was sure of it; and just then Gambril, the austere Gambril, treated us to another vocal performance. He began to sing out for relief. His voice wailed pitifully in the darkness: 'Come aft, somebody! I can't stand this. Here she'll be off again directly and I can't . . . '

I dashed aft myself meeting on my way a hard gust of wind whose approach Gambril's ear had detected from afar and which filled the sails on the main in a series of muffled reports mingled with the low plaint of the spars. I was just in time to seize the wheel while Frenchy, who had followed me, caught up the collapsing Gambril. He hauled him out of the way, admonished him to lie still where he was, and then stepped up to relieve me, asking calmly: 'How am I to steer her, sir.'

'Dead before it, for the present. I'll get you a light in a moment.'

But going forward I met Ransome bringing up the spare binnacle lamp. That man noticed everything, attended to everything, shed comfort around him as he moved. As he passed me he remarked in a soothing tone that the stars were coming out. They were. The breeze was sweeping clear the sooty sky, breaking through the indolent silence of the sea.

The barrier of awful stillness which had encompassed us for so many days as though we had been accursed was broken. I felt that. I let myself fall on to the skylight seat. A faint white ridge of foam, thin, very thin, broke alongside. The first for ages – for ages. I could have cheered, if it hadn't been for the sense of guilt which clung to all my thoughts secretly. Ransome stood before me.

'What about the mate,' I asked anxiously. 'Still unconscious?'

'Well, sir – it's funny.' Ransome was evidently puzzled. 'He hasn't spoken a word, and his eyes are shut. But it looks to me more like sound sleep than anything else.'

I accepted this view as the least troublesome of any, or at any rate, least disturbing. Dead faint or deep slumber, Mr Burns had to be left to himself for the present. Ransome remarked suddenly: 'I believe you want a coat, sir.'

'I believe I do,' I sighed out.

But I did not move. What I felt I wanted were new limbs. My arms and legs seemed utterly useless, fairly worn out. They didn't even ache. But I stood up all the same to put on the coat when Ransome brought it up. And when he suggested that he had better now 'take Gambril forward', I said: 'All right. I'll help you to get him down on the main deck.'

I found that I was quite able to help, too. We raised Gambril up between us. He tried to help himself along like a man, but all the time he was enquiring piteously: 'You won't let me go when we come to the ladder? You won't let me go when we come to the ladder?'

The breeze kept on freshening and blew true, true to a hair. At daylight by careful manipulation of the helm we got the foreyards to run square by themselves (the water keeping smooth) and then went about hauling the ropes tight. Of the four men I had had with me at night, I could see now only two. I didn't enquire as to the others. They had given in. For a time only I hoped.

Our various tasks forward occupied us for hours, the two men with me moved so slowly and had to rest so often. One of them remarked that 'every blamed thing in the ship felt about a hundred times heavier than its proper weight'. This was the only complaint uttered. I don't know what we should have done without Ransome. He worked with us, silent too, with a little smile frozen on his lips. From time to time I murmured to him: 'Go steady' – 'Take it easy, Ransome' – and received a quick glance in reply.

When we had done all we could do to make things safe, he disappeared into his galley. Some time afterwards, going forward for a look round, I caught sight of him through the open door. He sat upright on the locker in front of the stove, with his head leaning back against the bulkhead. His eyes were closed; his capable hands held open the front of his thin cotton shirt baring tragically his powerful chest, which heaved in painful and laboured gasps. He didn't hear me.

I retreated quietly and went straight on to the poop to relieve Frenchy, who by that time was beginning to look very sick. He gave me the course with great formality and tried to go off with a jaunty step, but reeled widely twice before getting out of my sight.

And then I remained all alone aft, steering my ship, which ran before the wind with a buoyant lift now and then, and even rolling a little. Presently Ransome appeared before me with a tray. The sight of food made me ravenous all at once. He took the wheel while I sat down on the after grating to eat my breakfast.

'This breeze seems to have done for our crowd,' he murmured. 'It just laid them low – all hands.'

'Yes,' I said. 'I suppose you and I are the only two fit men in the ship.'

'Frenchy says there's still a jump left in him. I don't know. It can't be much,' continued Ransome with his wistful smile. 'Good little man that. But suppose, sir, that this wind flies round when we are close to the land – what are we going to do with her?'

'If the wind shifts round heavily after we close in with the land she will either run ashore or get dismasted or both. We won't be able to do anything with her. She's running away with us now. All we can do is to steer her. She's a ship without a crew.'

'Yes. All laid low,' repeated Ransome quietly. 'I do give them a look-in forward every now and then, but it's precious little I can do for them.'

'I, and the ship, and everyone on board of her, are very much indebted to you, Ransome,' I said warmly.

He made as though he had not heard me, and steered in silence till I was ready to relieve him. He surrendered the wheel, picked up the tray, and for a parting shot informed me that Mr Burns was awake and seemed to have a mind to come up on deck.

'I don't know how to prevent him, sir. I can't very well stop down below all the time.'

It was clear that he couldn't. And sure enough Mr Burns came on deck dragging himself painfully aft in his enormous overcoat. I beheld him with a natural dread. To have him around and raving about the wiles of a dead man while I had to steer a wildly rushing ship full of dying men was a rather dreadful prospect.

But his first remarks were quite sensible in meaning and tone. Apparently he had no recollection of the night scene. And if he had he didn't betray himself once. Neither did he talk very much. He sat on the skylight looking desperately ill at first, but that strong breeze, before which the last remnant of my crew had wilted down, seemed to blow a fresh stock of vigour into his frame with every gust. One could almost see the process.

By way of sanity test I alluded on purpose to the late captain. I was delighted to find that Mr Burns did not display undue interest in the subject. He ran over the old tale of that savage ruffian's iniquities with a certain vindictive gusto and then concluded unexpectedly: 'I do believe, sir, that his brain began to go a year or more before he died.'

A wonderful recovery. I could hardly spare it as much admiration as it deserved, for I had to give all my mind to the steering.

In comparison with the hopeless languor of the preceding days this was dizzy speed. Two ridges of foam streamed from the ship's bows; the wind sang in a strenuous note which under other circumstances would have expressed to me all the joy of life. Whenever the hauled-up mainsail started trying to slat and bang itself to pieces in its gear, Mr Burns would look at me apprehensively.

'What would you have me do, Mr Burns? We can neither furl it nor set it. I only wish the old thing would thrash itself to pieces and be done with it. This beastly racket confuses me.'

Mr Burns wrung his hands, and cried out suddenly: 'How will you get the ship into harbour, sir, without men to handle her?'

And I couldn't tell him.

Well – it did get done about forty hours afterwards. By the exorcising virtue of Mr Burns' awful laugh, the malicious spectre had been laid, the evil spell broken, the curse removed. We were now in the hands of a kind and energetic Providence. It was rushing us on . . .

I shall never forget the last night, dark, windy, and starry. I steered. Mr Burns, after having obtained from me a solemn promise to give him a kick if anything happened, went frankly to sleep on the deck close to the binnacle. Convalescents need sleep. Ransome, his back propped against the mizzenmast and a blanket over his legs, remained perfectly still, but I don't suppose he closed his eyes for a moment. That embodiment of jauntiness, Frenchy, still under the delusion that there was 'a jump' left in him, had insisted on joining us; but mindful of discipline, had laid himself down as far on the forepart of the poop as he could get, alongside the bucket-rack.

And I steered, too tired for anxiety, too tired for connected thought. I had moments of grim exultation and then my heart would sink awfully at the thought of that forecastle at the other end of the dark deck, full of fever-stricken men – some of them dying. By my fault. But never mind. Remorse must wait. I had to steer.

In the small hours the breeze weakened, then failed altogether. About five it returned, gentle enough, enabling us to head for the roadstead. Daybreak found Mr Burns sitting wedged up with coils of rope on the stern-grating, and from the depths of his overcoat steering the ship with very white bony hands; while Ransome and I rushed along the decks letting go all the sheets and halliards by the run. We dashed next up on to the forecastle head. The perspiration of labour and sheer nervousness simply poured off our heads as we toiled to get the anchors cock-billed. I dared not look at Ransome as we worked side by side. We exchanged curt words; I could hear him panting close to me and I avoided turning my eyes his way for fear of seeing him fall down and expire in the act of putting out his strength – for what? Indeed for some distinct ideal.

The consummate seaman in him was aroused. He needed no directions. He knew what to do. Every effort, every movement was an act of consistent heroism. It was not for me to look at a man thus inspired.

At last all was ready, and I heard him say, 'Hadn't I better go down and open the compressors now, sir?'

'Yes. Do,' I said. And even then I did not glance his way. After a time his voice came up from the main-deck: 'When you like, sir. All clear on the windlass here.'

I made a sign to Mr Burns to put the helm down and then I let both anchors go one after another, leaving the ship to take as much cable as she wanted. She took the best part of them both before she brought up. The loose sails coming aback ceased their maddening racket above my head. A perfect stillness reigned in the ship. And while I stood forward feeling a little giddy in that sudden peace, I caught faintly a moan or two and the incoherent mutterings of the sick in the forecastle.

As we had a signal for medical assistance flying on the mizzen it is a fact that before the ship was fairly at rest three steam-launches from various men-of-war arrived alongside; and at least five naval surgeons clambered on board. They stood in a knot gazing up and down the empty main deck, then looked aloft – where not a man could be seen either.

I went towards them – a solitary figure in a blue-and-grey-striped sleeping-suit and a pipe-clayed cork helmet on its head. Their disgust was extreme. They had expected surgical cases. Each one had brought his carving tools with him. But they soon got over their little disappointment. In less than five minutes one of the steam-launches was rushing shorewards to order a big boat and some hospital people for the removal of the crew. The big steam-pinnace went off to her ship to bring over a few bluejackets to furl my sails for me.

One of the surgeons had remained on board. He came out of the forecastle looking impenetrable, and noticed my enquiring gaze.

'There's nobody dead in there, if that's what you want to know,' he said deliberately. Then added in a tone of wonder: 'The whole crew!'

'And very bad?'

'And very bad,' he repeated. His eyes were roaming all over the ship. 'Heavens! What's that?'

'That,' I said, glancing aft, 'is Mr Burns, my chief officer.'

Mr Burns with his moribund head nodding on the stalk of his lean neck was a sight for anyone to exclaim at. The surgeon asked: 'Is he going to the hospital too?'

'Oh, no,' I said jocosely. 'Mr Burns can't go on shore till the mainmast goes. I am very proud of him. He's my only convalescent.'

'You look . . . ' began the doctor staring at me. But I interrupted him angrily: 'I am not ill.'

'No . . . You look queer.'

'Well, you see, I have been seventeen days on deck.'

'Seventeen! . . . But you must have slept.'

'I suppose I must have. I don't know. But I'm certain that I didn't sleep for the last forty hours.'

'Phew! . . . You will be going ashore presently, I suppose?'

'As soon as ever I can. There's no end of business waiting for me there.'

The surgeon released my hand, which he had taken while we talked, pulled out his pocket book, wrote in it rapidly, tore out the page, and offered it to me.

'I strongly advise you to get this prescription made up for yourself ashore. Unless I am much mistaken you will need it this evening.'

'What is it then?' I asked with suspicion.

'Sleeping draught,' answered the surgeon curtly; and moving with an air of interest towards Mr Burns he engaged him in conversation.

As I went below to dress to go ashore, Ransome followed me. He begged my pardon; he wished, too, to be sent ashore and paid off.

I looked at him in surprise. He was waiting for my answer with an air of anxiety.

'You don't mean to leave the ship!' I cried out.

'I do really, sir. I want to go and be quiet somewhere. Anywhere. The hospital will do.'

'But, Ransome,' I said, 'I hate the idea of parting with you.'

'I must go,' he broke in. 'I have a right!' He gasped and a look of almost savage determination passed over his face. For an instant he was another being. And I saw under the worth and the comeliness of the man the humble reality of things. Life was a boon to him – this precarious hard life – and he was thoroughly alarmed about himself.

'Of course I shall pay you off if you wish it,' I hastened to say. 'Only I must ask you to remain on board till this afternoon. I can't leave Mr Burns absolutely by himself in the ship for hours.'

He softened at once and assured me with a smile and in his natural pleasant voice that he understood that very well.

When I returned on deck everything was ready for the removal of the men. It was the last ordeal of that episode which had been maturing and tempering my character – though I did not know it.

It was awful. They passed under my eyes one after another – each of them an embodied reproach of the bitterest kind, till I felt a sort of revolt wake up in me. Poor Frenchy had gone suddenly under. He was carried past me insensible, his comic face horribly flushed and as if swollen, breathing stertorously. He looked more like Mr Punch than ever; a disgracefully intoxicated Mr Punch.

The austere Gambril, on the contrary, had improved temporarily. He insisted on walking on his own feet to the rail – of course with assistance on each side of him. But he gave way to a sudden panic at the moment of being swung over the side and began to wail pitifully: 'Don't let them drop me, sir. Don't let them drop me, sir!' While I kept on shouting to him in most soothing accents: 'All right, Gambril. They won't! They won't!'

It was no doubt very ridiculous. The bluejackets on our deck were grinning quietly, while even Ransome himself (much to the fore in lending a hand) had to enlarge his wistful smile for a fleeting moment.

I left for the shore in the steam-pinnace, and on looking back beheld Mr Burns actually standing up by the taffrail, still in his enormous woolly overcoat. The bright sunlight brought out his weirdness amazingly. He looked like a frightful and elaborate scarecrow set up on the poop of a death-stricken ship, to keep the seabirds from the corpses.

Our story had got about already in town and everybody on shore was most kind. The marine office let me off the port dues, and as there happened to be a shipwrecked crew staying in the Home I had no difficulty in obtaining as many men as I wanted. But when I enquired if I could see Captain Ellis for a moment, I was told in accents of pity for my ignorance that our deputy-Neptune had retired and gone home on a pension about three weeks after I left the port. So I suppose that my appointment was the last act, outside the daily routine, of his official life.

It is strange how on coming ashore I was struck by the springy step, the lively eyes, the strong vitality of everyone I met. It impressed me enormously. And amongst those I met there was Captain Giles of course. It would have been very extraordinary if I had not met him. A prolonged stroll in the business part of the town was the regular employment of all his mornings when he was ashore.

I caught the glitter of the gold watch-chain across his chest ever so far away. He radiated benevolence.

'What is it I hear?' he queried with a 'kind uncle' smile, after shaking hands. 'Twenty-one days from Bankok?'

'Is this all you've heard?' I said. 'You must come to tiffin with me. I want you to know exactly what you have let me in for.'

He hesitated for almost a minute.

'Well – I will,' he decided condescendingly at last.

We turned into the hotel. I found to my surprise that I could eat quite a lot. Then over the cleared table-cloth I unfolded to Captain Giles all the story since I took command in all its professional and emotional aspects, while he smoked patiently the big cigar I had given him.

Then he observed sagely: 'You must feel jolly well tired by this time.'

'No,' I said. 'Not tired. But I'll tell you, Captain Giles, how I feel. I feel old. And I must be. All of you on shore look to me just a lot of skittish youngsters that have never known a care in the world.'

He didn't smile. He looked insufferably exemplary. He declared: 'That will pass. But you do look older – it's a fact.'

'Aha!' I said.

'No! No! The truth is that one must not make too much of anything in life, good or bad.'

'Live at half-speed,' I murmured perversely. 'Not everybody can do that.'

'You'll be glad enough presently if you can keep going even at that rate,' he retorted with his air of conscious virtue. 'And there's another thing: a man should stand up to his bad luck, to his mistakes, to his conscience, and all that sort of thing. Why – what else would you have to fight against?'

I kept silent. I don't know what he saw in my face, but he asked abruptly: 'Why – you aren't faint-hearted?'

'God only knows, Captain Giles,' was my sincere answer.

'That's all right,' he said calmly. 'You will learn soon how not to be faint-hearted. A man has got to learn everything – and that's what so many of those youngsters don't understand.'

'Well I am no longer a youngster.'

'No,' he conceded. 'Are you leaving soon?'

'I am going on board directly,' I said. 'I shall pick up one of my anchors and heave in to half-cable on the other as soon as my new crew comes on board and I shall be off at daylight tomorrow.'

'You will?' grunted Captain Giles approvingly. 'That's the way. You'll do.'

'What did you expect? That I would want to take a week ashore for a rest?' I said, irritated by his tone. 'There's no rest for me till she's out in the Indian Ocean and not much of it even then.'

He puffed at the cigar moodily, as if transformed.

'Yes, that's what it amounts to,' he said in a musing tone. It was as if a ponderous curtain had rolled up disclosing an unexpected Captain Giles. But it was only for a moment, merely the time to let him add: 'Precious little rest in life for anybody. Better not think of it.'

We rose, left the hotel, and parted from each other in the street with a warm handshake, just as he began to interest me for the first time in our intercourse.

The first thing I saw when I got back to the ship was Ransome on the quarter-deck sitting quietly on his neatly lashed sea-chest.

I beckoned him to follow me into the saloon where I sat down to write a letter of recommendation for him to a man I knew on shore.

When finished I pushed it across the table. 'It may be of some good to you when you leave the hospital.'

He took it, put it in his pocket. His eyes were looking away from me – nowhere. His face was anxiously set.

'How are you feeling now?' I asked.

'I don't feel bad now, sir,' he answered stiffly. 'But I am afraid of its coming on . . . ' The wistful smile came back on his lips for a moment. 'I – I am in a blue funk about my heart, sir.'

I approached him with extended hand. His eyes, not looking at me, had a strained expression. He was like a man listening for a warning call.

'Won't you shake hands, Ransome?' I said gently.

He exclaimed, flushed up dusky red, gave my hand a hard wrench – and next moment, left alone in the cabin, I listened to him going up the companion stairs cautiously, step by step, in mortal fear of starting into sudden anger our common enemy it was his hard fate to carry consciously within his faithful breast.

GLOSSARY OF NAUTICAL TERMS

Works consulted include *Collins Concise English Dictionary* (Harper Collins, London 1992), Gersham Bradford's *A Glossary of Sea Terms* (Cassell, London 1954) and Robert Kimbrough's edition of *The Nigger of the 'Narcissus'* (W. W. Norton & Co., New York 1979).

all aback: to have the sails pressing against the front of the masts

athwartship: running across the width of the ship

after-deck: upper deck at the *stern* of the ship, behind the *mizzenmast*

amidships: in the centre of the ship

anchor-watchman: person on *watch* while the ship is at anchor

aneroid glass: face of an aneroid barometer – a device of clock-like appearance registering changes in atmospheric pressure

awning: roof of canvas, or other material, protecting part of the ship's deck from the weather

ballast: heavy material placed in the hold to steady a ship, especially when empty. Thus 'in ballast' implies that a ship is not carrying any cargo.

bar: a bank or shoal across the mouth of a river

barque: three-masted ship, square-rigged on the *fore* and *mainmasts* (at right-angles to the *keel*), with the *mizzenmast* rigged *fore-and-aft*

beam: breadth of a ship at its widest point

belaying pin: pin around which ropes are secured

bend: to tie or fasten a sail

bilges: the turn of a ship's hull, below the waterline, where the sides curve inwards to form the bottom of the vessel. Also the area between the lower floorboards and the *keelson*, hence 'bilge water'.

billet: berth in a ship and colloquial term for a job

binnacle: box made of non-magnetic material, housing the ship's compass and fitted with a lamp

block: small wooden casing housing one or more pulleys

blue-jackets: military sailors

boatswain/bosun: foreman of the crew- a petty officer immediately responsible for the deck-hands

bows: forward end of the ship, from where it begins to curve to the *stem*

bowsprit: *spar* projecting forward from the *stem*

brace: line by which a *yard* is adjusted horizontally

bridge: elevated platform *amidships* from which the ship is navigated

bulkhead: upright partition separating the ship into watertight compartments

capstan: vertically revolving drum for hauling in the anchor cable

chain-sheet: chain attached to the lower corner of a sail for changing its position and extending it over the sides of the vessel

charter-party: business agreement between the ship's owner and the merchant who owns the cargo

chronometer-box: contains the ship's chronometer, a highly accurate nautical clock fitted with *gimbals*

cleat: anvil-shaped pin for securing ropes

coamings: raised frame around deck-openings to keep out water

companion-way: covered entrance to a staircase from the deck to a cabin, the term often standing for the staircase itself

compass card: compass in the form of a card, representing the plane of the horizon, that rotates so that 0° points to magnetic north

compressors: levers for braking the anchor cable as it runs out

coxswain: the *helm*sman of a small boat

crank arrested on the cant: shaft-arm stopped in a slanting position

cuddy: small cabin in a boat, situated fore or aft

davits: small deck-mounted cranes for raising and lowering the ship's boats

demurrage: costs incurred due to the charterer's failure to load or unload the vessel by the agreed time

derrick: simple crane, with lifting tackle slung from a boom

dredging with the anchor down: using a dropped anchor to gauge the water's depth and control the ship's movements, thereby assisting passage downstream in unfamiliar waters

dry-dock: dock that can be pumped empty of water to allow work on a vessel's bottom

ebb: period in which the tide flows out from high to low water

fall: end of a line, to which power is applied to hoist it

fiddle: steel grating hatch over the boiler room

fife-rail: rail running round the *mainmast* for holding *belaying pins*

forecastle: enclosed area beneath the *fore-deck*, usually the crew's living quarters

fore-and-aft: the length of the vessel, from *stem* to *stern*, running parallel to the *keel*

fore-deck: upper-deck forward of the *fore-mast*

forefoot: head of the *keel*, supporting the ship's *stem*

fore-mast: the front mast of a three-masted ship

fore-royal: uppermost sail on the *fore-mast*

forward 'tween-deck: front deck in between the upper and lower decks.

friction winch: hoisting machine fitted with an operator's foot brake

gaskets: line or canvas strap, lashing furled sails to *spars*

German Ocean: North Sea

gimbals: two metal rings, one pivoting within the other, permitting the object in their centre to remain horizontal, regardless of the ship's motion

gig: ship's boat

gins: pulleys for hoisting cargo

halyards: light ropes for hoisting or lowering flags, sails and *spars*

hawse pipe: iron fitting through which the anchor-chain runs, preventing it from cutting into the wooden bows or stern of the vessel

hawser: large heavy rope

headgear: generic term for hoisting equipment, at the front (head) of the vessel

heave-to: to *trim* the sails so that the wind acts on their forward surfaces in order to slow or stop the ship; in strong winds, to take in nearly all of the sails and 'put the *helm* down', thus keeping the ship's *bows* to the wind, enabling her to ride out the gale but at the expense of onward progress

helm: steering apparatus, more specifically a wheel or *tiller*, situated on the *bridge*. To 'put the helm up' is to bring the rudder to *leeward* and thus manoeuvre the ship so as the wind is behind her, to 'put the helm down' steers the ship into the wind by bringing the rudder to windward.

jury rudder: makeshift rudder

keel: centre-line timber running on the under-side of the vessel from *stem* to *stern*, to which the framework of the hull is attached

keelson: an internal *keel* running the length of the hull, directly above and bolted to the *keel*, thus fastening the vessel's floor timbers in between

lanyard: line for adjusting rigging

launch: small powered boat

lead-line: line weighted with lead, used to measure the water's depth

leech-line: line attached to the vertical edge of a square sail or the after edge of a *fore-and-aft* sail, used for furling the sail

leeward: in the direction in which the wind is blowing, and thus on the side away from the wind

lighter: barge-like boat, open or partly-decked, used for the loading and unloading of ships

lobby: small ante-chamber to the main cabin

lug: a square sail *bent* on a *yard* that hangs obliquely from a mast

man-of-war: warship

mainmast: the middle mast of a three-masted ship

main-sail: first sail above deck on the *mainmast*

main-yard: the lowest *yard* on the *mainmast*

masthead: top of a mast

mizzen-mast: the end mast of a three-masted ship

mooring-bitts: large posts, affixed in pairs to the deck, for the fastening of mooring ropes when the ship is alongside a quay

paddle-tug: small but powerful steam-powered boat used for towing larger ships

painter: line attached to the bow of a boat for towing, or tying it up

pilot: person qualified to steer or guide a ship into and out of a port

pintles: pin or bolt on a rudder's hinge, attaching it to the vessel.

point: a division of 1⁄32 of a *compass card*, equivalent to 11.25°

pole-masts: masts bare of *yards* or sails

poop: raised deck at the *stern* of a ship containing the officers' living quarters

port: the left side of a vessel when facing the *bows*

ports: openings for light and ventilation

quarter-deck: the rear maindeck between the *poop* and the *mainmast*

rail: fitted at the forward edge of the *poop*

ring-bolt: a bolt fastened to the deck with a ring attached to which tackle is fastened

roads: short for roadstead, a partly sheltered anchorage

rolling chocks: fins fitted on the outside of the hull, at the turn of the *bilges*, to reduce rolling

rudder-casing: wooden casing around the ship's rudder, projecting into the rear cabin

running gear: ropes used to haul *spars* and sails

scudding: running before a gale

scuppers: holes in a ship's side that allow water to drain off the deck

sextant: navigational instrument for determining the angular distance of a heavenly body from the horizon, consisting of a telescope mounted on a graduated arc of one sixth of a circle

sidelights: navigational running lights used by vessels at night, a red light on *port* and green on *starboard*

shoal: stretch of shallow water, or a sandbank/rocky area visible at low water

shore-fasts: ropes attaching the ship to the quay

slat: to flap violently

slice: a large poker-like implement, fitted with a flat blade and used for clearing the ship's furnaces

sou'-wester: a waterproof hat with a very wide back rim.

spars: generic term for masts, *yards* and other sail-holding poles

stanchion: fixed, upright support

starboard: the right side of a vessel when facing the *bows*

state-rooms: private cabins

steam-pinnace: steam-powered boat, carried by a *man-of-war*

steering-gear: the rudder, *helm* and interconnecting parts that allow the ship's course to be controlled

stem: curved centre timber at the front of the ship to which the ship's timbers are attached

stern: rear of the ship

stern-sheets: stern part of an open-boat

stevedore: person employed to load and unload ships

steward: officers' waiter

stokehold: the hold for a ship's boilers

strop: small strap, formed by splicing – intertwining the strands on – the ends of a length of rope

suit: set of sails for a ship or mast

tack: to make a zigzag course; necessary when a sailing-vessel is heading against the wind

tackle: the lines and *blocks* that make up the rigging on a ship

taffrail: curved railing at the stern of a ship

tail-shaft: end of the propeller-shaft, exposed at the stern of the vessel

'thwartship: see *athwartship*

tiller: handle fixed to the top of a rudder-post for steering what is, usually, a small boat

topsail: second sail above the deck

towing-chock: an iron casting through which the towing-rope is guided

trim: to adjust something with reference to wind direction, and the ship's course

truck: disc-shaped cap fixed to the mast's head, with holes for receiving *halyards*

trysails: quadrilateral *fore-and-aft*-rigged sails

watch: a four-hour duty-period on board ship, divided into half-hour intervals marked by bells. Also, the company or person appointed to be on duty during that period.

weather-cloths: protective tarpaulins on the deck of a vessel

wheelhouse: small house built over the steering wheel, to protect the *helm*sman

whipping up: hoisting by means of a pulley

windlass: machine for hoisting the anchor, with a horizontal barrel around which the cable winds – cf. *capstan*

windward: the side against which the wind blows and thus into the wind

yard: *spar*, tapered at each end and crossing the mast horizontally, from which a square sail is spread

XAVIER BRICE

WORDSWORTH CLASSICS

General Editors: Marcus Clapham & Clive Reynard

JANE AUSTEN
Emma
Mansfield Park
Northanger Abbey
Persuasion
Pride and Prejudice
Sense and Sensibility

ARNOLD BENNETT
Anna of the Five Towns
The Old Wives' Tale

R. D. BLACKMORE
Lorna Doone

ANNE BRONTË
Agnes Grey
The Tenant of Wildfell Hall

CHARLOTTE BRONTË
Jane Eyre
The Professor
Shirley
Villette

EMILY BRONTË
Wuthering Heights

JOHN BUCHAN
Greenmantle
The Island of Sheep
John Macnab
Mr Standfast
The Three Hostages
The Thirty-Nine Steps

SAMUEL BUTLER
Erewhon
The Way of All Flesh

LEWIS CARROLL
Alice in Wonderland

CERVANTES
Don Quixote

ANTON CHEKHOV
Selected Stories

G. K. CHESTERTON
Father Brown: Selected Stories
The Club of Queer Trades
The Man who was Thursday
The Napoleon of Notting Hill

ERSKINE CHILDERS
The Riddle of the Sands

JOHN CLELAND
Memoirs of a Woman of Pleasure: Fanny Hill

SELECTED BY
REX COLLINGS
Classic Victorian and Edwardian Ghost Stories

WILKIE COLLINS
The Moonstone
The Woman in White

JOSEPH CONRAD
Almayer's Folly
Heart of Darkness
Lord Jim
Nostromo
The Secret Agent
Selected Short Stories
Victory

J. FENIMORE COOPER
The Last of the Mohicans

STEPHEN CRANE
The Red Badge of Courage

THOMAS DE QUINCEY
Confessions of an English Opium Eater

DANIEL DEFOE
Moll Flanders
Robinson Crusoe

CHARLES DICKENS
Bleak House
Christmas Books
David Copperfield
Dombey and Son
Great Expectations
Hard Times
Little Dorrit
Martin Chuzzlewit
Nicholas Nickleby
Old Curiosity Shop
Oliver Twist
Our Mutual Friend
Pickwick Papers
A Tale of Two Cities

BENJAMIN DISRAELI
Sybil

THEODOR DOSTOEVSKY
Crime and Punishment
The Idiot

SIR ARTHUR CONAN DOYLE
The Adventures of Sherlock Holmes
The Case-Book of Sherlock Holmes
The Lost World & other stories
The Return of Sherlock Holmes
Sir Nigel
The White Company

GEORGE DU MAURIER
Trilby

ALEXANDRE DUMAS
The Three Musketeers

MARIA EDGEWORTH
Castle Rackrent

GEORGE ELIOT
Adam Bede
Daniel Deronda

WORDSWORTH CLASSICS

The Mill on the Floss
Middlemarch
Silas Marner

HENRY FIELDING
Tom Jones

RONALD FIRBANK
Valmouth & other stories

TRANSLATED BY
EDWARD FITZGERALD
The Rubaiyat of Omar Khayyam

F. SCOTT FITZGERALD
The Diamond as Big as the Ritz & other stories
The Great Gatsby
Tender is the Night

GUSTAVE FLAUBERT
Madame Bovary

JOHN GALSWORTHY
In Chancery
The Man of Property
To Let

ELIZABETH GASKELL
Cranford
North and South

GEORGE GISSING
New Grub Street

KENNETH GRAHAME
The Wind in the Willows

GEORGE & WEEDON GROSSMITH
Diary of a Nobody

RIDER HAGGARD
She

THOMAS HARDY
Far from the Madding Crowd
Jude the Obscure
The Mayor of Casterbridge
A Pair of Blue Eyes
The Return of the Native
Selected Short Stories
Tess of the D'Urbervilles
The Trumpet Major
Under the Greenwood Tree
Wessex Tales
The Woodlanders

NATHANIEL HAWTHORNE
The Scarlet Letter

O. HENRY
Selected Stories

JAMES HOGG
The Private Memoirs and Confessions of a Justified Sinner

HOMER
The Iliad
The Odyssey

E. W. HORNUNG
Raffles: The Amateur Cracksman

VICTOR HUGO
The Hunchback of Notre Dame
Les Misérables
IN TWO VOLUMES

HENRY JAMES
The Ambassadors
Daisy Miller & other stories
The Europeans
The Golden Bowl
The Portrait of a Lady
The Turn of the Screw & The Aspern Papers

M. R. JAMES
Ghost Stories

JEROME K. JEROME
Three Men in a Boat

JAMES JOYCE
Dubliners
A Portrait of the Artist as a Young Man

RUDYARD KIPLING
The Best Short Stories
Captains Courageous
Kim
The Man Who Would Be King & other stories
Plain Tales from the Hills

D. H. LAWRENCE
Lady Chatterley's Lover
The Plumed Serpent
The Rainbow
Sons and Lovers
The Virgin and the Gypsy & selected stories
Women in Love

SHERIDAN LE FANU
(EDITED BY M. R. JAMES)
Madam Crowl's Ghost & other stories
In a Glass Darkly

GASTON LEROUX
The Phantom of the Opera

JACK LONDON
Call of the Wild & White Fang

GUY DE MAUPASSANT
The Best Short Stories

HERMAN MELVILLE
Moby Dick
Typee

GEORGE MEREDITH
The Egoist

H. H. MUNRO
The Complete Stories of Saki

WORDSWORTH CLASSICS

THOMAS LOVE PEACOCK
Headlong Hall & Nightmare Abbey

EDGAR ALLAN POE
Tales of Mystery and Imagination

FREDERICK ROLFE
Hadrian the Seventh

SIR WALTER SCOTT
Ivanhoe
Rob Roy

WILLIAM SHAKESPEARE
All's Well that Ends Well
Antony and Cleopatra
As You Like It
The Comedy of Errors
Coriolanus
Hamlet
Henry IV Part 1
Henry IV Part 2
Henry V
Julius Caesar
King John
King Lear
Love's Labours Lost
Macbeth
Measure for Measure
The Merchant of Venice
The Merry Wives of Windsor
A Midsummer Night's Dream
Much Ado About Nothing
Othello
Pericles
Richard II
Richard III
Romeo and Juliet
The Taming of the Shrew
The Tempest
Titus Andronicus
Troilus and Cressida
Twelfth Night
Two Gentlemen of Verona
A Winter's Tale

MARY SHELLEY
Frankenstein

TOBIAS SMOLLETT
Humphry Clinker

LAURENCE STERNE
A Sentimental Journey
Tristram Shandy

ROBERT LOUIS STEVENSON
Dr Jekyll and Mr Hyde
The Master of Ballantrae & Weir of Hermiston

BRAM STOKER
Dracula

R. S. SURTEES
Mr Sponge's Sporting Tour

JONATHAN SWIFT
Gulliver's Travels

W. M. THACKERAY
Vanity Fair

TOLSTOY
Anna Karenina
War and Peace

ANTHONY TROLLOPE
Barchester Towers
Can You Forgive Her?
Dr Thorne
The Eustace Diamonds
Framley Parsonage
The Last Chronicle of Barset
Phineas Finn
Phineas Redux
The Small House at Allington
The Way We Live Now
The Warden

IVAN SERGEYEVICH TURGENEV
Fathers and Sons

MARK TWAIN
Tom Sawyer & Huckleberry Finn

JULES VERNE
Around the World in Eighty Days & Five Weeks in a Balloon
Journey to the Centre of the Earth
Twenty Thousand Leagues Under the Sea

VIRGIL
The Aeneid

VOLTAIRE
Candide

LEW WALLACE
Ben Hur

ISAAC WALTON
The Compleat Angler

EDITH WHARTON
The Age of Innocence

GILBERT WHITE
The Natural History of Selborne

OSCAR WILDE
Lord Arthur Savile's Crime & other stories
The Picture of Dorian Gray
The Plays
IN TWO VOLUMES

VIRGINIA WOOLF
Mrs Dalloway
Orlando
To the Lighthouse

P. C. WREN
Beau Geste

Bhagavad Gita

Distribution

AUSTRALIA & PAPUA NEW GUINEA
Peribo Pty Ltd
58 Beaumont Road, Mount Kuring-Gai
NSW 2080, Australia
Tel: (02) 457 0011 Fax: (02) 457 0022

CZECH REPUBLIC
Bohemian Ventures s r. o.,
Delnicka 13, 170 00 Prague 7
Tel: 042 2 877837 Fax: 042 2 801498

FRANCE
Copernicus Diffusion
81 Rue des Entrepreneurs, Paris 75015
Tel: 01 53 95 38 00 Fax: 01 53 95 38 01

GERMANY & AUSTRIA
Taschenbuch-Vertrieb
Ingeborg Blank GmbH
Lager und Buro Rohrmooser Str 1
85256 Vierkirchen/Pasenbach
Tel: 08139-8130/8184 Fax: 08139-8140

Tradis Verlag und Vertrieb GmbH (Bookshops)
Postfach 90 03 69, D-51113 Köln
Tel: 022 03 31059 Fax: 022 03 39340

GREAT BRITAIN
Wordsworth Editions Ltd
Cumberland House, Crib Street
Ware, Hertfordshire SG12 9ET
Tel: 01920 465167 Fax: 01920 462267

INDIA
Rupa & Co
Post Box No 7071,
7/16 Makhanlal Street, Ansari Road,
Daryaganj, New Delhi – 110 002
Tel: 3278586 Fax: (011) 3277294

IRELAND
Easons & Son Limited
Furry Park Industrial Estate
Santry 9, Eire
Tel: 003531 8733811 Fax: 003531 8733945

ISRAEL
Sole Agent —**Timmy Marketing Limited**
Israel Ben Zeev 12, Ramont Gimmel, Jerusalem
Tel: 972-2-5865266 Fax: 972-2-5860035
Sole Distributor – Sefer ve Sefel Ltd
Tel & Fax: 972-2-6248237

ITALY
Logos — Edizioni e distribuzione libri
Via Curtatona 5/J
41100 Modena, Italy
Tel: 059-418820/418821 Fax: 059-280123

NEW ZEALAND & FIJI
Allphy Book Distributors Ltd
4-6 Charles Street, Eden Terrace, Auckland,
Tel: (09) 3773096 Fax: (09) 3022770

MALAYSIA & [illegible]
[illegible] BHD
[illegible]ng Datuk Sulaiman 7
Taman Tun Dr Ismail
60000 Kuala Lumpur, Malaysia
Tel: (603) 717 3333 Fax: (603) 719 2942

MALTA & GOZO
Agius & Agius Ltd
42A South Street, Valletta VLT 11
Tel: 234038 - 220347 Fax: 241175

PHILIPPINES
I J Sagun Enterprises
P O Box 4322 CPO Manila
2 Topaz Road, Greenheights Village,
Taytay, Rizal
Tel: 631 80 61 TO 66

SOUTH AFRICA
Chapter Book Agencies
Postnet Private bag X10016
Edenvale, 1610 Gauteng
South Africa
Tel: (++27) 11 425 5990
Fax: (++27) 11 425 5997

SLOVAK REPUBLIC
Slovak Ventures s r. o.,
Stefanikova 128, 949 01 Nitra
Tel/Fax: 042 87 525105/6/7

SPAIN
Ribera Libros, S.L.
Poligono Martiartu, Calle 1 - no 6
48480 Arrigorriaga, Vizcaya
Tel: 34 4 6713607 (Almacen)
34 4 4418787 (Libreria)
Fax: 34 4 6713608 (Almacen)
34 4 4418029 (Libreria)

UNITED STATES OF AMERICA
NTC/Contemporary Publishing Company
4225 West Touhy Avenue
Lincolnwood (Chicago)
Illinois 60646-4622
USA
Tel: (847) 679 5500 Fax: (847) 679 2494

DIRECT MAIL
Bibliophile Books
5 Thomas Road, London E14 7BN,
Tel: 0171-515 9222 Fax: 0171-538 4115
Order hotline 24 hours Tel: 0171-515 9555
Cash with order + £2.50 p&p (UK)

23123A